EXPERIMENTAL HEART

REBORN

BOOK 6

SHANNON PEMRICK

Reborn
Experimental Heart | Book Six

Copyright © 2020 Shannon Pemrick
www.shannonpemrick.com

Cover Illustration by Jackson Tjota
Cover Typography by Amalia Chitulescu
Editing by Sandra Nguyen and Cody Anne Arko-Omori

ISBN 978-1-950128-17-4 (paperback)
ISBN 978-1-950128-16-7 (hardcover)
ISBN 978-1-950128-18-1 (e-book)

For my eternal dragon
You know why.

BOOKS BY SHANNON PEMRICK

EXPERIMENTAL HEART
Destiny
Pieces
Secrets
Exposed
Surrendered
Reborn

ORACLE'S PATH
Prophecy of Convergence

Prophecy Tested
Prophecy Chosen

LOOKING FOR GROUP
Spellbinding His Ranger
Protecting His Priestess
Summoning Their Elementalist

CHAPTER 1

A failure… Something I wasn't. Not anymore.

Dappled light scattered across the worn forest path. Songbirds trilled and insects buzzed. A warm spring breeze rustled the canopy above. We set a steady pace toward the village to meet up with some others for a "top secret" meeting with the gods—at least it was a secret for me, because no one wanted to tell me what it was about.

Stella's chattering carried through the air, drowning out Rosa's grumbling. The succubus and her incubus mate, Zaedrix, trailed behind us. They'd been the ones to collect us for this meeting, as I had a pseudo-contract with them—one that bound them to work for me without costing me my soul.

My and Raikidan's adopted daughter showed no fear of my "contracted" demons, and, typical of a fearless seven-year-old, she fired off non-stop questions at the pair. Wasn't much of a surprise, given she lived with Raikidan and me in the West Tribe, exposing her to all kinds of unusual individuals—ourselves included.

"Little one," Zaedrix said, his voice unnaturally smooth. I had to resist the desire to set my full, unwavering attention on him. If incubi couldn't outright hypnotize you with eye contact, their voice certainly could. And that was if their too-perfect appearance, when disguised, didn't lure you in first. Thankfully, these two had switched to a half-disguise, only hiding their wings for the sake of convenience. This made it easier to resist them. "If you keep asking questions, we can't answer you."

Stella let out a dramatic sigh and leaned over Raikidan's head from where she sat up on his shoulders, her dark hair spilling in front of his face before falling to the side. "But I have *so* many questions! Papa, make them answer me."

"You need to be patient, Stella. Allow them time to answer you," Raikidan said, his slightly gravelly, low-pitched voice chasing away Zaedrix's unintentional pull.

Stella pouted. "Fine."

Raikidan chuckled, his stunning blue eyes dancing alongside his amusement, and continued our forward path to the village. His acceptance of these demons' presence impressed me. He never once reprimanded me for making my pseudo-deal with them in order to deal with Kir, and he never had an issue with them showing up, as long as they weren't interrupting anything.

"Where do you come from?" Stella asked the incubus.

Zaedrix ran a talon-like hand through his short, light-colored hair, narrowly missing his single pair of horns. "Another plane of existence."

"What do you call it?"

"Its name is not pronounceable by your species' tongue."

Stella tipped backward to gaze at him upside-down, holding onto the dark sides of Raikidan's two-toned hair to keep from falling. "How did you get here?"

Zaedrix's intense golden eyes danced, seemingly amused by my adopted daughter's antics. "I came here through a summoning Rosa performed… when she was human."

Stella's brown eyes flicked to the dark-haired succubus. "You were a human?"

Rosa took a breath and put on a brave face. I could only guess she was either not a particular fan of children, or just didn't like being probed. "Yes, a very long time ago."

Like her counterpart, she, too, had a disturbingly smooth voice. However I noticed, just as with Zaedrix, it didn't seem to have any effect on Stella. I theorized that their specific demon nature may only affect those who had reached sexual maturity.

The young girl cocked her head. "How are you a demon now?"

Rosa wrapped herself around one of Zaedrix's arms, her talon-like hands pressing just enough into his tan skin to show her claim to him and prevent the incubus from pulling away, as if he ever would. A slight purr rolled out of her throat. "My beloved turned me into one."

Stella blinked and then looked at me. "Momma, what does 'be-levid' mean?"

I smiled, trying not laugh at her mispronunciation. "*Beloved* is an endearing term some give their mate."

"Oh, okay." Stella may not have been originally raised in an inter-species home, but she'd adapted to our way of life rather quickly. She understood Raikidan and I preferred to call each other mates, over husband and wife—not that we would be seen as such in any modern human legal system. She also understood Papa Raikidan had trouble grasping why he needed to wear pants around the house. Most of the time, she found our squabbling about the subject funny, rather than a tough topic of contention between the two of us.

And of course, she'd adapted well to my connection with Rashta. That may have been the fastest part of her adaptation to her new life with us. She loved spending time with the goddess when she popped out from time to time, and was proud to announce to anyone who would listen that she had the "most special momma in all Lumaraeon." The way she said it, I definitely felt extraordinary.

"You are special," Rashta said in my mind, our connection stronger than ever, which, according to the goddess, was thanks to Raikidan's presence continuing to purify her.

"Yeah, yeah." A year after Dalatrend's liberation from Zarda's heinous grasp, and my subsequent freedom from the darkness, I still struggled, finding it difficult to come to terms with my position with the god-dess. Grasping that I was truly free was hard enough. I had a feeling it'd take quite a bit more time before everything felt normal.

"Why did you turn into a demon?" Stella's voice cut into my musing. She'd refocused on Rosa.

The demoness didn't answer, too preoccupied with cuddling up to her mate, her face rubbing on his shoulder like a feline. I was surprised her dual set of horns managed to not gouge the incubus' skin. Zaedrix spoke for her, though his voice was a bit tighter than before. *No doubt*

Rosa's actions are causing some weird demonic reaction for him. "I turned her into what she is to save her life. After everything we'd gone through, I wasn't going to allow her to be taken from me like that."

His jaw tightened when Rosa wrapped her tail around his. I rolled my eyes. "Either go take care of her needs, or douse her with cold water."

Rosa narrowed her golden eyes at me. "You have no room to talk, newly mated."

"I at least have some semblance of decency to keep everything behind closed doors."

Zaedrix tossed his chin Raikidan's way. "Unless he has a say."

Raikidan chuckled, unashamed of his behavior, and even Rashta snickered in my head.

Then suddenly, the two demons were gone, their talon-like feet leaving scores in the dirt path, making me aware they hadn't vanished into thin air. A rush of wind followed their inhuman exit, the last indicator they hadn't disappeared using some sort of demonic magic—if demons even had magic. Though I did catch Rosa complaining about not wanting a quickie. *Their speed is terrifyingly impressive.*

"So, do we continue on?" Raikidan asked. "They didn't tell us where we were ultimately going, just meeting up with others at the crystal."

I tucked my hand into his. "They'll be back. And until they do, I'd like to enjoy a family walk."

A suggestive smile slipped up half of his handsome face, one that made my pulse quicken and a need build in my core. His hand squeezed mine. "Or, we could have Stella run ahead of us to Shva'sika."

I calmed my carnal reaction and narrowed my eyes. "Raikidan… behave."

Stella cocked her head. "Momma Eira, what are you two talking about?"

"Momma and papa things," I said, trying to dismiss the topic. I wasn't quite comfortable with Stella learning about such deep relationship intricacies so early. Raikidan, of course, coming from a different background, didn't understand why I went to such great lengths to keep her in the dark.

Stella smiled brightly. "Like when you're gonna bring home a little sister for me?"

A muscle in my neck twitched and Raikidan's grip tightened. His eyes shifted away. The past month, Stella had regularly brought this up. And unfortunately, it'd become a point of contention between Raikidan and me. "No, Stella, we're not talking about that."

She frowned. "How come? I want a little sister." She tugged on Raikidan's hair. "Papa, why can't I have a little sister?"

"It's not the right time," he said, parroting the words I'd said to him. I caught the irritation in his tone that he tried to keep at bay. My hand slipped from his and I crossed my arms. His gaze fell on me, but I wouldn't look at him.

The last six months with Stella hadn't been easy for me. It had its nice moments, but it brought back all the things I struggled with when attempting to raise Ryder, which I had sucked at.

You didn't suck at raising him," Rashta said.

I ignored her. It'd be a waste of "breath," given we would never agree on that.

Raikidan lifted Stella over his head and set her feet on the ground. "Why don't you run ahead and meet up with your aunt?"

The young girl blinked up at us. "Why?"

Raikidan's eyes darted to me before focusing back on Stella. "Your mother and I have some things to talk about."

My shoulders tensed, and my fingers curled. I did not want to argue more about this. Stella gazed at me and I forced a smile and a nod. "We won't be long. Promise."

She hesitated, then took several steps down the path before looking back. I motioned with my hands for her to keep going. A few more hesitant steps and then she ran off beyond the bend.

A tense silence fell between us. I wasn't going to start this conversation. In my mind, there was nothing to talk about.

"When do we want to tell Stella about Es'tla?" Raikidan finally said.

I stumbled on an answer. Es'tla was an early-teen half-elven boy who came into the care of Sha'hiri, the North Tribe leader, and the North Tribe as a whole after years of neglect and abuse at the hands of his father. The despicable man justified his unmentionable behavior because he had blamed his son for the death of the boy's mother.

I'd had the chance to test Es'tla's skill near the end of the rebellion. I'd gotten along with him, once I broke through some of the trauma his father caused. It sparked a recent request from Sha'hiri—one I hadn't expected Raikidan to want to talk about. "What about it? We haven't come to a decision."

His brow furrowed. "I thought you did."

I stopped walking. "I told Sha'hiri I'd be happy to train him. But when she told me I'd have to take him in and raise him, too, given his specific circumstance, I brought it up with you, and you weren't keen on the idea, so I told her we'd have to put it on hold."

Raikidan stared at me for a moment. "I didn't say I wasn't okay with it."

I crossed my arms. "You didn't have to, Rai. It was the way you acted when I brought it up. You were apprehensive about taking in Stella, but after seeing her again, you changed your mind. I understand the concept of adoption is difficult for you; that's why I didn't press."

His gaze fell to the ground. After a few moments I dipped my head to catch his attention. "Rai?"

This was a strange reaction from him.

I squeaked when he reached out suddenly and wrapped me up into his arms, resting his face on the top of my head.

"I'm sorry," he murmured.

My brow quirked up. "Um, for?"

He inhaled deeply into my hair, tangling his fingers into long violet strands I'd been having a go at growing out. "For being selfish. You're taking the time to understand and be tolerant of the differences I struggle with, and I'm not doing the same for you."

"I'm selfish, too, ya know. And I haven't been willing to talk about my stance in all this. I've pushed against a hard wall without explaining why, expecting you to just accept it." I pressed my face into his chest, taking in a strong inhale of his musky scent. "There isn't a need to rush this kind of decision. I'm not going to die from old age on you any time soon."

Raikidan snickered, though he allowed me to continue without any further interruption.

"I want more time with you, just the two of us. Stella was a surprise. She's a bump in that plan I'm still struggling to maneuver around. Parenting isn't coming as naturally to me as it is for you. And adding Es'tla to our odd family unit won't exactly make it easier, but I've been around older children and teens more than I have infants."

I exhaled. "And don't get me started on the complexities and risks of pregnancy."

Raikidan's grip tightened. "I get it. You're asking me to understand the human side of this and live in the moment of what we have right now." He kissed my head. "I'll do my best to try. I want everything with you. That includes the dragon desire for a large brood."

I shook my head. "*If* we come to that path, there's only so many children I'll be capable of bearing before my body stops being able to handle it."

Raikidan pushed me to arm's length, gazing down at me with his typical intensity. "We need to talk more about how that all works for you. Risks? Wearing down your body? This is all foreign to me, and frankly it's not settling well."

I pressed my lips into a thin line. "Yes, we are going to have to teach you all that. Though, that's something for another day. I think I hear Stella and Shva'sika coming our way." I listened closer. "And my uncle."

Raikidan framed my face with his strong hands and leaned in for a soft kiss. "We'll tell Stella about the brother she's getting."

I grasped his hands tight with mine. "Are you sure? There's no pres—"

He kissed me again. "Even when you don't think I am, I'm learning a lot from you. Stella is *ours* even if she didn't start that way. Ryder has become mine as much as he is Rylan's. And now Es'tla will be the same."

I smiled at the mention of Ryder. I hadn't gotten the chance to see him often in the last year, between my and Raikidan's agreement and him off doing his own special research with the scholars. But when he was around, Raikidan did the same as he had with Stella, taking my son under his wing, so to speak. I was so proud of him.

Stella's voice carried through the forest. She was yammering on so fast, it was difficult to figure out what exactly Shva'sika and my uncle had to endure listening to. Tangling my fingers with Raikidan's, we met the trio halfway.

Stella skipped alongside Shva'sika, the alluring, tall elven woman focused on the nu-human girl, her long, wrapped and beaded dark blue hair framing her porcelain, angular face. Zane walked beside her, their hands entwined. A large rock of a diamond ring sparkled around Shva'sika's left ring finger. The sight brought a smile to my face.

Zane noticed us first, waving in greeting. Shva'sika's gaze shifted up, and she greeted us with a smile, her captivating crystal-blue eyes sparkling. "Afternoon, you two."

I returned her greeting and then honed in on Zane's attire. A dark green tunic with gold embellishments covered his torso. A black belt cinched at his waist, and tall, black leather boots hugged his feet. He'd even forgone his bandana, showing off his "shaved" head.

Rashta snickered. *We both know he shaves it to hide his balding issue.*

"Uncle, did you lose your work clothes again?"

I couldn't help but tease him. For as long as I could remember, this man only wore his mechanic jumpsuit or some grungy t-shirt and old, worn-out pants. Then in came Shva'sika, and his wardrobe practically changed overnight, including more traditional elvish styles.

He smoothed his long red mustache. "I won't dignify that quip with a response."

I snorted, rolling my eyes. It also made him pretend to be more sophisticated than he was.

Shva'sika rested her hand on Zane's chest. "I think he looks handsome."

"Bias," I coughed out into my hand. Raikidan snickered. Shva'sika shook her head, her eyes narrowed in a silent scolding.

I noticed Stella hiding behind Shva'sika's legs, clinging to the woman's dress. I cocked my head. "Stella? What's wrong?"

My daughter's eyes fell to the ground and I frowned.

Shva'sika patted the little girl on the head. "Seems, from the grand story she was telling me, she thinks you're mad at her."

My brow furrowed. "Huh? Stella, no one is mad at you."

"But… but you sent me away when I asked too much for a baby sister…"

I let out a quiet exhale and exchanged a glance with Raikidan before kneeling down and holding out my arms. "Come here, sweetie."

Stella hesitated and then ran into my waiting embrace. I pulled her close and she snuggled deep. "We're not mad, Stella."

"Are you sure?" she mumbled into my neck.

I rose to my feet with her held close. "I promise. Papa and I just needed to talk about when to tell you some big news."

Stella lifted her face to gaze up at me with wide eyes. "News?"

I smiled and brushed a strand of hair out of her face. "I know you really want a little sister. But we can't promise that right now. However, we want to know how you'd feel about having another older brother."

Shva'sika's bright expression caught my peripheral. She knew exactly what this was about.

Stella blinked. "A big brother? Like Brother Ryder?"

I rocked my head back and forth. "Sorta. He's younger than Ryder; a few years older than you. He doesn't have a mom or dad, and Papa and I thought we'd change that."

Stella pursed her lips. "Can I have an older sister instead?"

All of the adults laughed. While most of us agreed that Valene was my adopted daughter unofficially, Stella saw her as a cousin. "No. Older brother is the only option right now."

The little girl let out a dramatic sigh. "I guess so, since he doesn't have a momma or papa."

I kissed her on the forehead. "I promise, his addition to our family won't be painful."

Raikidan rested his hand on her head and smiled.

Stella wrapped her arms around my neck. "I love you, Momma."

"I love you, too."

Raikidan's hand found purchase on my lower back, but I noticed it was a little firmer than usual when he made the action. I stole a glance, and caught the lingering traces of disappointment in his face.

"You know, you've still not said those three special words to him," Rashta said.

My stomach tightened. She was right. I hadn't even thought of that. The whole year we'd been together, I'd not come out and said those words to him, even though now, I could honestly say I believed them. *Shit.* I'd need to be more conscious about making an effort to use that phrase finally. He deserved to hear it, but I wasn't going to just say it randomly to him. That'd be silly.

"No, you're overthinking things. Come out and say it. There doesn't need to be any context."

I set Stella down on the ground to address Shva'sika and Zane. "So, were you two on your way to our place when you ran into Stella?"

Shva'sika home wasn't too far away from ours, but not close enough for Stella to get there and back so quickly.

My elven friend nodded. "Maka'shi asked me to fetch you two."

Maka'shi? If our tribe leader was sending Shva'sika, that meant Rosa was telling the truth. This secret event was a big deal. I had wondered why she insisted I choose my shaman attire for this mystery event. *What exactly is this event with the gods going to entail?*

That was really all I knew, and only because I forced Rashta to spill that much. I didn't know why the goddess was being just as cryptic, but I could only assume it was for kicks.

"But, from the way you're dressed," Shva'sika continued, "and Stella's mention about demons, I suspect you've already been informed."

I caught the tension in her voice at the mention of demons.

The familiar voice of Rosa chuckled near my ear. "Yes. We were told to fetch her by another important individual."

My eyes darted to my right, where the succubus now stood. Zaedrix was also with her. They both looked rather pleased.

Shva'sika's eyes darkened. "I can't imagine they're too important if they consort with the likes of you."

Rosa wagged a finger. "Tsk, tsk, watch your thoughts, young elf. Your precious Eira is among those."

Shva'sika's hardened gaze flicked to me for a brief moment. Shva'sika still hadn't forgiven me for making my pseudo-deal with the two demons. And when she found out I'd enlisted their help for another matter a few months ago, she'd made her displeasure clear.

I understood demons weren't liked—I didn't have a positive opinion about them to begin with, either. But as I'd learned more about their kind, I was starting to see where there was a possibility of everyone coexisting. Even a need to feast on souls could be worked around. *But Shva'sika's hostility toward Rosa and Zaedrix is a new level I don't comprehend.* It was as if her issue was far more personal.

Sure, the two sex demons had attacked the West Tribe about two years ago now, but most of the villagers had let that go, and accepted my dealings with the demons now. So what could possibly cause someone like Shva'sika to continue such hostility?

"You could ask her," Rashta said.

"I did, remember? And she got uncharacteristically huffy with me."

"I'm sure she'll tell you when she's ready," Isis, said, startling me a bit. She was the first life my soul had lived, and the reason Rashta and I were bound in the first place, it was still a little jarring having access to her

and all my other past soul-lives. They had let me be for the first part of my and Raikidan's mating rite gig, but the moment things were interrupted more frequently, starting six months ago, they'd made themselves more known. Luckily, they'd still remained respectful of the rites, when Raikidan and I needed time to each other. I attributed that behavior to them being as much dragon as I was, and having full-dragon mates too—Raikidan's past soul-lives.

"We should head into the village." Shva'sika spun on her heels, making sure Zane followed. He didn't protest, though his eyes were tight with concern.

Stella trailed after them. "Auntie Shiva, do you not like them?"

A smile tugged at my lips. Stella had struggled with both of Shva'sika's names, and for some reason didn't like her human equivalent name, so Me'kunar, a scholar I was close with, had come up with a strong nickname. From what little he mentioned, Shiva was an elven folk hero that supposedly had some relation to Shva'sika. Raina, my fourth life, and the first Shaman Ambassador, revealed she was related to said hero as well, but didn't go into details.

Shva'sika took a controlled breath. "No, I do not like demons. No one should."

My jaw clenched. But before I could step in, Stella spoke up. "Well, I like them. They answer my questions."

Zaedrix laughed. "Your daughter is growing on me."

My brow lifted. These two never ceased to surprise me. Not saying any more, Zaedrix encouraged the rest of us to follow down the path.

2
CHAPTER

Stella skipped ahead of everyone, searching for the birds flitting about in the canopy above, only to be distracted by a beetle or spider minding its own business on some plant or rock. A corvid cawed and swooped from a tree branch, winging close to the young girl's head. It was one of the crows she liked giving food to from time to time. Stella giggled and gave chase for a moment before getting distracted again.

The tension from Shva'sika had lessened, and she was willing to hold conversation with me, though completely ignored the presence of the demons.

"Sha'hiri will be happy to hear the two of you changed your mind," she said. "Though, we both know Es'tla will be the most excited."

My lip twitched. "If he's forgiven me for rejecting the initial request."

I remembered his reaction when I told Sha'hiri we'd have to hold off on the move. I didn't know he was nearby. And even though I'd been careful with my wording to Sha'hiri, explaining that it wasn't because we didn't want him part of our family, he'd been devastated.

Shva'sika rested her hand on my shoulder. "He has. I kept tabs on him, since I figured your and Raikidan's situation would change eventually. It didn't take him long to calm down and allow Sha'hiri to explain the situation to him." She laughed. "A few days ago, she told me he still hasn't unpacked his bag, waiting for the news he'd finally be moving."

I inhaled a breath and smiled. "Well, then it sounds like he'll be moving in before I get his room ready."

The corner of her eyes crinkled when a large grin spread over her face. "Don't worry. I'll make sure he's got a bed before nightfall."

I shook my head, not doubting for a second she would. Even though we weren't related, and I tended to call her friend, we were more like family. We'd been through a lot together, and even when we had our differences, we still had each other's backs. I doubted anything could break the bond we shared.

"How's the wedding planning going?" I asked, my gaze darting to Zane. His reaction would be better.

He let out a slow, heavy breath through his lips, his eyes wide. "You didn't warn me how involved this stuff is."

I bit my lip, trying not to laugh. Shva'sika patted his arm. "I'm trying to be fair and go easy. I'm aware elven weddings are generally far more extravagant than human ones."

Zane's eyes remained wide, as if he'd just returned from his first war. "I thought we humans went too crazy as it was. But this…"

My lips pressed tight, struggling not to let any of my internal laughter out. I'd only seen a fraction of the frenzy, and I wasn't sure how all of this hadn't sent him running for the hills.

"You really think she'd let him go now?" Rashta said.

"Not a chance. But the imagery is fun." I pushed my awareness outward again. "You'll make it. You've survived far worse, Uncle."

Stella, not so subtly listening in, turned her attention to Zaedrix. "Are you and Rosa married?"

Rosa's tails swished and Zaedrix chuckled. "No. Demons have no need for marriage rituals."

"Oh, so like Mama and Papa then… okay." Satisfied, she skipped ahead again.

Shva'sika's lips twitched. "Though you should have one."

I rolled my eyes. "It's not necessary."

"We'll see about that."

The forest path widened until we reached the village clearing. The buildings had little pattern to their layout. Some were stacked on top of each other, while others had more room, allowing for gardens or crop patches. Shops had signs hanging above or next to their entrances.

And well-maintained cobblestone paths weaved through the throng of structures.

People milled about their day, most stopping their tasks momentarily to wave in greeting. None flinched at the presence of the demons with us. Reaching the rustic building of the inn, I spotted a young, light olive-skinned elven boy with black and red hair around Stella's age. He wore no shoes or shirt, but he at least remembered pants. *He's picking up habits from his father and older brothers.*

The boy smiled wide when he noticed our approach and rush toward us. I opened my mouth to greet him, but the words died on my lips when I saw his focused gaze.

He held his hand to Stella. "C'mon, Stel. Everybody is waiting!"

Stella grinned and linked her hand with his. "Okay!"

The two kids disappeared around the inn. I huffed. "It's official. I've been replaced."

Zane's head flew back as he laughed. "Well, now that Sethal has his little girlfriend, he doesn't care about anything else."

Raikidan twitched. "She's too young to be spoken of like that."

Shva'sika and Zane chuckled at his expense. Even the two demons were amused by his reaction.

I squeezed his hand. "It's just a teasing expression. They're best friends and practically inseparable. It's cute."

Raikidan shook his head, his jaw tight. I did my best to repress my amused smile. Just another thing for us to work on.

Rounding the corner of the inn, the ice-blue eyes belonging to Valene greeted us. "About time you showed up. Everyone's been waiting!"

The laughter of her adopted father, Daren, boomed beyond the front door left ajar. The stout, pot-bellied human man emerged a moment later, speaking with his usual thick accent. "Ye need tae be patient, Valene."

The young woman huffed.

I stretched and then jabbed my thumb Raikidan's way. "Between taking care of Stella and him, I need my beauty sleep."

Laughter erupted around me, Raikidan rolling his eyes. Valene latched onto my arm, pulling me toward the center of the village. "C'mon, let's not make everyone wait any more."

I still wasn't sure what this *everyone* bit was about, but with Daren joining our small group, I was sure it would be interesting to find out. He didn't do large crowds or big gatherings. Made him uncomfortable. But if he was willingly tagging along, despite that possibility, this event had to be a big deal.

Weaving through the street, we came to a clearing in the homes. Lush grass carpeted the ground, and tended bushes and flowers dotted the perimeter. In the center, a colossal glowing crystal hovered above the ground in an elegant wooden structure, acting as an accent, rather than a cage or a dais. I'd learned that the crystal defied gravity by the enormous output of spiritual energy it emitted.

Dozens of people gathered in the garden, most from the village, but I recognized a few who were not. Blaze's familiar face stuck out. He watched Ken'ichi toss Stella high into the air and then catch her with ease. My heart momentarily stopped. Stella shrieked with delight, begging Ken'ichi to do it again. Sethal held up his hand, reminding Ken'ichi he promised his turn was next.

Blaze shook his head. "Eira is going to murder you."

I snickered, and spoke up, making my presence known. "If I wasn't so accustomed to what he's doing, you might be right."

Eyes turned my way, much of the current conversation buzzing in the gathering petering out. Blaze crossed his arms. "Well, looks like sleeping beauty finally decided to join us."

I flipped him my middle finger and he shrugged, opening his arms. "I mean, if you want."

A smirk tugged at his lips, his eyes sparkling. I snorted out a laugh and his smile grew, arms still held open. "It's good to see you, Eira."

We embraced in a quick hug, the spicy scent of his cologne and grease invading my senses. "You too, Blaze. You look good." Like most of my friends, I didn't see him much. While Zane made frequent visits to the village, Blaze was usually stuck working at the shop. I'd maybe seen his face twice in the last year.

Raikidan drew up beside me, his expression unusually tight. I suspected it had to do with him still fighting his protective instinct. He was getting better each day, especially now that my *mate voice*—a unique mental sensory input that dragon males received when their time to find their mate came—had disappeared a few days ago, but it would be a while longer before he would act like a semi-rational, non-overly possessive dragon. Or, so my past soul-lives indicated.

Blaze extended his hand, and Raikidan exchanged a firm grip, but to my relief it ended in a friendly handshake. I released the tension building in my shoulders. Raikidan was a little too unpredictable sometimes right now. *Must be how he felt with me and my mood swings.*

"That's how we all felt," Rashta teased.

I ignored her and reached out to muss Blaze's short spiky black hair. "I see you have grown your *mane* out again."

Blaze did his best to hide his wince by running his hand through his hair before shoving them into his pockets, as if his past words embarrassed him now. "Yeah, I still like it this way.

Valene poked out from behind me. The loose curling ringlets of her long brown hair bounced around her shoulders from the movement. "She showed me a picture of you with your longer hair, it's definitely better this way."

Blaze took a step back, as if he'd been startled. "Oh, uh, hey, Valene."

A small smile twisted her lips. "Hey to you too, stranger."

"He wouldn't be such a stranger if he came with me more often," Zane complained, drawing up next to Blaze and wrapping his arm around our friend's neck.

Blaze let out a snort. "With you prancing off into the woods with your fiancé, and Argus, Rylan, and Ryoko no longer working at the shop, at least not full-time, someone has to keep the projects from going over their deadlines."

Zane rolled his eyes and Shva'sika and Valene laughed. My uncle did do a lot less working these days.

I scanned the gathering for familiar faces. "Speaking of the others, where are they?"

Blaze leaned back on his heels. "Seda and Argus went to get Ryoko and Rylan. They said they'd meet us there. But Ryder and Genesis are here."

My back straightened. "Really? They weren't due back for another few weeks."

I bobbed my head trying to find the pair.

"We're right here, mom," came a familiar voice in the crowd. Not long after, Ryder pushed his way through, Genesis close behind him. His dual colored eyes—one silver-ringed blue, one gold-ringed green—squinted as he smiled. He ran his fingers through his white hair, one of his hands no longer sporting a protective glove.

I rushed over to him and wrapped my arms around his neck. He didn't hesitate to embrace me back. "I missed you."

He chuckled. "You saw me a month ago."

"Doesn't mean I can't miss you," I muttered.

I embraced him for a moment longer, maybe a little too long, before letting go. Genesis took advantage of the moment and swooped in, wrapping her arms around my waist. "Don't forget me now."

I chuckled and embraced her back. "Yes, I missed you too. I hope this newest adventure, as short as it was, worked out as you hoped."

She pulled away, her eyes unable to meet mine. "You could… say that."

Genesis tucked strands of her long raven hair behind her ear and took a step back, close to Ryder. I noticed a pink tinge to her cheeks. Movement between them caught my eye. My gaze flicked down to find their hands together, fingers entwined.

My brow quirked up and I placed my hands on my hips. "When did that happen?"

Genesis still couldn't meet my gaze, and Ryder turned his eyes to her, a smile on his lips. "Recently."

"Is that so?" I pursed my lips, my eyes narrowing.

He sighed and focused on me. "Please don't do the overprotective thing."

My brow quirked up. "Overprotective? Did I just hear that out of your mouth?"

Blaze took a few steps back and Genesis ducked her head. "Ryder, don't make her mad…"

"Oh, big brother's in trouble," Stella egged.

I set firm eyes on Genesis. She flinched. An amused smirk cracked through the faux irritation Ryder thought I was legitimately experiencing. "I never expected you'd turn out to be a cradle robber."

Laughter erupted around us, and Genesis' pale complexion face grew redder. "Eira…"

I lost myself in laughter, joining the others. I couldn't help it. It was too fun to tease them. Once I calmed down, I couldn't keep the smirk off my lips.

"So… you're not mad?" Genesis asked, her words tentative. "You can get a little overprotective sometimes. And when Seda hinted this might happen last year, you did… well…"

I shook my head. "I've grown as a person. As long as you to treat each other well, I could care less my son is dating a woman twenty times his age."

Ryder's eyes widened, disbelief crossing his features. "Mom!"

I laughed some more. "Alright, I'll stop teasing—for now."

Ryder sighed. A familiar bemused voice cut through the crowd. "Be happy her parenting instincts aren't so strong, boy. You'd be in more than hot water if it was."

I turned my attention to the familiar elf faces of Del'karo and Alena. In Alena's arms, Vanya, now just over a year old, babbled away.

A teasing smile was plastered on Del'karo's face. "Our eldest daughter is a special one, after all."

I rolled my eyes and scoffed, though I struggled not to smile. I had always had a strong relationship with Alena and Del'karo. More like they had treated me like family from the start, Del'karo not only taking on a mentorship role as my shaman teacher, but surrogate father. However, it wasn't until this past year did they start to refer to me as such. It was honestly nice hearing the words come from their mouths. "Has nothing to do with my parenting instincts. I'm just not some crazy psycho."

"Sometimes," Blaze muttered.

I shot him a sidelong glance before holding out my hands for Vanya. Alena happily handed over her daughter. I held her close and tickled and cooed at the tiny elf girl. She smiled and giggled, showing off the few teeth she had.

"So, Mom, when you're done playing with the baby, can you explain why are we all gathered here?" Ryder said.

I stopped mid-tickle motion. "Um…"

My son hung his head as he sighed and the others around us laughed. "Isn't this event important? How do you not know what it's about?"

Strong energy welled up inside my body and then shot out, Rashta taking form beside me. Many people backed away or bowed, even though this wasn't a new occurrence. She enjoyed her freedom when it was appropriate for her to separate from me. And I preferred it too. She deserved that.

"She does know what's going on," Rashta said. Her lips twitched, her eyes giving away her amusement. "She's just been so preoccupied this past year she's forgotten."

I barely heard her jest, my attention focused on her presence. Her dark wings flexed, the light breeze wisping strands of her black and red hair. *Her form is more corporeal today.*

Over the last year, we'd noticed her physical state would change when she was projected out of me. Some days, she could be mistaken for a semi-corporeal spirit, while other days, you could mistake her presence as being free of our bond—god-like aura and all. The running theory was that it was related to her level of lingering corruption.

Corruption… I pinched my nose. "I remember now."

Rashta braced her hands on her hips as she belted out a hearty laugh. "I knew it wouldn't take you too long."

Raikidan rested his hand on my lower back. "I'm not caught up."

I smiled up at him. "It has to do with the corruption that still lingers in Rashta that I told you about." I couldn't stop myself from glancing at Rashta suspiciously. "Though I can't figure out why it's become such a spectacle."

Blaze nodded. "Same. Not complaining, if it's getting all of us together to catch up, but still…"

Rashta smiled. "In order to purify me, the other gods need to perform a special ritual. As a result, a once-in-a-lifetime opportunity for mortals will occur. We thought it would be appreciated if we allowed you to witness the event."

"That's why we were so quick to return from our expedition," a raspy male voice said.

I turned to see two older elven men approaching. They dressed in thick robes with various chains, pouches, books of different sizes, quills, and parchments hanging off them. Both had intricate designs painted on their weathered mocha-tan hands. The younger of the two had long black hair, smattered with bits of gray. The older man had long silver hair and gripped a gnarled staff to help him walk. An unusual glow emitted from etchings carved into the dark object.

I smiled. "Me'kunar, Lo'shen, good morning. You're both eager, as always."

Lo'shen, the older of the two, gave a toothy grin. "We receive a personal message from a god to attend an event involving you, and you expect my old scholar heart not to jump at that chance?" Before I could answer, he whipped up one of his hanging books and pulled out a quill. "Now, how to write this beginning…"

I shook my head and Me'kunar laughed. "Did you expect anything different from him?"

"Not at all." I turned to Rashta. "Should we get going?"

"In a moment—we need to wait for one more."

"I've brought it," a new female voice said.

Eyes turned to Maka'shi as she approached. Trailing behind the small, blue-haired half-elf was a tall humanoid figure with a shadowy appearance. *The Guardian?* I'd never known it to ever step foot in the village. One time over the last year, when I had been trying to learn more about it, thanks to my last encounter with it after my *temporary* banishment, it refused to get too close. *What is going on here?*

Rashta nodded at Maka'shi. "Good. Bring it here so I can remove the binding."

Maka'shi hesitated. "Is that really necessary?"

"You knew this day would come," Rashta said. "It was told to you when you became Va'len's wife. His vision of the guardian's unbinding became your responsibility upon his death."

Unbinding? I wanted to ask for clarification, but I suspected, with the way Rashta was wording herself so carefully, she wouldn't answer me. The goddess hadn't been too forthright with a lot of information over the past year. Raina theorized it had to do with the corruption, as she'd never been so reluctant to discuss things with my soul in the past. But she wasn't the only one who had issues. I had a lot to catch up on learning about my past soul-lives, but in the moments I had to myself, they also struggled to tell me things. *Maybe this corruption is affecting me, too.*

It was something I thought about from time to time, and made some sense, given my past and how the goddess and I were basically fused together.

The Guardian moved forward without waiting for Maka'shi to listen to Rashta's command, drawing up to me, rather than the goddess. The being towered over me, reaching out with a shadowy appendage that served as its hand. If I were a more easily intimidated person, this would be terrifying. The Guardian rested his hand on my head, the action not new, but no less strange, given its unusual nature. I felt a slight pressure, but it also wasn't particularly solid. A pulsing sensation ran through me.

"I'm looking forward to this trip with you, Ancient Soul. You will be safe. I will ensure that."

I smiled. "Thank you."

"Thank you?" Lo'shen ceased his note scribbling, and Me'kunar even leaned a little closer. "Did you thank the Guardian? As if it were… speaking with you?"

Oh, right… From what I'd gathered, few knew the Guardian had sentience, until this moment. I'd assumed Maka'shi knew, but that didn't appear to be the case, based on the shocked expression on her face.

I nodded. "It's sentient."

The villagers murmured, a mix of surprise and excitement, with a few clearly uneased. I suspected that was potentially due to how they treated the construct, thinking their actions didn't matter. Me'kunar snatched his book and jotted down the new discovery. Non-villagers had no clue why this was such an exciting moment.

Vanya babbled and blew a spit bubble, making grabby hands at the Guardian. The construct lifted its "hand" from me and reached for the small elf child. Del'karo and Alena took a step forward. It was clear they were unsure about the Guardian's actions. While it'd never hurt any of the villagers, it'd never interacted with us like this, either. Vanya giggled when the construct's shadowy appendage formed into a point and *booped* her nose. It then gently played with her hands and feet, the little elf showing no fear of the being. *She is something else.* I had a feeling Del'karo and Alena would have their hands full with the girl as she grew older.

Lo'shen shuffled closer to the Guardian, his wrinkled face scrutinizing the shadowy being. "Why were we not aware of your sentience, Guardian? Why have you not spoken to us? Did we offend you in some way in the past?"

The Guardian's hand found my head again. *"It was easier this way, when so many forgot."*

I relayed the comment, and Lo'shen frowned. "How lonely you must have been."

"I waited for a reason. That reason has come."

I cocked my head. "What do you mean?"

"You will understand soon." The Guardian removed its hand and faced Rashta, expectant.

Rashta approached, plucking a feather from her wing. She chanted in a language that had an air of familiarity, and it took me a moment to realize it was Old Tongue. Lo'shen furiously wrote down everything before him, refusing to miss a single moment. I couldn't help but shake my head. *He's dedicated, I'll give him that.*

The feather in Rashta's fingers emanated a golden aura and the goddess' chanting ended. She pressed the glowing feather to the Guardian's chest. Small tendrils of shadow pulled out of the construct's body and wrapped around the feather, absorbing it. A golden light pulsed through the Guardian, and then nothing.

No, I couldn't call it *nothing*. There was now a small, golden glowing orb resting at the base of its neck where the breastbone would be. Except... no one seemed to notice. They appeared confused about the ritual, as if expecting more.

Wait. I blinked and when my eyes opened, the glowing orb had disappeared. *I'm seeing things again...*

"No, you're not," Isis said. *"We saw it this time, too."*

I chewed my lip and glanced down at Vanya, the little girl now getting a little squirmy in my arms. My stomach turned when I spotted a golden orb glowing on her neck—in the same place it had been on the Guardian. I blinked rapidly, and the glowing disappeared.

I... wasn't seeing things. Ever since Dalatrend's liberation, I'd been experiencing strange happenings. Some had to do with my elemental abilities. Others, my spiritual. But, every now and then, the strangest of all was this light.

At first, I'd thought my eyes were playing tricks on me. I'd briefly glance at someone and spot it. When I focused on them, it'd be gone. But then, my past soul-lives began to notice as well. Though the most perplexing part was Rashta. She claimed to not know what we were talking about, as if I wasn't really seeing anything at all. I found it hard to believe I was seeing things if my other lives were also picking this up. Sylvia, my ninth life, even had the gall to accuse Rashta of lying to us. But the goddess didn't budge.

Now, I was more convinced than ever that Sylvia was right. Whatever I was seeing was truly happening, and it wasn't normal. And if I was seeing whatever this was, Rashta knew, without a doubt, but was trying to hide that fact. *Why, though?*

"Hopefully, we'll find out more after the purification process," Velsara, my most recent previous life, said. *"It's not like her."*

"I wonder what it could be." Ayuma, my tenth life, said. *"It feels…"*

"Familiar?" Raina said. *"I agree. There's something uniquely familiar, as if we're attuned to its very nature."*

I bit the inside of my cheek. They weren't wrong. Even though they were just brief glimpses, I wasn't immune to noticing the same pull. As strange as it all was, there was something about the orb—something calming and reassuring about it.

Raikidan rested his hand on my back, pulling me out of my thoughts. "Eira, are you okay?"

I blinked and looked up at him, vaguely aware everyone was staring at me now. "Yes, why?"

His brow furrowed with concern. "You haven't responded to anything anyone has said to you."

I smiled to reassure him. "I was having a private conversation with my other lives about something. Don't worry about it."

I didn't want to alarm him about this happening again. At least, not in front of anyone. I'd told him about the situation after the third time it had happened. Like everything else, he took it in stride—after his overprotective and easily alarmed side took hold for a moment—offering to help me uncover the meaning. I was thankful of his support. But right now wasn't the time to bring it up. I didn't need anyone over-reacting or getting nosey. *I'll just have to beg his forgiveness for the secret later.*

"Oh, he'll make you beg all right," my sixth life, Atria, teased. *"Won't be for forgiveness, though."*

My face heated. *"Quiet, you."*

My reaction didn't go unnoticed by my audience, based on some of the snickering. Raikidan's brow quirked up. "Should I ask?"

"No, they're just being jerks." I let out an *oof* when the Guardian's hand suddenly landed on my head—a bit harder than I would have expected, too. "Um, Guardian?"

It stood motionless, without speaking. Then, just as suddenly as it touched me, it withdrew its appendage. *What was that about?*

Maka'shi let out an audible breath. Rashta shook her head. "You have nothing to fear, young leader. Bound or not, the Guardian will never harm her. Now, we should get going, or we'll get the scolding of a lifetime." She grimaced. "And I don't want that."

I bit my lip, trying not to laugh. I was a bit curious which god or goddess she was referring to. But at the same time, I didn't want to be subjected to a lecture, either.

"Where is our destination?" Valene asked, though her eyes went to me instead of Rashta.

Where were we going, again? It took me a moment to remember what Rashta told me a year ago when I'd been recovering from my fatal wound. "To a temple in the Northwest."

Valene cocked her head. "That's not very specific."

I shrugged and turned my gaze to Rashta. "That's all I've been told."

She smirked and then returned to my body in a rush of energy. I sighed. "I really don't understand what's with her lately."

Maka'shi chuckled, approaching. "It's all right. I know roughly where to bring us."

"That doesn't sound much better than Laz's explanation," Valene muttered.

The shaman leader's lip twitched. "We'll be meeting someone who will guide us the rest of the way. It's a secret and sacred place. Only a select group knows the location."

I wonder why all the secrecy.

"You'll find out soon enough," Isis said.

I wanted to sigh, and my past soul-lives caught onto my irritation, laughing away. I really hated all the secrets and having no reason for them.

"Don't be like that," Isis said. *"It's a great surprise. We don't want to ruin it."*

"Yeah, yeah, whatever."

Maka'shi turned away, pulling a blue-and-black orb from a pouch attached to her side. "Now, make sure you have everything you need. We won't be returning for a few hours."

"They're not coming with us, right?" Shva'sika said, her question pulling my attention to her. She pointed at Zaedrix and Rosa.

"We are," Zaedrix said. "We have our reasons to accompany you."

Shva'sika's eyes narrowed. "Evil creatures such as yourselves have no place on sacred ground."

Rosa hung off her mate, her tail swishing lazily behind her. Her words came out nearly as a purr, "Aw, no need to bite, little elf. We've been welcomed by someone with more power and authority than you. And as Zaedrix said, we have our own reasons to be there. So, why don't you learn to deal with it, hmm? Would make everyone's lives easier if you didn't put up such a fuss every time we were in your sight."

Shva'sika took an aggressive step toward the succubus, her hand poised to strike up an electrical spark, but Maka'shi stepped in. "That's enough, Shva'sika. I understand you have your own personal reservations about their presence, but this decision is not yours to make. Even the Guardian, unbound with full autonomy, chooses to allow them here."

I turned my head to look up at the protective construct. Maka'shi had a point. Without its binding, it wouldn't have to listen to the command she and I gave it when I knew the two demons would be coming around from time to time to check in. And I seriously doubted Rashta had given any extra commands to the being. It seemed she had given it full freedom. *So, why does it stick around?*

The Guardian reached out and touched my head. *"If you trust them, then I shall as well."*

Its arm then dropped. *Okay, that was weird.* It was as if the binding that had been loosed kept it from communicating regularly, compounding its choice to not reveal its sentience to the villagers.

"The demons are coming with us," Maka'shi continued. "There is no negotiating."

Our half-elf leader turned away from the Dancing Light Shaman and activated the portal. Shva'sika ground her teeth together and then followed Maka'shi through the portal, Zane close behind.

Del'karo took Vanya from me and set her in a basket secured to Alena's back. The happy toddler squealed and waved her arms. The two then collected their children and headed through the portal.

Stella returned to my and Raikidan's sides, and watched with us while the others walked into the portal. As they did, a flash of light hit my eyes, the strange neck orbs appearing again. I averted my gaze and blinked. When I returned my attention to the passing people, the light was gone.

Raikidan rested his hand on my back and spoke in draconic. *"You are seeing it again, yes?"*

I nodded. *"The others should not know about it at this time."*

"I understand. We will learn more. If it were a serious concern, Rashta would have said so."

I couldn't find myself convinced. There was just something off about the whole situation.

Lo'shen leaned in closer, his quill poised for writing. "What secrets are you two hiding, hmm? What reason would you have to switch to a tongue not many aside from dragons know?"

I snickered and poked the old elf in the forehead. "Nosey. It's going to get you killed one day."

He snorted. "At my age, not a chance."

Me'kunar laughed and tried to give me a hand by distracting his father. Me'kunar wasn't much better sometimes, but he had nothing on the nosiness of his father.

I shook my head and then took Stella's hand. She gripped me tightly, Raikidan too, when he took her other free hand. Portals scared her for some reason, so she needed a little extra help going through. The Guardian, patient as ever, noticed our readied state and headed for the portal. Before it entered, Sethal emerged and ran around it, heading for Stella.

"Stel, c'mon—" He paused when he noticed her holding our hands. "Stel, you scared?"

Stella tipped her head down, her hair curtaining her face. "Yeah… Portals… they…"

Her grip on my hand tightened and the rest of her words died on her lips. Sethal nodded, seeming to understand, and zipped around Raikidan, standing behind Stella. He placed his hands on her shoulders. "I'm here for you, too."

Her lips twisted, though I thought I caught a smile trying to break through. "Thanks."

"So she's afraid of portals, but not demons," Zaedrix mused. "Interesting little girl she is."

"You're not scary," Stella mumbled.

I chuckled. She really was an unusual girl. But I wouldn't have her any other way.

Raikidan took a step toward the portal, encouraging Stella to follow. She did, and little by little we got her into the magical vortex. Blue, black, and white lights flashed and swirled, threatening to send the mind into an unbalanced state.

Stella trembled the whole way through, but didn't try to run or ask one of us to carry her.

Our destination lit up the exit of the portal, temporarily blinding us. And then, the sounds of a forest hit my ears. I blinked and gazed around to find us in a shaded area at the base of what appeared to be a mountain. A thick forest spread behind us. An unusual wave of homesickness and familiarity rushed through me.

I forced everything away and kneeled down, addressing Stella. "I'm proud of you, Stel. That was a great job."

Stella nodded, trying to put on a brave face. "I'm trying really hard, Momma. I don't want to be afraid."

I brushed her bangs out of her face and planted a kiss on her forehead. "One day you won't be. We'll continue to work on it, okay?"

"And I'll help!" Sethal declared.

She nodded, a smile spreading across her face.

A familiar female voice I hadn't heard in some time called out, "Laz!"

3
CHAPTER

Before I could search for the source of the voice, a muscled yet soft form crashed into me. Her large breasts pressing against my body offered little protection from her crushing grip, and her long brown hair spilled over my shoulders. A mossy-wood scent, with a slight tinge of grease, wafted into my nose.

"Ryoko?" I wheezed out.

She squealed and my body lifted in the air, the area around us spinning into a blur. The motion continued until I thought I might hurl my breakfast. I blinked furiously and took a few minutes to orient myself when my feet landed on the ground. Ryoko refused to release me. Instead, she buried her face into my neck.

I smiled and wrapped my arms around her from behind, noting my light complexion contrasted even more than before against her sun-kissed skin. "I missed you too, Ryo."

"You weren't supposed to go away for so long," she mumbled into my skin.

"You were aware of the mating rites, because Rai made sure of it." I snickered. "And it's not my fault you've been too busy to have any visitors, when I've been allowed to see others besides him."

"You make it sound like I took you hostage," Raikidan muttered.

Ryoko took a step away from him, pulling me with her. "You did, jerk."

Raikidan rolled his eyes and grabbed a hold of me, trying to pull me back. I sighed as the two played tug-o-war at my expense. "Can you two, not turn me into a human tug toy? Please?"

The area around us boomed with laughter. I honestly didn't expect anything less from these two, but really, it'd be nice if they could finally come to an agreement.

"You know they're not going to," Rashta said. *"It's inevitable they fight over you."*

"What's that supposed to mean?"

"You'll find out soon enough."

My mind buzzed as my past soul-lives perked up. I didn't understand what was going on, but I knew answers wouldn't be coming at this time.

Stella tugged on my skirt. "Momma Eira, who is this lady? And why is she trying to steal you from Papa Raikidan?"

I tried not to laugh, but a chuckle escaped. No one would say it was an inaccurate assessment. "This is Ryoko. Do you remember me talking about her?"

Stella nodded, gazing up at my half-wogron friend. They had never gotten a chance to meet. Ryoko released me and knelt, to be at eye level with the young girl. "Hi, Stella—I've heard quite a bit about you."

My daughter smiled, and jumped right into her million question mode. "Are you really a wogron? How long have you known Momma Eira? Are those ears real? Can I touch them? Momma, who is that?"

My brow quirked up at her sudden attention shift, my eyes following to where she pointed, beyond Ryoko. A tall, built man with a shaved head and red beard leaned against a nearby boulder, his green eyes with golden rings pinned intently on us. Dappled sunlight smattered his tan skin. "Father?"

I hadn't seen him at all over the year, along with any of the dragons I knew. They took the mating rites seriously, even after I had broken the tradition.

He smirked. "I'm glad to hear I haven't been downgraded again."

I chuckled. "There's still time."

He frowned, but before he could speak, I continued, not wanting my joke to cause an actual issue with him. "How long have you been here? Why *are* you here, for that matter?"

"I brought your friend here, though I was told to let her do her thing when she saw you," he said, his smirk returning. "It was entertaining."

My arms crossed. "And you didn't make your presence known because?"

My father's eyes flicked to Raikidan. "Wanted to be sure it was safe."

Raikidan snorted. "You're fine." His voice lowered, as he mumbled to himself. "Some others, we'll see."

My father grunted. "You don't keep a clan leader position as long as I have by not being cautious around newly mated males."

Newly mated? It's been a year.

"No, he's right," Velsara said. *"A year ain't all that long for dragons. Even if matin' rites end after the mate voice goes away, the urge for males to protect their mates is somethin' they need more time to get a handle on. For some, it can take years. Dragon pairs are considered newly mated for the first two decades they're together."*

"Two decades!" I was going to have to deal with this nonsense for at least two decades?

"Not that I don't sympathize," my father continued. "I'm all too familiar with that fight. And mine was a difficult one to get a handle on." He closed his eyes. "There's a reason I justified breaking the agreement for twelve years at the risk of endangering the clan. To be away from her as much as I had to be… the physical pain I experienced…"

I frowned, my chest tightening at the turn of the conversation. "Father… you don't have to talk about it."

Stella, who was in the midst of touching Ryoko's ears, abandoned her tactile curiosity and walked over to the disguised red dragon, grabbing him by the hand. "You don't have to be sad. Everything works out in the end." She smiled, her eyes squinting. "I was sad when I lost my momma and papa. But now I have a second momma and papa, and a brother, and more family, and lots of fun friends. And Momma Eira lets me talk to Momma whenever I need to, cause she has special powers. Maybe she can help you, too."

My father knelt, giving Stella his full attention. I watched on, curious how he'd interact with her. This would be the first time they met. I had sent word to him about her adoption, but this was the moment to see how he accepted her. "You must be Stella. I've heard many things about you from a few of my children who've been lucky enough to meet you."

Stella continued to smile. "Hi, Grandpa."

The stoic man froze, his eyes showing he was processing those words. After a moment, he reached out and wrapped his arms around her, his massive form practically swallowing her. Stella giggled. "Your face hair tickles!"

"Does it now?" My father rose to his feet, Stella held in one arm. He rubbed his beard against her cheek, and she giggled and squealed, pushing on his face.

I snickered and shook my head, approaching the two. My father ceased tormenting my daughter and opened his other arm for a hug. I reciprocated the embrace. "It's good to see you, Father."

"I'm happy to see you, Lazmira." He released me and set Stella down to address Maka'shi, who was approaching. He dipped his head respectfully to the shaman leader.

She made a small hand gesture in greeting. "It's good to see you again, Rizgar. Thank you for showing us the way."

"It's my pleasure." He noticed the Guardian standing behind me, and visibly swallowed. I wasn't sure if he knew what a Guardian was, or what it was capable of, but at the very least, he understood it was a powerful being. "I should get everyone moving. There's a lot to do."

He motioned for everyone to follow, heading down a worn path cutting into the mountain. I fell into step with him, Ryoko drawing up next to me. Stella slipped back to Raikidan, who followed close on my heels.

"Father," I said. "We're in the clan's territory, that much I've had time to gather, but I don't understand why. I don't remember seeing a temple when I was here last."

He chuckled. "I guess you didn't look hard enough."

I narrowed my eyes. But before I could spit out a retort, he spoke again. "It doesn't surprise me you weren't told. The temple's location is a heavily guarded secret. I had plans to show you myself, as you had a right to know, not only as my daughter, but as Rashta's host; however, your mate rites took precedence. It so happens, you need to be there for this event the gods are putting on."

"But, why is it here? Is it coincidence it's in our clan's territory, or is there more to this?"

"Patience, my daughter. You'll learn everything when we get there."

I huffed and blocked out the laughter in my head from Rashta and my past soul-lives. I hated how cryptic everyone was acting today. I didn't see why it was necessary.

"Hey, Grandpa," Stella began, before flowing into twenty questions before he could even respond. The questions weren't always related, and then she sidetracked into telling a long story about her and Sethal going on an adventure into the woods, looking for fairies. It was quite the elaborate tale that made absolutely no sense.

My father stared at me with wide eyes, whispering, "How do you handle this?"

I gave him a shit-eating grin. "Patience. You'll learn soon enough."

Laughter roared around me, while my father shot me an unamused look.

"Momma," Stella complained. "I'm telling a story!"

I smiled at her. "Yes, you're right. I'm sorry for interrupting. Please continue."

She shrugged. "I'm tired of telling that story. It was getting boring."

I bit my lip so I wouldn't laugh. That wasn't uncommon for her to do.

"Ryoko, why are your clothes so different than ours?" Stella asked.

She wore an outfit similar to the one Peacekeeper Ryoko gave her when I had my ambassador coronation. Ryoko played with the half-skirt. "This is the fashion in my pack. They closed themselves off for so long, the style hasn't changed much over the centuries."

I smiled. I was so glad she'd made contact with the wogron pack Peacekeeper Ryoko came from. It was a risky move, given she was a clone of their beloved half-wogron, but one Ryoko was willing to make.

My eyes caught something odd underneath her clothes in her fussing—something brown and fluffy. I cocked my head. "Ryoko, do you have a tail again?"

Blaze clasped his hands behind his head. "Can't be. Rylan said they fixed that."

Ryoko clasped her hands behind her back. "Yeah… about that. It was fixed. Just not how I had hoped it would be."

I sputtered a laugh. "It's permanent?"

Her cheeks tinted pink. "Don't laugh."

I did, and refused to feel guilty. "It's exactly what you didn't want! How can I not laugh?"

"And Peacekeeper Ryoko is super salty about it, too," Ryoko muttered.

"She seriously carried on for an entire week how unfair it was she didn't get a tail!"

I held my sides, nearly falling over. I couldn't take it.

"Momma, can I have a tail?" Stella asked.

I was laughing too hard to answer, so Raikidan took over. "No, you can't have a tail."

"But Ryoko and the moody demon lady get tails. Why can't I? It's not fair!"

Rosa scoffed. "I'm not moody."

Others around me chuckled. Zaedrix wisely refrained from making any comments, but it all only made me laugh more. Wind rushed past me, and before I knew it, Rosa stood in my path, her eyes narrowed. "Enough of the mockery, *human*."

I rolled my eyes and slipped around her. "Chill. It's just some light teasing. And really, you acting like this only proves the point."

Rosa stomped her foot; the audible sound of her tail angrily swishing hit my ears. I shook my head.

"You handled her well," my father commented.

I shrugged. "I've learned she's not all that scary."

"Oh really," Rosa hissed. "I'll show you—"

"Rosa, please," Zaedrix said. "Let it go."

Silence fell over the group until Blaze chuckled. "Someone is sleeping on the couch tonight."

Zaedrix grunted. "She'll forgive me within a few hours. She's terrible at staying mad." He chuckled. "Especially when she wants something."

There was silence for a moment, and then Blaze sucked in a breath. "That look even felt like a cold bucket of water to me. Good luck."

I rolled my eyes. At least they were getting along with the others, relatively speaking. Under different circumstances, someone would be screaming, some more trying to kill the demons indiscriminately, and the incubus and succubus would probably be causing havoc in their own way. It was nice seeing the probability of co-existence, even if that was a lofty goal.

"You're handling their presence well," I said to my father. "I do believe this is the first time you've had contact with these two."

"I was given a rundown of your dealings with them," he said. "And you have a friend waiting for you. Talon, I believe his name was."

I blinked. Talon was here? Thinking about it, it made sense, if Tla'lli was as well. But it also explained why Rosa and Zaedrix tagged along.

"There's more to it than that," Raina said.

"What's that supposed to mean?"

"You'll see."

I rolled my eyes, though my father noticed. His brow ticked up. "Sorry, speaking with a past life."

"Ah." He nodded slowly. "I supposed it'll take me some time to get used to that."

Del'karo pulled up beside my father. "Don't fret if it takes you a while, Rizgar. Some of us are still getting used to the quirks that have come with the awakening."

Awakening. The term the scholars coined for my purified reconnection to Rashta and, subsequently my past soul-lives.

My father nodded. "I'll take your counsel to heart. Other than those quirks, I hope she's not causing any other trouble."

Del'karo laughed. "No, she's been uncharacteristically well-behaved. Though we can all thank Raikidan for that, keeping her busy and all."

My father grunted—whether in amusement or agreement, I couldn't be sure. I, on the other hand, rolled my eyes. *Acting like I can't hear them while they refer to me as some troublemaking child.*

"Oh, but you are," Rashta said. *"A moody troublemaker."*

However, I was glad the two men were getting along. They'd met after the Dalatrend liberation announcement at the party the North Tribe put on. My father was grateful to Del'karo for taking me in and acting as a surrogate father to me. And it seemed that respect was going to continue. *Now the two of them just have to meet Shyden.*

The terrain became a little more difficult to traverse, cutting off idle chat. I wiped a bead of sweat from my brow when we finally made to spot on the path wide enough for everyone to rest. A rocky ledge above shaded us from the sun, though the cool spring air of the mountains kept the area comfortable while we worked up a sweat—except the children. Naturally, they were made of energy that never quit.

Daren leaned against a boulder, breathing heavily. I snickered. "Tired, Daren?"

"Too old fer this," he said.

Valene poked him in the belly. "I don't think it's your age."

He scoffed and swatted her away. My father shook his head before pointing down a large tunnel carved through the mountain. The hole was large enough for an adult dragon to walk through without issue. "We're almost there."

Everyone collected themselves before continuing on. Not too far into the tunnel, fire elementalists produced lights to keep everyone from stumbling on their way through. I took in the tunnel, noting the blackened, semi-smoothed surface. It reminded me of a few lava tunnels I'd seen when training with Del'karo during my later years with the shamans, before I had been forced to leave. I was sure the clan had created the tunnel themselves.

This tunnel was longer and less straight than I expected it to be— winding in various directions with seemingly no end in sight. The children tried to run off ahead, but like the experienced clan leader he was, my father took command of their attention and explained to them why it was dangerous to run off, pointing out some of the branching tunnels that were hard to pick out. It seemed this tunnel system was one large maze to confuse those who were not welcomed. *Why hide a temple, though?*

"You'll see," Isis said.

Minutes passed before the tunnel became brighter, and the end of the tunnel came into sight. At that point, my father gave the children permission to run ahead. I wasn't so sure that was safe to allow, but he knew what lay beyond, so I bit back my doubt and trusted his judgment.

"Whoa!" Stella's voice echoed down the tunnel when she reached the exit.

"Well, what do we have here," a deep, rumbling voice in draconic said.

"Not a cave troll," another said, his throaty chuckle vibrating against the smooth walls.

"I don't know what you two are saying," Stella said. "But, hi."

Raikidan laughed and I shook my head. *What are we going to do with her?*

It wasn't long before we emerged as well; the tunnel opened to a cove. Rocky terrain rolled down into grass and flowers, with a few trees springing up here and there. A brook babbled in the distance. Mountain walls rose high on all sides, protecting the area.

"It's a lot different than in my time," Isis mused. *"It used to be so much more open."*

Stella stood to the right, checking out a red dragon lazing on a long stretch of smooth rock. My eyes flicked to the second dragon I'd heard. This one relaxed on the other side of the tunnel, watching the children with a careful eye. *Sentries, maybe?*

"No trouble?" my father said to them.

The dragon watching the children shook his head. *"Quiet as ever."*

"Good. Stay diligent. We do not know if the activities today will draw attention."

A knot formed in my stomach, unease crawling down my spine.

"Eira, what's wrong?" Rashta asked. *"That was a quick reaction."*

I slowed my breathing to control myself. *"I'm not sure. I guess, with how cryptic everyone is being, and Zaedrix's and Rosa's report about Kir, I'm getting a little unnerved."*

"It wasn't my intention to unsettle you," she said. *"I've just been having a little fun. This purification process will be harmless."*

"That's not… what I've been worried about…" Being harmed during this process hadn't even crossed my mind. Maybe it should have, but given how the gods talked about my importance as much as Rashta's, I naturally assumed that any ritual or task they'd perform wouldn't be likely to hurt me.

"Do you think Kir will attack?" Ayuma asked. *"I find it highly unlikely he knows you're outside the village."*

"Or that he'd come up with a plan to kill you when he knows how high-alert you and your allies will be," my fifth life, Nalia, said.

My fingers twitched. I wasn't convinced. *"What do you think, Isis? You know him better than anyone."*

It took her a moment to respond. *"I think you're wise to be cautious. As much as I hate that you have to look over your shoulder so much because of him, he is unpredictable. He learns things about us in ways he shouldn't, so to think he wouldn't potentially know of this meeting with the gods, even if he doesn't know the extent, would be foolish."*

"Lazmira," my father's voice cut through my mental conversation. I lifted my head to give him my attention. "Is everything all right? That was quite the serious expression you had."

I realized everyone was staring at me. Even Stella had returned to my side. "Sorry. Just having a private conversation."

The sentry my father had been speaking with rose to his feet. *"Did our conversation spark yours? Do you think Rizgar is right to be concerned there may be some sort of attack?"*

I nodded, choosing to speak in common so the others understood, even if it was only my half of the conversation. "None of us can say for sure, but the idea shouldn't be dismissed. Kir is unpredictable, and our last report on his activities weren't favorable."

The other sentry sat at attention. *"No one has been foolish enough to attack this sacred land in many generations. But if you believe it may happen, we will be extra diligent, Dragon-Phoenix."*

I nodded my thanks. I hoped this would turn out to be a false alarm, but something in the back of my mind continued to scream out in warning.

My father jerked his head toward the lush green below. "Let's get moving. There are many who are waiting on us."

CHAPTER 4

We followed Rizgar down a worn trail in the rocky terrain until we reached a worn cobblestone path. The children ran ahead again, many venturing off into the grass and flowers. I crouched down and investigated the road, dragging my fingers across the weathered and cracked surface.

"It's been some time since someone took care of these," Isis said, her tone sad.

"After the War of End, only the clan was ever allowed here," my father said, taking notice of my inspection. "We didn't trust others during the war to not desecrate the sacred land, and then when things calmed, outsiders all but forgot about this place, so we continued to guard it as a secret. Because we don't have a need for roads, we didn't continue with their upkeep."

I nodded. That was similar to the conclusion I had come to. I rose and gazed up at the towering cliffs hiding the cove before continuing down the path. "Isis said this used to be more open. Was the war the reason for the change? How did you manage to create such mountainous terrain?"

My father faltered, as if the mention of Isis' name startled him. "The dragons in this clan at the time chose seclusion over fighting in the conflict. For some reason, the war didn't extend this far north, so we chose not to get involved. We had a duty to protect this sacred land. But as a precaution, we contracted shamans from what became the North Tribe to work the land. It was no easy feat. Not only did these shamans have to alter the terrain enough to be a formidable obstacle if the war turned, it had to appear natural, else it would draw unwanted attention."

He paused, closing his eyes as if he were recalling something. "Since the element of red dragons is fire, and our clan has strong claws from living in the mountains for so long, we contributed by creating the tunnel system, digging out and liquefying the rock. The shamans, for their assistance, would be allowed to journey here freely, but we were crafty in the tunneling system as to not jeopardize the security we'd created."

"That makes a lot of sense," Isis said. *"A shame it had to happen, but I understand, too."*

I smiled. "Thank you for sharing that information. It explains what we hoped."

"You don't need to thank me, Lazmira." He smirked. "As much as it might seem that I'm teasing you with some information, this is your history as much as it is mine." His smile faded. "This is something you would have grown up knowing, had your mother and I been allowed to give you that life."

I grabbed his wrist, a wan smile on my lips. "Let's not talk about what could have been. It's better to live in the now."

He patted my hand and continued on, leading us through the meadow until a sheer cliff face came into view. At the base, dragons and people gathered—a lot of dragons and people. Not all were red dragons, and not all were human. Many of the faces I recognized.

Warm smiles and waves greeted us. My father scanned the area before placing a hand on my shoulder and addressing me. "I don't see our other guests of honor yet, so why don't you catch up with friends? There are a lot here waiting to see you."

Maka'shi drew up beside my father. "If you'd direct me to the other leaders, there are a few things I need to discuss with them."

My father nodded, but before he could break off with her, I spoke up. "Maka'shi, when you see Sha'hiri, let her know I have a new answer for her."

The half-elf woman smiled. "Shva'sika informed me before we left.

I made sure the message was passed along. I'll let you do some catching up before we finalize everything."

I gave a firm nod and allowed them to leave, Maka'shi calling for the Guardian to follow her, promising to find him some shade to rest in for now. The shadowy construct didn't hesitate.

"Poor thing," Raina said. *"It does better in the shadows."*

"Is that why it stays in the forest?" I asked.

"Mostly, yes."

"How much do you know about this construct?"

"Quite a bit. But I'll be able to explain that soon. You need to prepare for the incoming body, thirty degrees to your right."

My attention snapped in the instructed direction, but the warning came too late. A girly squeak escaped my mouth when someone running up to me bent over and threw me over their shoulder. Using their momentum, they spun us around. Those who hadn't moved on with my father and Maka'shi laughed, while I lost all sense of orientation. The only thing I could process was the clothing this person wore was similar to Ryoko's, though with a little less clothing on the torso, and the grip on my legs was so familiar the name just barely caught on my tongue. Then, I felt the faint familiar pull of the artificial bond Zarda had created for me and—"Rylan?"

He laughed. "Who else would be dumb enough to pick you up like this?"

Our spinning ceased a little too abruptly, leaving me dazed when my feet landed back on the ground. Familiar dark blue and gold mismatched eyes stared down at me, the corners crinkling from Rylan's broad smile.

Ry… Other than his clothes, and maybe slightly tanner skin, he hadn't changed a bit. I threw my arms around his neck. "Missed you."

He wrapped his arms around my waist. "You too, Laz."

I released him, allowing Rylan and Raikidan to engage in a friendly embrace, exchanging a few reuniting words. It brought a smile to my face. Out of all our friends, he'd bonded with Rylan the most. And it was great that wasn't tarnished with Raikidan's dragon instincts around me.

When Rylan pulled away, I took his wrist in my hand, gazing down at it. While he still had the synthetic metal shackle around his neck, the ones he used to have around his wrists were now gone. "I was told about the crazy procedure you went under recently. How are you feeling after it?"

Rylan pulled his wrist free and clasped his other hand around it, rubbing his thumb across his inner wrist. "Still going through therapy, and I have some residual pain here and there, but every day things get a little better."

I shook my head. I didn't know much about the procedure, but it was experimental, and had to do with cutting his hands off and utilizing the abilities of a healing shaman. And craziest of it all—it had been his idea. There were many risks theorized, some including permanent nerve damage. Even though spirit-based healing far exceeded the capabilities of modern medicine, it wasn't always perfect, and didn't always come without risks. "Are you able to play music again, at least?"

His lips twisted. "Yes, and no. No stringed instruments still. But some basic percussion and woodwind are doable, as long as I monitor how long I go at it."

Blaze sputtered a laugh and I rolled my eyes, knowing exactly where his brain went. "What are you, thirteen?"

He gave a half-hearted shrug. "At heart."

I shook my head. Some things never changed with him.

Ryoko slipped next to Rylan and wrapped her arms around him. "Don't worry, Blaze, there's other things he doesn't have to worry about how long he goes at it." She smirked. "I can assure you of that."

Blaze shoved his hands into his pockets. "Good. Bitchy, deprived Ryoko isn't someone I want to deal with anymore."

I laugh when Ryoko gasped. "Rude!"

Alena came up to Blaze and tugged his ear. "And watch your language, young man. There are children present." Her eyes cut to me. "I shouldn't be the only one to remind you, either."

I held up my hands. "I'm not getting parent of the year award."

My friends laughed. It was something I'd never been good about. Even when I was first doing the parenting thing with Ryder.

"Anyway," Ryoko said, getting back on topic. "What Rylan isn't saying is how good a teacher he is for the pups of the pack."

Rylan ran his hand through his white hair. "Yeah, that's been a highlight of all this. Forced me to reassess what I wanted to do with my life."

I smiled, happy it worked out in the end. It may not have been his first pick, but sometimes the best choice in life is far down that list. I should know, I'd finally embraced my craftsman abilities, and even found the spark needed to accept my Ambassador title. The latter wasn't easy, especially when it came to prepping for future meetings with nations wanting to heal relations, now that Zarda was out of the picture. But seeing the smile on people's faces when they saw me—their desire to talk to me to learn and grow—that was the real reward. I had worked hard on myself this last year, to be proud of my mixed blood. Raikidan helped wherever he could, encouraging me to rise above the lingering hate and show others that halflings belonged.

The sound of someone breathing hard pulled our attention. A young, athletically built man stood behind Rylan a little ways, bent over and breathing had as if he'd been running a while. He caught his breath and straightened, amber eyes dancing. "Hey, Eira."

I smiled, taking no time to recognize him. "Hey, Raid."

He ran his fingers through his short black hair and turned his attention to Rylan. "Did you really have to take off like a bullet like that? You knew she was here before Seda got the chance to say something."

Rylan shrugged. "The bond alerted me to her arrival and I was excited. Shoot me."

A muscle in Raikidan's arm twitched at the mention of the bond. He knew it wasn't something Rylan and I could be rid of, but I also was aware of how much its existence bothered Raikidan. I didn't blame him; it bothered Rylan and me as well. I'd tried to break it down like it had done naturally when I'd gone on the run over a decade ago, but a year hadn't been enough time. Maybe in a few years it'd be better, and maybe I'd be able to finally feel my mate bond with Raikidan.

I'd often thought about that, wondering if the artificial bond had somehow blocked me from properly connecting with Raikidan. From how some of my past soul-lives described their bond with their mates of the time, what I experienced wasn't even close to as intense a feeling. And given we were all half-dragon, the artificial bond was the only thing I could theorize as the contributing variable. *Now if only a miracle could be worked around that.*

"Yeah, well, let us know next time before you run off," Raid said to his brother. "You and Ryoko aren't the only ones who want to see them."

I rested my hand on my hips. "Well, then maybe you should escort us down, so they don't have to wait anymore."

Raid opened his arms. "First."

I shook my head and embraced him, though it was cut short when a low growl came from Raikidan. I pulled away from Raid and shot Raikidan a warning glare. As much as I understood, I wasn't going to allow him to get away with that behavior. The two of us locked intense gazes for a moment before Raikidan calmed.

Raid, however, backed off. "We were all given fair warning he might act this way. I should have been more careful."

"No," I said, my tone firm. "You've done nothing wrong. And Raikidan is responsible for keeping himself under control."

"Yeah, but still…" He turned away. "Let's get moving."

I nodded, figuring that was best. No point arguing, and it'd help Raikidan clear his head.

As everyone followed Raid toward the crowd, I fell into step with Raikidan, entwining my fingers with his and setting a warm gaze on him. He smiled back and squeezed my hand. I understood. He wasn't trying to come off as some controlling asshole to humans. Possessiveness was a prevalent and accepted trait for dragons. If I'd been raised with the dragons, I didn't doubt I'd have fewer issues with the behavior. It was just something the two of us needed to work on to get to some sort of compromise. I was his as much as he was mine.

When we reached the crowd, the first person to greedily push their way through was Yára. She threw her arms around my neck and squeezed. "I missed you!"

I smiled and hugged her, inhaling the sweet floral scent wafting off her dark blue hair. "It's good to see you, too. You're looking well."

She pulled away first. "I've been learning so much about the clan. And I've been training with the North Shamans, just like you advised. Thank you for that. Mom taught me what she could, for someone as inexperienced as me, but there was so much more for me out here."

I rested my hand on her cheek. "I had no doubts you'd handle that task. You're my sister, after all." I let out a long, exaggerated sigh. "Our brothers, on the other hand…"

She threw her head back in a fit of laughter when one of them called out, "We heard that!"

I peered around her to see all my brothers approaching. Rhaec and Trigon towered over them, as usual, though the female presence on Rhaec's shoulder caught my eye faster than anything. The familiar blonde psychic, Seda's sister Nyra, perched comfortably there, a bright smile on her face.

For a moment I wondered what she was doing up there, but Yára leaned close to whisper in my ear. "Don't focus too much attention on her and Rhaec's relationship. Trigon's been struggling with this change for some reason."

That explained it. I knew my brother was fond of her, so that didn't come as much of a surprise to me. Trigon's behavior, on the other hand, that wasn't as expected. I knew the two could get competitive, and they were close, so maybe that fueled the issue.

"My sister also gently turned him down after he'd spent so much time working up the courage to say anything," Nyra messaged telepathically.

And that explained everything else.

"He actually took it well. He wouldn't have known she wasn't interested in men, since she never talked about it. But he has been feeling lonely and hasn't had much success when they go prowling the town."

My brow lifted. *"Should I assume he's the issue, or does she not make a good wing-woman?"*

Nyra chuckled. *"Both."*

"All the half-dragons in one place finally," Lo'shen's rough voice said beside me suddenly.

I gasped and jumped back, triggering a chain reaction of laugher. "Don't do that, crazy old man!"

His old elven eyes squinted at me, and he let out a contemptible snort, whipping out a book. "Get your ears checked."

My lips pressed into a tight, unamused line while Raikidan snickered. He would say that.

Lo'shen scribed notes. I peered over his shoulder, finding some of the most elegant Elvish script I'd ever laid eyes on. "I can't believe how well you write."

"We elves pride ourselves on proper handwriting. Sloppy script would never be tolerated."

"Yes, I know that, but yours is still the best I've seen."

A wistful smile fell on his lips. "You should have seen my wife's."

My gazed softened. I never met her. Me'kunar told me she'd passed away a few months before I'd found the West Tribe in my exile. And knowing how rare it was for elves to live long after losing their life partner, Lo'shen was a rare bird. It clearly pained him to be without her, yet he continued on. Either because of his love for lost knowledge, or some other higher purpose, something kept him with us for a little while longer.

A massive log of an arm wrapped around my neck and pulled me into a tight hold. Trigon chuckled as he held me close. "Make sure you get our good side."

Lo'shen raised an eyebrow. "That'd take a lot of work."

Trigon pouted while I lost myself in laughter. "That's not nice. We make sure our sister stays alive."

"We keep you all alive," Yára said, placing her hands on her hip. "You numbskulls would be in so much trouble if it weren't for us."

"Oh yeah?" He released me and grabbed for Yára. She easily slipped away, sending him on a chase after her. This allowed for me to greet all my other brothers, Bone pushing his way to the front and hugging me tight.

"I missed you, too," I murmured into his shoulder. Even though I'd gotten to see them during this last year, it had only been twice. And it sucked. I wanted the time with Raikidan, but I also wanted to make up for lost time with my family and friends.

"It hasn't been the same without you around," he said.

I pulled away. "Well, I'll be able to get out more often now. I'll be sure to get on your nerves so much you'll wish I was gone again."

Bone narrowed his eyes. "Don't you dare."

Elgren, one of my other brothers, draped an arm over my shoulder. "I'd be interested to see our ultra-serious older sister be more annoying."

My nose scrunched. "I'm not ultra-serious. Just practical."

The two exchanged glances that screamed, "Same thing."

Nyra used her psychic abilities to levitate off Rhaec's shoulder and fly over to me, pulling me from Elgren's grip and into her own warm embrace. "You heard Yára. She needs that practical side to keep you all out of trouble." She snickered. "And boy, do you all get into it when they're not around."

Rhaec wrapped his massive arms around us. "You say it like it's a bad thing."

I opened my mouth to speak, but a new voice spoke for me. "With you lot, it is."

Turning my gaze, it wasn't hard to spot the familiar olive-tan face of Azriel forcing his way through. My face lit up, unbridled joy swelling in my chest. I slipped from my brother's grip and rushed Azriel. He opened his arms and my body crashed into his. Azriel wrapped me in a warm tight embrace. "I'm so happy to see you."

"I missed you, too," I mumbled into his chest. "At least this time I was only gone a year."

"I would have dragged you back kicking and screaming if you'd taken any longer."

I laughed. I had no doubts he would. After my surprise return to Dalatrend two years ago, we'd hung out and discussed things. His reaction to seeing me—the relief knowing I was still alive—it was nothing compared to the confessions he'd given me during that talk.

"Oh, so you're not going to react to that?" Raid said, presumably to Raikidan.

Azriel chuckled. "It's because I'm special."

Raikidan grunted. "You're something."

I laughed. It didn't surprise me Raikidan's instincts didn't see Azriel as a threat. We acted enough like siblings, it would be easy to trick his instincts to behave.

Azriel held onto me a moment longer than needed, before allowing me to slip away. "I hope you're staying out of trouble."

He placed a hand on his chest. "Me? Trouble?" He smirked, his dark eyes dancing. "You know I can't stay out of that."

My eyes squinted as I laughed.

"Course, I can't say it's as much trouble as you get into."

"Business good?"

"Better now that Zarda is gone."

That was good to hear. That club was his baby, and I wanted him to be happy and successful.

"Of course," he started, his eyes showing mischievous intent. "I'd do better if you came back to work for me."

I tugged one of his four ears in reprimand. "No." I then turned my attention back to Nyra. "Where is your sister? I expected to see her by now."

Nyra tossed her head in the direction of the gathered people. "Seda and Argus are handling something at the moment. Saléna is with Aurora, picking on Nioush."

My brow rose. *Aurora is here?* With her issue with sunlight, I never imagined she'd be caught dead out here, even with the specialized equipment she had at her disposal to help ease the issue. And why was she picking on Nioush? *Why is he here, for that matter?*

"Oh, and Telar is with them now, it seems." She cocked her head to the side. "He's insisting you know he and Avila must see you soon."

Excitement flooded over me. *They're here too?* But before I could inquire further, a child-like voice cried out, "Eira's here!"

I glanced over my shoulder to see a cluster of them, along with the feline-human form of Mocha approaching. I knew these child faces. Well, some of them. Others were new, while ones I expected to see weren't here. *The Dalatrend orphans.* There was one excitable face I wasn't surprised to see—little Myra. She was clearly a year older, hitting a bit of a growth spurt, but I'd recognize her cute face anywhere. Her attention was fixed on Raid as she ran over to him, wavy ebony hair flowing behind her. "Daddy, you found her!"

Raid lifted her up into his arms. "Of course I did."

I smiled. "Daddy?"

The corner of his lips quirked up. "Yeah, we decided to adopt her when we realized how attached we all were."

One of my eyebrows lifted. "Uh, we?"

Mocha sashayed over next to him and Raid wrapped an arm around her. "We."

Raid gazed at her with so much adoration, I didn't dare assume it was a joke. "I'm not going to pretend I'm not surprised."

She laughed. "Trust me, it was the last thing either of us expected as well." Her golden eyes shifted to him. "But that's life, and you won't hear me complaining."

Raid squeezed her close, bringing a smile to my face. Not only because of how happy they seemed, but because it was good to see Raid move on from Ryoko. I really didn't know how things would work out after he'd pined after her for so long.

Mocha held out her arms. "Now, I want the same proper greeting you're giving everyone else."

I snickered and hugged her.

A small hand tugged on my skirt. "Eira, pay attention to us, too!"

I turned my attention to the young red-haired girl vying for my attention. "Don't worry, Levi, I wouldn't dream of not saying hi to all of you."

She smiled wide, showing off a few teeth she'd lost. I knelt and gave them all my undivided attention, learning about the new children, what happened to the missing ones, and all around whatever they wanted to blab on about. Well, except Panga. The pale, dark-haired girl insisted on running over to Raikidan. She asked him to braid her hair, as was their ritual, though she didn't make it easy for him to resist, with the pleading look in her beautiful blue eyes.

As I spoke with them, I became more curious about something, turning to Raid. "I'm assuming they're all here because of you? Last I knew, you'd kept on helping out at the orphanage. Though, if you were taking them all, I expected the Matron to come along."

Raid's eyes flicked to Mocha. "She is here."

My head jerked back. "Huh?"

"Mocha and I run the orphanage now." He smiled. "And don't worry, nothing happened to Lyra. She's still working with us and the kids. She'll never give up her passion for them. We're just reducing the stress on her—"

"If you say it's because I'm old, I'm going to show you what this old woman can really do," a female voice said. I turned my gaze to the familiar, older nu-human face of Matron Lyra. While nearing the expected life span of the average born nu-human, her warm cerulean eyes showed her inner youth. With her were a number of adults, clearly from different walks of life, and the children that had been adopted out.

Jakcel was the first to break away and run up to me. He wore clothes I recognized as being associated with the North Tribe. Either he found a family there, or lived in a village near it. "Eira, I got a new family!"

I ruffled his auburn hair. "I was recently told this. I'm so happy for you. You'd better be behaving yourself and staying out of trouble."

He nodded. "I'm doing my best. And, and, they told me I am show-ing… um, promise for cool powers like them. They're powers like yours!"

Cool powers? I supposed some sort of elemental or spiritual ability would look like a super power to children. Though it did confirm where he'd been adopted out to.

I smiled. "I have no doubts you'll find this power, too, Jakcel. Promise me you'll work hard to master it once you discover what you can do?"

He nodded so hard, I thought his head might pop off.

Nari snatched my attention next, and I knelt to listen to them all, one by one. Elara had just finished telling me about her new life when a piercing dragon roar from the sky grabbed my attention. I rose to my feet, my head tilting up toward the sky. In the clouds, a dark shape had formed. A muscle in my neck twitched, my mind unable to tell if it was friendly or not.

Raikidan place a hand on my shoulder and murmured draconic in my ear. "*Calm. Zaith is announcing the arrival of his clan. It is required when entering territory belonging to other clans.*"

I let out a slow, quiet breath, my shoulder relaxing. He kissed the back of my head. "*You will learn.*"

The legion of red dragons and one black descended from the clouds. I'd forgotten how large the Velsara clan was. Velsara herself stirred in my mind, her excitement leaking into my senses. "*Calm down. You'll get to talk to him. We've been working hard to make that happen.*"

In what time I had to myself, my past soul-lives had been teaching me the technique to channel them. Isis and Velsara had been the easiest, partly because of their main element matching mine, and partly because of their placement in the rebirth timeline. Velsara was the life I'd lived immediately before this one, and Isis had been the first—everyone had an easier time connecting to her than any of our other lives when they had been the current life.

"*I know, I know. But it was so hard staying quiet when you interacted with him in the past. I want to see my boy so much.*"

"*The two of you will have to wait on that,*" Rashta said.

"*What? But why?*" Velsara asked. "*She's nearly perfected it with me. And it'll only be for a minute.*"

"*It will wait. The ceremony will start soon.*"

My past soul-life let out a resigned sigh and dropped it. I felt bad, but there would be more time after.

"*Prepare!*" a roughly familiar female dragon voice said.

They didn't need to warn me. I'd already spotted Rimu being carried by his father when he'd descended. I readied myself for the inevitable tackle, and listened to the feet tromping through the grass. People parted for the black and red, small-horse-sized dragon. But to my surprise, when he came within reach, he skidded to a halt instead of charging right into me.

"*Eira!*" he chirped, then ran around me a few times, before wrapping his body around mine and forced his head under my arm. "*Happy to see you.*"

I smiled and pulled him in for a quick snuggle. "*I am happy to see you.*"

"*I did good? Careful with small female.*"

I chuckled and let him go. So that's what it was about. Seemed his parents had finally gotten him to understand his size was something to be mindful about. I still didn't quite understand the growth of dragons, both physically and mentally, but it was only a matter of time. "*Yes. You did well.*"

He chirped and held his head high. His nose twitched, and his attention honed in on my mate mark. Rimu pressed his nose against the mark on the crook of my neck, inhaling the scent it gave off. I didn't notice any smell, but, as it was explained to me, that was because the mark was mine. Other dragons could smell it—for now. The scent would die down after a while, though when, I couldn't be sure.

Rimu let out a sorrowful sound I'd not heard from him before, and he deflated. I patted him on the head. Raikidan's mate claim meant Rimu could no longer fight the older dragon to claim me as his treasure. "*When you are older, Rashta and I will need you.*"

He perked up. "*I can protect still?*"

I nodded. His spirits restored, he ran in a circle.

"*You may regret that,*" the dragon voice from before said.

I looked up to see three dragons approaching—two red, one black. The frilled design on the smaller red helped me identify her over Zaith's more spine-and-plated appearance.

I smiled, speaking in common. "I would never regret saying that, Xaneth."

The lovely red dragon transformed into a beautiful red-haired woman with freckle-smattered pale skin. "Yes, I know. And it's something I am grateful for every day." She held out her arms for an embrace, and I didn't refuse her. "It's good to see you. And it appears you've come out of the mating rites in one piece."

My head flew back as I laughed. "Yes, I survived." My eyes flicked to Raikidan. "Him, on the other hand, we're still debating."

Raikidan let out a contemptible snort, crossing his arms.

Xaneth blocked her mouth with the back of her hand while she laughed. "As we all question for the first few decades. Don't worry, it does get better."

"As I've been assured a few times."

Zaith was the next to approach, transforming into his familiar tan-skinned nu-human form, sporting a two-toned red unsupported long mohawk, triggering Velsara to get excited again. "Hello, Eira."

"Hi to you too, Zaith. Did Xaneth relay my message?"

He nodded. "She did. You had it harder than normal, no? All is easily forgiven for that."

"Please, Rashta?" Velsara begged. *"Just for a moment."*

"No."

My past soul-life's energy deflated, but I wasn't going to let Rashta kill her excitement completely. *"Hey, what if we do that… thing you told me you'd do with him?"*

Velsara gasped. *"You'd do that?"*

I don't know why she asked the question. Of course I would.

I leaned in toward Zaith, one of my hands on my hips, just as I'd seen Velsara show me, and poked her adopted son's nose. "It'd better be forgiven. I expect you to be good and understanding of our situation."

I didn't have Velsara's accent, but by the way Zaith stared at me, frozen, my simulated action was enough.

Then, in a blur of motion, he pulled me into a crushing embrace, burying his face into my neck. Everything happened even faster after that. Velsara's happiness overwhelmed my senses, Raikidan snarled, Xaneth gasped, Rimu and his siblings yelped and hid, and the warm, powerful energy of Rashta left my body.

"This is why I told you to hold off," the goddess said through gritted teeth.

Zaith's presence disappeared, the young clan leader taking several paces back to put a safe distance between us. Velsara's happiness died along with the separation. "You're not her." He shook his head. "I know not to do that to a newly mated female."

I sighed and swiveled my attention back to Raikidan, only for my breath to catch. Teeth bared and murderous intent in his eyes, he fought against Rashta to get at Zaith. The goddess, fully corporeal, had her arms wrapped around his torso, doing her best to keep him back. But it was clear, her strengths as a goddess weren't on the physical side.

This was a new reaction to me. He'd never gotten this bad, even early into our mating, which is when I would have maybe expected such an overreaction, until he sorted out his will over his instincts. And honestly, it unsettled me. He was protective, but this just felt... off.

But as much as I should have been angry, I couldn't find myself to be. I was more disappointed than anything.

Stepping into his line of sight, I stood in front of Raikidan. I didn't speak. I wasn't sure I could put my disappointment into words. So, I hoped that feeling showed on my face. It seemed to, with the way Blaze sucked in a breath through his teeth and took a step back, mumbling to himself, "He fucked up."

Raikidan's gazed fixed on me. He froze, his eyes widening and brow pulling together. It didn't take him long to pull back from Rashta. He rested a hand on his forehead, his gaze downturned and unable to meet my stare. "What is going on with me?"

Ryoko placed her hands on her hips. "Seriously. You're *way* over-reacting."

Xaneth tapped a finger to her lips. "Normally I'd say that was normal, as I've seen far worse—"

"Worse?" Ryoko screeched, her eyes wide with disbelief. "You're trying to say you think that is normal?"

"Our species are different," Anahak said. "We're serious about protecting our treasure."

Xaneth flicked a finger and her mate backed off so she could continue. "As I was saying, normally we'd not question the behavior, as some males are just that sensitive to their instinct to protect their mate so soon after mating, but from the sounds of it, he's never acted this way after securing the mate bond. And I think it's wise to be concerned of the sudden change."

While the older she-dragon spoke, my attention had wandered to Rashta. She hadn't stopped watching Raikidan. "Rashta, what do you know?"

Attention fell on me and then the goddess. She didn't respond, her gaze transfixed on my mate. My lip curled. "You've been acting weird all day. What are you not saying?"

A few people exchanged astonished glances. Not many would be willing to speak to a god like I just had. But, when you shared a body with one, and had regular contact with others, you stopped a lot of the formalities and treated them like you did your friends and family.

Flame-like energy swirled around the winged goddess and then she shot back into me. Warmth welled in my chest, and then died as my body accepted her presence again. I crossed my arms, unwilling to let this go. *"Rashta."*

She sighed. *"It's not something I'm sure on. That's why I haven't wanted to talk about it."*

"Well, I'd rather hear theories than silence."

"I have been experiencing unsettling feelings these last few days. A disturbance, if you would. This isn't uncommon when I can't perform my appointed duty and there's a matter at hand I would have normally stepped in on. However, this sensation has felt more akin to situations I've experienced before with your past lives when they were in danger. It's made me alert and uneasy."

She paused a moment. *"I've noticed Raikidan has also acted strangely on the days I experienced the sensations. Though, as I've recounted the last year, and months leading to my near-purified state, he never showed signs until I tried that experiment on him."*

I drummed my fingers on my arm, trying to recall the day she was referring to. *"You're referring to the moment you connected him to his past lives?"*

"Yes. I'd never done this to any of his past lives, and I didn't think there'd be any harm trying with him. But now, I wonder if my action strengthened his connection to my power, even after the contact to his past lives disappeared."

"So… you think he's subconsciously reacting to your heightened awareness and he's now treating certain actions as a threat when he normally wouldn't?"

"That's exactly it. And why I didn't want you and Isis to do anything rash in case I was right."

I pinched my nose and sighed. *"So, I'll just have to be a little extra careful until we figure it out. I wish you'd said that to begin with. You know I'm not going to just do what you say because you tell me to, without giving reason."*

"She's got a point," Atria said. *"It would have been nice if we all knew—we could have helped sooner. Eira has access to us. That ability to connect with one's past in such a way shouldn't be taken for granted. You know this."*

Rashta sighed. *"I understand you're all upset. I didn't want to draw attention to things because it'd take away from everything else. Eira should be allowed to relish in these quiet moments. She didn't get them like the rest of you. I had hoped my vague warnings to be careful with Raikidan would be enough for now."*

I tapped my fingers again. *"And yet, if there's potential trouble, we need to prepare."*

"That's the thing, Eira. I don't know yet what this sensation is targeted toward. It may have nothing to do with you, and therefore not your concern. My distortion has severely impacted my abilities. More than I'd like to admit."

I sighed. *"All right, fine. But you must promise, the moment you think trouble is coming our way, you tell us."*

"You have my word."

Well that was one thing settled. *Now for Raikidan…*

"And your sister. She's returned."

My brow quirked up and I turned to find her nearby, but not where I'd last seen her after Trigon stopped chasing her around. *When had she run off?*

Yára pursed her lips. "Not sure what I missed when I slipped away, but everything good now?"

"Almost," I said slowly. "What's up?"

She shrugged. "Father needs Raikidan, and someone named Zaith. Something about a quick meeting."

"I'm not needed?"

She shook her head. "He said he wants you to be able to catch up with others. I guess he figures Raikidan will fill you in on anything important."

Must not be *that* important, if he was leaving it up to Raikidan to relay the details. I jammed my thumb in Zaith's direction. "That's Zaith."

Yára turned to the young dragon clan leader, whose gaze was already fixed on her with in unusually keen eye. "I don't think we've met."

"Uh, no," he said, his response lacking in his usual confidence.

Yára approached him, her hand outstretched. "Well, I'm Yára. Eira's clone—"

"Sister," I interjected. "She's my younger sister."

I wanted to put the clone bit behind us. Beyond health checks, it didn't matter that my siblings were clones or clone variants, and the more we treated each other like a normal family, the better.

"Yára…" he mumbled, his gaze lingering on her face before drifting to her extended hand.

What's with him?

"Hmm, I wonder…" Velsara mused. She didn't elaborate on that thought.

Trigon came up behind him and clamped a hand on Zaith's shoulder. Rhaec grinned and took up space behind the dragon leader on his other side. "She's our sister, too. So you'd best be careful around her."

Zaith didn't react to their clear threat. He reached out and grasped her hand, though not in a handshake motion. He'd slipped his fingers under hers to cup her hand, as if to perform some sort of human kiss greeting. But he didn't lift her hand or bend closer to her.

A grin slipped up half his face, his somewhat cocky and confident persona returning. "Nice meetin' you, water lily."

Yára cocked her head, but he released her and walked off without another word. My eyes flicked to Xaneth. Her eyebrows rose and she shrugged. Seemed even she was just as clueless about her young clan leader's behavior.

I brushed it off. He'd always acted strange in my book. Instead, I chose to focus on Raikidan. He'd remained withdrawn this whole time.

"Did you figure out what's going on with him, Laz?" Ryoko asked.

"Sorta." I drew up close to Raikidan and popped up on my toes to plant a soft kiss on his forehead. "Everything is going to be okay."

He grabbed my hand, his grip tighter than he would usually use. "What's wrong with me?"

I cupped his cheek and pulled him closer to rest his forehead on mine. "Nothing. As best as we can tell, you may be feeding off something Rashta is feeling. It's making you more agitated and reactive than you'd normally be."

Raikidan pulled me close and buried his face into my neck. "I'm sorry."

I wrapped my arms around him. "It's fine. We'll get through it."

Ryoko let out a long, pleased sigh, drawing my gaze. She had the stupidest grin on her face and looked as if she was about to fall over. "What's with you?"

"You two are just so sweet!"

I rolled my eyes. She was such a sap.

I patted Raikidan on the back and then pulled away. "Think you've got your head on straight enough to talk with my father now?"

He closed his eyes for a moment. "I think so. You won't be next to me, so that may help."

"How about I make things a little easier?" a new, but familiar hollow voice said.

We turned, spotting the unmistakable faces of Seda and Argus. And in Argus' arms, a rather large cat with tufted ears.

5
CHAPTER

The two of them hadn't changed at all in the last year. And while I'd planned to tease Seda a bit about her new career, my attention was fixated on the cat. My eyebrow arched. "Um… what's with the dog-sized cat?"

Seda laughed. "It's Crystal, Laz."

My eyes bugged and I shook my head, remembering the rambunctious ball of fluff that was practically attached to Raikidan. "No way that's Crystal."

Ryoko leaned in to get my attention and nodded vigorously, her eyes wider than normal, as if trying reinforce Seda's claim. *There's no way…* Sure, the kitten was a little larger than most would expect of a cat, especially a stray, but to get to this size?

Raikidan was gone from my side in an instant, lifting the cat out of Argus' arms and holding it in front of his face. The feline's long body now on display, I took in its brown, orange, and white coat pattern, and long bushy tail. And then noticed the tear in one of her ears. Reality sunk in. *That really is her.*

"Damn, she got big," Atria said.

Crystal pawed at Raikidan's nose and purred when he pressed his face against hers. He swept her up into a cradled position, on her back in his arms, scratching under her chin. Her loud purring carried past me, and the shadow of shame that had been lingering on Raikidan's face melted away.

Stella gasped and tugged on my skirt. "Momma, is that a kitty?"

"Yes, that's Crystal"—my brow spiked when Raikidan just walked off with her—"Rai, where are you going with her?"

He didn't answer, just continued off in the same direction Zaith had disappeared in.

"Momma, where is Papa going with the cat?"

"Um…"

Seda laughed. "Don't worry. She'll keep him calm. You know she has that effect on him."

I couldn't say I disagreed. He had such an unusual bond with that feline. I wanted to get him one of his own, but we'd been unsuccessful in finding any that weren't afraid of him.

"I can't believe you brought that thing with you," Blaze said, shaking his head. "You treat it like a dog, putting it on a harness and leash and all."

My brow spiked. "You walk her?"

Argus nodded. "She goes a little stir crazy if she's inside too much, but we don't want her running around on the street. So it was the best compromise we could come up with."

"Huh." I rested my hands on my hips. "Why did you bring her here? I don't think this purification process really warrants her tagging along."

The two exchanged glances and a meek smile appeared on Seda's lips. "Well, we were hoping you'd take her."

I blinked. "What?"

Stella gasped. "Momma, we're getting a kitty?"

I calmed her. "Hold on—Seda, what do you mean?"

"Between my studies and work, and meditation requirements, and Argus' equally long work hours, we don't have the time to dedicate to her in the way she really deserves. We figure… you and Raikidan have more time for her, and you have a family that can give her all the love she demands."

Argus ran his fingers through his dark hair. "And let's be honest. Even though I brought Crystal home for Seda, she bonded with Raikidan and claimed him as her 'person.' After you two left, she hasn't acted quite the same. So it makes sense to give her to you."

Stella tugged on my hand. "Momma, can we please have her? I want a kitty. I promise I'll take good care of her."

I blew out a breath. "I dunno, Stella. You're going to have a hard time wrestling Papa for the right to take care of her."

My daughter's eyes lit up and she wrapped her arms around me the best she could. "Thank you, Momma Eira!" She released me and ran off. "I'm gonna tell Papa the news!"

Sethal chased after her. "Stel, wait up!"

I chuckled and shook my head.

"Now," Seda said, before opening her arms, "I want the same greeting everyone else got."

I didn't refuse her, and Argus got his turn when Seda and I finally let go of each other. It was so good seeing them. "How are you both? Besides busy?"

Argus chuckled. "That about sums up our lives right now. I'm busy improving tech for everyone in a non-violent way." He turned his eyes to Seda, clear adoration reflecting in his eyes. "And this wonderful woman has really helped with not only improving psychic image and treatment by the general populace, but there've been some major improvement to psychological help for former soldiers and citizens, and it's not exclusive to just nu-humans."

A shade of red tinted Seda's cheeks and she brushed her sweeping bangs aside. The action was a poor attempt to cover her embarrassment, given she could easily see past the leather blindfold strapped to her face with her telekinetic abilities. "I work with a team. I can't take all the credit."

Ryoko hung her arm over my shoulder. "It's crazy to think so much has happened in just a year. For all of us."

I nodded. "It's a little surreal."

Blaze ran his fingers through his hair. "I don't know about all of you, but some days, it still doesn't feel real. I think I'm going to wake up in the middle of the night to Genesis barking out counter-measure battle plans."

Genesis scoffed and crossed her arms. "I didn't bark orders. That was Eira."

Rylan snickered. "I don't know if 'bark' quite describes the silent promise of murder if you didn't comply."

Everyone laughed, including me, unable to disagree.

Seda quieted and turned her head in the direction she and Argus had come. "Talon is ready to speak with you. And Telar is getting antsy, too. He's on the way."

I nodded and shifted my focus to where I thought Zaedrix and Rosa were, only to find them gone. "Oh. I guess they got impatient."

Lutha, one of my twin third lives, scoffed. *"No surprise there."*

"Yes, they've been with him for a while now."

I should have figured. "Alright, lead the way. Doesn't seem like this event is getting on as quickly as I expected."

Zane scratched his head. "I noticed that as well. I was under the impression this was more urgent than it's been treated so far."

Shva'sika patted his hand. "I'm sure they know Laz could benefit from some socialization and catch-up with her friends."

Blaze clasped his hands behind his head and leaned back on his heels. "I don't know. She could do that after this purification thing. There's no rush to catch up with everyone."

I pursed my lips, agreeing with him and my uncle. *"Rashta?"*

She was silent for a moment. *"I'm not sure why it hasn't started. Your uncle is right. While it was postponed because of your mating rites, this amount of waiting today is unusual. Unfortunately I can't contact them in my current state, so I can't check. I wouldn't worry about it. Enjoy the time you have with everyone."*

Ryoko cocked her head. "What's the verdict, Laz?"

I shrugged. "Rashta doesn't know, either. She doesn't seem concerned, though, so we might as well enjoy our time rather than worry about it."

Argus nodded, seeing no reason to argue, and beckoned for us to follow. Mocha and Raid encouraged the children to go off and play, Matron Lyra volunteering to watch them, allowing the pair to join us.

Not long after moving on, a lively ruckus caught my ear. *Sounds like a bunch of dwarves.* I peered out, curious whether I was right. While I'd met all kinds of individuals in my life, Vorn had been the only dwarf I'd formed any sort of bond with. I could see him showing up, especially if he assumed there was some sort of party going on, but it didn't sound like one dwarf, which threw me off. *Of course, it could be him bringing the party.*

It didn't take me long to locate them. Clustered around a wagon with crates and kegs strewn about, was a gathering of dwarves. They laughed, clapped, danced, and were really making fools of themselves without a care. Most had mugs in their hands, and from the tapped casks, it wasn't hard figuring out what the mugs contained. *How did they get that wagon in here?* I could see the two mules grazing nearby, but with the harsh terrain just getting to the mountain tunnel, it'd be difficult to get that in here.

"Well, looks like the day drinking has already begun," Genesis said, rolling her eyes.

I snorted. "You think dwarves ever stop? They're perpetually drunk."

"Not all of 'em, lass," Daren said. "But yer mostly right."

A familiar dwarf with a large septum ring in his bulbous nose, and blonde beard braided with metal rings and claps with decorative plates, turned our way and frantically waved his hand, holding his mug of ale, some of the contents spilling over onto the ground.

I laughed as Vorn cursed. *Only him.* But at least I was right about him showing up.

"Did you really think we wouldn't invite him?" Rashta said.

"No, I suppose not."

The other dwarves took notice of us, though two of them particularly stuck out to me due to their reactions. The man, burly, tan-skinned with well-groomed red hair and beard, and dressed in expensive-looking clothing, outright dropped his drink while the woman, busty and dark-skinned, with curly black hair pulled into a high bun, audibly gasped.

"Daren?" they both said.

I blinked and turned to my human friend. Did he know these two?

"Mither? Faither?" Daren said, taking a step forward.

My eyes widened. *Wait… did he just call them his parents?*

Faster than I'd ever seen Daren move, which was more like a fast paced lumber for him, he rushed to the now two sprinting dwarves. He of course wasn't on his feet for long, when the pair barreled into him. Joyful cries and laughter came from the pile of people.

I turned to Valene with my unspoken question. She cocked her head. "Wait, did he not tell you?" When my expression didn't change, she blinked. "I guess not. Daren was adopted as a boy by dwarves. They're traveling traders, and just found him wandering alone one day. He'd had a head injury, and couldn't recall much of what happened to him or his family."

My brow furrowed as I thought about this. Daren had told me he'd stumbled upon the West Tribe in his early adult hood, but never spoke much of his past. But it would explain a lot about the man. "Why did he never talk about them?"

She shrugged. "I don't know why it never came up with you. He talked about them a lot with me and Mom. And they have come to the town every now and then." She tapped her lips with a finger. "Now that I think of it, you weren't ever around when they did."

"If he had such a good relationship with them, how did he end up at the tribe?"

"Daren decided he wanted a change of pace, and struck out on his own. I guess the innkeeper life suited him better, because he's never seriously thought about leaving to rejoin the family business."

"I can answer yer questions maself, lass," Daren called out.

I turned to see him sitting up, his parents still clinging to him. The joy etched into their faces brought a smile to my lips. "I didn't want to interrupt your reunion."

He shook his head, his signature smile on his face. Not my best attempt at a lie, but he was too nice of a person to call me out on it.

"I'm going to spend some time catching up with them," Valene said. "We'll catch up after."

I nodded. I had no issue with anyone wanting to split off at any point.

She sauntered over to the trio, Daren's parents eagerly greeting her—his mother even gushing about her being a stouter, or something like that. I was already too busy moving on with everyone else to really catch the conversation correctly—not that I always understood some of the phrases dwarves used.

We passed groups of individuals from various walks of life hanging about and socializing. Many stopped to wave, or welcomed us, paying particular attention to me, even if I didn't know them—something I was getting used to as my status as Dragon-Phoenix became more widespread. As we continued, the sheer cliff face towering over us became hard for me to ignore. An unusual tugging sensation deep within me called me to break off from my friends and venture closer for some reason.

I shook the feeling and searched for a mysterious temple that was supposed to be hidden here. I expected to see some sort of building, or even an open shrine of sorts. I hadn't spotted it on the descent from the tunnel entrance. Unfortunately, I couldn't see it here, either. *Where the hell is this thing?*

"You're so close," Isis said.

"Since you know where it is, why are you keeping it a secret?"

She laughed. *"Because your frustration is amusing."*

The gathered people morphed into faces I knew or had seen from the South Tribe. Most nodded their acknowledgement of me, moving out of our path so as not to be a hindrance.

"Hey, Sweet Thing. About time you came my way." My back straightened. *I know that voice.* The individual in question popped into view a moment later, standing in the shade of a large tree. He was a tall, athletically built man with bronze skin, a strong jaw, and short black hair and facial hair. A blue cloth with a golden hexagram painted on it was wrapped around his head, covering his eyes. *Telar!*

Before I could even think to run to him, my body became weightless. Had I not been used to such a sensation, it would have been frightening. My breath *wooshed* out of my lungs when I flew forward and into Telar's waiting arms. His peppermint scent wafted into my nose. I stared up at him, momentarily dazed.

He grinned. "Looks like I can still steal your breath away."

I rolled my eyes and Ryoko sputtered out a laugh. A woman behind him groaned. "That was bad, even for you."

"He's also lucky Raikidan isn't here to murder him," Azriel said.

Ryoko snickered. "Not that Eira's faithful dragon-man didn't want to do that before they became official."

Telar chuckled. "That's why I'm getting this in now."

I shook my head and then wrapped my arms around him to finally give him a hug. "I wouldn't let you die."

"I'd let your man maim him for making me continue to wait to get my hug," a woman said, her voice vaguely familiar.

I pulled away from Telar and peered around him. Sitting on a bench at the base of the tree were two women. One woman, a half-elf from the looks of it, I didn't know. She was a pale thing, with strawberry blond hair, angular facial features, and a curvy figure. She surprisingly lacked in height, given her elven nature. Her feet were a good three inches off the ground from her position on the bench. A nose-mounted monocle covered one of her blue eyes and attached to a pointed ear with an ear cuff.

In her hand she held a book, and an inkwell with a quill sat beside her on the bench. That had me noticing the other ways she adorned her body, making me wonder if she was a scholar of some sort, even if it wasn't the usual attire I was used to—a side bag with parchment scrolls, over-the-knee leather boots, and a long white shirt with billowing sleeves, cinched at the waist with a corset.

The woman beside her, however, I couldn't forget. Long raven hair, violet cloth eye wrap with a golden hexagram, septum piercing, plump lips, bronze skin, and curves that didn't quit under her elven made clothes; besides the tired slump in her shoulders, I knew Avila when I saw her.

She held out her arms. "You, come here."

Before I could think to take a step toward her, her fingers twitched and my body shot away from Telar. I gasped and then found my face smothered in her large bosom. Avila's arms wrapped around my head, preventing me from pulling away. "Oh, how I've missed you!"

This wouldn't have been so bad had it not been for the fact I could hardly breathe. I tapped her arm. "I need air."

My words came out muffled, but she heard me well enough since she gasped and let up, though didn't release me. "I'm so sorry."

I chuckled, wrapping my arms around her. "It's okay. I missed these hugs."

"Momma Avila always gives the most comfortable hugs," Ryoko said.

I chuckled again at her mention of *momma*. Avila and Telar were just a little older than us, and as a strange result, she ended up taking on a motherly role. Something about the way she held you, it made you forget your worries.

Relaxing against Avila, I caught Telar muttering about how unfair it was his sister was getting a better reunion embrace, making me snicker a bit. "And honestly, I'm just glad you have the strength to do half of this."

She smiled. "Yes. You sent me the best remedy I could have asked for. I've got a ways to go, but this is the best I've felt in thirty years."

"That makes me happy." My attention turned to the woman next to her. She watched everyone, but hadn't engaged yet. She seemed a little unsure with the new crowd. "And who is this?"

The woman blinked and turned her attention to me. When she spoke, her words were soft. "Oh, um… I'm Taryn. Telar and Avila have been staying with me. It's nice to finally meet you."

She held out a tentative hand. Avila released me so I could reciprocate the gesture. This woman's grip was as soft as her voice.

"Even though I was sure Ravenward would be a safe place for them to hide out during Zarda's reign, there was still risk for your family," I said. "It means a lot to us. You have our gratitude and debt."

Taryn shook her head. "You don't need to thank me. They've been wonderful guests. And Avila has been a great help at our library on her healthy days."

Telar held up his arms. "Hey, don't forget about me, now. I helped a lot, too."

She narrowed her eyes at him. "Hardly. You are constantly coming in and messing up the order of our books because you're bored."

He waved a hand, lifting the book on her lap. "Only because you needed to get away from that desk of yours."

She gasped and reached for the tome, her fingers only gripping the edges of the exposed parchment inside the hard binding. "Telar, be careful! The ink is still wet."

His head moved in a way that told me he was rolling his eyes behind his blindfold. He released the book and then wrapped an arm around her shoulder, flashing her a devilish smirk. "You know I wouldn't ruin your book."

I noticed the pink rising in her cheeks, and she struggled to form the words to respond. I called out to Avila mentally, hoping she'd catch my words before any other psychic did. *Should I ask?*"

"Oh, don't worry. I'm already working on that." Avila responded, knowing I was assuming she'd meddle in her brother's affairs if I was right in my observation. *"I told him there was someone perfect for him out there, and she's it. Quite a bit different from you, but her calmer personality is what my crazy brother needs."*

"Has Telar gotten over… you know…"

"Don't worry. There's only a little bit of lingering regret. You're stuck with him as a friend for the rest of your life."

I bit back a chuckle so no one would know about our private conversation. But it seemed it still didn't go unnoticed by Telar. "I see your facial expressions, Sweet Thing. What are you two scheming over there?"

I placed a hand on my chest, feigning hurt. "Me, scheming? What would ever give you such an outrageous idea?"

Ryoko burst into laughter and Telar shook his head. "That was beyond fake."

I rose to my feet, Avila reluctantly allowing it, my mind racing for a good excuse. It didn't take long. "I was merely asking her where Aurora went. I was told she was with you three."

Telar scoffed. "Right. If that were the case, you'd say it out loud."

He wasn't wrong. That idea wasn't as well thought out as I planned. A wicked grin spread up my face when an awful idea came to me. All my past soul-lives cackled. "I just didn't want to interrupt you two lovebirds. It would have been rude."

Telar's mouth parted, and in a rare moment of success for me, he struggled to find words. Taryn's eyes bugged out and her face turned scarlet. "W–what? T–that's not… I mean, w–we're not… That's not to say…"

Her words tumbled to another language—Elvish was the best I could discern—and her pace quickened. Telar pulled away from her, his head turned in her direction, brows rising as if he were staring wide-eyed behind his blindfold. Avila's lips pressed together, a wicked smile formed on them.

"I think you broke her, Eira," Blaze said.

Shva'sika bent forward, her head cocking. "I'll be honest, she's not making much sense in Elvish, either."

Ryoko held her sides as she laughed, and I bit my lip. I shouldn't have found it funny, but I did.

Taryn's words came to an abrupt halt and she lifted her book, hiding her face from the audience she had attracted. Laughter rumbled through the onlookers, prompting her to duck her head farther into her book.

To give them—mostly poor Taryn—a break, I turned to Avila, and decided to fall back on my little lie from earlier. "So, where exactly is Aurora? You never finished telling me that."

She pointed with her chin. "Miss Head of the Dalatrend Cyber Security Network is over by that other tree, speaking with Arnia and

Jaybird. Aurora was getting hot in the sun, and Jaybird offered to keep her cool."

I looked in the direction she gestured, finding six people conversing under another nearby tree, some North Tribe Shaman clustered just beyond them. Arnia and Jaybird were the first I noticed. From the looks of their clothes, the twins had chosen to stay with the North Tribe. And from the way Arnia hung off the shoulder of Ven'lar, the Cleansing Spirit shaman who'd tended to her and her brother when they'd been marked as traitors by Zarda and subsequently tortured before their escape, she'd been given a good reason to stick around.

Jaybird circled a finger, using his air elemental mastery to push a breeze toward Aurora, who sat on the ground next to Seda's twin brother, Nioush. Leaning against the tree behind him was his and Seda's younger sister Saléna, Nyra's twin.

Nioush's presence still perplexed me. He was an arrogant prick on the best of days, and had always acted like everyone was inferior to him. But here he was, hanging around like he had always fit in.

My thoughts traveled over to Aurora not long after, when I noticed she wasn't wearing any protective clothes. "So, someone want to explain to me why Aurora isn't protecting herself from the sun before I go freak out at her?"

Avila leaned back. "Well, it's quite simple. Nioush is able to use his psychic abilities to shield her from the UV rays that harm her."

I pursed my lips. "And why would he do that?"

Mocha placed her hands on her hips. "Oh, you're going to be floored by this. You thought my and Raid's relationship was out in left field? Those two are an item now."

Both my eyebrows rose and I turned my full attention to Seda. "What? When? How?"

She shrugged. "I'm not in on all the details, but it started because she'd frequent the café he was working at and he'd 'spike' her coffee."

"Spike, as in slip blood into it?" He'd been around when Aurora's vampire bat DNA splice secret was revealed, so it didn't surprise me that he figured out her blood sustenance needs.

She nodded, though before she could speak, Ryoko piped up. "Um, can we back up and talk about Nioush being a barista? What?"

Seda shrugged again. "Like a lot of ex-soldiers, he didn't know what he was going to do, so he tried a few different jobs"—her mouth slipped into a frown—"while also having to navigate the prejudice against us psychics. And it just so happens, he was good with coffee. He's opening his own café next week. All the employees are psychics."

Ryoko gasped, her eyes sparkling. "That sounds amazing! We all have to go to the grand opening."

"You're not getting anything for free," Nioush called out.

Ryoko crossed her arms. "I wasn't going to ask for that, jerk."

Aurora smacked him on the arm. "Be nice." She then waved to me. "Don't be a stranger, Babe, come say hi."

I should. It'd be good to catch up with them all. But before I could answer her, Rosa suddenly appeared in front of me. Her hands rested on her hips. "Enough dallying. You can catch up with your friends later."

The succubus grabbed my wrist and dragged me away. I shot Aurora and the others an apologetic look. "Later, I guess."

Arnia laughed and waved me off. If I wasn't fighting the demoness, then they'd roll with it like me. I'd have time later to catch up with them.

Rosa set a direct path, her focus intense. Those who stood in her way were quick to move. The crowd eventually thinned to just South Tribe Shaman; they were also not high in numbers, and it wasn't hard to see why. In the shade of a large tree, Zaedrix stood speaking with a number of individuals, none of them human. My eyes scanned the beings. They were all demons. Well, Tla'lli and Talon were with them, so that wasn't entirely accurate.

"Can you classify Talon as human, though?" Atria asked.

That was a good question. He had human DNA, but that was only about a third of his makeup. *Are cambions classified as demon or human? Did it matter?* Not in my book.

Tla'lli was the first to notice us. The young elf woman brushed some loose braids from her tri-hawk over her shoulder and waved, drawing the attention of Talon and then the other demons. Rosa released me, and in a blink joined Zaedrix by his side, hanging off him as she usually did.

Talon smiled my way, his crimson eyes piercing through me. While he and Blaze shared that same unusual trait, Talon's more recent transformation had caused that look to feel more intimidating, no matter how gentle and kind he tried to appear. But I wasn't easily intimidated.

I smiled back and took a good look at him. Like Arnia and Jaybird, he'd exchanged his military attire for shaman fashion, though his were South Tribe. Bone spikes protruded from parts of his body, particularly his arms and upper body, including his spine. His ivory skin had actual color to it, compared to how pale he looked when I'd seen him several months ago.

Talon crossed his arms. "I've already gotten an assessment."

I shrugged. "I'm doing my version. You're looking much better than when I last saw you."

While some of the paths others had taken after their liberations were surprising, nothing had prepared me for Talon's transformation—or him, for that matter. Like many experiments, he never talked about his genetic makeup. But he'd done it because it'd seemed so absurd it couldn't have been real to him.

Two types of demon DNA spliced in with nu-human.

Given demons were so rare, he thought it was some sort of joke or code used by the geneticists. Until all the fighting stopped and his relationship with Tla'lli progressed did it become clear that information was, in fact, truthful. That's when I'd enlisted the help of Rosa and Zaedrix and found myself thrust into the world of demons. That included me finding out there were far more of them on Lumaraeon than anyone thought.

"Everything is under control now, from what Rosa and I can sense," Zaedrix said. "No bloodlust and no unsated hunger. There is no struggle between his human side and demon side. His beloved is feeding him well."

"I have a name," Tla'lli muttered, red spreading across her cheeks. "And must you talk about it so flippantly?"

One of Zaedrix's eyebrows rose. "I don't understand. He must feed to survive."

The redness in Tla'lli's face deepened. It was obvious she wasn't comfortable articulating the problem that I understood easily, and the incubus wasn't getting it.

A nearby succubus chuckled. "Zaedrix has always struggled to understand the privacy you elves and humans require."

Her point was proven when the incubus became even more confused. Rosa shook her head and left his side, her fingers trailing over his shoulder. "He may not, but my more recent transformation allows me to understand."

My eye brow rose a bit. *More recent transformation?* My understanding was the succubus had been turned during the Dark Wars. That was well before my soul's time. Plus her wording insinuated Zaedrix had been transformed as well, but I never got that impression from him by the way he acted.

Rosa drew up to the elf shaman and lifted her chin, the action sensual as much as it was tender and caring. This was not something I'd seen from her before. "Talon is as much an incubus as he is bone demon and human. He must fuck to feed. You understand this, that much is clear. But because of our nature, we do not find it embarrassing to speak out. It is as natural as discussing the desire to eat an apple." Her lips pulled into a kind smile. "You'll get used to it in time."

Tla'lli struggled to find words with the demoness' gaze on her. Her eyes darted to the demons standing behind them, particularly to the towering pale demon with crimson eyes and enormous spikes protruding out of his body and down his spine and tail. Wings made of bone, but no membrane to allow the creature to fly, protruded from the being's back.

The bone demon chuckled, as if he found the interaction amusing. His mouth opened, revealing razor-sharp teeth, and his voice rumbled deep, "It does get easier, child. Even we non-sex demons have learned to accept how they speak."

Another succubus, this one with reddish-brown skin and crimson hair, drew up next to the bone demon, wrapping her arms around one of his massive ones. "And you've done well these few months, Tla'lli. We had our doubts outsiders would be able to handle our existence beyond our secluded borders. Even though we do have some non-demons living amongst us, they have been few in numbers for a reason." She smiled. "But you and your tribe have shown us there is potential, especially in how you treat our son."

Talon's face lit up, and I couldn't blame him. Experiments never held out any hope to hear those words in their lifetime. It was the nature of being created and thrown away as tools of war. But it didn't stop many from dreaming of the possibility, especially as the rebellion came to an end. And Talon had found that. Didn't matter that the side he found wasn't the human one.

The demoness smiled, continuing. "I'm confident it won't take you long to find yourself comfortable speaking as we do."

Tla'lli nodded slowly.

The bone demon turned his gaze to me. "It is good to see you again, Eira."

I dipped my head respectfully. "I hope you take no offence to us checking on Talon, Xithoz. I know you all have been helping him."

He chuckled. "I'd been more concerned if you hadn't checked him yourself. Why else help him if you despised what he was? I hope you don't mind us crashing your event. We received a personal invitation from Nazir."

I shook my head. "I don't have an issue in the slightest. I've been learning quite a bit about all of you these last few months. It's broadened my perspective on many things." My eyes narrowed. "However, I'll be honest. Nazir's involvement in your presence has me more concerned."

"I doubt you have much to worry about," the succubus hanging from Xithoz's arm said. "He understands how important today is."

"You're probably right, Nemora. However, I trust the trickster about as far as I can throw him."

I'd come to see Nazir in a bit of a better light than I had in the past, but that didn't mean I trusted him. Rashta snorted but refrained from any verbal comment. She had her own issues with the god for whom she still harbored feelings.

"I do not, Eira."

"Sure, you don't."

My past soul-lives laughed.

Nemora peered past me, her head cocking. "Are your friends afraid of us?"

I glanced over my shoulders to see the others hanging back. I honestly didn't expect them to come as close as they did. The whole demon situation was not going to be easy for most to understand.

"Eira sent word about the situation when it all went down," Blaze said. "She let us know we shouldn't get too close to Talon until he was comfortable. We're just waiting for that indicator."

"Ladies should stay about as far away as Eira for now," Talon said. "I try to keep them about that far for now, until I get more of a handle on all this."

Ryoko placed her hands on her hips. "As long as you're not telling us to get lost. That's just rude."

He smirked. "Never to you, Ryoko."

Rosa leaned closer to him, her eyes narrowed. But she relaxed soon after, seemingly not finding anything off about him.

The others ventured closer, a few nervous to be around so many demons, while the others merely curious.

"So, this is your extended family, huh?" Ryoko said. No surprise that she wasn't afraid of all this.

"In a way, yes," Talon said. "Where is yours?"

She shrugged. "Somewhere here. I'm sure you'll see them eventually. Ashnard wanted to meet Laz." She turned her golden eyes to the gathered demons. "Is this all of you, or…"

Xithoz shook his head. "No. Many of the Xolral clan chose to stay behind."

"Huh…" She cocked her head in contemplation. "There are a lot more of you here in Lumaraeon than we were led to believe."

A few demons exchanged unsure glances. I didn't blame them. They'd hidden away in secret since the Dark Wars because, unlike a majority of demons, the Xolral clan was peaceful—or more accurately, they were as peaceful as was allowed per their nature to survive. It was a choice they made, which was why I had any sort of hope of coexistence with them. I wasn't under the delusion that all demons were like them. But just as the rest of us made a choice in our morals, so did they.

Ryoko realized the reaction she'd caused. She gasped. "Oh, no, I didn't mean that in a negative way."

An incubus of a much bulkier build than Zaedrix, lounging under a tree with a succubus, chuckled. "No need to get worked up. We know our clan's ways are not the norm"—his eyes darted to Rosa and Zaedrix—"even in the eyes of our kind."

Rosa scoffed. "You all, including the empress, are fools to think peace can come. Only death awaits you on that path."

The incubus shook his head, choosing not to push the matter. Zaedrix, to his credit, didn't speak. He had a more subdued expression, as if he were thinking on the other demon's words.

In my time dealing with the two sex demons, I'd learned that Rosa was the more aggressive and impulsive of the two. Why, I wasn't sure. Maybe it was an effect of demonic conversion. Possibly it was a personality trait from the time she was human. Or maybe succubi were just more aggressive by nature. Either way, it wasn't a dynamic I expected from such demons.

"Momma Eira," Stella called out.

I turned to see her scurrying my way, Sethal hot on her heels, and Raikidan a little bit behind. From the look of Crystal perched on Raikidan's shoulders, she'd been unsuccessful at wrestling the cat away from him.

"No surprise there," Rashta said. I agreed.

"Momma, I—" She halted, gazing up wide-eyed at the demons gathered, particularly Talon and Xithoz. Many of the demons shifted their weight, their body posture readying for screaming. But they didn't know Stella.

"Whoa, cool." She turned her gaze to me, her eyes still wide. "Momma Eira, can I look that cool?"

Nemora rested a hand on her chest, her features going soft. "Oh, she's as precious as Zaedrix said."

I raised a brow in the incubus' direction. He shook his head. "I didn't say that."

"I get the feeling he's lying," Raina mused.

"Yes, you did," Rosa said, rolling her eyes. "You're a little too fascinated with the girl's fearless behavior."

"I'm not fascinated," he said, his posture a bit defensive.

Rosa crossed her arms and her eyes narrowed. She spoke, but not in a language I'd heard before, making it impossible for me to keep up. Zaedrix shook his head and replied in the same tongue. A bemused grin appeared on Nemora's face as she shamelessly listened, making me realize that this was probably some sort of demonic language.

Stella tugged on my skirt to grab my attention, ignoring the two bickering demons. "Please, Momma Eira? I wanna look like that."

I did my best to hold back my amusement with her insistence. "No, Stella, you can't look like these demons."

She turned her gaze to Raikidan as he finally joined my side. "Papa, can I?"

He shook his head. "That appearance is specific to their species."

She pouted and kicked a rock. "That's not fair."

Nemora sashayed her way over, and stroked Stella's hair affectionately. "When you're older, you could always choose to become one of us." A low purr vibrated in her throat. "I'd be more than happy to help with that."

A muscle in my neck tensed, and a low warning growl reverberated in Raikidan's chest. *No way in—*

Stella pulled away from the scantily clad demoness and shook her head. "No, I don't want to *be* a demon. I want to have cool spikes and wings."

Sethal latched onto her and pulled Stella a few more steps away from the sex demon. "She's fine this way."

A bemused smile spread across Nemora's lips. "How lucky she is to already have a protector."

The demoness turned with liquid-like movement, and headed back to Xithoz. Stella cocked her head, looking at Sethal, who still hadn't let her go, and then to me. "Momma, what did she mean?"

I pursed my lips to think how to explain it to her when a dragon's roar pierced the air.

6
CHAPTER

Just like before when Zaith had announced his clan's presence, my body went rigid. Raikidan rested a hand on my lower back. *"Calm. You know the call of Corliss."*

He was right. I should have caught that. *"Rashta, am I that on edge?"*

"It would seem so," she said. *"Though I can't say if it's because you're aware of possibilities, or if it's due to my heightened state. Just do your best to be calm."*

Apparently that was easier said than done. I took a deep breath anyway and turned my attention skyward, hoping to spy Corliss and Mana. I hadn't gotten the chance to see them during the mating rites, though I heard Corliss call to Raikidan now and then when we were in the territory.

They weren't in visual range yet, so I spoke to Raikidan, figuring Stella had already moved on to different thought topics. *If not, she'll remind me.* "How'd the meeting go?"

He gave a half-hearted shrug, Crystal making it difficult for him. "Fine, I guess. Your father just wanted to gather the various leaders here to discuss the concern of your safety and put a plan into place if something does happen."

Tla'lli took a step toward us. "Is that something I should get details about with my father? He told me I wouldn't be needed this time, but if it's about Eira's safety, I'd like to be part of those preparations. I should be anyway, since my father is preparing me to take over the tribe, but he wanted me to handle things here."

Raikidan shook his head. "I doubt it. The agreed-upon plans are simple."

Talon glanced at Tla'lli and smirked. "Knowing your father, his idea is just smash them the moment trouble shows its ugly face."

Tla'lli and I burst out laughing. It wouldn't be an inaccurate assumption. Ir'esh was a straightforward and predictable man.

"That about sums up half the votes," Raikidan said, his face deadpan.

My laughter increased. *So glad I'm in good hands.*

"Not a bad base plan, no?" Velsara said.

"It doesn't even qualify as a plan at all," Raina argued.

"Attack first, ask questions later. My kind of plan," Nalia said.

Corliss roared again, drawing my gaze. His large green body with smattered black scales was easy to spot against the blue sky, and he wasn't alone. The beautiful green body of his mate, Mana, flew beside him, along with a black dragon with four horns curling in different directions, and a black dragon with red scales in a stripe-like pattern— Ebon, Raikidan's brother. That meant the other dragon was Ebon's mate, Nyoki. I'd never seen her in her true form before.

But what took my breath was the enormous black dragon flying behind them. Even from this distance, he was easily the size of my father. An old feeling of familiarity washed over me—like a long-distant memory.

"You know who that is," Rashta said.

Raikidan's grip on my back tightened at the same moment she spoke, making me already aware why I experienced the sensation. *That's his father.*

I wasn't sure how to feel about this situation already. Raikidan and his father didn't have a good relationship, not after his father blamed him for his mother's death eighty-seven years ago. *What are the others thinking?*

"Don't get too defensive," Atria said. *"It's been a long time since that day. Even an older black dragon can change."*

I sucked in a tight breath through my teeth. I hoped she was right, or this could get messy.

Mana folded her wings and dove, breaking away from the family unit straight for us at an unsettling speed. Corliss called after her, but the excitable female ignored him.

Ryoko jumped up and down, flailing her arms, as if they hadn't seen us yet. The distance between us and Mana lessened and before I knew it, her large form was practically on top of us. She shifted to her nu-human body, her long green hair flowing behind her. The moment Mana's bare feet touched the ground, she launched herself into Ryoko's waiting arms, the two embracing in a tight hug.

Mana held on for a few moments before pulling away and throwing herself at me. Luckily for her, I anticipated this, and managed to catch her in a proper hug. "I missed you all so much."

I smiled into her hair, her floral and pine scent wafting into my nose. "Missed you, too."

We separated and she went to give Raikidan a hug, but stopped when she noticed his intense stare toward the sky. "Raikidan, just… keep an open mind, okay?"

He didn't respond. Mana shuffled her feet, struggling to maintain any sort of confidence. "Please…"

When he still refused to acknowledge her, she frowned. I grabbed her hand and squeezed. We'd just have to wait this out. Raikidan couldn't be made to speak with his father.

Corliss and Ebon landed first, then Nyoki. The three of them shifted to their nu-human forms, though no reunion embraces transpired. Corliss kept a close eye on Raikidan while Nyoki stuck close to Ebon, who looked up to his father and nodded. The large black dragon descended. The moment his claws touched the ground, he shifted, transforming into a nu-human man with jet black hair and matching thin mustache and goatee. He appeared similar in age as my father, and shared many physical characteristics of both his sons.

His clothes were quite plain, comprising of a simple tunic, leather pants and boots. *I suppose we should be glad he put some on, given Raikidan's account of him not having any interest in interacting with humanoids and their customs.*

"Prude," Velsara quipped in a whisper.

Ignoring my dragon-raised past soul-life, my eyes focused on the rectangular object in the older dragon's hand. It was a little less than a foot long, rather thick, and wrapped in leather. *I wonder what that is.*

Raikidan's father set his piercing blue gaze on his youngest son, and took deliberate steps toward him. Raikidan didn't move, his intense gaze never leaving his father.

The older dragon drew closer until he was a little less than an arm's reach away. *Well, now I know where Rai gets his personal space issues from.*

Rashta snorted and my other lives lost themselves in a fit of laughter.

To my surprise, it wasn't the older dragon who broke the tense silence. "Father," Raikidan greeted, his tone pensive.

His father didn't respond verbally. He took his time assessing his son. The longer this continued, the more I noticed Raikidan's muscles tensing. I left Mana's side and slipped next to Raikidan, tucking my hand into his. The touch instantly relaxed him, though I could tell it didn't ease all of his tension.

The older dragon's piercing blue eyes shifted to me for the briefest of moments before he refocused on his son. He then held out the rectangular object in his hand. The older dragon spoke, though his northern accent was so thick it required my full attention to understand him. "I was told you needed this to finish some research."

Without breaking eye contact, Raikidan took the offering. When Raikidan refused to budge in this stare-down, even to sate any possible curiosity about this package, I reached out and took it from him, finding it far heavier than I expected. My eyes flicked between the two males to make sure I wasn't going to cause any issues and then I carefully lifted the stiff, old leather wrapping. *From the feel, I don't think anyone has conditioned this leather in centuries.*

My breath caught when the object within was revealed—a large leather-bound tome. A large buckle held the warped and yellowed pages bound within. Intricate designs had been embossed into the corner of the cover, but it otherwise lacked any indicator of what lay within. Of course, I already knew. There was only one book in Raikidan's father's possession that we needed for a particular piece of research.

Early into my mating rites, I'd asked Shva'sika to act as a messenger to Ebon to see if he would be willing to negotiate with their father for this book. I thought it'd help get it into our hands faster, since Ebon had a more practiced silver tongue over Raikidan, and because I didn't want to stress Raikidan out by forcing him to have contact with the older dragon, when he'd shown clear signs of reluctance when he had our first conversation about the book.

I released the old buckle and opened the pages. The musty, and slight chocolate scent, wafted in my nose. I had to resist the urge to sigh. Old books had such a pleasant smell.

Scrawled across the weathered and torn pages were two types of script. One was rough, as if carved into the page with a fingernail or talon. The other was more scripted and elegant, like Elvish, but it wasn't, not even one of the rarer dialects still used today.

Me'kunar stepped forward, his eyes gleaming at the sight of the old book. "Eira, please tell me what you have there."

I hesitated, glancing to Raikidan. I'd promised him I wouldn't allow anyone to know about this book unless he gave his blessing. It was special, and with how secretive dragons were these days, especially with the potential subject hidden within, I wasn't going to overstep his boundaries and his trust.

"You can tell him," Raikidan said. His gaze never wavered off his father.

Despite the tense situation, a smile spread across my face. He'd come such a long way from the secretive dragon I'd first met. In the past, the potential information contained within these pages would have sent him on the defensive, trying everything he could to make sure no one saw the contents. But now, the idea of others knowing more about the dragons, and what secrets the past may hold about them… that didn't seem to bother him anymore.

"This book was found by Xephrya in an abandoned library," I said. "The contents potentially discuss a color of dragon that may or may not be controversial. And there's mention of another element that may play a part in unraveling the mystery."

"It's not actually all that controversial," Zalia mumbled. *"Everyone just forgot and made up their own stories because of it."*

My brow rose. Zalia was my seventh life. She wasn't as talkative as some of my other lives, but when she did speak, it was with purpose.

"She's right," Sylvia agreed. She then chuckled. *"The two of us know from personal experience."*

My forehead knitted together. *"Are you two serious? You couldn't have mentioned this sooner?"*

"Calm your tits. You were busy with your mating rites," she said. *"We'd planned to talk about it when that ended. I was going to bring it up after the ceremony. I didn't anticipate that book would be handed to you."*

Me'kunar tilted his head. "Eira? Is everything okay?"

The concern in his voice snapped Raikidan out of his intense staring contest with his father, and he focused on me, placing a hand on my lower back. I sighed. "It seems Sylvia and Zalia know about some of these contents and only just now told me." I shook my head. "However, it's still important to have it translated, as I'm sure not even they know everything contained in these pages. Unfortunately, it's so old, it's written in both Draconic and Old Tongue."

The older scholar's eyes shone, reaching out for the book excitedly. "You can't tease me like this, girl. Give it here."

I snickered, holding it out of reach. "You haven't even asked what we think this book details."

He shook his head. "No need. I'll find out once I dive in."

Lo'shen tapped his staff on the hard ground. "Boy, let her tell us. You may not want to wait to dive into those pages, but my old heart can't take this suspense."

I pressed my lips together when Me'kunar glowered at his father. "Fine, Eira, tell us what we should expect."

"Well, I can't say for sure, because I haven't even read the contents," I said, trying not to laugh at the irritated face he shot me. "But I've been told two words are used regularly. *Chromatic*, which is written in the draconic, and *Spectral*, which is in Old Tongue."

Me'kunar pursed his lips, his brow furrowing. "And you said this may have something to do with dragon colors?"

I nodded. "Something about a chromatic color, potentially. I'm not sure what the spectral refers to, but I'm sure it's related." Truth was, somewhere deep within, I felt like I knew the answer. Maybe it was because of what Sylvia and Zalia said. I had lived those lives as them, after all. But there was something even further, with the spectral references, that screamed that I was merely forgetting something vital. "Naturally, that makes it important we translate and learn what we can."

"Yes, I understand." He held out his hand for the book, calmer this time. "You have my word I'll be careful with this tome."

My gaze flicked to Raikidan and then the other dragons to make sure they weren't going to object at the last minute. Raikidan remained calm, and his family, except for his father, seemed eager to know what this book was about. I hadn't exactly told Ebon why I needed the book—just that it was for some important research.

When no one objected, I handed the book over to the elven scholar. He smiled brightly and opened the book, scrawling over the text. Mana slipped up next to him, offering her services to help with the draconic side of the translations. Her approach didn't surprise me. She had a love for lore and obscure ancient texts, thanks to her grandfather.

With the book translations being worked on, I wanted to ask Sylvia and Zalia to provide more details, but Raikidan had gone back to his staring match with his father, concerning me. This forced my attention to remain on the current matter at hand for now.

The two continued to face each other in silence for a few moments before Raikidan's father suddenly grabbed Raikidan and pulled him into a tight hug. "You were right. It was my fault."

Raikidan froze in father's embrace, most likely too shocked to react.

His father paused a moment as if his tongue had trouble speaking the words that followed. "I shouldn't… have blamed you."

Raikidan remained stock still for another few seconds before returning his father's embrace. A smile slipped up my face, and the tension in my shoulders eased out. Ebon and Corliss both let out audible breaths, and I noticed the others around us relaxed as well.

The two embraced like this for several minutes without saying a word before Raikidan's father pulled away. He patted his son on the shoulder before looking at me, as if that were all that was needed to patch up the rift between them.

"They're simple males," Rashta said. *"What more do you expect?"*

"This is her, then?" Raikidan's father said, his attention still on me.

Raikidan nodded. "Yes."

The older dragon grunted. "Ironic. Your mother's death created life, and for her most loyal friend at that."

I couldn't tell if that was an insult or not. It wasn't necessarily a kind comment, but Raikidan's father didn't come off as the most tactful dragon out there, especially from what little Raikidan told me about him.

"Now you know where Raikidan gets it from."

I did my best not to laugh.

Raikidan didn't seem to like how he phrased it, because he glowered at his father. But the older dragon didn't care about his son's reaction and I chose not to react myself.

"Raiden," he said as he extended his hand.

I returned the gesture. "Eira."

The older dragon's attention skewed to Stella when she shuffled her feet. Apparently, she'd taken to hiding behind me without me noticing.

"Momma, is Papa and him done fighting?" she asked.

She's getting better at picking up the non-verbal cues. I knew that could be hard when it came to dragons. They were more complicated than it seemed on the surface.

I ran my fingers through her hair. "Yes.

Raiden inclined his head, his eyes darting to Raikidan. "Papa? She's too old to be yours."

Raikidan's lip curled. "She is mine."

The older dragon turned his gaze back to Stella and then to me. I rolled my eyes. "It's called adoption, dipshit. I know it's not common with dragons, but even at your age, you can grasp the concept."

Nyoki and Ryoko sputtered out laughter. Ebon lost himself in his own, holding onto Corliss to stay upright, the latter covering his face with a hand and trying hard to contain himself.

Raiden's eyes flicked up and down as he assessed me. A smirk suddenly cracked his stoic expression. "Careful, I might start to like you if you keep talking like that."

Ryoko's laughter increased. "Her mouth got someone to like her!"

I jammed my thumb in Raikidan's direction. "You mean that's not how I got him?"

Ryoko lost it and fell over. Raikidan rolled his eyes and then pulled me close to his side.

Raiden's expression has returned to its neutral, observing one. "I will get that book back, yes?"

And there's the jumpy thought process Raikidan shares. "You will once we're done with it."

"And that will be?" His tone showed his lack of patience.

I gave a non-committal shrug. "When the translation is done and I am able to use it for the purposes I need it for."

His eyes narrowed, and then he scowled, but from the way his eyes flicked beyond me, I wasn't the cause of his displeasure. Curious, I turned to find my father approaching.

"Hi, Grandpa," Stella greeted for us.

He briefly smiled at her before focusing on Raiden. The two locked such intense stares, it was almost as unsettling as the fight between Raikidan and Raiden. And then, for some reason, Raikidan pulled me a few steps back from the two males, Stella following. I shot him a questioning glance.

"They don't get along," Raikidan murmured. "My mother always had to be present so they wouldn't fight."

My eyebrow quirked up. I knew Xephrya and my father had been close friends, but I never would have guessed he and Raiden had such issues that they would fight over merely being in each other's presence.

"I see you've finally crawled out of your hole of shame, Raiden," my father said.

The black dragon sneered. "And you're still breathing. Pity. I was looking forward to pissing on your corpse."

I shook my head. I really didn't want to act as a referee here. "Father, did you come here for a reason, or just so the two of you could act like idiots in front on an audience?"

My brothers laughed, though it was cut short with a warning glance from our father. He then set his stern gaze on me. "I originally came this way to fetch you. Sha'hiri is ready for you and your mate."

All at once, excitement and fear washed over me. It was finally happening. But what if he didn't settle in? What if he wasn't happy, or it became too hard on Stella? What if I screwed this all up because I can't be trusted as a parent? *Okay, calm down. It's going to work out.*

I shared a glance with Raikidan. He nodded, calm as ever. I fed off that energy, allowing me to shove away the lingering doubt. Taking a deep breath, I knelt and faced Stella. "Hey, Stel?"

The little girl cocked her head. "Do you have something to tell me, Momma?"

I nodded. "Yes. You remember how we talked earlier about you getting another brother?"

Ryoko gasped, cutting off any response my daughter had. I turned my attention to my friend, my brow cocked. She began squealing, her eyes shining with uncontained excitement. I realized a moment too late how my words would have sounded to those not in the loop about Es'tla.

The idea circulating in Ryoko's head burst from her lips. "We're finally getting purple-haired dragon babies!"

My head jerked back, and my brow knitted. "Purple... what?"

Laughter echoed around me. Ryoko let out an exasperated sigh and gestured to me, then Raikidan. "Purple hair. Dragon babies."

I snickered. "I suppose I shouldn't have expected anything different. But, no, I'm not pregnant."

Her ears drooped. "What? No. You have to be." Her hands rested on the lower part of her stomach. "Our little one needs someone to grow up with."

Everything in my brain stopped. "W—what?"

A big smile pulled up her face until it met the corners of her eyes, those golden orbs sparkling with delight. She nodded. I was on my feet and closing the distance between us before I'd fully processed the news.

I grabbed a hold of Ryoko, pulling her close, and spinning her around, unable to contain my excitement for her. I vaguely processed the cheers and other shouts of excitement around us. When I pulled away, I didn't hesitate to interrupt Raid's and Blaze's congratulatory heckling to give Rylan a strong hug.

After a moment, I released him. "This is exciting news." My eyes cut to Ryoko. "But no, our own news isn't like yours."

Ryoko pouted, as if that would somehow change reality. Raid laughed. "I really want to understand how she even came to that conclusion, when just before, Eira's father clearly said someone was waiting for them. I highly doubt there's already trouble in paradise and that the two of them need some sort of professional help right now."

"But she said Stella was getting a brother!" Ryoko tried to defend herself.

"Laz and Raikidan are adopting again," Shva'sika said for me. "This has been in the works for a while."

"Momma Eira told me about the brother I'm getting because I kept asking for a baby sister," Stella said, a little too loud for my liking.

A few of my friends laughed. I pinched my nose, and Ryoko held out a hand toward Stella. "See, she gets it."

Rylan shook his head. "Let it go, Ryo. You can't force something like that."

Her nose scrunched. "Fine."

Raikidan came up and patted Ryoko on the shoulder, as if to

congratulate her in his own way, and then turned his attention to me. He tossed his head toward the direction my father had come from. "We shouldn't keep Es'tla waiting."

Stella latched onto me. "I'm ready to meet my new brother now."

I smiled and waved for Ryder to come with us. "You too."

He nodded, leaving Genesis' side and joining mine. Rizgar led the way, my friends trailing behind us. As strange as it was, I was getting used to having this entourage.

"Do you have any questions?" I asked Ryder. "You weren't with us when we made the decision this morning, and I hadn't found any time to bring it up with you."

He shook his head. "No. You and I talked about the adoption possibility before. I figured it was only a matter of time before it happened."

"And you, Father?"

"Not at all." Rizgar turned a soft gaze on me. "I may be an older dragon, but I understand adoption and why others do it. And if this makes you happy, I will support you."

I smiled, grateful he was so good at adapting and accepting. I still had some lingering resentment with him, but I was working on that.

Weaving through a cluster of gathered scholars, my father set a course for the sheer cliff. As we drew closer, that strange tugging sensation from earlier returned. I didn't have time to stop and work it out, however, as Sha'hiri came into view. The tall nu-human woman with violet eyes, porcelain skin, and snow-white hair sat on a bench made of ice. Like many of the shamans, because Zarda was no longer around to force his pact onto them, she no longer sported a cloak, allowing her northern-style clothing made of high quality cloth, fur, and hand-crafted accessories to be on display. Several colors of paint dotted and swirled up her right arm.

She conversed with a half-elf teen with light skin and copper hair, similarly dressed as her. An overstuffed bag sat at his feet. My pulse slowed, as did everything else around me seem to. *Es'tla.* He'd grown a bit from what I could see, but otherwise appeared as I'd last seen him.

The two looked up when they caught our approach. Es'tla's face lit up, and before Sha'hiri could stop him, he leapt to his feet and rushed toward me. I barely had time to prepare before he crashed into me. I was acutely aware of how inaccurate my assessment of his growth was. Last I'd seen him, his face came up to my chest. Now? He was as tall as me.

I shouldn't have been surprised. Even though only half-elf, he had the potential to be just as tall as a full elf. Xye, Shva'sika's brother, was a prime example of that. And at his age, Es'tla would start going through large growth spurts.

Wrapping his arms around me, Es'tla buried his face into my neck. "Thank you… Thank you for changing your mind."

I embraced him, rubbing his back reassuringly. "I never meant for you to think you were unwanted. I'm sorry."

"Just…" His grip tightened. "Just don't send me away."

"Never." I murmured. "You'll always be loved in this family."

I held him like this for several long moments before he finally pulled away. He had an uncontained smile that he turned on to Stella when she approached him.

"I'm Stella. I'm gonna be your sister." She pointed to Crystal on Raikidan's shoulders. "And that's our new kitty. Well, she's Papa's kitty that we can play with"—her nose scrunched—"if he isn't hogging her."

I choked on a laugh. Es'tla stared at the large feline, murmuring about her size.

Stella continued talking. "I'm happy to meet you. Momma Eira and Papa Raikidan adopted me, too."

Es'tla knelt in front of her. The two gazed at each other for a moment before a wicked grin spread up half of Es'tla's face. He reached out and ruffled her hair, making it one big mess.

Stella screeched and pulled away, holding her head. "Momma! Momma, he messed up my hair. I don't like him no more, send him back."

I rested my face in my hand and sighed. Things were going to get real interesting in this family. "We're not sending him back because of that, Stella."

"But he messed up my hair."

"Don't worry, Stel," Ryder said, right before pulling Es'tla into a headlock. "I'll make sure he's set straight."

"And if he doesn't, we will," Trigon called out.

"Stop picking on him," Yára scolded.

"He started it."

Es'tla, calm in his "imprisonment," shot Ryder a questioning glance. "Who are they?"

"Some of your many aunts and uncles. You've been welcomed into quite the large family."

The teen half-elf's brow knitted together, and he glanced at me with a slight panicked expression. "How much time do I get to remember everyone?"

A soft, reassuring smile appeared on my face. I understood he was going to need time to get over the trauma his father inflicted. Even I was still working through my own. "There's no rush. Take things in as you can."

He nodded, relaxing a bit.

Stella tugged on my skirt. "Momma Eira, what about my hair?"

I chuckled and knelt, then I motioned for her to turn around. I ran my fingers through her hair; it wasn't all that bad. Just a quick brushing and it'd be fine. Her running around like a maniac did more to dishevel her appearance than Es'tla had.

While I took care of her, Ryder released Es'tla, who turned to Sha'hiri. She approached with his bag in hand. "Thank you, for everything you've done for me this last year and a half."

The nu-human shaman leader smiled, moisture brimming her eyes. "We'll miss you, Es'tla. But I know you're in good hands. I'm looking forward to seeing you achieve so much under Laz'shika's guidance."

The corner of my eye twitched. I'd made the decision to forego my appointed shaman name, and requested no one call me by it anymore. As much as the shaman culture asked you to let go of the past and become a new you with a new future—at least how it worked now after the War of End—my past defined me. It may not have been the best history, but I wouldn't be me had I not gone through it. I was Eira, or Lazmira if you were my father, who desired to call me by my given dragon name instead of middle human one.

Ayuma snickered. *"Or Raikidan when he's got you alone."*

I did my best not to physically react, as her words ignited heat in my body. I quite enjoyed it when he called me that name.

Sha'hiri turned her gaze to me just as I finished fixing Stella's hair. "You've got your hands full, but I'm confident you'll be able to meet the challenge."

I opened my mouth to speak when the wind picked up and a voice, soft and airy, tickled my ear. "Eira…"

CHAPTER 7

My gaze turned toward the wind, my eyes landing on the sheer cliff again. The moment I did, that same sensation tugged at me again, this time even stronger than either of the previous two times. I found myself unable to ignore it this time, my feet moving on their own.

I couldn't quite understand why I experienced this need to walk closer, but I also wasn't able to stop myself—not even when Ryoko called out my name, and Raikidan's, who I assumed was following me because that's what he did.

"Come, this way," the whispering voice said, the blowing wind carrying it around me.

Pebbles on the ground scattered and crunched under my boots, the terrain becoming rockier, still I persisted. I came within inches of the cliff, my fingers reaching out and running across the jagged surface. My feet continued to move, following the arching curve I hadn't noticed before, until I came to a break in the hard surface.

A vertical scar carved up the cliff face, the widest point barely large enough for a human to squeeze through. *How did I not see this before?*

"Eira," the voice called again, this time as if originating from deep within the cave.

I slipped through the crevice, the squeeze a little tighter than I expected. Somehow I managed, though Raikidan struggling behind me pulled me out of my trance-like state. I laughed when I noticed the trouble had been caused by his broad shoulders wedging into a particularly narrow section. Crystal wasn't with him, thankfully. I guessed he'd left her with the kids.

"Well, that's what you get for following me into this tight space," I teased, helping him contort until his shoulders fit through.

He rolled both of his shoulders. "I actually wasn't. I heard a voice and then couldn't stop myself from walking toward it."

I gazed down the narrow tunnel stretching before us, the area lit up just enough from the entrance to see up to a bend. "At least I'm not crazy, then."

He chuckled and nudged me. "Only a little."

I rolled my eyes and pointed with my chin farther into the cave. "Might as well keep going. I can't imagine anything evil lurking about in some sacred place. My father hasn't come rushing after us, and Rashta and my other lives aren't warning me in any way."

My brow furrowed when I realized how oddly quiet they were. I waited to see if they'd pipe up, but they didn't. *"Um, hello?"*

No response.

Raikidan bent over to be a little more eye level with me. "What's wrong?"

"They're not responding at all to me. It's so strange."

He slipped his arm around my waist, pulling me close. "Well, if something evil has snuck into this place, I'll be here."

I gazed up at him, meeting his determined, protective gaze. It sent both a shiver down my spine and an aching desire between my thighs. *Okay, not great timing.*

As if my reaction was displayed clear as day for him, the sapphire color of his eyes deepened, turning almost molten. He bent closer, capturing my lips with fevered need. A groan escaped me, and my pulse quickened. But as quickly as the kiss started, it ended with him pulling away first and leaving me a little breathless.

He grinned. "I needed that."

I reached up and brushed the back of my hand across his cheek. "I know today has been difficult on you."

Raikidan rested his forehead on mine and closed his eyes. "You've no idea. But I'm trying my best, for you."

My eyes hooded and I smiled. I desperately wanted to take this moment to use those special three words, but they tangled on my tongue. Almost as if this wasn't that right moment I'd been waiting for.

Instead, I threaded my fingers with his and pulled away, encouraging him to follow me deeper into the cave. He complied without a fuss, though we didn't go far in the end. The bend opened to an enormous cavern. Despite the many stalactites and stalagmites covering the floor and ceiling, the space could easily fit several adult dragons, even older ones of my father's size. Light poured in from a hole from the ceiling, illuminating the most fascinating sight.

The largest tree I'd ever laid eyes on—one that even surpassed the sizes of those in the Velsara Wilds—stood in the center of the cave, its large roots sprawling across the rocky floor.

Pink flowers grew from the branches, with talismans hanging from the thick boughs. Sparkling light dripped from the flowers, like shimmering liquid. On their descent, some transformed into flying creatures, such as birds or insects. Those that continued to fall pooled by the roots, occasionally transforming into land animals, like fox or deer. Then they'd wink out, as if they hadn't really existed.

Symbols of various origins were scrawled into the bark of the tree, emitting a red light that pulsed like a heartbeat.

An overwhelming sense of homesickness came over me, as if I yearned to rejoin a place I didn't even remember. But I knew this place—a place so etched into my history, I'd never be allowed to forget, even though this was the first I'd ever laid eyes on this tree… in this life.

"Welcome to the temple of Lusaria," Isis said.

Raikidan's grip on my hip tightened. "Eira, what is this place?"

The sensation of awe I was experiencing being in such close proximity to the tree—one I lacked when I came near its sister version on the Plane of Between—delayed my response. "It's… the Birth Heart."

Rocks scattered behind me. I turned to see my father approaching. "It seems I don't have to explain anything to you. Though, I suppose I shouldn't be surprised."

"I came into contact with a version of this tree on the spiritual plane. Arcadia told me about its nature when I'd inquired with her." My gaze turned back to the magnificent tree. "She told me this place was protected, to keep her safe. I hadn't realized our clan was that protector."

"Yes, we've guarded this tree longer than any of our stories can remember." He regarded me a moment. "Though, I would have thought Isis would give you that information."

"My connection with my past lives has only been good for this past year. Before that, the corruption that caused problems for Rashta and me also caught them up into it. And since my mating rites, I haven't had a whole lot of time to catch up on my own history through their eyes." My brow furrowed. "Though I'm not sure why you've singled her out specifically."

"Because I'm also North Hyberian Clan," Isis said.

Both my brows lifted. I supposed I shouldn't have been surprised, since she seemed to know this area well, but I had assumed she'd just visited, rather than lived in these mountains.

My father tilted his head. "Based on that reaction, it's safe to assume she just told you?"

I nodded, gazing up at him. "How ironic that I'm reborn into this clan again."

Rizgar smirked. "You're not the only one of the clan who's said that. I don't know if it was intentional, or just how things worked out—"

"Oh, it was intentional," Rashta said. *"Make no mistake about that."*

"But we thank the gods that they would bless us like this," my father continued before I could tell him about Rashta's input. He smiled so genuinely, his next words penetrated deep. "I know I thank them regularly, for allowing me the honor of having the Dragon-Phoenix as my daughter. As much as I need to make so much up to you."

My lip quivered, a mix of emotions rising up. I was trying my best to forgive him for staying away for so long. I was doing what I could to remind myself he hadn't abandoned me, at least not in the way I'd always claimed he had.

"I don't mean to interrupt, but... I'm still lost about this Birth Heart bit," Raikidan said.

Ayuma let out a deep sigh. *"Well, we all have agreed he's not the most tactful or brightest of his lives."*

"But, he's also not the worst," Aria, my eighth life, said.

"Oh, don't be so hard on Reve," Raina scolded. *"He wasn't stupid. Just impulsive."*

"I can't say those are entirely different in my book," Aria said, her voice a bit exasperated.

I shut them all out to focus on Raikidan. "The Birth Heart is a direct line to Lumaraeon, who isn't just the land we live on, but also the prime goddess."

Raikidan blinked. "Oh." A few more moments passed before his face skewed. "Wait, what?"

I laughed, as did my past soul-lives. That was a little too predictable. "I don't know how to explain it better since Arcadia provided me that information, but the quick version is this—Lumaraeon is the only primordial god, and the Birth Heart is the way to contact her. There are three of them, one for each plane. That's really all I know."

Raikidan scratched the back of his head. "Alright."

A gust of wind swirled around us, the voice I'd heard before carrying on it. "You can just show him."

The moving air whipped toward the tree, as if it were alive, drawing my attention. To my shock, sitting on the tree was a young elf woman in a blue dress, with a light complexion and long blonde hair. Her crystal blue eyes sparkled alongside her carefree smile. *Anila…*

The voice in the wind now made sense. It was said the goddess couldn't speak herself, so instead she used the wind to do that for her.

As I gazed up at her, I realized how young she appeared. When I'd seen her during Zarda's sentencing, I thought she was older than the maybe-eighteen-year-old before me.

"She's always appeared this age," Rashta said.

It must have been the situation. I didn't really have much time to take in all the details.

Anila patted the tree limb she sat on and kicked her feet. Between the behavior and her words earlier, I understood the concept she was trying to convey.

Grasping Raikidan by the hand, I guided us closer to the Birth Heart, my father following. A mix of emotions rose up in me slowly, and I did my best to sort them out. It was one thing for me to have contact with the gods I was familiar with, but this was something entirely different.

We came to a halt when we were only an arm's reach from the trunk. I took in the glowing runes, and then flicked my attention to a rabbit that formed from the dripping lights. The illusion hopped away, disappearing into nothing soon after.

Lifting a shaking hand, I reached for the tree, but stopped short. Doubt and unworthiness clawed at my senses. *Is it right for someone like me to speak with her?* My eyes clamped shut and I desperately tried to banish the thoughts.

Raikidan squeezed our entwined hands, reassuring me as if he knew the negative judgment plaguing me—I was worthy.

Taking a deep breath, I bit the bullet and pressed my hand against the rough bark. Immediately, warmth seeped into my skin, crawling up my arm and into my body, along with a voice.

"Hello, my dearest Eira."

My breath caught, and my knees nearly buckled underneath me. Tears prickled the corner of my eyes. Her voice was so warm and soothing, like a mother cradling a child in her arms.

"I'm so happy to speak with you. You've been through so much, child. I wish things could have gone as I'd planned. You deserved that far better."

My lips quivering, my gaze cast downward. *"I'm sorry… that I'm such a dis—"*

She hushed me. *"No, dear. You're not a disappointment. Please don't ever think that. You are so far from it. Only you could have survived those unpredicted trials. You did all you could, and that is all I have ever expected of you."*

She chuckled, her voice dropping a bit. *"And really, had you not, that fine mate of yours would have been a much harder match."*

My eyes flicked to Raikidan, a smile tugging at the corner of my lips. *"I'm sure I would have been better for him if I were a bit different."*

"Not in the slightest. Your quirkiness is the perfect match for his… uniqueness."

Warmth not belonging to Lumaraeon welled in my chest, and before I knew it, I was giggling away. Raikidan turned his attention to me, his eyebrow cocked, but his confusion made it continue.

I released his hand and pressed the back of mine over my mouth, trying not to lose my connection with the prime goddess at the same time, but it did nothing for my laugher.

"Treasure what you have with him. It's everything you deserve and more." There was a bit of a pause, allowing me to calm down, and then she continued. *"I won't keep you any longer, dear. You've got quite the trial before you. And your father will need some help out of here."*

My forehead creased, and I shifted my attention to Rizgar. He'd gone stock still, frozen in his communication with Lumaraeon.

"What's wrong with him?" I asked her.

"Oh, I might have let him know that his deepest dream was about to become a reality."

Everything in me slowed. *"Mom is here?"*

It wasn't much of a guess on my part. She was the only thing I knew that could cause my father this sort of reaction without him actually laying eyes on her yet. And given the gods were involved in this purification process, it wasn't a hard stretch to believe she'd shown up for the occasion in some form as well.

"Help him through this," Lumaraeon said. *"It's important he face her. I look forward to speaking with you again, Eira."*

Her warmth receded from my body, leaving me cold and uncomfortable. Everything inside me cried desperately to not allow her to leave me. I understood the sensation, the instinctual desire to be close to where we'd all originated in our purest form. But now wasn't the time to linger on such things. She wasn't gone forever, and I had other matters to worry about.

Turning my attention to Raikidan first, I caught him pulling away from the Birth Heart. From the looks of it, he'd pressed his forehead against the tree's trunk. That possessive side of me wanted to be a little miffed he'd chosen to be so close with Lumaraeon like that, but the logical side snuffed that out.

I instead turned to my father. He'd stopped communicating with Lumaraeon, and when I took a step closer, he turned a fear-stricken gaze on me. I smiled at him reassuringly and held out my hand. "It's going to be okay. You can do this."

His eyes shifted to my hand, but he didn't take it. The unspoken words were clear to me.

"Just be yourself and act as you normally had with her in the past."

My father swallowed hard. "I don't know if… I have the right to do that."

I stretched my hand farther. "You need to face the past, like I did."

"Your ability to be this calm is slightly alarming, Lazmira. I hope you understand that."

I smirked. "Remember, I'm a shaman. I speak with the dead on a frequent basis." One of my shoulders lifted in a half-hearted shrug. "And I've been in contact with her before because of it."

His lips pressed into a thin line. "Has she… said anything about me?"

I shook my head. "No. But, so you know, she never said anything negative about you in front of me."

His brow quirked up. "Never?"

"No. The only time I ever heard anything remotely negative from her mouth was when I'd overheard her last conversation with Largren. And those words were more disappointment than anything."

Largren was my father's lieutenant. While my father was capable of leading the clan himself, a little help didn't hurt. Due to his half-color lineage, he also was able to pass messages between Rizgar and my mother when she was alive. It was the only way to ensure the pact wasn't broken, sending Zarda on a dragon-extermination path.

My father sucked in a deep breath through tight lips and then grasped my hand. "Okay, I'm ready."

Anila, who hadn't left, giggled and jumped away from her perch. The wind carried her safely to the ground, as if she were as light as the petals from the Birth Heart. The moment her feet touched the ground, she twirled and danced her way toward the entrance, beckoning us to follow.

I turned to Raikidan, who nodded, and then tugged my father. Both dragons fell into step beside me. However, halfway through the cave, my father's steps slowed. *I need a quick distraction.*

"Ask him a clan question," Isis suggested. *"As much as I could tell you, his knowledge would be more current."*

That was a good idea. It also helped that my father was the clan leader. It'd be easy to distract him with that topic. *But what to ask… Oh!* "Father, given our clan has such an important job protecting the Birth Heart, is there a way to identify a dragon who comes from this clan?"

I noticed the tension in his arm lessen a bit. "Excellent question. There's an unmistakable physical indicator that all dragons know. And it's one that you're familiar with."

I shot him a side glance, finding him grinning. He was having too much fun with his cryptic response. *But if it distracts him, I'll put up with it.*

He then tapped the corner of his eye, drawing my focus. A vivid green with an unusual golden ring around the pupil—a trait I inherited from him—*Wait!*

I blinked, thinking about the time I'd come into contact with Isis.

She, too, had the trait—it was the first thing I'd picked up. The same with Raikidan's mother, Xephrya, who had come from this clan as well. And then there was Ryder; he'd inherited it from me. Even all my siblings had it.

My father nodded. "Yes, it's the eyes. Our gift from Lumaraeon for our continued service to her."

That made a lot of sense, though I was surprised such service didn't give more of a boon. But that wasn't all that important if the clan didn't want anything more. "Has there ever been a time where a dragon lost the trait? Or is there a point where it's not hereditary?"

My thoughts slipped to Raikidan. Unlike Ebon, he hadn't acquired the trait.

Rizgar's jaw worked as he thought. "For those who have the boon, it's rare to lose it. I've never seen it in my lifetime, but had been told those who are sent away dishonorably lose the gift."

"I can confirm this," Isis said. *"Those who left the clan because of my parent's mating also lost Lumaraeon's favor. It was a quick process, too."*

I nodded, relaying her words to my father. He took the information in well. "Makes sense. Those who leave the clan these days do so because they take mates and choose to relocate. Lumaraeon has always welcomed this choice, and as such their offspring inherit the gift—so long as they come back to pay their respects every so often."

My brow furrowed, a few things coming to mind. "Ryder inherited the gift from me. I've no doubt that's due to my favor with the goddess. However"—my attention shifted to Raikidan—"Raikidan didn't get this trait, while his brother did, and that doesn't make sense to me."

"Hmm, yes, that was something that had always perplexed me as well," my father said. "He was the only one of Xephrya's offspring to not receive the gift."

Anila giggled and the wind picked up. "Because you wouldn't have trusted him otherwise, Eira."

Raikidan grunted. "She didn't trust me even without it."

I tapped my lips. "That's true, but I get what's she's playing at. If you'd had the eye trait, even if I didn't consciously know the meaning, I did on an instinctual level. I didn't trust Largren. And, remember when that red dragon came into your brother's shop while we were there helping Rylan design that gift for Ryoko? I had felt instant distrust toward him as well. I'm sure now it was because of his eyes." I shook my head. "If you carried that trait in some form, I would have never agreed to your help."

My attention turned to the wind goddess. "Anila, given he and I are together now, would Lumaraeon give him the trait?"

The young woman shrugged. "I doubt it. While she has taken the gift away for disloyalty, it is not common for her to give it to even the most dedicated of dragons who join this clan. That's not to say she doesn't favor your champion." She smiled. "He is as treasured as you. But dragons are a stubborn race, and even if it showed her favor, they're not likely to change their appearance. It is why his first life did not receive the gift."

"Did she offer it?" Raikidan asked.

Anila nodded. "Yes, but she was not surprised when you rejected the offer. Nor did she take offense."

"Good, I have no interest in changing how I look."

The wind goddess laughed and then whisked herself out of the cave. Raikidan's response also brought a smile to my face. I understood the undertone of his words. He'd come a long way from the shame he felt for being a half-color. I was happy he accepted that part of him.

My musing was interrupted when my father lagged behind, resulting in my arm going taut. Based on my view of the tunnel, I didn't need to look at him to know the reason. *Just a bit further.* "So, our clan has a physical indicator. What about other clans? Or is that just something to learn over time with contact with them?"

My father didn't respond right away. "I wasn't aware you couldn't tell the difference in clans."

I shot him a questioning glance and he nodded, understanding the unspoken question. "I assumed, due to your contact with the Velsara Wilds Clan, that you were either told or caught on, since your siblings were quick to. It's a scent-based indicator."

That made sense, as did my brothers and sister catching on. Unlike them, I didn't have the same full contact with the dragons to learn from them. Even during the rebellion, I hadn't spent long periods of time with the various dragons who offered their help. *And my mind was a little more focused on our goal, rather than figuring out how the dragons worked as a whole.*

The cave tunnel narrowed and I let out a quiet, relieved breath. "Rai, can you take up the rear?" My eyes flicked to my father. "I don't need someone making a break for it at the last minute."

Rizgar's eyes narrowed while Raikidan chuckled and agreed to my request. Given I'd have to release my grip on my father to squeeze through the rest of the way, it was my only way of ensuring the outcome we needed.

I slipped through without much trouble in comparison to the larger men. I squinted my eyes to protect them from the harsh outside light when I emerged. Anila was waiting, a big smile on her face.

She tossed her head to my left and then used the wind to lift her into the air, where she perched on a small protrusion on the sheer cliff face. I turned my attention to where she'd directed, to find my family gathered nearby. But their numbers had changed. As in, they'd grown… by a lot.

It took me a moment to recognize that some of the new faces were brothers who either Zarda had executed, or who had died in battle before I'd ever gotten the chance to meet them. Though, given some of their looks—full half-dragon traits on display—I knew some of Zarda's reasoning for killing them.

Before I could think to go over, Ryoko ran up to me, her eyes sparkling. "So, how was it? Yára said we had to wait until later to see for ourselves, so you've got to give me details."

It didn't surprise me my siblings knew of the Birth Heart, given they were living here. The responsibility of protecting her fell on them as well.

I worked my jaw, trying to think. "It's a little hard to put into words the feelings you get being in her presence, let alone talking to her."

"So it's true, this… Birth Heart really is a connection to Lumaraeon?" She pulled her hands close to her chest when I nodded. "It's crazy to think, we live on a goddess… That she's more than just this entity existing beyond a physical form that our minds can't quite comprehend but simultaneously accept her existence."

If someone could smell a brain cooking from thinking too hard, this would be the moment.

Ryoko shook her head vigorously and blew out a breath. "Well, I guess I'm just gonna have to wait to find out myself. In the meantime, there's someone who wants to meet you real quick."

She turned, drawing my gaze to a towering figure standing just beyond us, with Rylan. The unmistakable appearance of a wolfish head, black and grey fur, piercing golden eyes, and fluffy tail… I was looking at a wogron. From the shape of its barrel chest and clothing, the wogron appeared to be male, and he easily reached eight feet in height.

Noticing our attention, the wogron approached. Ryoko gestured to him. "Laz, this is Ashnard, Alpha of the Asholta Pack."

I almost reached out for a hand shake—or paw shake in his case—only to remember their poisonous curse. Given wogrons had large, sharp claws they couldn't retract, even the smallest nick would infect me. With that mental reminder, I nodded my head in a respectful greeting instead.

His lips pulled back into what seemed to be a grin, though was hard to tell with his sharp teeth exposed. "Smart choice."

He then dipped his head in the same way I had. "It's a pleasure to meet you, Eira. Ryoko and Rylan have nothing but praise for you. And even some of the Dalatrend Council."

Ryoko snorted. "Should be more than just *some*."

I shook my head. "Don't let it get to you, Ryoko. I don't care about their opinions of me. I didn't do things for their approval then, and I don't now."

While the Dalatrend Council was much larger than just the rebellion council, thanks to how the citizens had voted after Zarda's fall, all but Genesis of the original council had been elected into some of those seats. With Genesis choosing not to take part in politics, it left me with one less council member that had any sort of love for me, and that number to start with wasn't great.

Ashnard grinned again. "Sounds as though you have as decent a head on your shoulders as I was led to believe. I will be interested in seeing how your presence changes talks. That is—if I'm not mistaken, you will be present more during peace talks with the other nations?"

I nodded. "I should be there for at least a few."

Ryoko snickered. "That'll get their panties in a knot."

I shook my head. She was getting too much enjoyment with these ideas in her head.

"I won't keep you anymore," Ashnard said. "You have my thanks for allowing my pack to attend such a special event. I'm aware how private of an individual you are."

I smiled. "I don't mind at all. I look forward to learning more about your pack and the wogrons in general. And you have my thanks as well, for giving Ryoko a chance."

The alpha wogron's eyes shifted to my friend. "Yes, while the initial reception to her hadn't been as warm as I'd requested, I am glad it worked out. She and Rylan have added a great deal to the pack. I'm looking forward to seeing us grow."

Ryoko ducked her head, and her hands rested on her abdomen. A meek smile spread across her face.

Ashnard nodded at me once before walking off for his pack. With him gone, Ryoko started to say something. "Oh, Laz, something you should—"

"Sis!" Trigon called out. "What's the hold up?"

We both turned to my family. Trigon waved me over and gestured to my brothers I'd never had the chance to meet. "C'mon, you've got a lot of catching up to do, too."

My eyes darted to Ryoko, who nodded. "I was about to tell you what comes next."

A familiar head of aqua-colored hair pushed through my grouping of brothers before I could question my half-wogron friend. *Mom…* Her green eyes sparkled. "But before you do anything else, I need a proper hug."

I didn't need to be asked twice. I ran to her waiting arms. She held me tight, her embrace achingly familiar. But as I rested my face in the crook of her neck, I noticed some indicators that this was just a temporary pseudo-physical state. Her scent was muted, she didn't breathe, and where I'd feel the warmth of her skin, it barely registered. This pseudo living form was nice, but sometimes a spirit form was easier to handle.

She was the first to pull away from the embrace and turned, allowing me to see the lithe form of my aunt, Jasmine. She tucked a strand of her long raven hair behind her ears with a pale hand, and then adjusted her thin-rimmed glasses that partially obscured her violet eyes. Jasmine smiled. "My turn."

I grinned and embraced her as well. It wasn't a long hug. She wasn't always one for that, but I'd take what I could get.

A quick flash in my vision had me blinking. In that brief moment, the golden glowing orbs from before had returned, taking up position on everyone's necks around me. Another blink of my eyes, and they were gone again. I shook it from my mind. It was time to meet my brothers, and I wouldn't let anything distract me.

It took a bit. I wanted to memorize all their faces, learn what I could in this short window I had. My heart swelled the longer I had this. It was all I'd ever wanted in the past, the family I'd been denied for so long. Even if many of them weren't coming home at the end of the day, I still relished in this small sliver of time.

When everything began to die down, my mother placed her hands on my shoulder. "Now, where is your father? He'd better not be hiding."

I went to speak when he called out from the cave. "I'm not hiding."

My brow rose. *Doesn't look that way to me.* It wasn't like I'd sped through my reunion with my family.

"He's stuck," Raikidan called out.

A long sigh escaped my lips as I hid my face in my hand and the others outside the cave lost it in laughter. My mother managed to calm herself a bit before speaking. "Need help?"

There was a pause and then my father spoke. "No, I've got it."

She chuckled. "Well, just shout if you change your mind."

I watched her, noting the twinkle in her eye. She was getting so much enjoyment out of this.

After a bit of grunting, and a whole lot of complaining in Draconic, my father broke free of the crevice, nearly losing his footing in the process. He wound one of his shoulders, muttering to himself, "Why do we keep that so damn small?"

Raikidan pushed on his back as he tried to squeeze out of the crack himself. "I don't know, but muse about that after you move your ass out of the way so I can get out."

I bit my cheek so I wouldn't laugh. From the limited exposure I'd had with the dragons, clan leaders got a lot of respect, especially if they were as large as the North Hyberia Clan. But Raikidan really didn't care about any of that. *I think I might be rubbing off on him.* It made me wonder how his and my father's relationship would form over the next few years.

Of course, my father didn't listen, though that had more to do with my mother than with him not wanting to heed a younger dragon's demands. She'd taken several steps toward him now, drawing his attention. His eyes firmly locked on her, my father froze up. Raikidan grumbled and shouldered his way around the older dragon and headed our way.

My mother reached out and grabbed his hand for a brief moment, passing him a warm smile. He returned the gesture before continuing toward me.

Rizgar swallowed when my mother stopped an arm's reach from him. He attempted to speak, but the words took a moment to form on his tongue. When he finally did, he stumbled over his words—some sort of apology, from what I could decipher. My mother crossed her arms, her weight shifting to one side, listening to him ramble.

Raikidan made it to my side, though he didn't remain. He kissed me on the temple and murmured low. "I'll be right back."

I blinked and then nodded, unsure where he could possibly need to slip away to. My gaze followed him as he maneuvered through my gathered family. He set a direct path toward his father, and a familiar woman with flaming red hair. *Xephrya*. The spirits were out in full force today. That could only mean Arcadia was nearby. No surprise, given the gods should have shown up sooner.

When Xephrya tore her attention away from Raiden, an enormous smile lit up her face. She opened her arms and Raikidan broke out into a run. I smiled when the two embraced. This was something he deserved. He may have gotten some closure with the spiritual walk I performed with him, but these kinds of moments with her could really help heal the rest of his heart. *More people deserved this kind of closure.*

I turned my attention back to my parents. My father's blathering had cut off, though I wasn't sure whether it was due to my mother's stare or if he'd run out of words. "Amara…"

She rested her hands on her hips. "You going to kiss me, or keep rambling? Because I haven't waited all these years to see you, to listen to you apologize for something that wasn't your fault."

Rizgar struggled. I assumed he was looking for more words, but in the end, action proved to be a stronger pull. He reached out for her with his large hands and pulled her close, crashing his lips into hers for that kiss she demanded. My mother wrapped her arms around his neck and the two embraced for several long moments before she pulled away.

She let out a pleased hum. "That's more like it."

My father's head lowered. "I'm sorry I failed you, Amara."

Her eyes softened, and she rested her palm on his cheek. "No, you did exactly as I asked of you. I forced you into the agreement because I knew you wouldn't be able to accomplish the task otherwise. I assigned Largren with a specific message, because I wanted to spare you the pain of the inevitable, even if I had to tell a lie to do so."

My brow furrowed. "Mom, what do you mean by save him from the inevitable?"

"Hmm, why indeed," a smooth and commanding voice said. A muscular arm hung over my shoulder, drawing my gaze to the amber-eyed, dark tan-skinned human now clinging to me.

My brow quirked up. "Oh, hey, Phyre."

The fire god chuckled, having always enjoyed our casual interactions. "She can explain what she means later. Your time has come."

I grunted. "What, Nazir taking the day off, so you've become the harbinger of death?"

He winked. "You'd go out in a blaze of glory."

Several of my past soul-lives laughed while I shook my head. "Been there, done that."

My comment had those around me roaring, including the fire god. My one-time ability to defy death under certain circumstances had become quite the story from what I'd heard, given it was more exaggerated fiction than fact most of the time.

Phyre patted my shoulder and motioned for me to follow him. He'd also grabbed Raikidan's attention to join us. I was curious why, but figured I'd find out shortly.

The three of us picked our way through the throng of people now eagerly clustering up to get their view of the event they'd waited so patiently now to witness. The scholars were the worst, doing whatever they could to slip in front of everyone else, their books and quills at the ready.

Though, there was one place that remained clear, as if the onlookers were repelled—an area where many other gods had already gathered.

My eyes shifted to a few I had met in the past—Gina, the goddess of health and healing; Arcadia, the goddess of spirits, and her faithful wolf companion, Maiyun. Raisu, the god of dreams, nodded to me, with a twinkle in his eye that screamed, "I told you so." I knew he meant the dreams he'd sent me about Raikidan and me changing the fate I thought I was destined for. Nazir had also joined the gathering.

All the gods fanned out in a semi-circle pattern around two people. One was a man with ebon hair, dark skin, and blue eyes, and the other was a woman with blonde hair, light skin, and eyes that shimmered with all the colors imaginable. Both wore white tunics with elegant embroidery around the long collar and on the sleeves. The god of matter, Zoltan, and the goddess of time, Genesis—also known as the gods of life.

Genesis smiled, her eyes twinkling. "So glad you could join us, Eira."

I nodded, finding my pulse quickening a bit. The attention of so many gods was a little unnerving, even for me. "What do I need to do?"

A man sighed, drawing my attention to an unusual-appearing individual leaning against a rock. "Keep on waiting, because one of us can't seem to track *time* properly and is still not here."

I couldn't put an accurate description to this god, as each feature I focused on changed in some way, sometimes to something that wasn't remotely humanoid, like his fingers shifting to talons and then a fuzzy paw of sorts.

"That's Koseba," Rashta said. *"He's always dramatic."*

Koseba was the god of shapeshifting, so that explained his morphing features. I had no comment about his personality, but I had noticed amused reactions to when he'd mentioned "time." What did they know?

"All of you were late," I said, not afraid to shoot that in Koseba's direction. "You don't really have a right to complain, now do you?"

More amusement rumbled through the gathered gods. Phyre draped his arm over my shoulder. "She does have a fair point."

Koseba rolled his eyes. "We had a reason for being late."

"As does Zion," Genesis said, her eyes flashing. "He is handling the remnants of what we were doing earlier."

Raikidan tensed beside me, not that I blamed him. As far as I'd been led to believe, no mortals outside the dragons knew who Zion was. And based on the confused murmuring from the scholars behind me, that may have been entirely accurate. And if he were to make an appearance, then… I didn't know, honestly. For all I could surmise, the entire keep-him-secret deal was some holdover from the War of End.

"Bingo!" Ayuma said, her voice far too cheery.

I refrained a sigh. I had a wealth of knowledge in my head that could talk to me, and here I was, having to discover all this on my own because that knowledge had too many minds of their own.

"Oh, you love it."

Like hell. I took a breath and refocused my thoughts. "Why were you all so late? It was bad enough that Rashta noticed."

"There was a situation we had to look into," Zoltan said.

"Does it have anything to do with the weird feeling Rashta has been getting lately?"

The god's brow furrowed, his lips pulling tight. "What does she know?"

I shrugged. "She isn't sure what is causing the feeling, just that there's something wrong somewhere. And it's affecting Raikidan, and making me even more paranoid than usual."

Zoltan's eyes flicked to Raikidan. "So, her little stunt did have a lasting effect."

"I don't think that's important right now," Raikidan said, his eyes narrowed. "You're avoiding Eira's inquiry. What are you hiding?"

The god turned out his hands, showing his palms. "Calm down, I'm doing nothing of the sort. Just trying to gather any information we may be missing."

A tall, light-skinned human woman stepped forward. Armor reminiscent of that worn by valkyries in historical texts adorned her sultry form. Her long black hair blew with the light breeze, and her golden eyes pinned to us. *Satria.* She was the goddess of war we experiments revered. "I do believe what Rashta is sensing is related to the matter we dealt with. Zion is finishing the rest."

"But what is it that's the problem?" I asked, a little off put by their cryptic behavior at present.

"There is nothing you need worry about," Zoltan insisted. "We've handled it."

"Rashta, am I wrong to find their behavior—"

"No, I'm not happy with it either," she said. *"Especially since I can tell something is still wrong."*

Zoltan scrutinized me. "You're not letting this go."

"Rashta says something is still wrong." I had no reservations telling them the truth.

A muscular human man with tan skin and flaming red hair, wearing ancient fighter attire similar to the ones Phyre wore, right down to the tonfas, stepped forward. *Solund, the god of the sun.* Or, as I'd come to learn, more accurately the god of sunlight bending. But it was due to the people's belief that he harnessed the sun that he had obtained the sun as his particular domain when he earned his ascension.

Solund's amber eyes set hard on me. "This must be the work of the corruption. We did our due diligence."

The tall human woman next to him with porcelain skin and white hair, wearing ancient swordsman attire similar to the ones Arcadia wore, placed a light hand on Solund's arm. "Do not dismiss her words so carelessly, Husband. Even afflicted with corruption, Rashta's domain remains as it is. She senses these threats better than any of us."

She turned her grey eyes on me. "That is why Eira doesn't disagree. I can see that she, too, is in tune with Rashta's power right now."

This woman was Lunaria, goddess of the moon, or more accurately as I'd also learned, much like Solund, she, too, was a bender of light, though of moonlight. *Light bending…* an elemental form that was so rare now, hardly anyone knew it even existed.

Before I could answer the goddess, thunder cracked overhead and the sky darkened.

Phyre chuckled. "Well, looks like he's finally here."

8
CHAPTER

The blue sky continued to darken until the stars shone. My breath slowed, the sight of a portion of the sky altering in this way both mesmerizing and unsettling. The stars began to swirl up, like they were being pulled into a vortex, and disappeared into a dull yellowish white light peeking through the center of the vortex.

Then, out of the swirling came the most magnificent creature I had ever laid eyes on. A dragon easily five times the size of my father descended; shimmering scales of all manner of iridescent colors covered his body. Black claws gleamed in the sunlight, and black horns grew from his head. The horns branched like a deer or an elk, much like Mana's. They were the only two dragons I've ever seen with such unique horns.

His powerful wings beat, the black webbing translucent. Within the colored membrane, lights pulsed as if made of stars.

This dragon wasn't the only one to fly out of this massive portal. Smaller dragons, of sizes I was more accustomed to, shot out in great numbers. Their scales, too, shimmered in the same colors as the enormous dragon before us. I realized the colors of the two types of dragons I was seeing. "Rai, I don't think we need a translation on that book anymore…"

He made a quiet, non-committal sound, drawing my curious gaze. Raikidan had fallen to his knees, his wide eyes pinned on the enormous dragon landing behind the gathered gods. My eyes scanned the gathered mortals, finding all dragons present lowering themselves in the presence of their god.

The ground trembled under my feet when Zion landed. His massive wings folded tight against his body and he gazed down at us with multi-colored eyes. *Those eyes… look familiar.*

The chromatic dragons with him found perches of their own, though none settled close to the gathered mortals.

"You're late, Zion," Phyre called out.

The dragon god's voice rumbled, reverberating in my chest. "I am the Keeper of Time. I am never late."

I was taken aback by his proficiency with the common tongue. No dragon had the capacity to speak common while in their natural form. *Maybe it's because he's a god… and what's this Keeper business?* If his domain was over more than just dragons, and covered time as well, which I surmised it did, given the evidence before me, I'd never heard a god call themselves a "keeper" of their domain.

"You kept Eira waiting," Phyre called up.

I snorted. "So did all of you."

He shot me a "not helping" glare, and Zion barked out a hearty laugh before lowering his head to be more on my level. "There is a reason I am fond of you, Ancient Soul."

A heavy ozone smell with a slightly sweetened burnt undertone wafted out of his mouth and surrounded me. It was both comforting and unsettling.

I dipped my head respectfully. "It's a pleasure to meet you, Zion."

"No, it is mine. I have watched your soul since its first birth, and now I am able to meet you a second time."

My eyebrow spiked. *Second time?*

His gaze went contemplative. "Did Sylvia not tell you?"

"She said she'd planned to explain a few things after all this. I guess she didn't anticipate you showing up."

"No, but I should have," Sylvia said.

Zion chuckled, as if he could hear her words. "Yes, you should have, child." *How did he hear her?* "But, no matter. I will introduce myself as"—his gaze swept over the gathered mortals as he straightened— "my image has been distorted over the centuries. I am Zion, god of dragons, prophecies, and fate, and Keeper of Time. I am a chromatic dragon, as are my clan here. We are not a forbidden color, but the precursor, with the ability to touch time."

I blinked slowly. A precursor color? *Man, what I wouldn't give to have Ambrose hear those words.* As Raikidan's grandfather was bigoted, I didn't have much love for the dragon. It'd be nice to see his held ideologies crumble beneath him.

Rashta chuckled. *"Oh, he's here. He, Salir, and Rennek arrived while you were conversing with Lumaraeon. His reaction is as priceless as you'd hoped."*

That brought a smug smile to my face. *"So, Sylvia and Zalia, was this the information hidden in that book?"*

"While I can't say for sure, since we haven't read it, I would assume so," Zalia said. *"At the very least, it was what we were going to reveal to you."*

"So, this whole time, you knew about the chromatic dragons?"

Sylvia chuckled. *"Oh, girl, you've got no idea."*

I pursed my lips, thinking about what she meant. Suddenly an image of Zalia flashed through my mind so quickly that I missed a majority of her features. Except her eyes—kaleidoscopic. So mesmerizing and hard to forget, much like Chameleon. I blinked slowly, my gaze turning to the dragon god. *And him.* He had the same eyes.

I snapped my attention to the closest chromatic dragon. The dragon tilted their head, confused by my sudden attention. The movement, however, gave me the sight I needed. *Same eyes. Holy shit.* "Are you a chromatic dragon hybrid?"

Zalia chuckled. *"In a way, I am. My father was fourth-generation after the initial mix pairing."*

I took a moment to absorb that information. *"And you, Sylvia?"*

"Nah, but my champion was."

I blinked and then whipped my head toward Raikidan. He jerked back and shot me a questioning glance. Things started piecing together in my mind. All the lives I'd lived. Things I'd experienced. The people I'd met. *People I've met…* A face that had taunted me since first meeting him surfaced in my mind. Multi-colored hair and eyes matching—my head jerked in several directions as I searched for him. "Nal? Nal where the hell are you hiding?"

Zion's head canted, throaty laughter rumbling out of him. "That did not take her long. Better show yourself."

Behind Zion, a chromatic dragon with black curling horns and heavy plating along his body slowly poked his head into view. I narrowed my eyes when he winked and then spoke in draconic. "*Hello again, Eira.*"

Raikidan's gaze flicked between us. "You know a chromatic dragon?"

I crossed my arms. "I didn't know that's what he was until right now. He's the guy I told you about. The one who helped me out one day on an assignment, then just up and disappeared at the end, only to reappear randomly to mess with me."

Nal chuckled. "*I will not apologize for that.*"

My lip curled, but before I could spit out any more words, he spoke again. "*I will answer your questions. You deserve them. After the purification. That is more important.*"

My tongue slid over my teeth. He had a point, but still… "Fine, but you have to give me your real name right now."

He shook his head, though resigned to my terms. "*My name is Naloth. Nal for short, as you had guessed that day.*"

Well, there was that. I turned to Phyre. "With those terms out of the way, is there anything left to do to prepare for this purification?"

Phyre turned his attention to Zion. "Did you finish rooting out that issue?"

The dragon god nodded. "The problem has been taken care of."
Rashta stirred. "*No, it hasn't.*"

Resting my hand on my chest, my brow furrowed. "*Are you sure?*"
"*Yes. The sensation has worsened.*"

I looked up at Zion to find his keen eyes on me. "I heard her, Dragon-Phoenix, do not worry. I am concerned by her words. Care was taken in rooting out the issue."

Naloth dipped his head. "*I am willing to check some more, Zion.*"

The god thought for a moment before flicking his barbed tail in the direction of three chromatic dragons on his other side. "You three go check. Naloth will stay. Be careful, though. If they're evading my sight and yet Rashta is sensing them, they are not to be underestimated."

The trio nodded and unfurled their wings, leaping into the air and flying into the vortex above.

"Zion, what is going on?" I asked. "Don't sugar coat."

He let out a deep breath. "We call them time defilers. They have the unusual ability to mess with the timelines. It is our job to stop them."

I pursed my lips. "This has something to do with me, doesn't it? I can't imagine Rashta would be feeling this way if it were just something you regularly dealt with in your domain."

He nodded. "Yes, that is true. These defilers are targeting moments in your life, as well as your past lives. It is not the first time this has happened, and most of the time, it is a minor nuisance, as they just cause a new timeline to emerge from the main. But, if left unchecked, it could possibly corrupt the main timeline, which we cannot allow."

I chewed my lip. This timeline stuff was difficult for me to grasp on a good day when conversing with Seda, given psychics could see potentials in the timelines. But I did understand one thing. "This is a big deal though, isn't it? Bigger than normal."

Zion nodded. "Yes. The attacks we dealt with were sporadic, but frequent. I was sure we had quelled the last of them, but if Rashta still senses their meddling, then it means something sinister is lurking. And as the Keeper of Time, it does not sit well with me that I cannot see what it is."

"Was it smart to only send three dragons to check it out?" Raikidan asked.

Zion shook his head. "Do not worry about them. They are some of the fastest in the clan. If trouble arises, they will return to report back before anything happens."

Raikidan scowled and I was with him. I didn't like this one bit. Something was definitely off. "Let's get this purification done, then. The faster we do, the less likely this will be an issue at all."

Zion agreed. He lifted a claw and motioned for Raikidan and me to step back a few paces before gesturing to a buxom elf woman with tan skin. She had gauged ears, a septum piercing, wide ring-like necklaces around her neck, and other jewelry adorning her body, as well as an off-the-shoulder short dress with underbust corset and leather pants and boots. She held herself with an almost regal air, commanding attention. *Valena, goddess of earth.*

Even though it had been a wordless command, she acted without hesitation. The earth beneath us rumbled and pillars of stone shot out of the ground. With a motion of her arm, the pillars bent toward each other, though not entirely connecting, creating half-arches. This drew my eyes to their spacing. Each row of pairs was evenly spaced, and each of the half-arches was positioned within the invisible circle the other mortals had subconsciously formed.

Zion reached for one of the pillars and carved his claw into the hard surface. The mark emitted a golden glow when he pulled away to carve another mark on the stone. I didn't recognize the symbols he carved.

When the first half-arch was done, Zion moved to its other half. Upon finishing the second curved rock pillar, the lights in the two arches pulsed and a translucent wave shot out to its paired pillar, the energy colliding and creating a shimmering wall of pale golden light. *They now look like a completed arch.*

This continued until he finished with all the arches. I took in the sight and realized there were fifteen of them. *That was done with a purpose.* Though I couldn't say what that purpose was just yet.

Phyre rested his hand on my shoulder. "Ready?"

"Wait," Ryoko said. I turned to see her shouldering an overexcited scholar aside to stay in front of them all. "What are you doing to her?"

Phyre smirked. "Nothing harmful, I can assure you."

Her golden eyes narrowed at the god, and she poked a finger in his direction. "You'd better hope not, or so help you, I'm going to pummel you into the ground."

Several scholars stared at my friend, wide-eyed. Lo'shen and Me'kunar laughed, as did Phyre.

When he got himself under control, he turned his gaze to Valena. "She's definitely yours, child."

She brushed her long, curly brown hair over her shoulder. A deep smile curved her plump lips, and her green-flecked brown eyes shimmered with amusement. When she spoke, her voice was huskier than I expected—the octave a little deeper than the average woman's—though still soothing. "Yes, n' this one makes it hard to not pick favorites o' my children." She shot the fire god an accusatory glare. "Though that ain't stopped you so far."

He showed his palms and gave a half-hearted shrug. "I'm not good at following rules." His gaze swept to me and then out to the gathered mortals. "And, as you said, some just make it too difficult not to."

Ryoko cocked her head. "Huh? Child? What are you two talking about?"

The goddess laughed. "Those bestowed elemental gifts are our children. You, like all Brutes, are mine. It was my way o' protectin' you all from the life we wished we could have avoided." A smirk slipped up half her face. "You just went and figured out how to go beyond that."

"Oh." She paused for a moment and then cut narrowed eyes to Phyre again. "My threat still stands."

He threw up his hands and I laughed. This wasn't something she'd let go.

I turned to Zion. "Back to the matter at hand, so Ryoko doesn't turn our resident fire god into cinder dust, what exactly do Raikidan and I need to do?"

A smile pulled back the dragon god's lips, showing off his toothy maw. "You and your champion will walk through these time arches. Each one represents a moment when your souls lived a life. Upon touching the time field, your past lives will be released. This is a necessary step to combat the corruption."

Seemed simple enough. A bit excessive if you asked me, but what did I know? I wasn't a god. *Though, that doesn't account for the last arch.*

"A word of caution," Zion said. "The two of you must maintain contact in some way through this process. If you lose contact at any point, it could severely damage your soul. This is especially true for the last arch. In this moment of time, Rashta will be pulled out. Your soul will try to combat this process the most."

I instinctively took a step back. I didn't like the sound of that possibly.

Ryoko stomped her foot. "Phyre, you lying bastard. You said Laz was going to be fine."

The fire god sighed. "Why am I the one she's mad at?"

Zion laughed. "Little wogron girl. I am pleased to see your devotion to the Dragon-Phoenix is as strong as ever in this life."

Ryoko cocked her head to the side and opened her mouth to question him, but he continued. "However, as long as Eira and Raikidan do as I have said, they will only feel slight discomfort when they pass through the time gates. And they are tenacious lives. I have no doubts they will pass through the last arch successfully. I merely mention the caution so they are not taken by surprise."

Ryoko's nose scrunched and she narrowed her eyes at the large dragon. She didn't voice an argument, but the wordless threat was clear. She'd take on the whole pantheon if something happened to us.

Phyre patted my shoulder and then gestured for Raikidan and me to step in front of the first set of time arches. I exchanged a glance with Raikidan, who nodded, and we took our directed place. The energy before us hummed, making me aware of how powerful it had to be for me to sense it. The realization shot my heart rate up, a mix of fear and anticipation swirling in my gut. My past soul-lives stirred in my mind. They'd stayed quiet during all this, but given how they were acting earlier, I suspected they knew this, or something along these lines was going to happen.

Nalia chuckled. *"We didn't know the process, but Rashta made us aware of the needed result. We just weren't allowed to say."*

Raikidan threaded his fingers with mine and gripped my hand tightly. His calm nature seeped into me through our contact, helping to ground me. Taking a deep breath, we both stepped into the first time arch.

Power jolted through me, stealing my breath. Images flashed through my mind, but they were so quick it was hard to process any of them. Velsara's laughter rose up into my head, and then she disappeared. The sensation was uncomfortable, as if a piece of me were missing.

The power around me died down a bit as I forced my feet to keep moving, my eyes on the next arch, but a thrumming power remained in my body, as if I'd been given the energy shot of a lifetime.

Reaching the next arch, the same process happened again, this time Xenia's presence leaving me. Over and over, I experienced the removal of my soul-lives, from my most recent back to my oldest, never looking back or allowing myself to stop. Even when the exceptionally difficult moment came for both Lutha and Lina to leave me, or when Raikidan experienced a similar situation a few arches before, when Aria separated from me.

However, as we continued on, I was able to sort out the images and other mental input thrown at me from the time arches. I could hear laughter and crying, the sounds of battle and confessions of feelings. I could see children, families, and people walking around the street. I witnessed moments of war, people arguing, and particular couples—my and Raikidan's lives—embracing and enjoying each other's company.

My breath came harder as we approached the fourteenth time arch. This had taken its toll on me, but I wouldn't back down. *I have to do this.*

We walked through my last life's arch, Isis whispering quick words of encouragement before disappearing. I gasped when I came out the other side of the arch, a floating sensation pulsing in my head. It felt so wrong to be pulled apart like this, and we still had one last time field to pass through.

I took slow, shaky steps toward the pillars. *"Are you ready for this, Rashta?"*

"I'm more concerned about you," she admitted. *"I sense this will be more unpleasant than the others originally anticipated."*

I worked my jaw, trying to keep my nerves down. *"The corruption acting up?"*

Thanks to Rashta's ongoing purification, I rarely felt that nasty little side effect from Zarda's meddling anymore, although it did occasionally rear up, affecting both our moods and actions. Rashta always tried to endure the brunt of it, but if a particular day was bad, all bets were off.

"Yes. I'm doing what I can to combat it."

I took in a steady breath. Then for her sake, I couldn't hesitate in this time field. I squeezed Raikidan's hand and he did the same back. My ears picked up his breathing coming as hard as mine. He may be out of lives to expel, but we were in this together.

We stepped into the shimmering light of the last time arch, and everything inside me came to a halt. Discomfort crawled over my skin. Fear and anguish turned in my gut. I clamped my eyes shut. Breathing became difficult, and every fiber of my being screamed to step back.

"You can do this Eira," Rashta said. *"Fight the corruption's grasp on your soul. You're stronger than it is."*

Raikidan tugged me forward, as if he'd already stepped through, yet I struggled to comply. My entire being reeled, crying out for me to run away. He grabbed my other hand and tightened his grip. I clenched my teeth, biting back the pain wracking my body.

Then, I stepped through. My eyes flew open and I gasped for air. My knees trembled and I stumbled on my next step. Raikidan caught me and held me close. "Easy."

Tears streamed down my cheeks as I buried my face into his chest, my fingers digging into his skin. My lip quivered, my mind struggling to cope with the empty sensation that lingered in my mind and body. It felt so… wrong, like my soul was fractured.

I vaguely sensed Zion lowering his head and murmuring something.

Raikidan ran his fingers through my hair, the action encouraging my mind to focus.

"Lazmira," he murmured. The sound of my name in his gravelly tone sent a shiver down my spine. It also pulled me back into awareness. My ears picked up footsteps shuffling on the ground around us. It wasn't just Zion checking on me.

Taking deep, slow, but still shaky breaths, I found myself centering, and strength returning to my drained body. Or maybe it was the soft hand resting on my hip and radiating warm energy. Either way, my senses returned.

Taking in one last deep breath, I pulled away from Raikidan. He reached out, his thumb caressing my cheekbone where a tear still lingered. I gasped and furiously rubbed my face with an arm. Raikidan chuckled. "She's back with us."

The hand on my hip retracted, and its owner let out a relieved breath, speaking in a brogue much lighter and airier than I was prepared to hear. "Good. I was gettin' a bit worried there."

I peered down at the stout dwarven woman with braided blonde hair. "Were you healing me, Gina?"

The goddess nodded, her soft blue eyes gazing up at me. "Yer reaction was stronger than we anticipated. Feelin' better?"

I nodded, gulping in some more air. "I still feel off, but I can at least stand now."

What I wasn't quite willing to say, though, was that in this moment of recovering, that ability to see the unusual glowing orbs had returned, and blinking wasn't sending them away this time. Even the gods had them, theirs a little more powerful than any others I'd seen. It didn't help my ability to recover in the least.

Arcadia stepped forward. She turned her sullen gaze to me. Her irises and pupil were such a pale gray, they nearly melted into the whites of her eyes. A rather unsettling sight, I could only compare their appearance to plate crystal. "That is to be expected. A soul does not like to be fragmented in any way. It's even difficult separating a pure spirit from the corrupted one when a soul is sentenced to hell."

I blinked slowly. I always wondered how that worked for reborn souls.

"Laz?" Ryoko called out tentatively. "Do I get to beat a god up or not?"

I looked over my shoulder to see her poised on her tip-toes, trying to see around the moving gods. I snickered. "Not this time, Ryo."

She landed hard on her heels, her nose scrunching and ears drooping. "No fun."

Valena threw her head back in a laugh. Her partner, the god of nature and a dark skinned elf of muscular physique, Tarin, stood next to her shaking his head. Though, I did catch a flicker of amusement in his vibrant green eyes.

I turned my gaze to Phyre to see how he was reacting, only to find his focus fixed on the time arches. Not a muscle in him twitched. He wasn't the only one, though. Satria had also set her full attention in that direction. My curiosity piqued, I turned. My breath caught at the sight before me.

Floating in the energy field in the last arch I passed through was Rashta. Her long black wings wrapped around her, as if to protect her from prying eyes, and her hair splayed out, as if caught up in wind and then frozen. She wasn't the only one in these fields. As Zion mentioned, my past soul-lives stood in their respective time fields, eyes closed. With them were Raikidan's lives, mated hands firmly clasping each other. Even where Lutha and Lina shared a single mate of Raikidan's life, and Aria shared two of Raikidan's in the same manner, they all held hands in some way.

That wasn't all. Even with the glow of the time field, on the necks of each of our lives were glowing orbs like I'd seen on everyone else, but unlike the others, theirs were dimmer—smaller, even. I took a quick glance down at my chest to find my own body glowing with this same light, and while it was difficult to tell for sure, mine did seem smaller. My heart beat slowed. *Could this glow I'm seeing possibly be...*

Zion repositioned himself by the arches, pulling my thoughts away. He assessed each one, and then made one swift raking motion with his claws. The time-field energy glowed brighter and then shattered, making an audible sound like glass breaking. I jumped back, and Raikidan grabbed my waist.

In one collective gasp, all of our lives breathed in, their eyes fluttering open. Rashta, however, collapsed onto the ground. Almost faster than my mind could process, both Phyre and Satria rushed to the goddess' inert form, fussing over her. Zoltan and Genesis approached, the former cautioning the two to be careful, as they still didn't know the full extent of the corruption. He then motioned for Gina, Lunaria, and Solund to join them.

Satria and Phyre continued to fuss, as if not hearing the older god's words. My head tilted. Something about their worry resonated with me as something more than surface concern for their fellow goddess.

Arcadia drew up next to me. "Parents always worry about their children, even after they've grown and made something of themselves."

It took me a moment to process her words. When I did, I turned wide-eyed to the spirit goddess. "Her parents?"

"Yes," Satria murmured, brushing some of Rashta's hair from her face. "She's ours."

A part of the reveal made sense to me, but something also didn't add up. "What exactly is Rashta, species-wise?"

"A valkyrie."

I blinked slowly. Rashta was a… valkyrie? To some extent, that made sense. In my mind temple, where Rashta had been locked away, there was a mural that displayed my past soul-lives with Raikidan's. It also depicted a valkyrie. I'd instantly recognized the portrayal. And up until now I'd never questioned that depiction, which had obviously been her.

But now… another part of me wasn't so sure. Valkyries had gone extinct so long ago. I was certain, even with some of the incorrect information Zarda had fed us about the gods I was still trying to sort through, Rashta came after that moment in time had happened.

Gina patted the war goddess on the shoulder, encouraging her to step aside. Whatever needed to happen to fix Rashta, it seemed Satria was powerless to help, and her fussing would only put her in the way.

Satria reluctantly complied, her eyes constantly darting to Rashta as Lunaria hovered with outstretched glowing hands. The war goddess came my way, guided by Phyre, who had also been sent away.

"Satria," I said tentatively. "Can you… explain? I thought the Valkyries—"

When a bittersweet smile appeared on her face, my words caught. I knew the answer. The traces of pain in her eyes told them. *She's the goddess of war…* "You're a valkyrie, too."

The goddess turned around, revealing a detail on her back no statue I'd ever seen had depicted. Her armor had two purposefully made cutouts where black feathered nubs stuck out of her back by her shoulder blades. "I am a fallen valkyrie."

I blinked slowly, processing this new information.

The goddess continued, turning back to face me. "Much like the chromatic dragons, my race was touched with time manipulation as well, but in a much different way. We found ourselves able to not only predict the outcomes of battles, but change it to our own desires."

Satria closed her eyes. "At first, we merely watched over warriors in battle. But, every now and then my sisters would change an outcome. And then, as time passed, their meddling became harmful, and they began to revel in the games they played."

She shook her head. "I did not share these sadistic whims, and refused to do more than see outcomes and guide fallen souls to the spiritual plane. Of course this did not sit well with my sisters. They did their best to sway me, but I remained neutral, as I felt was intended for us. Angered, my sisters deemed me unworthy of flying beside them. They tore off my wings and banished me."

Pain contorted her face. "It wasn't long after that, my sisters' meddling caught up to them, and the Valkyrian War started. One of the bloodiest genocides I've ever had to witness."

"But, you were spared," I said.

She nodded. "Yes. Due to my neutral standing in war, man did not see me as an enemy. I wept at the sight of my sisters dying one by one, but I couldn't turn back from the path I'd chosen. And, in the end I became the last valkyrie."

Phyre grabbed her hand. She smiled fondly at him, giving his hand a quick squeeze, and then swept her gaze over to Rashta. "That is, until after my ascension, when I bore Rashta."

I pursed my lips, my mind trying to process it all, and one bit of understanding I couldn't grasp. "But, if Phyre is her father, and he's human, doesn't that make her the first halfling, and not me?"

Satria shook her head. "No. Valkyries are always and only female. We take mates of other races and bear only female children—only valkyries. It has always been that way, since we first came to be."

I worked my jaw. I wasn't quite sure how well that made sense on a scientific level, but I also didn't have enough knowledge to say much about it. Instead, I focused on something smaller, and possibly trivial, but it tickled my curiosity. "Your statues don't depict you with your broken wings. Why is that?"

"I asked early sculptors to alter my appearance," she said, her face neutral, as if that type of request wasn't an odd one. Before I could ask her why she would do something like that, she continued. "There are times in our lives we wish to forget who we are—where we came from. Wouldn't you agree, Phoenix?"

I nodded, now understanding. Phyre, on the other hand, didn't particularly like her comment, based on the displeasure on his face. He pulled the goddess closer. "I still think we need to fix those statues."

Before she could protest, I spoke up. "I agree with him."

Her brow rose with interest, urging me to continue. I did.

"Something I've learned is that running from what you are does you no favors. *What* you are makes up a part of *who* you are, so denying that piece of you is rejecting your own self."

A subdued expression glazed her face. "Perhaps you're right. I will have to think on that further."

I glanced beyond them to Rashta and the gods tending to her. "How long will it take to purify her?"

Phyre turned concerned eyes on his daughter. "A while at this rate. We understood it was bad, but this is…"

He trailed off and I waited for him to finish his thought, but he never did. "Have you seen this corruption before?"

"We have. Once."

When he didn't elaborate and Satria didn't jump in, irritation flared in my chest, but I tried to not let it get the better of me. It was clear they weren't in a good headspace to be talking about it. And as long as Rashta was purified, that's what mattered in the end. *Right?*

I wanted to believe that, but something about the other corrupted individual stuck with me. Were they ever able to fix them? What if they weren't, and that's why Phyre and Satria were so worried?

My attention lifted to the sky vortex. Could that individual be the presence Rashta sensed and they were really still out there causing trouble?

Zion noticed my fixed attention. "Do not worry, Dragon-Phoenix. I can sense they are safe."

I worked my jaw. Even though he said those words, I couldn't believe them. It didn't matter Rashta had been removed from my body, I still sensed… something wrong.

The dragon god sighed. "Focus on something else, child. This is the first time your lives have been together on the living plane. And there are many who have questions." His head canted, as if he were listening to something I couldn't hear. "It seems Lumaraeon is also permitting questions to us gods, within reason. I believe all that will keep you busy."

I pursed my lips and sucked in a breath through my nose. I didn't like his attempts to distract me with trivial matters, but he wasn't wrong either.

"He's right," the familiar, accented voice belonging to Velsara spoke.

I turned to face the buxom nu-human woman with beaded and braided multi-shaded red hair as she approached. Painted marks covered her tan skin. With her was a tan-skinned man with red hair, cut and styled similarly to Zaith—Taiegh, her mate and Raikidan's previous life. "Better to focus on somethin' productive, no?"

I resigned myself. Not like arguing would get me anywhere. My attention slipped to the gathered scholars. *And from their eager faces, it might be good to ensure there aren't any unnecessary heart attacks.*

Ryoko also wasn't immune to her curious nature. She pressed against what was now clearly an invisible barrier, her golden eyes wide and taking everything in. Next to her was Lo'shen. Though, unlike my half-wogron friend, his attention was more focused. I pinpointed his gaze to Velsara.

She wasn't ignorant of his attention. Velsara turned to the gods. "Would you please be so kind as to let down the barrier?

Most of the gods looked to Zion for the answer of what to do. I knew he hadn't put the barrier up, but I wondered if his ability to split me from my past soul-lives made this request more difficult to approve without his input.

The dragon god thought for a moment and then swept his gaze over the crowd. "Mortals, I sense your excitement. I will permit you into the circle as long as you do not rush the Dragon-Phoenixes and their champions, or the time arches. This state they're in is not stable. We do not want anything to happen to them."

The mention of those arches drew my eyes to them. I'd assumed, after the time fields broke, they'd become inactive. But, the symbols Zion had carved into the stone still glowed with golden light. *I think I'm starting to get a grasp on how this is all working.*

I wasn't disconnected from my past soul-lives or Rashta—not really. The fracturing was only a temporary state, and thus an anchor was needed. Otherwise they'd have done this a long time ago, instead of my soul and Rashta entering the rebirth cycle.

Murmurs of agreement rolled through the crowd in response to Zion's request. The dragon god nodded and twitched one of his wings. A moment passed before anything happened, and that something was an adorable squeak from Ryoko when she suddenly tumbled forward. I laughed.

She took a breath and dusted her legs as if trying to fix her dignity. "Not funny."

"To you, maybe," I quipped.

She narrowed her eyes, but instead of words coming from her lips, she yipped when Lo'shen pushed her aside. "Velsara…"

Her eyes squinted as a wide smile pulled up her cheeks and she opened her arms. The older elf hobbled forward, tears pricking the corner of his eyes. The spryer woman closed the distance faster and swept him up in a tight embrace. "Lo'shen, my dear friend."

My brow lifted. *Dear friend?*

The old elf sobbed in her arms. Me'kunar came up behind him, a bittersweet smile on his face. Beyond them, South Tribe shamans pushed forward, a raucous of chants growing from them. I smiled.

Velsara was a shaman of their tribe. Her death hit them the hardest, and now they could have a reunion with her and obtain the closure they deserved.

Lo'shen finally calmed and pulled out of Velsara's embrace. "I'm sorry, child. I didn't mean to lose my composure like that."

She reached out and brushed a stray tear from his cheek. "Ain't no reason to start apologizin' on me."

He took a calming breath before patting her on the cheek and smiling. The older elf then turned his attention to me, chuckling to himself while Me'kunar and Velsara exchanged an embrace. "I bet you have a number of questions, Eira."

I blinked. "Uh, that's an understatement. You know each other?"

He smiled. "Of course. For five hundred years, in fact. I'm no spring chicken, after all. Even Me'kunar, while just a young boy, knew her."

I rubbed my temples. "So you knew… this whole time I was—"

Lo'shen shook his head. "No. When we first met you, we had no idea. As we got to know you, we both had our suspicions, but it wasn't until you were given the Ambassador title did we get out answer."

"And yet, you didn't say anything. You played things off as if you knew nothing."

He nodded. "It was a request from Arcadia. While we weren't given details at the time, we understood there were issues and it was best to play ignorant until the situation was fixed."

I worked my jaw. That made sense, but I couldn't entirely push back the small amount of betrayal I felt. If they'd just been able to help me, maybe things would have gone a little smoother.

I turned my attention to Me'kunar. "So, what you said at my coronation after party, about the Ambassadors…"

He nodded. "Some truth, some not. The Ambassador is only ever one soul, the Dragon-Phoenix's. Ever since Raina started the shaman way, that title has only ever been reserved for you. That is why it is such a special title, and why it is only ever been bestowed to a few women in history."

My other past soul-lives approached, giving the onlookers a better view of them. The lives I lived as shamans stepped toward Lo'shen and Me'kunar, Raikidan's lives not leaving their sides.

Lo'shen's eyes shone, and he gestured to Raina, a lithe elf woman of light skin with braided long dark green hair and green eyes, and her mate, a light-skinned, lean elven man with piercing lilac-purple eyes, long white hair, and groomed mustache and facial hair around his chin. A scar cut from the bridge of his nose to this jaw. Based on his features, I guessed him to be the now-extinct white dragon color. "Raina, the first Ambassador, and her Guard, Xanthus."

He turned to Nalia, a stocky, dark-skinned human woman with amber eyes and long brown hair braided on one side, and her mate, a tan-skinned human of a lean muscle build, sporting some light facial scruff, and blue-streaked white, medium-length wavy hair pulled back into a ponytail. From the double-colored nature of his features, he had to be a half-color, of two extinct colors—white and blue. "Nalia, our second, and Razeth, her Guard."

Next was Xenia, a human woman of dark complexion, with white and dark blue hair, and mismatched eyes—one amber, the other pure white, a clearly injured or prosthetic one, based on the deep, long scar that ran vertically down her face. Her mate stood beside her, taking the form of a light-skinned human of an athletic build, with silver eyes and violet hair. My heart slowed as I took in those features of his. He was a violet dragon—the rarest of all the colors before their extinction. "Xenia, the third Ambassador, and her Guard, Madorai."

Lo'shen faced Velsara and Taiegh, who had come up behind her and placed his hands on her shoulders. "Our fourth Ambassador, Velsara, and her Guard, Taiegh."

He then turned to me and Raikidan. "And our fifth and current Ambassador and Guard." Moisture brimmed his eyes. "I never thought I'd see a day where I'd be so lucky to witness you all in one place. It makes this old scholar so happy."

The tearful realization didn't last long. He whipped out his note-taking tome hanging from his side and began scribing in Elvish. He grinned from ear to ear and giggled from time to time.

I snickered. "You're a little too excited about this."

Lo'shen's eyes cut up to me. "Coming from the person who gets excited over maps?"

I snorted. "At least I don't giggle like a school girl."

He opened his mouth to reply, but nothing came out. He struggled with a comeback and I snickered again. Lo'shen dove back into his scribing.

I turned my attention to Ryoko. She'd been unusually quiet so far. I found her gaping at the sight of all my soul-lives. "Ryo, you okay?"

Her head bobbed in a slow nod. "Yeah… just… taking this all in. I'm not really sure where to start with my questions."

Isis stepped up, her copper hair flowing in the light breeze. "I'd be happy to do the introductions and explain things to everyone. I know those details the best since I'm the one who sent everything in motion. That should help reduce the number of questions."

I nodded and allowed her take center stage. While she went about introducing herself, and telling the story that started all this chaos, I turned to Naloth. "Don't think you've escaped giving me answers."

He let out a dramatic sigh and shifted to his nu-human form, taking the appearance of a broad-shouldered, muscular nu-human with bronzed skin and multi-colored hair. "The short answer is I'm tasked with watching over your timeline. I'm not supposed to interfere."

My brow ticked up. "And the long answer?"

Sylvia, a heavily pierced human woman with long, dark, wavy brown hair smattered with bits of red, bounded up to him and wrapped her arms around his waist. An unusual form-fitting, sleeveless, knee-length dress with a high cowl and hood, and tight pants covered her mocha-tan skinned, curvy athletic frame. On her arm she sported an intricate device that appeared to connect to her dress through wires and tubes. "He's my great-grandson, so he broke rules out of biased emotions."

Ryoko cocked her head, surprising me. I figured she'd be trying to listen to Isis, but maybe she was attempting both. *That can't go wrong in any way.* "What? No way. You two look the same age."

"We take on an appearance of a similar age to Eira unless we've never reached that point," Raina explained. "So while some of us lived much longer than Eira has now, we won't look that way until she ages."

That made sense. Spirits did something similar, either taking on an age appearance that would resonate best with the one they conversed with, or one they recognized better, if they had a personal relationship.

Ryoko tapped her lips with a finger. "Okay, that makes sense. But how can he only be your great-grandson? From the lineup you gave us, there's no way you were born recently enough for that to make sense."

"We chromatic dragons live beyond the constraints of the timelines," Naloth explained. "It allows us to insert ourselves into any part of the time streams to do our jobs."

"My head already hurts." Ryoko rubbed her temples, not that I blamed her. This time stuff wasn't easy for me, either.

"Why don't we back up to why you've interfered lately," I said. "Bias toward my soul because of Sylvia isn't really that great of an excuse."

Naloth shrugged. "For me it is. I'm known for being impulsive."

Sylvia snorted ironically, as if that claim was an understatement.

He continued. "Initially I was denied my requests to watch over your life, because of the threat of bias and meddling. But when we found out about your corruption, I was allowed to monitor your timeline. I'd proven with other tasks to have a good eye at catching meddlers, and given your vulnerable state, it made you an even bigger target."

He shoved his hands into his pockets. "I did well at first proving I could handle the task. But, as we both know, in the end I failed to stay away."

I nodded. "First during the infiltration assignment. Then, at the sandwich shop."

Raikidan fixed me with a concerned stared. "Sandwich shop? What incident at a sandwich shop?"

I rubbed the back of my neck. "Oh, I guess I forgot to tell you about that. One day, when I was out getting lunch alone, Kir tried to attack me. Naloth showed up to give me a hand."

Raikidan sighed, pinching his nose and muttering under his breath about not knowing what he was going to do with me.

I rolled my eyes and turned my attention back to the chromatic dragon. "While I know why you interfered with Kir, why did you step in during that assignment? And why did I notice you more after that time?"

He shrugged. "Weakness. I knew you'd be able to get out of there eventually, but I saw how difficult it would have been for you had I not stepped in. The other times were because once we're noticed by our charges, it's difficult to stay hidden." The chromatic dragon chuckled. "I will admit, the day I reacted to your attention, that was me messing with you intentionally. I couldn't help myself."

I crossed my arms and leaned my weight to one leg. "You'd gone so long not helping me, though. How could that one moment trigger you to act all of a sudden?"

"Well…" He rubbed the back of his neck. "That wasn't actually the first time I had meddled in your timeline. Just the first time you witnessed me."

My brow ticked up. "Go on."

"When you ran from Zarda, it presented the moment needed to begin your purification process. Lumaraeon and Zion instructed me to use the Hunters Zarda sent after you to our advantage and nudge you toward the shamans and Raikidan." I opened my mouth to speak, but he held up a hand and continued. "Yes, it reinforces the fact those events were guided rather than accidental; however, I will assure you, they would have still happened had I not done anything. It would have just taken longer." His voice lowered, and he mumbled more to himself than anyone. "Not that you made it easy to speed things up."

An amused snort escaped me. Sounded about right for me, even if I didn't know some of my path had been manipulated. "How about any other time? That moment was Lumaraeon's direct command. I can't see just that recent of an event creating that much weakness."

He shook his head. "No, the exact moment was during your time in service. It was an assassination mission you had particular trouble with, when you shouldn't have. Something was off about the troubles you received on that assignment. With the skills you'd acquired, it should have been simple to complete. And yet, you nearly died."

My pulse slowed. I knew that moment he was referring to. It was just as he said—I barely made it back from what should have been an easy mission. "So… you're the reason I lived through that?"

He shook his head again. "Not exactly. I was going to intervene, not only because of personal bias, but because I knew you dying before Rashta could be purified would cause catastrophic problems for your soul. However, when I appeared in the timeline, whatever was causing you harm vanished." He closed his eyes. "It was difficult for me to step back at that point. I wanted to save you. But I managed to stand by my oath, and you saved yourself in the end. Unfortunately for me, that set me on a difficult path of fighting my instincts to meddle when I wasn't allowed to."

I nodded slowly, understanding how strong a dragon's desire to protect was. *It must have been so hard to fight that for so long.* "Did you ever figure out what caused me issues that day?"

"Not right away, but once we found out Kir knew of your existence, I went back to that moment to observe at a different angle and found it had been him who'd gone at you that day."

I scowled. "So, he knew about me even back then. If that doesn't cement my theory he was Zarda's puppet master, I don't know what does."

Naloth nodded. "We've found evidence in our more recent investigation that you are correct on that. Nazir gave Zarda power, but it was Kir who was the master manipulator. How he knew to use Zarda, we're still not sure. It's far too convenient, based on how closely the two events transpired for it to be a mere coincidence."

I chewed my thumbnail. He wasn't wrong. Somehow Kir found out about the meeting between the god and the deranged mortal. *But how?*

"Alright, I now have even more questions," Ryoko announced, pulling my awareness out of my head.

CHAPTER 9

I want to back up and understand more about something with you," Ryoko said, addressing Velsara. "I've gotten a chance to take in the races Laz has lived, but you're the only nu-human. And you said you know these two book nerds here"—Lo'shen and Me'kunar chuckled at their nicknames—"From where you came out in that time stuff, my guess is you were Laz's most recent past life. How long ago did you live, compared to Laz?"

A mixed expression crossed Velsara's face, and the energy around us died down, melancholy falling over the South Tribe. "I died fightin' the Purge."

Ryoko's ears drooped. "Oh…"

My past soul-life smiled for her. "Ain't no reason to be sad. Sure, I have some regrets, but I lived a good life, an' it was my choice to fight when I knew the chances of me comin' back alive was slim."

"So, um, how old were you when you… died?"

Velsara thought for a moment. "About six hundred."

"Huh…" Ryoko counted on her fingers and then looked to our Genesis, standing next to Ryder. "That means you have to be a lot older than we first thought."

"Genesis is about three hundred years older than me," Velsara said.

Genesis blinked. "You sure?"

Velsara nodded. "I remember your name. My mother spoke about you. The first nu-human."

Genesis did some mental counting, her fingers twitching every so often. "Fifteen hundred years… has it really been that long?"

Velsara smiled. "Time flies, doesn't it?"

Genesis nodded, her mind no longer present with us as she thought in her own head. If we weren't sure she was a demi-god before, we were now. No way could she live that long otherwise, especially being such an early experimental nu-human. *Now that I think of it…*

Her abilities for necromancy were unusual as well. From what I'd found during some leisurely searches in the Eternal Library, necromancy was an old form of arcane magic that twisted spiritual energy. While Genesis had some books growing up to help her learn, the ones I'd found were far more in-depth, and she'd learned more about how unique her skill was.

The way Genesis described it, her power was more innate than any necromancy spell depicted in the books.

No… it can't be.

As discreetly as I possibly could, my gaze scanned the gathered gods until Nazir came into sight. The giant of a man, clad in black metal armor that matched depictions of ancient warriors found in library texts, hung back from most of the gods. Given his nature and domains, I never really saw him as the type to have too many strong relations with the other deities.

The man's ebon hair, pulled into a high ponytail, drifted in the breeze, his lavender eyes focused on the gods tending to Rashta. My attention remained on him, wondering if my theory would be proven correct by him switching focus, but it never happened. After another moment, I gave up. It was a decent assumption, but not the right—

Nazir's eyes flicked in Genesis' direction. It was brief, but long enough for my suspicions to bubble up again.

Zaith suddenly burst through the crowd of South Tribe shamans, drawing my focus and cutting Ryoko off in the middle of a question she was asking, his eyes intent on Velsara. Peacekeeper Pyralis followed behind him, his demeanor much calmer. "Sorry, my little sunflower, I held him back as long as I could."

Velsara smiled at the two dragons and opened her arms in invitation.

Zaith didn't hesitate. He ran to his mother and embraced her in a strong hug. Pyralis approached at a slow pace, to allow the two a moment.

My past soul-life gazed up at him when Zaith refused to let her go, long after he should have. "I'd greet you, too, Father, but I'm currently having the life squeezed from me."

I chortled and Pyralis threw his head back in a boisterous laugh. Ryoko poked my arm, her mouth agape. "You're related to a Peacekeeper?"

I snorted. "No, my past life was. You're the one who is related to a Peacekeeper."

An arm draped over her shoulder, Peacekeeper Ryoko suddenly appearing next to us. "Yeah, get it right."

Ryoko ducked her head. "Oops. Guess my brain is a little over-whelmed."

Peacekeeper Ryoko smirked. "Well, once you get it sorted out, Mom and Dad want to meet you finally."

My friend froze, eyes tightening. I wondered if that was the first time Peacekeeper Ryoko had worded that to her. I knew the fabled hero of Lumaraeon paid her visits now and then through the Spiritual Crystal at the South Tribe to help Ryoko out, but I wasn't privy to their conversations.

And, my mother was the closest to a mother Ryoko ever had. It wasn't an uncommon situation in the military. Squads made close bonds with each other, creating our own family unit of sorts. So while no experiment held their breath that they would ever meet their biological parents, they may have bonded with someone who would have been willing to fill that void.

"So, um, is that why you're here?" Ryoko asked, trying to work her brain out of its stalled state.

Peacekeeper Ryoko shrugged. "Yes, and no. All the Peacekeepers are here. We aren't the only infamous souls in Lumaraeon. We wanted to see all this go down, too."

My eyes fell over the gathered crowd. It'd be hard to pick them out, given the numbers, but Peacekeeper Varro, a healing shaman from the South Tribe and Peacekeeper Ryoko's mate, wasn't too far away from her, looking on. He nodded in acknowledgement when he noticed my attention, a warm expression on his face.

Peacekeeper Ryoko smiled and patted Ryoko's shoulder before walking off. "I'll catch up with you after all this is done."

I turned my eyes to Pyralis, who was now able to embrace his daughter, thanks to Taiegh pulling Zaith away to connect with his son. Even though the Peacekeeper focused on his daughter, his attention did shift for a moment to me. He winked and a knowing smile spread over my lips.

He'd always known I was the Dragon-Phoenix. But like so many others, he feigned ignorance for my sake. As much as I hated it, I did appreciate his intentions, even if it was potentially only out of respect for his daughter.

Before Ryoko had the chance to fully recover, Stella ran out of the crowd. Barely contained in her arms was Crystal. "Momma Eira! Papa Raikidan! I... oh."

Her wide eyes gazed over my gathered lives. "Who are they?"

Nisha, a buxom, light-skinned elven woman bent forward, her violet hair spilling over her shoulders, the movement exposing some red strands. "You know us, Stella. You've tried to talk to us a few times."

My daughter cocked her head. "I've never met you before. But you're really pretty. I like your dress."

Nisha wore clothes that looked like something between a dancer's outfit and a mage's robe depicted in historical texts. While I wouldn't call it a dress, I could see how Stella would see it as one.

My past soul-life's captivating silver eyes twinkled before she wiggled her fingers. Sparks of color shot from her fingers and coalesced around Stella's body. The young girl gasped when translucent billowing sleeves draped off her arms, and her t-shirt and pants transformed into a cute dress. "Wow! How did you do that, lady?"

Nisha chuckled and spoke before I could correct Stella for being so rude. "With magic."

My daughter pursed her lips and turned a confused gaze to me. "But there is no more magic, right?"

I smiled at her. "Nisha is from a different time, when we used to be able to practice magic."

"Yeah, about that," Ryoko said, now recovered. "This adds even more questions."

I chuckled. "Okay, we'll stop interrupting you." My eyes darted to Stella. "Is that okay, hon?"

She put Crystal down on the ground and let out an exhausted breath.

I was surprised she'd been able to hold the large cat that long… and that Crystal put up with it. "Yeah, that's fine. Can I stay and listen before I go back to play with the others kids?"

"Of course."

She joined my and Raikidan's side, struggling a bit to get Crystal to comply with the direction. I was thankful Seda and Argus had the cat on a harness and leash. I hated the thought of having to track her down if she ran off during all this.

I refocused on Ryoko. "Okay, you've got center stage."

"Magic?" Her eyes were wide. "No one has been able to use that in… like forever! How long ago did you live?"

"I was the second life of our soul, so…" Nisha pursed her lips. "Over fifteen thousand years ago, at least. Given how many times we've been reborn, and our extended lives because of our dragon blood, we've stopped counting the specific number of years at this point."

Ryoko's mouth fell open. "Over fifteen thousand? Are you serious?" She turned her shocked expression to me. "When did we lose magic again?"

I chuckled. If her brain was already unable to process things, the gods only knew how she'd react to answers for her other questions. "About two thousand years ago."

"Didn't lose it," I thought I heard Naloth mumble. I turned a perplexed gaze to him, only to find him engrossed in a game of rock-paper-scissors with Sylvia and Ayuma, an incredibly short human woman who had assets that more than made up for her lack of height.

Ayuma threw her hand flat while Sylvia and Naloth threw fists. She sprang into the air, her hands flying up. "I win!"

When her feet landed back on the ground, she brushed a lock of her short, curly black hair with green tips out of her face.

"Wow, you were really short," Ryoko said.

Ayuma winked a green eye. "We only grow until we're perfect, right Ryoko?"

I bit back a laugh. Ryoko wasn't tall by nu-human standards, though she was still considerably taller than Ayuma. A tall, well-built human man with a slicked back, black mohawk fade and black beard came up behind her and placed his hands on her shoulders. *I think his name is Zephyr… if I'm remembering right.* At one point, my soul-lives told me all of Raikidan's past names.

"Whoa," Ryoko said, her voice a bit breathy as she looked the man over. "Man, you were built like a brick house, Rai." Her eyes darted to his other lives. "Like, seriously. He's the biggest one here."

She wasn't wrong. Compared to his other lives, this guy was a giant.

Zephyr chuckled. "It's good to see you again, too."

Ryoko cocked her head, but before she could question him, Blaze called out, "Can we back up and talk about their size difference? She's like… child-sized, especially compared to him."

Ayuma stuck her tongue out. "I'm not child-sized, and we just have to be more creative and fun than you're capable of."

I choked, and Ryoko bent over in a fit of laughter. Blaze, to his credit, brushed off the insult relatively easily.

About the time Ryoko got herself under control, Ayuma skipped over to her and wrapped my friend up in a hug. "But Zephyr is right, it's been so long since we've seen you."

Ryoko blinked. "I don't understand."

The broad smile spreading on Ayuma's face caused her green eyes to squint. "We were best friends."

My friend's eyes widened. "Wait… you mean… I lived another life before?"

"Duh."

Nisha ran over to her and latched onto Ryoko's arm, "Same here."

Ryoko's eyes lit up. "Could I do magic?"

Nisha nodded. "Yep. You were also my dance partner."

Ryoko snorted. "Awesome, I used up my cool powers and coordination in another life."

Laughter rolled through the gathered people.

Isis pointed to herself. "You were also my friend."

Ryoko snapped her attention to me. "Did you know this?"

I shook my head. "If I had, I would have told you." I tapped my thumb against my chin. *I wonder…* "Who else was friends with her soul?"

Atria, Rinneth, Pheydra, Aria, and Xenia all raised their hands.

"Well, that explains a lot." I always wondered why Ryoko and I got along so well, when it really didn't make sense for us to. Now it did.

Arcadia approached. "Souls resonate with each other in many ways, and they can resonate with more than one. This is why many mortals will disagree with the concept that soul mates are only romantic connections. Your two souls are a good example. It's why, when you two are reborn at similar times, you find yourselves coming together. We don't plan this, as not even I can control when a soul is reborn."

"Does anyone control that?" Mana asked. "While mortals call Rashta the goddess of rebirth, that's not a true domain of hers. I don't recall any gods with those abilities, and there's overlap with some of you."

The goddess shook her head. "There is no deity that resides over that domain."

Mana went to thinking. I rapped my fingers against my thigh. It was strange. People didn't ascend to godhood these days. I wasn't even sure one had come into power in some time before Isis had been born. I assumed all domains were covered because of it. How could they not be, with so many people coming into existence?

Ayuma turned to Zion. "Can we show her? Please?"

"Hmm, I do not know," the dragon god said. "Your soul is a particular case. And this split is not without its risks."

His eyes narrowed when she popped out her lower lip into a pout. "Child, do not do that."

Nisha came up behind her and tilted her head while quivering her bottom lip.

"Not you, too." It wasn't hard to see this was not a look he could handle. I honestly found it entertaining to see who was and wasn't affected by such a tactic.

A devious chuckle came from Ryoko and she joined in, using her perfected skill to droop her ears alongside the matching sets of pleading eyes.

I bit back laughter when the dragon god closed his eyes and let out a long sigh. "I will not risk her safety. You will have to—"

"I have another way," Arcadia announced. "Lumaraeon has given me a temporary alternative. More for show than anything, but it should suffice."

The three women cheered and gave each other high-fives. While they celebrated their small victory, Arcadia walked off, motioning for Valena to join her. The two spoke in low tones, making it hard for me to pick up their conversation. But from the way Arcadia motioned to an area near the time arches belonging to my soul-lives, I got the vague sense they were going to make something similar.

The goddess of earth nodded and raised her arms. A flick of her wrist was all it took for four half-arches to shoot out of the ground. Her power was fascinating and intimidating.

Arcadia drew a thin-bladed, dagger-like weapon from her sash and sliced into her finger; she barely flinched. While blood bubbled up through the wound, she sheathed her weapon and approached the stone arches.

All watched her trace symbols onto the hard surface with her blood. I couldn't quite figure out why she had to do this with her blood. My time fields hadn't required some sort of weird blood ritual.

When the goddess finished with all four half-arches she stepped away and turned her attention to Zion. "If you'd be so kind as to breathe on it."

The dragon god eyed her for a moment, as if he wasn't ready to trust this plan of hers. He swiveled his large head over the arches and released a shallow exhale. A pale golden mist expelled from his mouth, rolling over the arches. The blood on the stone sparked, and a field of energy rushed between the stone half-arches, much like it had done for mine. However, unlike my time fields, these didn't stop at just connecting with their pairs. The magic shot out, creating a semi-cylindrical field of light between the arches.

Arcadia nodded her thanks, then motioned for Ryoko to approach. "Walk into the tunnel from one side, and do not stop until you get to the other end. Be sure you don't leave. If you do, your spirits will return to your body, and we will not be able to try again."

Ryoko eyed the time magic cautiously. "Will it hurt?"

"No. Unlike Eira, your soul will not be split. This is merely creating a field where your past spirits can exist outside your body while your soul is in use."

Ryoko took a deep breath. "Okay, let's do this."

She positioned herself in front of a time field and then walked through. She didn't flinch upon entry, and she didn't appear to have any signs of pain as she walked to the other side of the containment field, just as Arcadia claimed.

The time magic pulsed and warped, figures coalescing outside of her body in a strange liquid movement. *Was this how it looked when Raikidan and I walked through ours? Or is hers different due to the modified nature?*

When Ryoko reached the end, she turned around and blinked. All her past soul-lives greeted her in their own way. She gawked, especially at one life in particular—a large man with jet black hair. Ryoko pointed his way with a thumb, while turning her gaze to me. "I was a dude."

I snickered. "No one said a soul couldn't change like that."

She walked up to him and gave him a good once-over. "I was a buff dude."

Her past soul-life chuckled and lifted his arm into a flex. Ryoko threw a fist into the air. "All right!"

I shook my head, a smile on my face. She was so easily excited, but I wasn't going to kill her fun. This was an interesting situation, after all.

Nisha, Ayuma, and my other lives with a connection to Ryoko approached the time cylinder they were trapped in, happily greeting their old friends. It was Rinneth who had been friends with Ryoko's male past soul-life, greeting him by attempting to bump fists against the barrier.

As this interaction transpired, I noticed something peculiar. While I could see the glowing orbs at the bases of the necks of my soul-lives and of Ryoko herself, her extracted spirits didn't have this. I discreetly scanned a few nearby spirits, only to find they were also missing this feature.

I massaged my eyes with one hand, hoping—maybe a bit too desperately—the orbs I was seeing would go away. My spine prickled when they remained. *That means—*

"Eira, are you okay?" Arcadia asked, her question drawing the attention of everyone around me.

"Yeah, I'm…" I rubbed my eyes some more, pretending they were bothering me while I tried to make something up. I wasn't ready to discuss this with a god of all people, let alone with an audience watching. "Feeling tired from all this, I guess. It's a lot for my brain."

The goddess regarded me, her plate-crystal eyes piercing through me. Could she see my lie? "Do you have something you wish to ask? Something that would ease the burden? We all know you tend to overthink, and this is a safe place to ask questions."

"It's nothing major; I'm just trying to grasp the difference between spirits and souls. And yes, I know I've been taught they're different, but seeing how my past lives are here and being discussed as split souls, and then Ryoko is over there in some magic bubble with her spirits, it's all bleeding together."

Acadia's usual solemn expression softened to an understanding one. "I see. It's a bit simpler than you may think. The soul is the essence of life that resides in a body. The spirit is the manifestation the soul takes on when inside a body. When a soul dies, it goes to rest in the spiritual plane, and the spirits it has lived are released. This is how a single soul can have several identities, as you see with your friend here."

She paused a moment to allow those who weren't aware of all this information to process and keep up. "Your pasts have been imbued with a piece of your soul, fragmenting it. While dangerous, this was done so we could combat the corruption Rashta absorbed. For the spirits around you given temporary bodies, and Ryoko's pasts, they are not connected to their souls. Theirs are still at rest—as they should be—or in the case of Ryoko, active."

"So, is that why I'm in a bubble?" Ryoko asked.

The goddess nodded. "When a soul is not at rest, all past spirits are pulled back into it before the reincarnation process. We cannot give spirits temporary bodies if their soul is active."

Everything in me slowed. I was worried that would be her answer to the topic. *That means, what I'm seeing really is—*

"What we're all seeing," Lutha cut in telepathically.

I did my best to hide the fright she'd given me. *"So, it's not just me."*

"No. While we sometimes struggled to see it when you did, it's as clear to us now as it is for you."

Unfortunately, my interaction with her didn't go unnoticed. Arcadia, who had continued to watch me far too closely, spoke up. "What is wrong, Eira?"

I bit the inside of my cheek. I didn't want to talk about yet. But it looked like I wasn't going to have a choice.

"We should tell her," Velsara said. "We won't get answers by privately speculating."

She had a point.

"Laz, what's going on?" Ryoko said, exiting her time bubble. The past soul-lives that'd come out of her had already disappeared before she'd stepped out, and upon her departure, the time magic fizzled, instead of breaking like it had done for my soul-lives.

I let out a breath. *No going back now.* "We're seeing souls."

The entire cove stilled. When the silence spoke, it was for clarification from Arcadia. "Come again?"

I sighed. "I'm seeing souls."

She shook her head. "That's not possible."

Motioning to the base of my neck, I persisted. "It's an orb of golden light that sits right here. Everyone but the spirits have them. Even the demons have them, though theirs are different in appearance. Mine and my lives don't glow as brightly, because of our fragmented state, and you gods have the most powerful glow I've seen. It actually hurts my eyes after a while."

"How long has this been going on?" Satria asked.

I worked my jaw. "A few months now. It's been on and off the whole time, but today it's happened more often. And then when my soul was split, it turned on, and won't go away."

Several gods exchanged glances, piquing my curiosity. Their eyes showed a silent understanding passing between them. *Velsara was right in having us bring it up.* They knew something.

"It isn't possible for a mortal to see souls," Arcadia insisted.

"Isn't it, though?" Telar said. "A year ago, you said it shouldn't have been possible for her to rend a soul, yet she did."

He was right. As much as I wanted to bury those dark moments so I wouldn't relive them again, it wasn't something I could forget.

A woman with an anthropomorphic form approached. Unlike Mocha, who had more human traits beyond her tails, ears, and altered face shape, this woman looked entirely feline, like wogrons did canine. She had white fur with black spots, and a fluffy tail swished behind her. *Solstice.*

She was the last Leocona in existence. And even though her domain was ice and winter, she wore a fur-lined dress over her curvy figure.

"We have noticed a change in your soul as of late." She spoke with a raspy voice, thickened by an accent. "It was around the time your Champion made an attempt to sacrifice his life in place of yours. This new development may be related."

Arcadia shot the goddess an icy warning stare, which didn't go unnoticed by me or my past soul-lives. "What don't you want me to know, Arcadia? Is it something related to Rashta denying I was seeing anything at all?"

The spirit goddess set her jaw. "We have no proof of anything. There is no reason to discuss theory right now."

My eyes narrowed. "But we're not working with theory. I can see these souls and I don't know why. You can deny it all you want, but that doesn't change what is happening to me. So if you know what's going on, even just an inkling, I deserve to know."

Arcadia sucked in a breath through her nose. "When your soul is reformed, this light will go away. It won't matter."

Irritation flared in my chest. "Why are you acting like this? Is it so bad that I can see souls? Is it terrible you were wrong about a mortal gaining the ability to? I didn't ask for this, but I sure as hell would like answers."

Still the goddess didn't speak, her eyes hard. And no other gods stepped in, as if this talk of souls removed their ability to speak out against her decision to shut the conversation down.

Typical of Ryoko, she jumped in to diffuse the building tension. "I've got a question about souls, if I'm allowed to ask."

I didn't like that she was changing the subject, but at this rate, it was probably for the best. Neither of us was going to bend.

Arcadia turned her pale eyes to my half-wogron friend, doing her best to be pleasant. "What is your question?"

Ryoko pointed to Lutha and Lina, the two fair-skinned women, nearly identical with white and red hair and sultry figures, save for their different haircuts—Lutha's, a short mohawk-like style, and Lina's long and flowing. "How does that work? Like, Laz is one soul, so how does a twin situation work?"

To my surprise, it wasn't Arcadia who answered. Stepping forward were the psychic god twins, Sela, a woman with fair skin and hair, and her twin brother, Tyro, a man of dark skin and hair. They both sported dark blindfolds, golden hexagrams painted on them.

Sela spoke first, her voice hollow, much like Seda's. "Identical twins have what we call a *split soul*. This is when the soul naturally creates more than one spirit, and divides itself willingly to harbor more than one vessel. It only occurs in identical twins, and is the main reason why they, of all twin types, are more likely to be psychics."

Ryoko tapped her lips. "Huh, and fraternal twins?"

"They have their own souls," Tyro said, his voice smooth and inviting.

"But they are bonded souls, much like how your and Eira's souls are bonded. This is why a psychic ability can manifest between them. These soul connections are also how twins have special awareness abilities if they don't manifest true psychic power."

"Wow…" Ryoko turned her attention to Jasmine, who was hanging back with my uncle, mother, and father. "Hear that? We have answers!"

A contemplative expression graced my aunt's face. "Yes, and it explains how physic bonds were capable of forming for tank-born fraternal twins."

Ryoko turned to Raikidan for her next question. She pointed to two of his past soul-lives—green dragons, from their green hair and golden eyes. They were Reve and Zetan, Aria's mates. While they looked similar enough to be called identical, they had slightly different body types. The one with the muscular build had a mohawk, while the leaner, more athletically built one had a more run-of-the-mill short, tousled cut. "You were a twin, too. How common is that for dragons?"

"By definition, all eggs laid in a single clutch would be fraternal twins. It doesn't have the same effect on us as it does on humans or elves." He shook his head. "Identical twins, though, are rare. Most of the time, they don't hatch. Those that do, it's not uncommon for at least one of them to die within the first few days. Our shells just don't have enough room or nutrients."

"I'll admit I'm not exactly the healthiest of dragons either," Zetan, the smaller framed of the twins said. I thought I detected a bit of a wheeze from him.

Ryoko pursed her lips. "Do you two have that twin connection humans have? You're clearly not psychics."

"Dragons can develop similar traits, but they're not as consistent," Reve, the broader of the two, said. "We have some base emotional sensory connection, but our bond isn't strong enough to cause anything life-threatening."

I rapped my fingers on my arm. "Xephrya was a twin, too, if I'm remembering correctly."

The female dragon in question appeared in the gathered mortals. "That's right. My sister, though, didn't make it. I received some Seer-sight type abilities. Of course, it's nothing as intense as what a human or elf psychic would develop."

Ryoko tapped her lips. "So Laz has been human, elf, and nu-human, psychic, and able to harness more than one type of element of magic. Is there anything she hasn't been? Besides a dwarf, of course, as we can see."

Atria, a tall, voluptuous woman with olive-tan skin and long, slightly wavy black-to-red ombre hair snickered. Her sapphire eyes twinkled with amusement. "If you don't count Ayuma as a dwarf."

Ayuma rolled her eyes. "Ha, ha."

Raina stepped forward, shooting Atria a scolding glance. "The only element our soul hasn't harnessed is wind. Even sub-elements and variants have been covered."

Before Ryoko could mouth anything else, Shva'sika gasped and rushed up to my elven past soul-life. "That sash… may I?"

Raina smiled, a peculiar, knowing glint in her eyes. "Please, have a look."

Ryoko shot me a questioning glance while Shva'sika inspected the cloth. I worked my jaw, trying to remember clothing significance in elven culture. "If I'm remembering right, clothing is embroidered and designed differently, depending on the family. Even stitching patterns can reflect who made a textile."

My eyes flicked to Nisha. "Right?"

She nodded. "That's right. And it's not uncommon, even in this time, for house crests to be embroidered and proudly displayed on prominent parts of their clothes, too." She turned around and pointed to the back of her skirt. "I wear mine."

Ryoko's brow rose. "On your ass?"

Nisha threw her head back in a laugh, while her mate, Aser, a blue dragon with tousled dark blue hair and tan skin, hid his copper eyes behind his hand. "Are we sure she's not able to channel Vestele?"

Ryoko cocked her head. "What did I do?"

Nisha struggled to get herself under control. "Vestele said the same thing when I revealed this outfit."

I choked on a laugh. That would figure.

"I put it there so people could see it while I was performing." Nisha spun fluidly, her practiced skill on full display. Her dress lifted with the movement, but to my surprise, her house crest stayed visible enough to remain recognizable. "Up on a stage, I needed it to be visible by everyone. So why wouldn't I choose to embroider it on the back of my skirt?"

I barely heard her last few words, my eyes glued on the embroidered image. Two dragons entwined together, what looked like a butterfly marked between them.

Fingers snapped in front of my face. My eyes fluttered and I found Ryoko half-bent in front of me. "Laz? You back on Lumaraeon with us?"

I snorted amusedly. "Sorry about that."

"You totally went blank on us. What's got you?"

I shook my head, trying to clear my mind. "It's just that crest. It's… familiar."

A knowing smile spread across Nisha's lips. "It's because of the Ambassador crest." Her shoulders lifted in a half-shrug. "Well, the Dragon-Phoenix crest, technically."

My eyes shifted to Raikidan. He'd been acting his usual self, taking things in quietly. I reached out and lifted the front cloth of his waist cape.

"Whoa, good thing he's wearing pants under that," Ryoko teased.

I snorted. "Not like you'd complain if he wasn't, Miss Rear-View-Mirror Peeker."

She opened her mouth as if to protest, then shrugged instead. She had no shame.

My attention turned to the symbol on Raikidan's clothes. "So this…"

Nisha nodded. "…came from my family crest."

I gazed at her quizzically and she continued, taking a heavy breath first. "My mother had a… strained relationship with her family. So when she mated with my father, they started our new family name, Wysaven. Though, we remained crestless until I was born. When our soul was reborn for the first time, it caused quite the stir." She smiled. "But it brought the inspiration to our family crest, and then an altered version was bestowed to our soul specifically around Raina's time, to match our title."

That made a lot of sense. Though, what was the significance to the butterfly? I had assumed it was related to me, but clearly this was something older.

I turned to Shva'sika, who was deeply engaged in an animated Elvish conversation with Raina. "So, care to share which part of her outfit got you excited?"

Shva'sika smiled, her eyes sparkling. "All of it. I noticed two patterns not used since the Kitansyr royal family and Falaelon working-class family were combined. And then there was a stitching that resembled the Lightshine family. It's because Raina created the Lightshine family."

I blinked, looking to Raina for confirmation. She nodded. "I was born into the Falaelon family. However, due to certain circumstances, I'd gone to live with my aunt, who had married into the Kitansyr family. There was a rivalry between the houses, and my aunt's marriage did nothing to improve things, so I took it upon myself to sort out the differences and merge the families."

Xanthus, standing patiently beside her, shook his head. "Don't ask how she managed that feat, because even I'm not sure."

Raina took Shva'sika's hand in hers. "And Shva'sika is more than just from the same family. She's a descendant of my maternal uncle."

My eyes widened. "Please tell me that's just a coincidence."

The elf woman laughed. "Well, I'd be partially lying if I did. I told the gods it would be a good idea for Shva'sika to take up the mentorship role for you because of our connection; however, that wasn't what convinced them."

I tilted my head to urge her to go on when Velsara spoke up. "It was me. Shva'sika was born the same year I died. It felt only natural for her to be chosen."

"Huh…" I tapped a finger against my lips. "This relation to each other, is this how you're both related to Shiva?"

Raina nodded. "Yes, she's a shared ancestor of ours."

My eye twitched when the scratching of a quill came too close to my ear. I turned to Lo'shen, who had taken the liberty of creeping closer to get a better eavesdropping vantage. "Can you record your nosey notes quieter?"

He squinted an eye at me, dipping his quill into his inkwell before scratching the tip against parchment even louder in defiance. I held his indignant stare for a moment, only to sputter out laughter. Lo'shen chuckled and patted me on the back.

Mana took a tentative step toward the gods, her hands held together and her shoulders tight. "Um, I have a question for one of you, if I could ask it?"

Satria looked past Mana's nervousness and smiled. "What would you like to ask?"

"We've been so focused on the concept of Eira's past lives, and they've all been half-dragon, for reasons Isis explained earlier. But I, uh, just need to know something about the biological compatibility of dragons with humans and elves."

The goddess' expression didn't change. "You already know the answer to that."

Mana blinked slowly and then a grin spread across her face. She jumped around. "I knew it! I knew it!"

Many of us, including myself, laughed at her excitement.

"Mana, calm down," Corliss said through his laughter.

"But I knew my family's theory was right."

He chuckled some more. "I know, but I'd rather not lose my head from your flailing arms."

She stopped and ducked her head. "Oops, sorry."

He hugged her. "It's all right."

"Is someone going to explain for the rest who don't know this little secret?" Nyoki asked.

"Dragons used to be human!" Mana blurted out without any pause.

Silence fell over the crowd. Every pair of eyes fell on her, and then shifted to Satria for further clarification.

Satria chuckled. "It's as she says. Humans and dwarves are the oldest races on Lumaraeon. Sometime along the life span of humans, many of them evolved into elves, and both, because they were nearly the same genetically, developed the ability to shapeshift. This is where the dragons came from."

Ryoko cocked her head. "They came about because of shapeshifting? That's weird."

"At some point many of the shifters ceased shifting back and eventually became their own viable race," the goddess said. "Then all three races forgot their origins and the rest is history, as mortals like to say these days."

Ryoko nodded. "Okay, that makes sense."

Blaze clasped his hands behind his head. "Wow, now I feel dumb because she figured it out better than me."

Ryoko stuck her tongue out at him. "That's because you are dumb."

She sucked her tongue back in and turned her gaze to the war goddess again. "I'd like to know something, given this topic of compatibility. I witnessed Raikidan's ability to sleep in a human form not once, but twice, and he claimed it shouldn't be possible for dragons. How was he able to do it? Is it because humans and dragons were once the same, or is it more complicated than that?"

"It's a bit more complicated than that." Satria thought for a moment. "As a dragon ages, and they use their shapeshifting ability more often, they become more capable at maintaining a shifted form. However, this ability is enhanced the longer a dragon remains in his or her shell to grow—this includes times of sleep." She grinned. "Of course, we only need to ensure this happens to those dragons destined for non-dragon partners."

Raikidan crossed his arms. "Why didn't I know about it?"

Her shoulders lifted. "Because no one told you."

He looked to his mother, who pressed her lips together. "It occurred so spontaneously, I thought it best not to tell you until you were older, as I believed age would sort it out."

Xephrya's eyes darted to me. "That, of course, didn't happen until she came around."

I pointed to myself. "Why me?"

"The destined mate is the key to control in an unconscious state," Satria explained. "Your constant presence and bonding with your Champion allowed the ability to mature properly."

Ryoko snapped her fingers. "Knew it wasn't a fluke."

I chuckled, and Raikidan rolled his eyes.

"So, one more question, if I can," Mana said.

"Ask away," Satria said.

"This connection between our two species, is it why Old Tongue and our ancient dragon language that has lost its original name are so similar?"

Lo'shen stopped scribbling in his book, his eyes snapping up to the god. Me'kunar also showed interest.

Satria nodded. "Yes. The two languages came from the first language that is now only known to Genesis and Zoltan."

Lo'shen peered over to the two gods still purifying Rashta. "I can presume they will keep that secret."

Satria laughed. "They claim there's no need for others to know it. But I'm sure it's because they like to talk to each other in a way others can't possibly understand."

"Your theory is wrong, Satria," Genesis called over.

"Yeah, sure."

I laughed. I'd be one to side with Satria's theory.

An uncomfortable sensation crawled up my spine, cutting my fun short. My pulse raced and my eyes darted around, everything within me suddenly going on edge.

I wasn't the only one, though. Every one of my soul-lives searched for something unknown.

Raikidan rested his hand on my lower back. "Eira? What is it?"

"I… don't know," I said, my words slow as I focused on finding the source of this unknown disturbance. "Something feels… off."

Suddenly, Naloth, Zalia, and Rylar, Sylvia's chromatic dragon mate, snapped their attention to the time vortex above, as did all the chromatic dragons and Zion. I gazed up, and my eyes widened when a multi-colored dragon fell through.

"Move!" Lutha shouted before she and Lina used their psychic ability to shove everyone out of the way in time to miss being crushed by the dragon colliding with the ground.

Sprawled on the ground from the graceless landing, I propped myself up on my arms. My stomach lurched at the sound of the sickening, lifeless *thud* the dragon's body made. *Oh no…*

Sylvia jumped to her feet and rushed over to the chromatic dragon—or, what I was sure was a chromatic dragon. Half the body was blackened and smoldering.

My past soul-life reached for the unmoving body, only to gasp and retract her hand before she touched the dragon. Her eyes were wide, and her voice barely registered above a whisper. "He's… dead."

Naloth sprinted over to the dead dragon, checking his fallen clan member. Another chromatic dragon roared and ran over to him as well. The dragon frantically nudged the dead dragon's body. The pain in both sets of eyes was too much.

I rose to my feet, things slowing around me and my heart pounding in my ears. "Zion, where are the other two?"

When he didn't answer, my gaze snapped to the dragon god. His head was tilted skyward, eyes nearly glazed over. I spoke louder, my racing pulse putting me even more on edge. "Zion, where are the other two dragons?"

Silence permeated the tense air. No one even seemed to want to breathe. When the god finally spoke, my stomach dropped. "I don't know. I can't find them."

"How…" I licked my lips. "How can you not find them?"

The god didn't answer, his attention still on the timelines. The chromatic dragons around us also searched, their eyes glazing over just like their god's. Even Rylar fell into the trance.

Stella grabbed my skirt. "Momma… I'm scared…"

I rested my hand on her head, wishing desperately I could tell her everything was going to be okay. But I couldn't.

"Uh, guys," Ryoko said. "What's in the sky over there?"

Before I could see for myself, the ground underneath us quaked.

CHAPTER 10

The tremor only lasted a moment, but it'd certainly gotten everyone's attention. My breath came slowly, my nerves frayed. Then another tremor, this one more violent.

I braced myself the best I could. From the corner of my eye, I spotted Raikidan grabbing Stella and Crystal protectively. Nothing would happen to those two as long as he had a say—which was good, because as the shaking ceased, it allowed me to focus.

Lutha and Lina's mate, Rhaegos, a built man with a long, deep brown mohawk, short beard, septum piercing, and scarred terracotta skin, knelt and placed a hand on the ground, his amber gaze focused. Nalia did the same. Valena's and Tarin's focus dulled, as if they, too, were searching for something.

"Something is coming," Rhaegos said in a deep, rumbling voice.

"What is it?" I asked.

"Hard to say," Nalia said. "Sometimes it feels large, and then other parts feel small."

"It's… an army," Raina whispered. Attention snapped to her. She had her eyes closed, brow creased in concentration. Roots had grown up from deep within the ground and wrapped around her arms. "I've seen this kind of pattern before. But the tremors… don't know how they're causing them."

"Maybe if you all look at the sky, you can figure it out," Ryoko said.

I turned and then took a startled step back. Beyond the rim of the mountains surrounding us, dark clouds rolled in. My eyes squinted. No, they weren't just dark, they were black—unnaturally so. The mass moved in at an unnatural pace, and something akin to lightning flashed within, but no sound could be heard. What was clear were the shapes illuminated in the cloud with each strike.

"W–what is that?" someone said.

I didn't have an answer. However, it did send a prickle of unease down my spine. "Get all non-combatives into the temple."

No one moved, all too stunned to process my command. "I said… Everyone who can't fight, into the temple, now!"

My raised voice sent people into a scramble. Raikidan hauled Stella into his arms. Ryder and Est'la ran up to us. I had Raikidan hand Stella off to Est'la, who protested. "I want to help."

I opened my mouth, but he continued. "I've been training. I have a lot of control."

My heart clenched. His eyes pleaded, but I couldn't put him in this kind of danger unless he absolutely needed to be. I placed my hands on his shoulders. "You will be helping."

"But—"

"Est'la, you're part of this family now." I made sure to hold his stare so he understood how serious my words were. "That means you need to protect your sister and the Birth Heart. If something happens out here, and that wall protecting the sanctuary comes down, everyone inside is going to need you to fight for them. Do you understand?"

His face steeled and he nodded, taking Stella. Ryder took Crystal, and the two dashed off, joining my uncle and Genesis. Ryder wasn't a fighter, either, but he'd take up that mantle if he needed to. I prayed that moment wouldn't come.

Another violent quake shook the ground. I gasped when I lost my balance, but before I fell, or Raikidan could react, clawed hands grasped my arms. Zaedrix pressed his chest against my back, and wrapped his tail around my leg to hold me steady. I noticed Rosa had done the same for Raina. *Oh, that's right, they'd made a deal with her once, too.*

It surprised me Rosa was assisting my past soul-life. I would have thought, given that their deal had ended with Raina's death, they'd feel no obligation to help her in any way. *Maybe they're a bit more loyal than they like to let on.*

"It's them," Zaedrix murmured in a half growl. "The ones you've sent us chasing after. I can smell them."

My heart rate sped up and I had to force myself to breathe. The Crimson Sanctuary was here? I knew it was a possibility, but I really wanted to believe it was paranoia. *How did they know to attack here?*

More violent quaking. Boulders broke off the mountain on the far side, crashing to the ground. An echo of cracking sounds bounced off the walls of the cove. *That sounds like—*

Nalia jumped to her feet. "Not good."

"Something is breaking through the mountain," Valena murmured, her glazed-over eyes focused toward the towering landform.

I gasped when the ground shook beneath me. Zaedrix kept his hold, but the increasingly violent tremors made it difficult for even him to stay upright. More chunks of rock fell from the mountain cliffs, and fissures broke the ground, weaving their way toward us.

A plan would be good right about now. Relaying what Zaedrix told me would be the smart thing to do, but my mind was racing too much, and the frenzy behind us to hide the vulnerable made it too hard to think straight.

The ominous cloud in the sky continued to spread. Another loud crack from the mountain, and an enormous boulder fell, revealing more damage within. My heart pounded in my ears. *Are we really just standing here waiting? What's wrong with us? Especially us experiments. We should be better than this.*

Rhaegos snarled, the muscles in his arms tight with effort. "I can't stop it. Whatever is causing this is too strong."

"I'm having no better luck," Nalia added. "Every time I touch the earth, something stronger wrestles it from me."

I took a breath. "We need to prepare. All earth elementalists should try to hold them off as long as we can."

"Who's them?" Ryoko asked.

My gut twisted as I uttered the name. "The Crimson Sanctuary."

Everyone stilled, even those seeking shelter.

"Are you sure?" Ryoko asked, her fists clenching and unclenching.

"Rosa and I have been chasing them long enough to know their smell," Zaedrix said.

"Safe to guess Kir will be among them?" Rylan asked.

I nodded. "As their leader and the orchestrator of their attack on Dalatrend, I can't see him sitting this out."

Isis turned to Lutha and Lina. "What do you sense? Can you confirm he's with them?"

I hadn't noticed the two women had turned their focus to the mountain wall, hair standing on end—an indicator of using a great deal of psychic power.

"Nothing," Lina mumbled. "We're not sensing a single thought."

Seda stepped forward and tried her luck, only to fail. Every psychic in the vicinity searched, and every one of them came up empty-handed. That was not comforting.

I turned to Sela and Tyro. *There is no way this organization could get past two gods.* My stomach knotted when Sela frowned. "This shouldn't be possible."

Tyro's fingers curled. "How can they hide from us?"

People murmured around us. Blaze took a caution step forward. "Please tell me you two are making a poorly timed joke."

Instead of answering him, they turned to Zion. He was no longer searching the timeline. Instead, he gazed out toward the mountain.

Silence.

"Zion," I hedged.

"She's here," he murmured.

She? I had no idea who the god meant, but from the conflict flickering in his eye, it was more complicated than we had time for. The ground quaked again, harder than it had before. Zaedrix's grip on me still held. *No more stalling.*

"Earth elementalists, try to hold that mountain together as long as you can." My eye flicked up to the sky, the dark cloud now rolling over the mountain. "And we need to figure out what the hell that thing is."

"Nothing you'll be able to do anything about," Satria said. She turned her attention to us. "We gods will not be able to help you in this. We're sorry."

Ryoko threw her hands out, the fissures that formed between us and the mountain closing shut. "Why not? You helped with Zarda."

The war goddess shook her head. "No, we only witnessed Rashta's judgment. Nazir fought Zarda because the man was foolish enough to attack. Rashta's involvement was also unique."

"What about us?" Ayuma asked. "It's obvious Rashta's purification still isn't finished."

Satria's lips pressed into a thin line. "The time arches will be under our protection. But all of you need to be careful. If anything happens to one of you, it could spell disaster."

A dark shape moved under my feet. Raikidan, Zaedrix, and I jumped back. The shape rose up from the ground and the Guardian formed, taking position between us and the mountain.

Raina smiled. "Kharis is refreshed and ready to protect us. Our enemies will have trouble with him around."

"Kharis? That's the true name of the Guardian?" I asked.

She nodded. "That was his name before he became one of several Guardians my family created."

My brow furrowed. "A—are you saying he used to be a human?"

"Yes." Her tone was so matter-of-fact. "A dire situation forced us to use an ancient spell. It would turn a willing individual into a being of guardian power. We didn't know the specifics beyond that." She smiled kindly at the Guardian. "Kharis was a good friend of mine, and one of my personal guards. He willingly offered himself for the spell, accepting whatever fate would befall him."

That explained the soul orb I'd seen within him. Deep inside the shadowy form were the remnants of a soul who would do anything to protect his people—and Raina.

"It pained me to know he and the Guardians who had survived over the millennia had been subjugated. They were never meant to be bound that way."

There are more? "We wouldn't happen to have access to the others, would we?" I didn't want to sound desperately hopeful, but we needed all the help we could get. And an army of Guardians would be one hell of a miracle.

"As a matter of fact, my lady, we do," a male voice I vaguely recognized said.

I turned, facing a half-elven man clad in ancient armor. My brow quirked up. "Lazei?"

The dead warrior, whom I'd met once by chance two summers ago, protecting a library entrance through the use of a spiritual crystal, smiled. "It's a pleasure to see you again, Eira."

He turned to Raina and knelt. "Lady Raina, it's my honor to serve you again."

"Lazei…" she whispered, tears welling in her eyes. "My old friend."

I struggled to find words. He knew Raina? That certainly explained his actions toward me when we'd met.

The warrior raised his head to gaze at the first Ambassador. "If you permit…"

Raina blinked back her tears, taking a deep breath and straightening her spine. A regal air rolled off her in an instant. "Lazei of house Ravadi, son of Naertho, you were tasked in protecting the Falaelon family library as an Eternal Guardian when you could no longer perform the duty of guarding me. Since then, you have safeguarded this entrance even after your mortal body failed you and the city fell to ruin. Today I ask you to once again take up arms and fight the darkness that threatened us long ago."

"My sword is yours to command, Ambassador Raina."

Her lower lip quivered and then her features softened, her arms opening. Lazei was on his feet and embracing her in a blink. "I've missed you, my friend."

"And I you."

The ground vibrated again, reminding us not to forget our task. "Okay, mushy reunion is over. Lazei, you said you had an army for us?"

He chuckled and gestured in the way he'd come from. "An army who would fight once again for the Dragon-Phoenix. And all the Guardians remaining in the land."

My jaw dropped at the amassed warriors. There had to be at least a thousand souls gathered. And with them, beings much like Kharis, but of more than just shadow—fire, air, earth, even one that looked like some sort of cloud vortex with lightning sparking within.

"Lazei, are any of them…" Raina's words broke off, as if she were afraid to ask a question that didn't have a favorable answer.

The warrior nodded. "Aias, Ruvyn, Naexi, and Zestari have survived this long, and are as devoted as ever."

A single tear trickled down Raina's cheek. Xanthus wiped it away with a finger, gaining him a grateful smile. She composed herself as best as she could. Me, on the other hand… I was still struggling with comprehending this army.

I turned to Arcadia. She gazed out at the mountain under attack. She spoke, though didn't turn to address me. "Like the other gods, I cannot help in any way."

The corner of her lip twitched, as if she were holding back an amused smile. "However, I cannot stop spirits from utilizing the gateway I created earlier to allow some to attend the purification event. And I cannot stop them from pledging their services to defend you or any other mortal there."

A grin spread up half my face. *Clever.* There were always ways around rules, you just needed to know how to exploit those weaknesses.

A large presence came up behind me. I whirled around, only to regret it a moment later when another large quake tried to knock me off my feet. Luckily Zaedrix had remained at my side and caught me.

His and Rosa's continued presence perplexed me. I may have had an agreement with them to assist in dealing with the Crimson Sanctuary, but even this was a bit much to expect from them, in my eyes. Taking out members one-by-one was vastly different from fighting a battle, and there was no doubt in my mind it'd come to that.

Of course, those two demons weren't the only ones I was surprised to see still hanging around. Xithoz loomed over me, Nemora stuck to his side.

Before I could question their presence, the bone demon spoke. "We will be fighting alongside you."

I blinked slowly.

"Lumaraeon is our home. This Crimson Sanctuary threatens the peaceful living we seek, as we do not fit in their vision any more than you do, half-breed."

I did my best to refrain from twitching. I knew that in this instance, he wasn't insulting me.

"We've sent one of our own for more reinforcements from our village," Nemora said, though her gaze was oddly fixed in a scowl aimed beyond me. Following her projection, I found it landed on Arcadia. That piqued my interest. I didn't doubt demons and gods would have issues being in the vicinity of each other, but her malice was unmistakably narrowed and focused. *Does she have something against the goddess?*

"Nemora," Xithoz murmured. "Please focus."

So I wasn't jumping to conclusions.

The succubus turned her piercing gaze to me. "Our fastest has gone, but I can't say how quickly they'll return with more numbers."

I worked my jaw. Demons were frighteningly quick. But even with speed on their side, battles could turn at any moment. *Wait, speed…*

My back straightened. "How many can we spare to do some recon?"

"Couldn't spirits do that?" Rylan asked.

I crossed my arms. "Yes, but given Kir's nature, he'll expect that. And if that's the case, I'm concerned what kind of damage he could inflict without us knowing what we're up against yet." I rapped my fingers. "But demons, I doubt he'll expect."

"There's another benefit as well," someone said.

We all turned to see Aurora approaching with Nioush. In her hands she carried a large silver case. "We haven't been idle this last year. Mobile communication has been spotty at best, especially in areas like this. We made assumptions that travel would require the tech to be improved."

She opened the case in her hands, revealing objects that resembled communicators, but smaller, and black boxes with straps. "With connections built through the scholars, we were able to obtain old tech specs for communicators. While we weren't able to recreate them, as we were still missing some valuable information, we utilized the design to improve the ones we use today."

I removed one of the communicator earpieces, turning it in my hand. In a lot of ways, it looked like the device I was used to, just smaller. Not quite as tiny as the earpiece I'd seen soldiers use when not utilizing their helmets, but from the looks of it, this design allowed for digital visor use, whereas the smaller design removed that ability.

Zaedrix lifted one of the black boxes out of the case and secured it to his arm. A slip of his finger activated the face plate screen, and it lit up. My eyes widened at all the information displayed. It was like the communicator, but easier to read as it wasn't so close to your eyes. And the larger screen helped, too.

I activated the earpiece in my hand, the digital visor sliding out as I'd expect from a communicator. As I anticipated, the display was much sleeker, most of the usual features transferred to the arm device.

"Make sure you grab the correctly matched pieces," Aurora said when Nemora reached for one. "They won't work otherwise. I've color coded them to make sure they're not mixed up."

I peered at my earpiece to find a small red dot painted on it. Searching through the case, I found its corresponding arm device and strapped it on. "How many of these do we have?"

"Not enough for everyone here, so we'll have to be sparing. Amara has taken charge of mobilizing combatants into the best unit combinations, so we will hopefully be able to distribute them that way."

It didn't surprise me that my mother stepped up so quickly. She'd been a high-ranking soldier for so long, it came second nature to take up the mantle. And it put me a bit at ease, knowing someone with more experience was leading this defense. There was only so much I could do.

"So as to not to take too many of these, I will represent the Xolral clan for the scouting," Nemora said. Her eyes flicked to Rosa and Zaedrix. "Will you two join for that?"

Right, my demons weren't technically part of the clan.

Zaedrix nodded. "I want to see firsthand what we're dealing with."

Rosa murmured something in the demonic tongue that I assumed was a confirmation, based on how she reached for a device of her own. Aurora went over how to attach the communicator combo for the demon's benefit, and then explained how they worked.

A lot of it went over my head, but the jist I understood was that the pieces connected through a unique signal and the arm device contained most of the controls. The ear communicator still acted as a speaking device, and had a button to filter through the visor-specific modes, though the arm device could do this as well. It seemed they kept the ear options in case you didn't have the arm attachment with you. Made sense, though I wasn't quite convinced having the extra piece was less inconvenient than what we used to have.

She went over the basics of controlling the new device and how to connect our signals. She had a portable antenna to ensure we could stay in contact, but she warned the demons to keep an eye on their distance. The trees and mountains tended to interfere, so she couldn't accurately say what kind of distance the antenna signal could produce.

When the trio were set, and we did a test check to make sure they were connected up to me, I gave them one last warning. "Given our enemy can stop psychics, expect possible jamming signals for tech. If we lose contact at any point, that could be why."

The demons nodded and in a blink, disappeared from sight. Their speed made my pulse skip. I wasn't sure if I'd ever get used to that.

With that done, I took in the preparations. Those with battle experience worked to coordinate plans. I should join them to make sure I was on the same page.

That was stalled when Sylvia grabbed my arm to look at my device. "Uh, is this the right time?"

"It looks remarkably similar to mine," she said. "I just want to see if luck is on our side."

"You think yours can potentially work with ours?" I couldn't hide the skepticism from my voice. I knew they had physical bodies and all through some special god-magic, but I really wasn't sure how much they had on them was more for show or was actually functional.

Sylvia shrugged and lifted her arm, drawing my attention to the device strapped to her arm. In some respects, it shared a likeness to the one I now used. But she also had a few more gadgets attached.

"I'm hoping this can be used in some way, because if we can't, I'm not going to be much help in all this. I can do some things with metal, when it's available, but I'm not a fighter."

Shit. I didn't think about that. My eyes flicked to all my soul-lives. Some, like Atria, who spun a dagger with her fingers, appeared ready to put the Crimson Sanctuary in their place, but Aria, Rinneth, Zalia, Ayuma, and Pheydra had clustered together away from all the commotion to watch. It was easy to see how out of place they were.

"Hey, I said non-combatants need to go seek shelter," I called out.

Ayuma winced. "We weren't sure what to do. We've got our elemental abilities, and have had to defend ourselves, but we're not really battle-trained."

My gaze softened. "It's okay. You don't have to explain yourselves. There's no shame in living a life that didn't require that kind of survival. This will ensure we have more who can act as a last defense."

"Are you sure?" Pheydra asked. "We're all connected here. It doesn't feel right to—"

"This isn't the time to play hero if you're not up to the task," I said. "Our soul is fragmented, and any minor miscalculation could destroy us. I'd rather play things safe than worry about cowardice and what's 'right.'"

Ayuma steeled herself, her usual carefree spunk replaced. She and Zephyr exchanged some words before she took off for the safety of the temple. Pheydra and Rinneth followed after speaking with their mates, Roan, a blue dragon, and Vesser, a green-black dragon. Zalia spoke with her black dragon mate Khalon—he insisting she go as well. It seemed that Zalia had some weapons and elemental fighting experience, but due to some sort of injury she had, her mate was concerned. She agreed with him.

However, Aria remained.

She gazed at her mates, hesitating to leave them. "Zetan..."

He smirked. "Everything is going to be okay."

She frowned. "You said that last time, and everything definitely didn't turn out okay."

Zetan drew her close, her hands pulled up against his chest. He rested his forehead on hers. Her eyes hooded. Her mate reached up and caressed her cheek with the back of his finger, one of his knuckles catching the corner of her lip.

Aria's lips parted as if she were going to speak, but he beat her to it, his voice pitching lower. "Everything is going to be okay."

Ryoko moved more earth to fill in a fissure that had formed nearby, and then turned to the couple, fanning herself.

"I promise," Zetan murmured.

Aria swallowed, her hands twisting in his shirt. Her back arched just a little, and her knees bowed, as if on the verge of buckling under her. I couldn't imagine the emotions churning within her right now. After being separated from both her mates for so long, and for Zetan to speak to her like this, only to worry if something would happen to him because she couldn't stay to watch his back.

Her senses returned suddenly—her back straightening and eyes snapping open, a fire burning in her gaze. "You'd better, or you're going to regret it."

Zetan blinked, taken aback by her sudden change. She turned her stare to Reve, who grinned. "Don't worry, babe, I'll keep him out of danger. You go and keep the Birth Heart safe. I'm also sure there are some scared children who could use a distraction."

She nodded once and then ran off without another word, leaving Zetan in his confused daze. "Why does she do that?"

I bit my lip so I wouldn't laugh.

Raikidan wrapped his pinky around mine and leaned in close, keeping his voice low. "I'm guessing I can't be so lucky as them, to convince you to not put your life at risk."

"You'd assume right." My eyes flicked to him. "We're going to be fine. We're a strong team. Not even Kir can take that from us."

Sylvia shouted in triumph, interrupting further conversation. It was at that moment that I realized she'd taken my communicator device from me.

I also didn't have my earpiece. Nioush made a motion and I spotted my communicator levitating in his hand.

"You were distracted," he messaged telepathically. *"Aurora took over until you could focus."*

My eyes darted to her. She activated prompts and made other gestures on the arm device, while speaking to someone on the other end. *Idiot.* I shouldn't have allowed myself to be so distracted.

But if she was willing to handle that, I could work with Sylvia. There was merit to sorting things out with my other lives.

A long cord now connected Sylvia's device to mine. She tapped away at her screen, muttering, "C'mon, c'mon. Juice up."

Atria chuckled, sparks of electricity arching between her fingers. "If you needed juice for it, you could have asked."

My two past soul-lives worked together, and the ancient device sprang to life. Holograms popped out of the display and other parts moved. Sylvia cheered in triumph before making attempts to interface the two different devices. It was the point of all this. Somehow... I still wasn't clear how this would make her battle-effective. Then again, I wasn't sure how her electronic device worked when she was a split soul, and not some sort of time traveler.

Wait... I turned to Naloth. "You're the reason it works."

He smirked, unashamed of his actions. "The gods can't interfere, but there aren't any rules about the chromatic flight fighting with you."

His expression grew serious. "The Crimson Sanctuary is going to regret what they did to Riket. He was a good mate and father, and his loyalty knew no bounds. He deserved better than that."

Tightness gripped my chest. I almost didn't want to ask. "Do we know what happened to the other two?"

A frown tugged down Naloth's lips. "They disappeared."

My brow spiked. "Disappeared? How does someone just disappear from those who can see time?"

His gazed turned to Zion, who still stared at the dark clouds rolling in. "We've got our suspicions, and if we're right, this is not going to be good."

"Here, catch," Sylvia said, forcing my attention back to her. I nearly fumbled the device she tossed to me, barely managing to keep it from hitting the ground.

"So, you good?" I asked, securing my input device to my arm. Nioush returned my earpiece.

"Oh yeah." Sylvia pull an earpiece, much like mine, from her arm gadget, and popped it into her ear before yanking out what looked to be a needle attached to her device with some sort of black tube.

Rylar stepped up next to her and took the needle, allowing Sylvia to check the wires and tubes attached to her dress. I jumped back when her mate jammed the needle into his arm. I wasn't sure if I should be horrified by the action, or by the fact he barely blinked. *No way would I have done that with a needle so willingly.*

Ryoko's face contorted. "What are you two doing?"

Sylvia held up a finger, her attention focused on her device. Suddenly the screen flashed, and then strips of light flickered on her dress.

Rylar removed the needle, blood oozing from his wound. The lights on Sylvia's dress blinked some more until they stayed on. She threw her fist into the air. "Yes!"

"Uh, so what does your dress do that will help us?" Raid asked.

Sylvia grinned and flipped the hood on her dress over her head, obscuring most of her face when combined with the outfit's high cowl. She winked and then disappeared.

I jerked back, my eyes darting around.

"Over there," Rylar said, pointing far to my right.

I turned to see Sylvia standing quite a bit away. She chuckled and then disappeared again, this time appearing a little ways to the left of where she'd stood. Four more times she blinked around.

My mouth fell open. "What is all this?"

"Portal tech," Rylar said. "A niche technological advancement we time watchers were sure to control once we discovered its creation. It caused quite a number of issues, but also kept Sylvia safe."

My past soul-life reappeared next to him, two guns now grasped in her hands. "I'm now ready. My aim isn't stellar, so I'll be most useful as interference… I think that's what you call it. That person who confuses the enemy."

"You're a diversion," I said. "Similar concepts."

She nodded. "Then that's what I am."

"I'll be doing the same," Atria said, pulling the scarf around her neck up over her nose. "My skills lie in thievery, and I learned a number of disabling techniques in the process. I'm also not new to taking lives when necessary."

Ryoko smirked. "Well, at least we know why Laz was such a good thief."

Atria chuckled. "Even half-dragons have the weakness to hoard. Makes us decent thieves by nature." She winked. "And some of us don't care much for morals due to that fact."

The ground violently shook again, more fissures cracking the earth and breaking the mountain. Rhaegos snarled and then shifted into a magnificent brown dragon. Though, he had features that weren't something I'd ever seen before. His body had a longer, more sinuous appearance compared to other dragons I'd seen. And he didn't have wings—instead, large plating resembling rocks or gems covered his back. And his claws were massive.

Rhaegos gouged those claws into the earth, and the ground groaned and shivered underneath us. It cracked and split, and in an instant the brown dragon disappeared beneath the earth, his club-like tail narrowly missing us in his descent. The ground closed up behind him.

"Uh…" Ryoko managed. "Is that… normal?"

Lutha laughed. "Brown dragons are masters of earth. It's how they get around. It's the equivalent of us swimming in water."

My eyebrows rose. That was impressive. Explained the lack of wings. I suspected they'd get in the way otherwise. "Given he doesn't have wings, how does that differ from drakes?"

"Drakes are beasts, dragons are not," Lutha said, her tone matter-of-fact. "Nothing else to it, really."

"So, where did the earth swimmer go?" Ryoko asked.

I would have laughed at the nickname, had it not been for Nalia's groaning as she tried to answer Ryoko's question. She hadn't moved from her kneeling position. "He's trying to find an underground weak point we're missing. Whatever they're doing on the other side, it's difficult to combat."

"How bad?" I asked.

She let out a strained breath. "Let's just say, my rite of passage fight with Tarin felt like a cake walk."

Aurora gasped, startling me. I spun around, finding her frantically punching at her display and asking the demon on the other end to repeat a number. The tightness in her wide eyes sent unease down my spine.

"Aurora, what's wrong?" I called out.

She continued to input something, then turned away from us, calling out, "Amara, what are our numbers?"

My mother rushed around one of the clusters of combatants. "What?"

"What are our numbers?" Aurora repeated. I caught the panicked strain in her voice. Something was very wrong.

My mother's brow creased. "Around fifteen hundred, why?"

Aurora gulped. "Are you sure?"

"We might have a few more, but I'm confident in my count."

My pulse slowed. "Aurora, what are their numbers?"

Eyes fell on her, a hush falling over the area. Aurora swallowed, her lip quivering. "Rosa reported in at least five thousand strong on their side. And that was a conservative estimate."

Silence.

"How… how is that possible?" Rylan said. "How could he amass that large an army? Weren't Rosa and Zaedrix thinning their numbers when we failed to find any followers?"

My lips twisted. "They tried, at least. They both mentioned something about losing their trails too many times. As if they'd up and disappeared in…"

I turned to Naloth, who had a grim expression on his face. "Into thin air?"

I nodded slowly.

His eyes darkened and then he tipped his head skyward. "Then it is her. But why would she…"

He trailed off, his eyes going distant.

"Who is this mysterious entity everyone is so worked up over?" I asked.

Naloth was silent for a moment, as if waiting for the gods to tell him to stay quiet. It wouldn't surprise me, given how Zion was acting earlier. But the reprimand never came. "Her name is Celesta."

I blinked. The name had familiarity, but I couldn't put a face to it. However, Rylar seemed to know exactly who Naloth was talking about. He took a step forward, his shoulders tight. "What do you mean? Celesta was sealed away."

Naloth closed his eyes, his face pained. "She escaped."

"She escaped?" Rylar bared his teeth, but his great-grandson didn't say any more. He turned his attention to Zion, expecting answers, but they also didn't come from the dragon god. He focused on something beyond mortal eyes, conflicting emotions flickering across his face.

Who was this Celesta that even Rylar was so worked up? What significance did she have to Kir and the Crimson Sanctuary? Was she the time defiler? It would explain the cold trails.

An image of Phyre and Satria's worried gazes for their daughter flashed through my mind. A prickle of dread ran up my spine. Or maybe this was something even worse than a problematic time defiler.

The earth shook violently, this one rocketing others off their feet. Raikidan grabbed onto me to keep me upright.

Nalia roared in frustration and fell over, her breath coming out hard. "I can't fight it anymore."

She wasn't the only one. The effort to prolong the advancing army had taken its toll on all the earth elementalists.

"Then we stop," I said. I raised my voice. "Stop reinforcing the mountains. Conserve your strength, and everyone get ready. Lutha, Lina, one of you tell Rhaegos to fall back."

Lutha nodded. "I've told him. He's ceased holding the earth but has chosen to wait beneath to spring the moment we give the command."

That choice impressed me, and also brought up questions on how he breathes, but that was for another time when our lives weren't hanging in the balance.

"Babe, we don't have the numbers," Aurora said. "They outnumber us ten to three."

I took a deep breath. "I know, but there's nothing we can do about that. There's no running from this." My eyes swept over those gathered around me. "If anyone wants to run, I won't blame you. These are shit-poor odds at best."

Someone chuckled. "Don't be like that, Fire Bug. We like these odds you give us."

A tall, tan and muscular man with dark brown eyes, and brown hair and mustache approached. A lit cigar was pinched between his lips.

"Raynn…"

He grinned. "Don't worry. Being dead has its perks. Can't die a second time."

I choked on a laugh, and the man with him also chuckled. He was a near-spitting image of Raynn, though human instead of nu-human. In his hands he carried some interesting-looking guns, his body covered in armor I'd never seen before, though it shared similarities with Sylvia and Rylar's clothes. Without a doubt, that was Peacekeeper Raynn, the man our Raynn was cloned from.

"We got yer back, little miss, don't you worry yer pretty head," Peacekeeper Raynn drawled.

Little miss? The two men couldn't be more different in their mannerisms if they tried. At least it'd be a little easier to tell them apart.

Maka'shi pushed her way toward me. "We've sent shamans to round up more help, including soldiers from Dalatrend and neighboring powers who are willing to fight. They've got portals to get back. As long as we hold off our enemy, we'll have the numbers."

My fists clenched and unclenched. I hoped she was right.

Isis walked out several paces toward the direction the Crimson Sanctuary would attack. "They'll think they've got us cornered in this cove."

I gazed at her, noting the way she stood. She didn't have the stance of a warrior. She barely had the stance of someone who had the confidence to defy these unbelievable odds. "Isis—"

"Don't tell me to hide away, Eira." She turned, her eyes blazing with a fiery determination. "I did that once before. I didn't face my uncle that day, listening to everyone else who told me it was for the best I wait the war out. I have regretted that choice every moment since. I will not repeat that mistake."

I took in a slow breath and nodded. If this was what she wanted, then so be it. I wouldn't be the one to ask her to repeat those actions again.

"You're going to need this then, dear," a feminine, light alto voice said.

Isis whirled around. A tall, fair-skinned woman with wavy ash-brown hair, deep brown eyes, and impressively muscular arms, and a man with an imposing build, scarred tan skin, piercing gold-ringed green eyes, and short red hair now suddenly stood before her. "Mother? Father?"

The woman smiled and held up a bow and quiver filled with arrows. "We wouldn't let you do this alone."

Isis took the weapon and nodded, her determination bolstered. She attached the quiver to her hip and tested her draw before pulling three arrows from their holster, as if she was readying to release them in quick succession. Something I noticed, though—these arrows didn't have piercing points. No, instead they were wrapped in some sort of cloth, and appeared to be rather weighty on that side.

That wasn't all. More spirits appeared, including some around my past soul-lives. Nisha's father, a magic user, and some mages allied with them were amongst the new additions. I didn't know what to expect from magic in battle, but it was sure to give us some sort of edge.

As well as this number swell. They were clearly spirits utilizing the opened gate, but where had they come from?

Lazei abruptly appeared next to Raina. "My lady, I've managed to collect more allies. Though not as many as I hoped, I believe it will improve our odds."

Raina smiled at him. "Thank you, Lazei. This is a great improvement. Isn't that right, Aurora?"

The first Ambassador turned her gaze to my friend, who hesitated. "Yes. It's still not ideal… but it's better than nothing, especially since we're dealing with spirits and no living bodies."

"Good, that means you can get to where it's safe," I said.

She hesitated again, but didn't fight. She wasn't a combatant, and that was okay. Her skills would lie in directing teams when she could, based on input from these devices.

Nioush kissed her on the forehead and seemed to speak with her telepathically from the way her eyes hooded. She then rushed off with her gear. Nioush joined his siblings, who were gathered with the few other psychics present.

The mountain broke some more, large boulders breaking off and crashing to the ground. It wasn't hard to see the damage that'd been done inside the formation any more. It wasn't going to last much longer.

Isis' father shifted to his natural dragon state, his form impressive and intimidating. An air of confidence I'd felt around my father radiated off him. *He's a former clan leader.* There was no mistaking that feeling.

My father also shifted, the two gazing at each other, not with hostility, but respect—former leader to current.

The two dragons bellowed out deep roars into the sky. A challenge to Kir. A signal we knew they were coming, and we weren't afraid.

More dragons joined in, first Zaith, then other smaller clan leaders. Raikidan's past soul-lives murmured a few words to their mates and shifted, joining in the cacophony.

Raikidan bent close to me, his lips pressed against my ear. "I will do whatever it takes to keep you safe."

I grabbed his hand and squeezed. "We're going to come out of this together. Kir won't win."

He kissed my temple and then shifted, positioning himself over me. Naloth slipped behind me, touching my hair.

"You're about to fight your nemesis," he said, before I could ask him what he was doing. "You can't face him with your hair in disarray."

My lips pressed in a thin line. I was pretty sure my hair was fine.

A thunderous crack echoed through the cove. A massive boulder, larger than any other before it, fell from the mountain, revealing a massive hole through the formation. I drew my special shape-altering dagger, gipping it tight to keep my calm. *No going back now.*

Our forces spread out, my mother and several others barking out formation orders.

A gust of wind hit me, and then Zaedrix, Rosa, and Nemora appeared out of thin air. The only sign of their quick run came in the form of claw marks on the ground. All three of them were out of breath, and blood dripped down Nemora's arm.

My brow creased. "What happened?"

"Somehow they spotted us," Rosa reported, her lip curled. "All three of us."

"It was the revenants who could see us," Zaedrix clarified. "The living were unaware."

A muscle in the back of my neck tensed. That was not a good sign. "Are you okay, Nemora?"

"Don't worry. A mere scratch." She bared her sharp teeth, malice burning in her golden eyes. "One I will make them pay for in full."

My pulse quickened. At that moment, I was glad she was on our side. Few creatures could strike fear in me so easily. But demons, they weren't to be trifled with—even the ones who tried to live in peace.

The mountain spat out more large chunks, the boulders shaking the ground upon impact. My past soul-lives fanned out around me, their mates taking up position over them like Raikidan did to me.

Then, the mountain exploded.

Wind and earth elementalists and psychics jumped into action, protecting us from the flying debris. The ground shook, but not in the way it had in the past. I knew this sensation. I'd been a cause for similar ones in my military days. *They're coming.*

The shaking continued; a rumbling soon followed. The reverberation grew louder, and then morphed into the sound of marching feet. A shadowy mass moved into sight, obscured by the dust kicked up from the falling rocks. And that wasn't all.

My eyes flicked up, the moving dark cloud now spread over us. Though, "cloud" wasn't quite accurate. While it had some fluffiness to its shape in some places, others were thin, like bleeding ink. A strange sparkling quality came with it, giving a night-sky feel, much like the vortex Zion had created.

The shapes within the cloud were more noticeable now. Large wings and bulky shapes—*Dragons.*

I wasn't sure what to expect with Kir's assembled army. He could have recruited anyone, as long as they were "pure blood." The fact he could assemble an army of thousands against us was unsettling enough, and I wasn't so foolish to believe he brought everyone at his disposal. Even if he was confident enough to think he could win today, he'd have a backup plan.

The army became visible, flag banners flapping in the wind depicting the Crimson Sanctuary's blood-drop-and-shield crest, their positioning clearly indicating that a single man led them. *Has to be Kir's doing.* He'd be old enough to stick with such archaic war traditions.

I took several steadying breaths. Waiting for a kill, I could do. Meditating for hours to take in a peaceful area was piece of cake. But waiting for this altercation really tried my training.

Raikidan bent his head, his nose pressed against my back. I reached up and rested my hand against him, thankful for his steady aura.

The advancing army came to a halt a few hundred yards from us, but the man leading them continued several more. Isis gripped her bow, and a few more of my soul-lives took preparing breaths. Lutha and Lina hovered a few inches off the ground, hair standing on end.

The man came into clear view, all features vaguely familiar enough to me to identify him—middle-aged, dark hair, and blue-veined ashen skin. It was Kir, but he'd shed his nu-human disguise back to his natural human one. His gray eyes shone with a slight red glow, a quality revenants displayed in low- to no-light situations the dark sky above currently produced.

My distorted sight allowed me to see his soul, but it wasn't like the lights I'd seen before. His was no longer golden, but dark and twisted. It made me think of the demons' souls I'd noticed within them. They'd also had a twisted look, though theirs had an orange glow.

Turning my gaze out to the gathered army, while I couldn't see much of their defining features, many out there also had this twisted orb. I suspected they were the revenants at Kir's command.

Kir came to a halt and shouted out, "Isis. Give yourself up now to save these poor souls any more trouble."

Isis scoffed and yelled back to him. "Like I'd believe you'd leave them alone. They've rightfully allied with us. You wouldn't allow half-breed sympathizers to live, and we will not bow to you."

My soul-lives and myself advanced forward, unafraid to face him. Kir watched us, but instead of any sort of shock at seeing any of us, or having a direct conversation with his niece instead of me, he grinned.

"Perfect," he said. "Most of you are here. No doubt the others are hiding, but we just need to deal with one of you to get rid of them." He laughed. "You made this too easy for me, Isis."

Tension built in my spine. He knew far too much. How the hell did he know our soul would be split for the purification? No one but the gods knew the extent of the ceremony.

"You're a fool, Uncle," Isis said. "And you'll pay for it today."

Taking in a deep breath, she exhaled a flame over the three arrows she held in her fingers. Nocking the first projectile, she angled its trajectory high, and in an impressive display, loosed the arrow. She repeated the action with the two arrows in quick succession.

The three projectiles roared through the air, over Kir and over his army. Her uncle grinned, as if mocking her aim, but as the flaming arrows arched down, I realized just how special they were.

A moment later, they landed in the middle of his army and exploded.

I latched onto the fire, feeling the will of an other—Velsara—take a hold of a separate part of the inferno. The two of us intensified and spread the flame. His army panicked and scattered, those caught up in the blaze screaming in agony. Kir turned and frowned, watching his force break formation, and ultimately split, the barrier Velsara and I creating cutting off at least half of his army on the other side of the mountain.

I grinned. *That'll even the odds.*

Suddenly, Kir laughed. My brow pulled together. He really was insane. "Such ill-informed children."

My breath caught when the raging inferno died. But it wasn't a natural snuff, like an elementalist had stolen control from us. The fires warped and twisted as if moving in reverse.

The flames diminished until they were three small lights soaring toward us. My eyes widened when, out of nowhere, a woman appeared next to Kir.

She was a beautiful woman of dark complexion. Her raven hair, tipped with white at the ends, floated and twisted with a life all its own. Her dark blue eyes with white flecks nearly melted into her black sclera—no irises to be seen. The sight was unsettlingly snaring.

The clothing adorning her tall and lithe form appeared as a mashed design of different periods, clashing with her otherwise elegant appearance. Talismans hung from her, though the language was unreadable, many smudged or partially ruined, either by age or damage. A paintbrush with sparkling material dripping from the ends hung from a sash alongside a pouch containing something bulky and rectangular.

The fire flying toward us dipped and careened down at her. The woman lifted her hand and caught the three arrows Isis had shot, and then a moment later the fires snuffed out and the projectiles crumpled to dust.

Naloth swore, speaking low, as if to himself. "It was her."

"Who is she, exactly?" I mumbled, hoping my words would only carry to those behind me.

"Celesta, the goddess of timelines."

CHAPTER 11

*G*oddess *of timelines?* I'd never heard of her. And yet, much like those who hadn't known Rashta by name, I felt like I knew her, as if my memory had been blocked in some way. *But if Zion is the Keeper of Time, how could she be…*

Rylar snarled. *"How is she here? She was locked up, and her corruption is still evident."*

Corruption? Phyre's and Satria's worried faces flashed through my mind again; the insistence of purifying Rashta fresh and hard on the surface of my mind.

"She escaped," Naloth said.

Rylar hissed. My attention turned up to Zion, his eyes fixed on Celesta. All manner of emotions flickered in them. *Keeper of Time… Keeper…* I now understood why he was the only god to use the keeper title. It wasn't his domain, not technically.

"Celesta," Zion rumbled. "Why are you here?"

"Oh, my love," the woman crooned. "After so many millennia, that's the reception you give me?"

Her love? Was that a literal call or something she just said?

"We have searched everywhere for you." His voice came out strained. "How could you align yourself like this?"

"How could I?" Her face twitched, her expression switching back and forth from an innocent and happy smile to a serious and dark one. "How could you bear to lock me up like some feral beast?"

"I did what I had to, to save you."

"Save me?" A tinkling laugh came from her lips as she spun around in an almost childlike way. "Save me from what? There was nothing to save me from." Her face snapped to a serious tone, one that matched her mature face. "The only thing I needed saving from was you. You tricked me into that cage so you could take my domain right from under me."

Goddess Genesis stepped forward. "Celesta—"

"Oh, Mother, there you are. Is Father here, too? Of course he is. He would also be needed to *save* Rashta."

Genesis is her mother? I could also guess Zoltan was her father, by the way he watched the unstable goddess. *Makes sense, given their domains.* And this corruption business would explain why her existence was hidden now. Who wanted the knowledge to get out that a goddess hadn't lost her ascended power when she fell? That was a dangerous being to exist.

She smiled, a wicked and unsettling gesture on her. "I escaped to fix a wrong. None of you were willing to stop her, and now look at what's happened. It's my turn to mend what she broke."

"Stop this, Celesta," Zion said. "You're helping those who seek to eliminate mortals who are the will of Lumaraeon."

The goddess' face darkened. "You all should have listened. I foresaw so much, and yet you ignored me in favor of a child trying to prove herself. This… *Dragon-Phoenix* was never meant to exist, and it is my duty to fix problems in the timelines."

The mocking tone made my eye twitch. "And who are you to tell us we don't belong?"

She slid her unsettling gaze to me, a malicious grin on her lips. "Because you have caused so much destruction in the wake of your continued existence."

"And you can say you're pure?" Isis challenged. "When you support those who create that chaos, instead of letting things be as they are ordained by Lumaraeon."

Kir spat on the ground. "Don't think you're something special, Isis. You're just an abomination, one that should have never existed."

I snorted. "Says who, a mortal man who died for false ideals and refuses to move on to the afterlife because his ego is so large he couldn't possibly be wrong? Because you've forgotten where we came from that allows such unions to exist?" My lip curled. "You're the fool, Kir."

He gestured to Celesta. "I have her on my side. The only god to not be swayed by your poisonous lies."

"You have one goddess, who has fallen from grace." I gestured to the gods gathered on our side of the invisibly drawn lines in the battlefield. "Unlike you, we do not have the support of the corrupted."

Kir snorted. "And yet you have demons."

"Your soul is just as twisted as ours." Nemora purred and licked her lips. "And while your soul would make for a terrible meal, you've brought so many delectable feasts right to us. How could we not agree to side with those who would risk it all to protect our home?"

If this weren't so serious, I'd laugh at the idea that Kir was so corrupted a demon wouldn't find him edible. Rosa had even told me that darker souls were a favorite of theirs. That was why it was so easy to get them to not kill innocent people in our agreement.

"You do not belong here, filth," Kir snapped.

"More than you do, angry spirit," she said.

He snorted with contempt. "We will purge this land of all tainted blood. Your demise will be the message we send. All half-breed filth will fear their imminent death. It is written. And Celesta will help me, because she agrees."

The goddess' face twitched, but due to her unstable nature, and possible dual personality due to the corruption, I couldn't be sure the cause.

It didn't matter, though. What Kir had revealed was enough to make me laugh and not try to hide it. The man scowled. "You dare mock us?"

"Mock you?" I partially hid my face in my hand, trying hard to contain myself. "Did you even hear yourself? Celesta is going to help you? Here I had been led to believe you knew everything there was in order to guarantee a win."

His eyes darkened. "I have all the advantages. You stare death in the face and—"

A grin twisted up my face, my eyes intent on him. "Death? You? You're no more than a yapping pup nipping annoyingly at the ankles. Your army? It is nothing. Your goddess? Powerless."

"She is the goddess of timelines! She has the power of—"

"Nothing!" My voice carried all through the area, bouncing off the mountain walls until stillness permeated the air. Even Kir was taken off guard by my declaration.

The only ones to remain unphased were my soul-lives. Even with them no longer in my mind, I felt just as deeply connected to them as before. Our shared soul kept us linked, and in some strange way, that allowed them to know the knowledge within me, what cemented my claim and my resolve—what Kir miscalculated.

"Celesta is still a goddess, no matter how fallen or corrupted," I said, my voice steady. "As we learned with Rashta, not even a god touched with corruption has the power to defy Cosmic Law. And that means, just as the other gods cannot directly interfere with this event, neither can she."

Murmurs rumbled through Kir's army, their confusion and dismay evident. My allies, on the other hand, their morale was bolstered by my revelation. The goddess' appearance and help for our enemy, when we received no help from the gods, had crushed their already wavering determination to make it out of this alive. But if she couldn't cause us issues, we stood a better chance.

Kir turned narrowed eyes to Celesta. "Does she speak truth? Did you lie to me?"

The goddess stared at me with cold, calculating eyes, and then suddenly clapped with glee and spun around. The child-like behavior had returned. Her unusual eyes sparkled and she grinned at me. "I've always liked you, Eira. I've liked many of your lives. So smart and resourceful. It's such a shame you aren't supposed to exist."

She laughed that tinkling laugh again. "And a shame you don't understand our plan. I never promised I could fight in this bloodshed. I helped up to the point where I was allowed—hiding them from your demons, bolstering their numbers by taking volunteers from the past, and offering information that would give an edge. All for the sake of righting a past wrong."

She smiled so wide her eyes squinted. It was disgusting how happy she was talking like this. "You'd be better off accepting your death quickly than prolonging your suffering any longer."

The screen on my communicator arm component flickered, various things flashing. I'd been casually glancing at it this whole time, watching the messages Jasmine was sending me. The feature was more robust than the old communicators, and in this moment, provided the handiest change. She wouldn't use the earpiece, for fear of alerting the enemy, but she'd shown me her plan. More tech that would show them we weren't going down easily. And she was in a position to reveal it.

"No." The word was simple and defiant. "And you shouldn't misjudge what we were up to beyond your sight."

Bang! A loud gunshot slapped into everyone's ears and echoed through the cove. Many people jumped; some screamed, presumably those who weren't used to hearing a rifle go off.

Kir's eyebrow quirked up, and then he laughed. "Was that supposed to scare me? Or does your sniper have terrible aim?"

I smirked. "Whoever said she was aiming for you?"

He would have expected that. And with Celesta's focus more on him than anyone else, it'd be smarter to pick a target she wouldn't care about.

His brow knitted and he turned to his army, still scattered out of formation from our previous attack. Three revenants who'd been dumb enough to line up perfectly in the panic stood stock still, their eyes wide and mouths hanging open. While too far for me to see the bullet holes in their bodies, I knew the shot met their marks.

A moment later, agonizing screams tore through them and they burst apart. A shockwave of energy rippled through the area. Nothing remained of them.

Kir didn't control his reaction, his shock plain as day on his face. A wicked grin curled up half of my face. "Did no one tell you? I'm able to rend souls."

He stiffly turned back to me, eyes tight. Celesta's serious side had returned. She assessed me with critical eyes. "That is not possible for a mortal."

I chuckled. "Is for this one. I did it once before, when Kir thought he could catch us off guard. I'm quite surprised no one noticed he didn't return. But maybe you don't care much for those of your cause. It wouldn't surprise me."

Kir laughed suddenly. "You almost had me. Someone shot my men. That wasn't you."

"Not this time." I exuded as much confidence as I could muster. "But only because we learned how to replicate it."

I wish I could take credit for the idea, but it'd been brought to me during my year with Raikidan. The shamans believed my ability to deal with revenants in the way I had was due to a special quality lingering in my spiritual energy.

Reincarnation had a potent effect on elemental power. So why wouldn't it do the same for the spirit? It just needed to be proven, and the East Tribe had the tools to help. Especially one I'd been acquainted with when Arnia and Jaybird were found to be moles by Zarda.

The device, once attached to a living host, drew out spiritual energy to a specified degree. If used in the way Zarda wanted, it could even suck a person dry, killing them.

It was for that reason Raikidan had tried to convince me not to participate in their experimental idea—harness enough condensed energy to use against revenants without anyone needing to risk their souls being attacked.

Of course, stubborn and independent me wasn't willing to give into his pleas. Though, I was sure to *reward* his patience with my "reckless-ness" even when testing took a great deal out of me. And test we did.

It took many energy harvests and experiments to realize how I'd done it. In my moment of desperation to live, I'd channeled not just the energy of one past soul-life, which I could so easily do with some training, but several. All my shaman past soul-lives to be exact—the lives that were most in tune with spiritual energy.

It'd been hard to channel it again on purpose, taking several attempts, but I'd managed it long enough for the device to draw enough spir-itual energy for one experiment. That'd been about two months ago. I didn't know the progress until this very moment, and that's how I found out Jasmine was helping this project from beyond the grave—so to speak. And why she chose to be the one to experimentally fire the first shot of bullets they'd created.

She may have been a scientist, but Jasmine had technically been created to be a war experiment. If it weren't for her unusual abilities causing her sight problems, thus needing the special glasses she wore, she wouldn't have been taken from front-line training. Luckily, her intelligence and enjoyment of scientific code landed her a position she relished more—until Zarda took over and used her as his own punching bag when he was angry.

"How…" Celesta murmured, her lip curling into a snarl. "How did you hide this from me?"

I gave a half-hearted shrug, a pleased smirk on my lips. "I guess you're not as good as you think you are. Especially considering we had no idea you'd been watching."

The corners of her cold eyes pinched and then her eyes flashed with a strange golden glow. "Deal with them, now, and quickly. They don't have enough of their weapon to win this."

Shit. Of course she'd look to see what we were packing. She may not be able to change our ammunition numbers, which admittedly wasn't great, but she couldn't be stopped from divulging that information.

A thirsty and wicked grin appeared on Kir's face. "Gladly. No half-breed or supporter of will walk away alive today."

He made a motion with his hand, sweeping it up and clenching into a fist. A *clank* echoed through the cove, then a *whoosh*. Three trebuchets behind the gathered army flung flaming boulders into the air. At the same time, the dragons still hidden in the strange clouds above descended. Their combined attack proved to be a mistake.

Lutha and Lina raised their hands in unison, their hair standing on end, and the sailing boulders arched up, careening with three unsuspecting dragons from Kir's force. The impact sent them off course, colliding with other dragons. Allied dragons sprung into the air, including Raikidan and his past soul-lives.

Then chaos erupted.

CHAPTER 12

Guns fired, elements flew—the chaos of war all too familiar to me. Guardians and allies rushed toward our enemy, ready to fight and even die if necessary. I wished so hard that all would be able to go home at the end of this. It was something they all deserved. But that wasn't how war usually went.

War was a harsh reality no slap to the face could ever compare to. It took no sides. It took casualties indiscriminately until only one was left standing—the stronger side.

It was why war experiments loved Satria. We accepted our fate, and were just glad to feel the warmth of someone who cared even if she couldn't pick a side. It was more than we'd ever been given as a result of our cruel existence.

And now, with our freedom, it was cruel to know that those who had fought so hard would not be allowed to feel that freedom for much longer.

Sylvia's clothes flickered with power and then she disappeared, no doubt going to be a pain in Kir's army's ass, potshotting them from different angles. Atria jumped behind Lina, directly into her shadow. My eyes bugged when a pair of hands reached out of the psychic's shadow and grabbed her ankles, pulling Atria down. She didn't struggle, as if she expected it.

"Don't worry," Lina messaged, while her face remained pointed at the sky where she was focusing most of her psychic efforts. *"It was an ally, one we know quite well."*

I blinked slowly, my hand shooting out when fire blasted our way, instinctively quenching it without thinking. I only knew of one person who had that ability. *"Shyden is here?"*

Lina smiled, her hand swiping crosswise over her body. Another flaming boulder changed directions. *"Your other assassin friends have joined the fray as well. They were hoping to see you after the purification."*

Chunks of earth crashed toward Kir, forcing him to jump away and drawing my attention back to the issue before us. Celesta, unbothered by the attack, stepped aside, her expression bored. But what caught me off guard was the fact it hadn't been any of my past soul-lives who'd attacked Kir. No, Isis' mother set her enraged attention on him.

"You will pay for your treachery, brother," the woman seethed before sending rocks flying at him.

He dodged and snorted. "That's cute coming from you, Shora. You're the one who betrayed your kind."

"The only thing I betrayed was your ego." Her eyes narrowed. "You, on the other hand, turned your back on your kin and spread lies, all to polish your pride in something that didn't truly exist."

More earth crashed his way. My eyes widened when, instead of dodging, Kir moved his arms and the ground beneath him bent to his will. *He's an earth elementalist?*

My only previous contact with him had been in the city, or just beyond the walls it used to have. During those encounters, he'd preferred close combat, mostly due to his attempt to pump me full of R-poison—a contact-based element that killed its victims within the hour if not dealt with by a spiritual energy user like a shaman. And Isis had never warned me.

But as I thought about it, him being an elementalist made sense. The ability to touch the elements was a hereditary trait. If Shora and Isis could harness an element, even if they were different types, there was a greater chance Kir could as well.

Kir attacked again with his ability, but a wave of earth intercepted him, the counter coming from Nalia. She didn't pause in attacking again, her movements strong and quick. It was impressive, and showed her skill as an elementalist. Not to be outdone, Velsara exhaled a hot flame and Raina shot plant roots out of the ground. Kir grinned and then disappeared from sight.

Shit. Should have known he'd pull that. Question was, where would he pop back up? The back of my neck prickled, a strange sensation of danger pulsating from my right. I turned, only to see Isis… standing alone, her bow poised and eyes darting around. Everything in me slowed. She'd made herself a target.

I drew another dagger, one I wasn't afraid to lose like the one Ryder had made me, and fused it with spiritual energy. No easy feat, even with the enchantment the shamans had placed on them.

"Isis, move!" I shouted, tossing the spiritual weapon.

She gasped and spun around just as Kir appeared behind her, as I predicted he would. His hand stretched out to grab her, intent on harming her vulnerable soul with R-poison. My sailing dagger met its mark in an exposed part of his arm. The revenant howled, his form distorting.

Isis stumbled backward, fear constricting her eyes. She fumbled with the arrow in her hands, dropping it. The momentum of the altered end falling caused it to propel toward Kir.

An opportunity presented itself, and my soul-lives took it. Nalia created an earth barrier over Isis, and Velsara breathed a heavy flame toward Kir. At the same time, Nisha, who had stepped back and had been chanting something this whole time, lifted two fingers in Kir's direction. Magic sparked off her fingertips.

Glowing symbols appeared in the air around Kir, and in the same moment Velsara's fire reached him and the dropped explosive arrow, the magic runes detonated in an explosion all their own.

A shockwave shot out, but we were protected thanks to a barrier Lutha and Lina placed before us. The vibrations made the rock formation protecting Isis break, and she scrambled away before it could collapse on her.

My muscles bunched with tension as we waited to see what kind of damage we'd done to our nemesis. I wasn't expecting it to kill him—he was a revenant, after all—but if we'd wounded him badly enough, it'd make it easier for my shaman soul-lives and myself to use our spiritual power to deal with his corrupted soul. I had no doubts we'd have to rend it. There was no way I'd take the chance of him crossing over to the spiritual plane, willing or not, so his soul could be judged.

Before the dust could clear, chunks of earth shot out toward us. I dove to the ground, narrowly dodging the projectiles, and gritted my teeth. *Should have known it would be too good to be true.* I sprang up and spat a fire into my hand, only to pause at the sight of sand flying from the nearby brook and swirling around Kir like some vortex. Xenia had her hand out, her one good eye focused hard on her task.

She had an unusual connection with the elements, only able to tap into a very specific part of each, and neither an opposite of each other. I'd never heard of an elementalist able to use both earth and ice, but she did, in the form of sand and snow.

Xenia twitched her hand and the whirling sand stopped for a moment, hanging in the air and exposing a confused Kir, and then shot inward toward him, acting like a billion-plus micro blades. They cut into the revenant's false body, slicing his clothes and skin, though he didn't bleed.

My past soul-life flexed her hand, the element redirecting, but before she could slice into him more, he blinked out again. He reappeared a moment later, just a few feet away. His eyes flicked between us all, unsure how to handle the situation.

"How are you all still so powerful?" he said, his voice low enough he may have been talking more to himself than us. "Your soul is split—you shouldn't have this kind of power individually."

Velsara grunted. "You really ain't as bright as you let on. The reincarnation may grant us strength built upon the previous life, but that don't mean we're only strong because we have access to that past. It's wholly our own, and ain't no soul split gonna diminish that."

Kir's lip curled, and he shot a look to the goddess to his side, as if expecting her to help with his miscalculation. But she was preoccupied. Zion was no longer present—at least, not in his dragon form. Circling Celesta was a tall, bronze-skinned man with a well-built physique. He had long black hair splattered with various colors pulled back in a loose tie by his shoulder blades.

A black and blue skirt hugged his hips, the length causing the fabric to pool at his feet and train out behind him. The skirt was secured at the waist by a wide sash-like belt. Several objects of unknown significance hung from the belt.

A sheer black sash was wrapped over one of his shoulders, tied down on either side by his belt; the ends hung loose at his hips. Leather armor wrapped around his biceps, the same sheer fabric as his sash was attached to the armguards, covering his forearms like a type of sleeve, billowing in the wind.

Miniature versions of his horns protruded from his head, and patches of scales covered his bare shoulders and arms. A beaded necklace hung around his neck, a wooden talisman strung onto it.

Celesta, for her part, now carried three cards in her hand—tarot cards, from the looks of it. Their shape matched that of whatever was in her pouch, so I guessed she had a full deck in there.

Zion's movements displayed a regal air while also having an eerily smooth, almost predatory gait. "Celesta, stop fighting me and come home."

"Oh, my love," she purred, tapping her tarot cards against her lips. "We both know my prison is no home."

There was that pet name again. I don't know why, but I really wanted to understand more about the dynamic between these two.

Pain shadowed his eyes. "It wasn't intended to be a prison. You were there to heal, but you fought for some reason. If you'd just let us heal you, you could have come back with me."

Celesta clicked her tongue. "Don't pretend you were some savior of mine."

"Celesta," Kir hissed. "Can you set aside your little lover's spat for a moment and focus?"

She gave the revenant a sidelong glance. "Your miscalculation is your own issue. My love and I have some things to sort out."

My chest clenched. I was afraid that was the meaning behind the pet name. If these two were mates, I couldn't imagine the pain Zion was suffering, seeing Celesta in this state.

Kir's lip curled. "You're supposed to help deal with this pest issue!"

"I am. My plans are still in motion, as I guaranteed." She looked away dismissively. "And if you won't properly utilize the army I assembled for you, then that's your problem."

Shit. She would remind him he was being impulsive, taking us all on like this. As powerful as Kir was, he couldn't hold out against our combined force indefinitely.

And unfortunately, he understood the goddess' meaning. Kir sent a wave of earth crashing toward us and then disappeared, reappearing closer to his army. He pointed to us, and shouted, "Focus your efforts on the Dragon-Phoenix! Destroy them."

His army reacted in an instant. My pulse quickened. *Just great.* I shot glances to my soul-lives. They nodded and we spread out, unleashing a torrent of elements while pushing forward. We couldn't allow Kir to get out of sight, and if his army pushed too hard, the temple would be at risk.

I rushed in, fire in one hand, blade in another. My past soul-lives weren't far behind, and together we unleashed a fury only the Dragon-Phoenix knew.

My and Velsara's fire scorched some of the Crimson members. Nalia crushed the ones I missed by opening the ground and slamming it closed, sickening screams and squelches the only sound her victims were able to make. Raina called upon the roots deep beneath us to rise up and strangle her targets. Nisha uttered incantations and flung all manner of spells I couldn't begin to comprehend. But the most disturbing retaliatory attack had to go to Xenia.

With barely a twitch of emotion on her face, she swirled sand and then shoved the particles into the lungs of Crimson Sanctuary members through their noses and mouths, suffocating them. I'd seen some cruel tactics, but this one was pretty high on that list. And to see her shut her emotions down so flawlessly, like a trained soldier, was both admirable and terrifying.

Lutha and Lina stayed behind us, focusing their energy on the flaming boulder streaking through the sky.

"We're also assisting in the revenant dragon-soul issues," Lutha messaged.

I swore as I ducked under a sword and thrust my dagger into the neck of an attacking enemy. I hadn't thought of that possibility. I knew any soul could become a revenant, but my only personal experience with them had come in the form of humans and elves.

"They don't appear to have the ability to create R-poison, so that helps."

I parried another attack, my lips pressed tight. That may be, but given they were undead, the dragons were rather powerless against them.

"Kir made a mistake," Lina chimed in. *"With Arcadia's gateway active, they have more solidified bodies. That's how you and the others were able to harm Kir."*

I hadn't thought about that. It was instinct to use my element in a situation like this. I never thought to question how we were all able to affect him, since it was working. Which meant…

"Yes," Lina confirmed. *"The dragons can injure the revenants enough for us psychics to inflict the key damage to remove them from the fight. At least, temporarily enough that it'll give us a better chance."*

While not ideal, it was something, and I wasn't going to take any advantage for granted.

I jammed my foot into a woman and then thrust my weapon into the side of her neck. She choked and gargled on her blood, swinging wildly with her club in a desperate attempt to harm me before she fell. She failed. I passed her fallen body nary a glance, focusing on my next target.

He was a large opponent, and heavily armored. The warrior loomed over me with an impossibly huge bludgeoning weapon, swinging it with far too much ease than I was comfortable with. I jumped out of the way, the weapon smashing down on the lifeless warrior I'd just dispatched. The sound of crunching bones and squelching of blood splattering hit my ears.

I rolled when he swung again with inhumanly quick reflexes, narrowly missing being crushed as his weapon slammed into the ground, breaking it. *He has to have some sort of connection to the earth. There's no way he could do that otherwise.*

To my displeasure, two more Crimson Sanctuary fighters closed in on me, putting me in a tight position. I glanced to my soul-lives, only to find them just as overwhelmed. *Shit.*

The ground rumbled beneath me. I jumped back, not sure what to expect. My enemies advanced, but the moment they stepped where I had stood previously, the ground beneath them exploded and Rhaegos' large head shot out of the earth. His toothy maw clamped down on three victims, their screams cut short with a spray of blood. He then pulled back down under the earth, his prey still in his jaws, and the ground closed up.

I blinked. *Okay… that was… disturbing…* I shook myself and steeled my emotions. I had gone soft in my year off.

Taking a deep breath, I exhaled a wave of fire at those trying to swarm in. It pushed them back for a moment, but it wasn't long enough to gain any edge.

My eyes darted around. Kir was nowhere in sight, but neither could I spot my other lives. I gritted my teeth. That wasn't good. We were to stay in range of each other to make sure nothing happened to our soul. And yet, we'd been so easily overwhelmed that the Crimson Sanctuary had seized an opportunity to isolate us. Even if it cost a few of their numbers, they were willing to accept those sacrifices for what they deemed the "greater good."

A blinding flash of light slashed at the enemies to my left like some sort of blade, cutting them clean through. They crumbled, gore and bile spilling over the ground. My nose wrinkled as the unpleasant bodily fluid smells mixed with charred flesh. To my right, earth shot up in a straight line, sending more enemies flying. *Who—*

A lithe woman with fair skin and a tall man with tanned skin flanked me. "Iana? Alistair?"

Iana smiled, her crystal blue eyes sparkling. "Thought you could use a hand."

She flicked her wrist, her hand clutching a small dagger. Light shot out of her extended appendage, cutting through more Crimson Sanctuary members. The attack kicked up enough wind to tease her long platinum blonde hair.

Like Lunaria and Solund, Iana was a light bender. The true nature of her abilities had been shrouded in mystery, though, until several months ago, due to some painful complications she had experienced with the ability. It took me sending her out to work for Alistair and some divine intervention for things to be sorted out.

"I see you're still progressing on your training." I looked her up and down for a quick assessment before I lobbed a ball of fire beyond the row of approaching enemies to scatter them. "And I see you you've finally kept your job on Alistair's ranch."

A small smile appeared on her lips, her cheeks tinting pink. "Yeah, he made sure I didn't run off again."

Alistair sent a wave of earth at three warriors and smirked at her, mirth glowing in his dark blue eyes. "There's no way I'm letting you run off again."

I rolled my eyes. "Fight now, flirt later."

The rancher snickered. "Careful there, Ambassador. I'll change plans to not bring the herd your way."

I snorted and lobbed another fireball. "You do that, and you can explain to a crying seven-year-old why she's not getting the horse she was promised and has been proving she is ready for by learning how to care for them—even going as far as to show her mom where she's made many mistakes herself and needed to learn more to be sure she was also ready for such a task."

He grimaced, running his fingers through his brown hair. "Yeah, how about I don't do that, then."

"We should be more concerned about living through this, don't you think?" Iana said.

Before I could say anything, the shadows around the enemies flanking us warped and twisted, rising up and swallowing their owners. My stomach twisted at the disturbing sight. "I guess you brought your long-lost brother with you?"

Iana had visibly paled. She nodded. "Yeah. Even though he still doesn't know you all that well, he wanted to see what the fuss was about." She shifted a brief glance my way before she began cutting into more enemies. "Don't feel bad about your reaction. I'm still getting used to his ability, too. It's not like Shyden's."

Contrary to what experiments had been told, Iana wasn't a tank creation. Zarda had stolen her life away in his attempt at controlling all those who could harness elements. And while light and darkness weren't considered elements, the madman wasn't going to allow his "collection" to be incomplete.

I hadn't known Shyden's shadow transportation fell into shadow bending until we'd found Iana's brother. Even when Shyden had used it in ways similar to Iana's brother, it wasn't quite the same. And seeing how both of them utilized their abilities differently, it gave me a new appreciation for the ability I still knew little about.

My ear piece crackled, but nothing came through. *Shit.* Looked like we were getting interference of some sort. I knew it would be a possibility, but it would have been nice not to have to rely on the psychics to relay messages when they'd be taxed already. *Wait...* "*Avila, are you—*"

Her exasperated sigh rang clearly in my head. "*Oh, yes, I'm here, in a dark cave acting as a human communicator because I wasn't allowed to fight.*"

I tried not to laugh. "*You're a great help, though. I don't know anyone more qualified to watch an entire battlefield and relay to so many people at once.*"

"Yes, well, I don't appreciate my brother getting to play hero while I'm stuck in here playing operator."

"You are a hero, Avila. Trust me."

She paused, as if the small bit of praise had gotten to her, and when she spoke, it was a casual warning. *"Watch your six."*

I spun, spotting the man trying to run up behind me. Snatching a nearby flame burning a charred corpse, I hurled the element at him. The warrior jumped out of the way, but before I could try to catch him with his guard down, a blur of a shape crashed into him.

Rosa pinned the man, her eyes fixed on his. He went slack in her grip, her hypnosis ability quickly taking hold. She dragged the back of her talon down his cheek, crooning, "You're going to be delicious."

Fear registered in his eyes, but his paralysis held fast. A wicked grin spread along Rosa's lips, and then she jammed her talons into his chest. Blood gushed, and the man let out a strangled gasp. Rosa yanked her hand back out, his bloody and still-beating heart pulsating in her grasp. The man's mouth gaped, but no sound came out. His body twitched as she opened her mouth, revealing her sharp canines, and bit into his organ.

I should look away from the display, I know I should. But for some reason, I couldn't tear my gaze from her. Was this how they fed on souls? My earlier searches in the Eternal Library when I first met her and Zaedrix didn't have accurate information. Their becoming a bonded pair did sate half of their needs to survive, but they continued to kill, not because they had an insatiable appetite for death, but to feast on souls.

While I'd learned this truth from these demons firsthand, I never asked how they ate souls, or how that affected their ability to cross over to the spiritual plane. I wasn't sure I wanted to know those exact details.

"Mesmerizing, isn't she?" someone purred close to my ear.

I gasped and spun, my dagger at the ready, only to find Zaedrix standing there with a victim of his own—not hypnotized, but squirming against a death grip on his throat.

"I've heard you were considered quite the demon in the past." A mischievous grin curved up his face. "We could make you one of us officially. Then you could be almost as enthralling as my beloved."

I rolled my eyes and tossed a ball of fire at a Crimson Sanctuary member who had been attempting to come up behind Zaedrix. The incubus' eyes flicked to the enemy now screaming in agony and flicked his tail; blood spurted out of a wound that now appeared on the man's neck. The man fell, and Zaedrix refocused on the victim in his hands.

The man struggled and panicked, even begged for his life, but the demon was uninterested, and I wasn't inclined to show mercy, either. Zaedrix slowly raked his claws over his victim, enjoying drawing out the pain. At this point I refocused on the battle.

Iana and Alistair had spread out, utilizing the demon presence that had increased around us to work against the pressing army. Kir was nowhere in sight. I darted my eyes to each of my fighting soul-lives; none were engaged with him. I wasn't sure whether I should be relieved by that or not. If he was hanging back, then the tactic was obvious— he'd wait for his underlings to wear us down and then swoop in at the last moment.

Fire shot toward me from my periphery. My hand shot up and quenched the flame. The elementalist, a revenant by the looks of him, grinned and attacked again. Taking a steadying breath and sheathing my weapon, I retaliated with my own fire, not holding back in the slightest.

Our flames collided, but to my surprise, they matched in power. *So that's how you play.* His first attack had merely been to grab my attention. Normally, I'd love a challenging opponent, but today, expending too much energy wasn't ideal.

Fireball after fireball, we exchanged blows. My breath came hard, and my arm burned where he'd managed to inflicted some damage. Zaedrix and Rosa jumped around us, taking on more opponents than was humanly possible, but were always kept too busy to step into my fight.

My only saving grace was that gateway Arcadia had made. My attacks were wearing this elementalist down. Even if he didn't breathe, his posture said it all.

We circled one another, trying to find an opening.

"Sweet Thing, move!" Telar shouted in my head.

Before I could process the warning, my body jerked back and I tumbled to the ground just as a dragon crashed to the ground where I'd been facing off with the revenant. I stared at the lifeless, smoking body, praying that it wasn't one of my allies.

I took a deep breath, steeling myself, and clambered back up to my feet, searching for the revenant. I found him spasming on the ground, Telar only a few feet away, focusing on destroying him. Taking that as my cue not to waste any more energy on this revenant, I set my sights on a woman clad in ancient armor. I guessed her to be another time traveler.

I drew my special dagger with the intent to morph it to a weapon that would be more suitable for direct combat when a ball of electricity shot past me, connecting with the warrior. She screamed and fell to the ground, writhing. Without hesitating, I lunged at her, driving my dagger through her throat. With a gargled cry she lurched, blood splattering out of her mouth, and then she went lifeless, her eyes dulling.

I withdrew my blade and turned back to face the elementalist who'd assisted me. My blood ran cold at the sight of Shva'sika readying another charge from her fingers.

"What are you doing on the battlefield?" I blurted out. She wasn't a killer. She was supposed to be where it was safe.

She set determined eyes on me. "Doing what I must to protect you and everything I hold dear."

Her conviction left no room to argue. Shva'sika snapped her fingers in rapid succession, lightning flying off her fingers into the encroaching army. "The energy this battle produces gives me a limitless supply of power."

Unlike a lot of lightning shamans I'd met, Shva'sika was unable to quickly produce her own. Over a matter of weeks, she could create a decent store, but once she depleted it, she'd have to wait again. However, she was able to use the energy of others to build the needed tension to fast-track her ability. I wasn't sure how it worked, but just as she'd mentioned, it had its perks in a situation like this. As long as she didn't physically tire too much to where she couldn't snap her fingers—how she ignited her sparks—producing the lightning wouldn't be an issue for the long haul, unlike other lightning elementalists.

My breath caught when an attacker ran up behind her, a gleaming broad sword poised to strike her down. By pure instinct, I flung one of my remaining daggers at him. The blade sliced into a bit of exposed flesh by the base of his neck, sinking deep. He choked, faltering his attack just enough for Shva'sika to whirl around and strike him with lightning. The man collapsed, writhing for a moment before going limp, his metal armor acting as a conductor to cook him alive.

I rushed past her to retrieve my weapon, praying it wasn't too damaged, and narrowly missed a sword swing from another enemy I hadn't noticed. While I was glad these fighters weren't brandishing guns, indicating they were most likely the warriors Celesta had brought through time, didn't make them any easier to fight. They clearly had battle skills and weapons prowess.

The warrior swung again, so fast that I only had enough time to raise my daggers up to catch the blade. I collapsed to one knee under the strain of his superior strength. I may have training and prowess with a few weapons, but it didn't come in the form of swordplay.

A wicked blade slammed down on my assailant, his body crumbling with a sickening squelch, blood splattering. I jumped back, startled and unsure about the new presence. I paused when I laid eyes on the woman clad in ancient armor.

She was a near-spitting image of Shva'sika. It was downright disturbing.

"Sh–Shiva?" Shva'sika stammered. The name of the ancient demon hunter coming from my friend's lips shocked me. This was Shiva?

The woman grinned, calculating brown eyes assessing her descendant. "I'm glad I can finally meet you, young spirit walker. I hope we can catch up. You and Raina. I would like to see how much has changed in the family over the long millennia." She turned toward the battle. "But of course, after we deal with this filth. Xithoz!"

I blinked when she called out the demon's name, and again when he responded with a grin and spoke. "Finally decided to join the fun, Shiva?"

She chuckled, and then spoke in that demonic language Rosa and Zaedrix had used earlier today. The demon nodded before calling out to his clan."

"You speak their language?" Shva'sika said, her brow pulling together. "I… I don't understand. Aren't you a demon hunter?"

The woman gave a curt nod. "I was. It was something I was good at, too. Until I met the Xolral Clan and learned the truth about them. It was then I swore I would never slay one unless they couldn't be reasoned with."

Truth about them? What did she mean about that?

The warrior launched herself into the fray alongside Xithoz and the other demons. Whatever she meant by that, it could wait until after we won.

Metal humming through the air caught my ear. I whirled and jumped back from a swinging sword. Wincing when the sharp metal grazed my arm, I strafed and lunged with my dagger, willing it to transform into a short sword in the same moment. My opponent skillfully evaded, my blade bouncing off his armor, and he followed up with a quick counter. I parried the strike, sucking in a hard breath under the strain. He came in for another strike so fast that I struggled to stay on the defensive.

In my periphery, I spotted motion and evaded a flying boulder careening in my direction. Unfortunately, that put me in the path of another earth attack, and I wasn't quick enough to get away. Pain shot through my side, something in my chest cracking. Agony flowed through my whole body as I bounced and rolled across the ground. When I came to a sliding halt, I lay splayed out on my front, momentarily stunned.

What a pitiful display from me. I'd grown too accustomed to Rashta watching my back when Raikidan wasn't around. Honestly, the lack of any presence in my mind was disconcerting after all these years of having something there.

Groaning, I weakly pushed myself to my knees. My vision was blurry, and it hurt to breathe. Several enemies converged on me, eager to claim my life. Inhaling deeply and feeding the burning flames in my chest, I unleashed a hot breath of fire, hoping it'd deter them.

The attempt was a wash as one of the approaching enemies blocked the blast with a slab of stone. I struggled to scramble away when she pushed the earth at me, pain shooting through my chest with every movement. I braced for the inevitable impact, but before it came, a wall of stone shot up in front of me.

Gunfire rang in my ear, and through my weakened vision, Ir'esh, the leader of the South Shaman Tribe, flew into sight on a wave of earth. With him were three identical men with partially shaven blue hair, and punky clothes. *Doppelganger!* I hadn't expected him to show up. But his unique ability to create copies of himself, even if it was dangerous to do so in a fight situation, helped tremendously.

The three replicas jumped off the wave while Ir'esh continued his collision course, a disturbingly intense look on his face. Each Doppelganger fanned out, taking position around me, firing at any enemy in sight. "Chameleon, get her out of here."

I blinked and then a pair of hands grabbed my shoulders. "Hold your breath."

The familiar command and voice took hold of age-old training and I inhaled a deep breath and clamped my eyes shut. My body's molecular structure altered and moved through several types of organic materials. As many times as he'd done this to me, the sensation still wasn't a pleasant one.

We popped out, my knees resting on hard stone, and I took a gasping breath. Chameleon kept a hand on me. "You okay?"

I nodded, taking in another few breaths. "This rib of mine made that extra uncomfortable."

His kaleidoscopic eyes flicked to somewhere behind us. "Well, it's a good thing we have a healer at the ready."

Brow furrowed, I took in my new surroundings. Towering stone surrounded us on three sides. In front of me was raised earth, but low enough to peer over. From the sounds of it, the battle raged just beyond the hidden pocket Chameleon had brought us to.

After I'd taken in my bearings, I turned around. Leaning against the cliff face was an elderly elven woman. Her eyes gazed out blankly, as if unaware of our presence. *I know her.* She was the blind woman I'd lent my sight to at my celebration party after my shaman test. *What is she doing out here?*

"Bring her here," her shaky voice said, not attempting to turn our way.

Chameleon nudged me to follow him. I complied, though prepared my questions.

The woman smiled at our approach. "I know you have questions, Ambassador, but for now, allow this old woman to be useful one last time."

I hedged closer. "You speak as if you're not going to make it past sun set."

"We elves become quite in tune with our bodies as we age. When you get to my age, you know when your time is coming. And I don't have much time left." A smile spread over her lips that felt too out of place. "But please, don't mourn, young Ambassador. I've lived a fulfilling life, and have not only been blessed to have met two Ambassadors in my life, but have heard the others with my own ears."

She lifted her hands toward me. "Now, come here for your healing. You have a Sanctuary to dismantle."

I swallowed and crawled the rest of the way. If this was truly one of her last days on Lumaraeon, I wouldn't dare refuse her.

Even though blind, the woman had no trouble finding the proper position to begin my healing session, the motions ingrained in her from so many long years of service. Knowing it wouldn't be good to distract her, I turned my questions to Chameleon. "Should I ask why she was allowed out here instead of kept inside?"

"The temple has some sort of enchantment that prevents me from phasing through it," he said. I blinked. I didn't think there was anything that could repel his ability. "So we found this safe spot, since she insisted on being of use to you and your lives."

My brow quirked up. "Safe? How is being outside safe?"

He jerked his thumb toward the shorter wall. "The gods are just beyond. No way the Crimson Sanctuary is going to be any threat to her."

"And if they get around? The gods can't lift a finger unless our enemy is attacking those time arches keeping my soul split."

"We have a backup plan, don't worry."

I frowned, not liking how laid back he was about this whole idea. But it wasn't like I had the power to make the woman go hide in the temple. And as the soothing sensation of her healing flowed over my damaged ribcage, I had to admit I was thankful for her stubborn insistence to help.

I winced when a bone popped back into place, then the pain I'd been experiencing disappeared. The woman let out a breath and pulled away, the glow around her hands dying out. "Your rib is repaired, but a more thorough session will be needed to get you back in top shape. Of course, time is of the essence, so this will have to do."

I reached out and squeezed her hand. "Thank you."

A sweet but still somehow determined smile spread over her weathered face. "Go show that revenant what you're made of."

My jaw set and I slipped away to Chameleon, who'd taken up a position by the short wall. A digital visor projected over his eyes from his communicator. "What's our status?"

His eyes remained fixed on the raging battle beyond. At this vantage point, everything looked like pure chaos. "Your lives are fine. You were the only one who had been separated." His gaze flicked to me from the corners of his eyes. "Not sure how that happened."

I grunted and activated my communicator visor, using the arm component to initiate the optical zoom. "Not even I can keep track of everything going on when chaos surrounds me."

"Kir remains elusive," he continued. "For someone so determined to destroy you, he does a lot of hanging back."

Zooming in, I started my search. "He tried the direct approach, and wasn't strong enough to take on so many of my lives. So of course he'd let his cult wear us down to make us easier targets for him. It's no different than the two of us sitting here."

As much as I wasn't thrilled to be back here, I understood the tactical advantage. I wasn't designed for close combat, even if I did decently at holding my own. This patient stakeout was more suited to my skill set.

Atria popped into my sight directly out of a shadow on the ground, thrusting her daggers into the back of another victim. Her shadow then warped and latched onto someone else, dragging its victim into the dark abyss. Atria then disappeared the same way she'd come. "Shyden and Atria work well together."

Chameleon nodded. "I was surprised at first that he chose to work with her and not you. But seeing you go hard at the Crimson Sanctuary with your flames, and seeing how more reserved your life's fight style is, it makes sense."

"She does seem comfortable, as if she's done this before." The thought of Ryoko's past soul-life having some sort of shadow-bending ability crossed my mind. It was certainly possible.

Thinking of Ryoko drew my eyes into searching for her. It didn't take me long to spot her and Peacekeeper Ryoko, working together to crush our enemies. Wogrons flanked them, attacking with a ferocity that made my stomach lurch. I would never want them to be my enemies.

Zeek, Ryoko's former lover and a fellow Brute-class, fought alongside her as well. But when I didn't spot Rylan among them, panic surged up. My focus darted, hoping he'd only been separated from the pack. I couldn't find him. Taking a deep breath, I turned my attention inward, feeling out our artificial bond. The connection tugged at the back of my mind, pain shooting through me like a knife to the back. I stifled a gasp and continued to probe, the pain ebbing.

Whatever Rylan had experienced, it was only temporary. I came to the conclusion he was fighting somewhere, but not near Ryoko right now. Even though the three of us had been trained to stick together in battle, and were quite successful at it, too, when we were paired with others, that training wasn't as easy to rely on.

Sylvia flashed into my vision. Her clothes still glowed with the power granted through her portal device. She no longer had the two hand guns she started with, and carried a much larger two-handed gun. I suspected she'd scrounged it off a fallen combatant.

My past soul-life fired a few rounds and then disappeared.

"Did you bring Aliyah here today?" My question to Chameleon came out sounding casual, as if we weren't in a life-or-death situation.

The random question certainly took him by surprise. "Uh, yeah."

"How's she doing?"

He frowned. "Still hasn't recovered a whole lot of her memory."

When we'd found her by chance as a captive during a mission, we thought we'd rescued and healed her in time to avoid any permanent issues. But after she woke, the poor thing could barely remember her own name, let alone recognize a single face from her past—not even Chameleon.

We'd learned Zarda had found out about her faked death, and it seemed Aliyah had been smuggled out shortly after she'd uncovered some information that could ruin him. Whatever that information was, it was never documented. And with the woman's memory gone, the chance to find out went with it.

"She remembered you recently," Chameleon said. "It's why I brought her with me. Thought it'd help her. Plus this was going to be such a big event, I wanted her to make a new memory."

I snorted when he mentioned "big event." My reaction made the corner of his lip quirk. "Yeah, not the event I thought I'd be subjecting her to. I hope it doesn't affect her too badly."

"Does she remember you?" I hated having to ask, as I saw how it'd affected him after Aliyah had admitted she didn't recall anything about him.

Chameleon worked his jaw. "Not really. Mocha called me by my real name a few weeks ago, and that sparked a recollection. She was one of the few back then to call me by my name, so it made sense." He frowned. "But, it didn't piece much else together."

I noticed the sag in his shoulders. Turning my gaze back out to the battle in search for Kir again, I asked, "How are you through all this?"

He sucked air through his teeth, hesitating on an answer. "It's complicated for me. Many days, I'm just happy she's alive and trying to live to her fullest even without a past to lean on. And sometimes I wonder if I'm doing more harm than good with her and should just back off. I constantly ask myself if I'm really doing this for her, or if I'm doing it for myself, trying to get the Aliyah I know back instead of embracing who she is now."

The corner of my lips lifted. "You love her too much to be that selfish."

When he didn't respond, I stole a glance. Red tinged his cheeks as he tried to focus on the battle at hand. As amused as I was, I wouldn't push. I knew his situation was a precarious one.

A black dragon fell from the sky, so close to us that it filled my vision. I jumped back, my heart racing. The dragon crashed to the ground, uncomfortably close to the gods.

The body lay motionless for a moment and then jerked, though not naturally. The dragon rose, its movement jerky, as if life had been forced into it—my eyes darted to the ground, finding one person I'd feared to see. *Genesis, what the hell are you doing?*

She wasn't a fighter. She'd helped once in a skirmish and I was certain it'd scared her. She wouldn't talk about it for days, not even to Seda so we could make sure she had handled everything the best she could. In no reality did it make sense for her to be out here. And I doubted Ryder would have allowed her to slip outside the safety of the Temple.

The black dragon body wasn't the only one to move. Riket's form shuddered as a soul entered his lifeless body. I bit the inside of my cheek. I hoped she knew what she was doing. As useful as risen bodies would be, it put her into a moral quandary that may not matter right now, but would after this battle was won. *Unless...*

My eyes flicked to Arcadia. Her attention was fixed on the chaos beyond, but that didn't mean she wasn't doing something with her god abilities, including receiving the okay from a spirit for their body to be used in such a way. Sure, she couldn't interfere, but relaying a spirit's wishes to a shaman, who could then speak to Genesis through a psychic, wasn't against the rules. My head spun from the convoluted concept, but it also made sense.

The dragons she controlled took flight, attacking ground troops instead of targeting their aerial force. I sucked in a tight breath when Crimson Sanctuary members broke through the line of defense and went for her.

Nazir stepped in their way, his sword poised to defend. My brow furrowed. *What is he doing?*

A sanctuary member grinned, their proximity close enough for me to hear him speak to Nazir. "You can't do anything, god of death. Don't try to pretend you can alter the fates of these misled fools."

Nazir refused to step aside, his shoulders squaring and his posture becoming more intimidating. "I cannot participate in this skirmish, true. But there is no law to prevent me from protecting my daughter."

I sucked in a deep breath. There was the true confirmation I'd looked for earlier. And now that I'd heard it, I wasn't quite sure how to handle the information.

Genesis, to her credit, didn't react. She remained focused on her control, spreading her influence among the bodies strewn about the battlefield. I lost count of the forms rising from the ground, their movements janky but suitable for battle. *She's controlling more than the last time.* Nazir must have given her some sort of instruction. I doubted she'd found ways to harness her ability like this from her finds with the scholars.

"Step aside," the Crimson Sanctuary member snarled. "She fights this battle. You cannot protect those who are involved."

Nazir positioned himself to attack. "I have merely struck a deal with her to instruct how to utilize her abilities properly, as her training was sorely lacking. The deal includes my protection until she's mastered her skill. How she demonstrates her ability to learn is her business. I must still abide by my end of our bargain."

A smirk lifted the corner of my mouth. If anyone knew how to deal with loopholes, it'd be the god of trickery and deceit. And, if Genesis were truly his daughter, he wouldn't make a soul-binding deal. A mere spit in the handshake would be enough.

The Crimson Sanctuary member growled and made the stupid decision to attack the defending god. In a flash, his blood spilled across the ground, his innards flying everywhere. Crimson liquid dripped from Nazir's blade and darkness shadowed his eyes. The remaining enemies hesitated, unsure how to proceed. They couldn't take on a god, but Genesis' new skill posed a great advantage to our low numbers.

Tearing my focus away from that now-handled situation, I continued my search for Kir.

"Found the bastard," Chameleon muttered.

He pointed in the direction I should look and I zoomed my visor. Sword down by his side, Kir lazily hung around Celesta. Not enough to be of any problem to her as she dealt with Zion, but he was certainly in the shadows biding his time.

Celesta, for her part, wasn't acting in a way I'd expect. *Why hasn't she attacked Zion or the other gods? And why haven't they attacked back? Is she toying with them? Waiting for something, maybe?*

My eyes flicked to the cards in her hand. She now only held two, but why did she have them in the first place? What was their significance? As unstable as she was, Celesta wouldn't pull them out unless there was a reason.

Taking in Kir's positioning to Celesta, I nudged Chameleon. "I've got a crazy idea."

He smirked. "Whatever it is, I'm in."

13
CHAPTER

Exhaling a deep breath, I adjusted my grip on the daggers in both my hands, trying not to clench too tightly, but keep a good hold for this plan. Chameleon took a swig of water from the water skin he had packed, preparing the right amount of energy needed for the plan.

"You sure about this?" he asked, storing the container away. "I won't stop you, but it's risky."

I nodded. "It's the only thing I can think of to get them to make a mistake. We don't have the numbers to outlast them, so we've got to try a different tactic."

He took a deep breath. "Okay—let me know when you're ready, then. Remember, we're taking a risk right up front. I can't tell if we'll be coming up behind our quarry or not."

"I know. He hasn't moved much, so I'm confident. I'm more concerned about the timing. I doubt I can be partially fused with anything while I'm trying to use my spiritual power."

Chameleon nodded. "After I let go, I'll move somewhere safer, but I'll try not to go too far in case the plan fails."

"Good call." I took a deep, calming breath, centering my mind with my spirit, and adjusted the grip on one of my daggers. "Let's get this done."

Chameleon positioned himself behind me and gripped me in a secure embrace that allowed for a quick breakaway when the time came. Then, after the elderly elven woman wished us luck, we disappeared into the ground.

While I knew our destination, my sense of direction disappeared in an instant. It was hard enough keeping my mental awareness around my weapons so I wouldn't lose them in all this molecular shifting.

Then we popped out of the ground. I inhaled deeply through my nose, using all my strength not to gasp and give away our presence. As we'd planned, Chameleon and I had popped out behind Kir. The arrogant spirit hadn't moved, surveying the damage and chaos his Crimson Sanctuary created. Not hesitating, I lunged for him, my blades at the ready and spiritual energy building within me.

He didn't sense me until it was too late. Before he could whirl around, my blades plunged into his back, penetrating deeply. He grunted, the weapons ineffective against his undead nature—until I forced the building spiritual energy within me into the blades. An ear-shattering scream of agony tore through him. The power in my energy overwhelmed his revenant strength and his knees buckled. Kir was left immobile, my daggers perfectly positioned to halt any ability to retaliate.

"No!" Celesta cried out. I wasn't expecting my attack to go unnoticed, not with how he screamed. But her distress caught me off guard. I'd doubted that she actually cared about Kir. It didn't seem she had, with the way she casually dismissed him earlier. "You aren't meant to do that. You can't change this plan!"

Ah, that explains it. But no matter what she wanted, she couldn't touch me. And for a moment, hope sparked. Maybe the second half of my plan wouldn't be needed. Maybe, just maybe, I was strong enough to defeat Kir myself, and not have to rely on Rashta or draw upon the power of my past soul-lives when they were within me. If I could pump enough spiritual energy into him, I could scatter his soul to the winds. A difficult feat, sure, given how much energy I'd expended already to get him to this point, but maybe—

The whistling of a bladed weapon caught my ears. I lurched back, my blades dislodging from Kir, freeing him. *Shit!* I took several more steps back as four Crimson Sanctuary members closed in.

Kir gasped and struggled away, turning a seething glare my way. "You're going to pay for that."

Okay, so part two of the plan would be needed. Not ideal, especially since it was far crazier than me thinking I could defeat Kir alone, but I'd come this far. There was no backing out now.

Kir rose to his feet, grabbing his dropped sword. He flourished the wide blade as if the action would scare me, and then rested the back side against his folded arm. It looked like he intended to run me through with it. Not that he'd get his wish.

A hungry grin pulled at his face, a cackle coming from his throat. "You got cocky, girl, separating yourself from the others like this. Now you're going to pay for it with your existence."

I flashed a smile, playing off his assumption I'd gotten ahead of myself, and feigned forward. Kir lunged and I jumped aside, disguising my backward movement. I made a half-hearted swipe at my adversary, and dodged back when he came in for a counter.

Kir swung three more times consecutively, the movements strong and harsh. His movements were faster than I'd expected, and he narrowly missed slicing my chest on all three attempts, the last swing nicking my shoulder. Blood dripped from the shallow cut.

He also left little room for me to keep track of his followers. They didn't rush in like their leader, but none had given up a pursuit, allowing Kir his fun. No doubt they were hoping for their own opening for glory.

Kir swung again, his frustration with his other misses causing him to arc too wide. Quick on the counter, I slashed his arm with a spirit-infused dagger. He hissed and jumped back. One of his subordinates lunged, hoping to catch me off guard, but I'd already noticed the way he'd shuffled for the spring, and deftly dodged, raking my blade across his back.

He cried out and crashed to the ground, twitching. It wasn't a fatal blow, but it certainly hit a number of important nerves. Normally I'd finish him off, but there were too many enemies to deal with to worry about that. He'd either bleed out or someone else would finish him.

Taking several steps back, I weaved around more of Kir's attacks, mindful of his attempt to drive me in a different direction—no doubt toward his minions, but I wouldn't allow him to mess up my carefully thought-out plan.

I swiveled my head, making it look like I was taking in my being surrounded, when I was actually gauging my positioning. *Almost there.*

I feigned a stumble, and Kir's lackeys took the bait, coming at me all at once. I dodged and they ran into each other. Kir snarled and insulted their stupidity, using earth to force them away. *Right, earth. Shit.* It was now or never, because at this point I'd been lucky he hadn't been using his elemental control.

Jumping back and forth, as if trying to figure out a way to get around him, I lured him closer and closer to being a pawn of mine. And when I sensed Celesta close by, I sprung. Feigning another lunge, Kir fell for the perceived opening and attacked. He overextended in his confidence and I deftly jumped to the side, slicing my dagger into his shoulder and down his arm. He roared and swung wide, trying to throw me off before any more of my spiritual energy could be forced into him.

Slipping under his arm, I slashed at his chest and then vaulted toward Celesta, my daggers already poised. She began to turn, noticing our proximity, but it was too late. I sliced one of my daggers into her exposed back, following up with a downward strike for her hip with my other.

The goddess screamed, dropping the cards in her hand, as well as that weird paintbrush of hers. Zion, more on reflex by the looks of it, snatched the falling artifacts. His eyes were on me, astonished I'd be stupid enough to attack a god—albeit a corrupted one, but a god nonetheless. All the other gods stared as well, as did warriors all around us.

Celesta whirled on me, rage contorting her face. "You bitch! How dare you."

I took a few steps back, a grin on my lips. "I've been told I'm a bit too reckless at times. Besides, I've fought Phyre. And I've fought other gods in previous lives. Don't think you're something special."

Her nostrils flared and she flicked her wrist. I took a step back, my heart leaping into my throat. This was the risky part of my plan. I didn't know what she could do, and the moment I attacked her, it allowed her to bypass the Cosmic Law.

But nothing happened.

She whipped her head to her hand, the one that had previously held the paintbrush.

"You've lost your privilege for that, Celesta," Zion murmured. He held a tight grip on her artifacts. "You've misused the gifts I'd given you. They're not yours to use here."

The goddess' lip curled. "Taking those won't stop me."

She reached for her hip, the one I'd injured, and grabbed for something that was no longer there. Her eyes widened and she searched again for her now missing bag.

I snickered and stepped back several paces, lifting my hand to reveal my secure hold on her deck of cards. "Looking for something, Celesta?"

Fury twisted her features. "Give that back!"

I clutched the bag tighter, a difficult feat with my dagger still in hand. "No, I think I'll keep it."

The goddess took a step toward me when water lashed out at her, and my mother appeared in a crashing wave that consumed several Crimson Sanctuary members around us. She held her weapon, an abnormally large great sword modeled after Satria's weapon Tamashi, poised to strike. I paused a moment, her wave giving me several precious seconds to think and process. While I'd seen her with the weapon earlier, like all other times I'd seen her as a spirit, I never asked how she was able to use it. It should have been nothing more than an illusionary prop, given her real weapon had gone missing after her death. But during my shaman test, and now, here she was, wielding it—and from the blood staining the blade, using it.

"You will not touch my daughter, you corrupted bitch," my mother snarled.

Celesta paused, her eyes focused on the sword. "How did you get that?"

My mother grinned. "It was a gift."

I blinked. Was there something special about her sword? A long time ago I wondered why she even had it, but never thought far enough into it to ask. And, really, what was so strange about a replica of Tamashi?

Movement behind Celesta caught my attention. Zion came up behind the goddess of timelines and wrapped his arm around her, pulling her into a tight hold. She gasped and struggled. Managing to break an arm free, she slammed her hand into his face just as he was about to… bite her? *What is this dragon, part vampire or something?*

The force of her hand into his face jarred him enough for Celesta to break free. She pointed at me. "Get my artifacts back! And kill her."

My mother swirled up the water around us and attacked our closest enemies. "Eira, go!"

I whirled and sprinted away. My heart thundered in my ears. Now came the part I hadn't quite planned out. I just needed to dodge all the swarming Crimson Sanctuary members and get to Chameleon. *Good thing running is a specialty of mine.*

A large mass of dragons dove from the sky. I glanced over my shoulder to see Raikidan and three of his past soul-lives—Anshur, Verrak, and Taiegh—swooping down and unleashing powerful breaths. A curtain for fire scorched the ground and raged, cutting off the larger wave of pursuers. My heart leapt. My dragon knew how to pick the perfect time to assist me. It would take a bit for elementalists to put out those powerful flames.

Ducking and weaving around sword swings and elemental attacks from enemies on my side of the blazing wall, I managed a decent distance from the enraged goddess. Allies swarmed in to assist, but overall it did little to halt our enemy with the numbers imbalance.

I threw out fire at bodies and the ground, letting instinct guide how I disrupted my pursuers. Changing up my path in erratic patterns effectively confused and frustrated them, causing them to make more glaring errors my allies took advantage of.

A hand slid up from the ground several feet ahead of me. The chaos of people I skirted around made it invisible to everyone but me, since I was the only one looking for him. *Right on time, Chameleon.* Picking up my pace, I closed the distance. When I was nearly upon Chameleon, I pretended to trip, rolling at the end of my supposed crash, and slipped the bag of cards into his grasp. He clamped down tight and sunk back into the earth as I rolled and sprung up on my feet. Wasting no time, I sprinted away, clutching my arm close as if I'd never let go of the object.

Something hard crashed into me from a blind spot. Agony raked over me as I slammed into the ground and rolled. When I came to a stop, I was on my back and staring up at a massive man with a crooked jaw towering over me. He grinned, revealing jagged yellow teeth, and lifted his foot to crush my chest in. I rolled, his foot slamming so hard into the ground it sunk several inches. *Shit, that was too close.*

Body still aching, I pushed through the pain and vaulted to my feet. I poised my dagger to fight, only to find out I no longer had my weapons. In my fall, they'd scattered in two separate directions. The daggers vibrated, the special nature of the weapon Ryder had crafted for me long ago trying to fuse itself back together now that it was no longer controlled by me.

Taking a steadying breath, I calculated how to get them without being crushed by the troll of a man. A base plan worked up, I jumped one way to throw him off, and then headed in the proper direction. As I assumed, he was less brains than brawns and he easily fell for my feint, allowing me to quickly snatch up one of my daggers and get a decent distance toward my other before he whirled on me.

Foot poised to strike, my battle-weary brain realized just a little too late this man was an earth elementalist and not some freakish gorilla creature. I brace for earth to fly at me, but before my adversary could stomp the ground, a white form slammed into him, the protruding spikes all over the body goring him clean through. The elementalist choked and then went limp.

Xithoz peeled the dead human off him, his spikes coated in a fresh coat of blood.

"Thanks," I said, picking up my other dagger.

"You're not hurt." It was more a statement than question.

I shook my head and readied myself when seven Crimson Sanctuary members swarmed us. "I'm good to take on these fools."

"Hand over the artifact," one of them said. "And we'll make this quick for you, Halfling."

I blinked, feigning confusion. "Artifact? What are you talking about?"

Before he could spit out a retort, I showed my palms, the best I could, at least, while keeping a firm grip on my weapons. My enemies blinked, confused.

In the distance, Celesta roared. "Find it!"

I smirked, and rushed my enemies before they could react to their new command. The closest man, I jammed my dagger deep under his ribcage from the side. My forward momentum carried me to the woman next him, my dagger slicing into the soft flesh of her neck. She choked, blood gurgling in her mouth. I yanked my weapons out of my victims' bodies.

The woman dropped, slowing choking to death. The man collapsed to one knee, gasping for air, my blade having just punctured one of his lungs. I swept up behind him and plunged my daggers down behind his clavicle. He choked and then his eyes rolled back when I withdrew my daggers and sliced on over his neck, blood spraying out across the ground.

I pivoted, ready to defend myself from the other four Crimson Sanctuary members, only to find Xithoz disposing of the last one. He was efficient, I could give him that.

The large demon turned crimson eyes to me. They looked… sad. "You've effortlessly slipped back into the killer they made you into."

My gut clenched. I'd been doing my best not to think about how easy it was to turn off my emotions and enter my assassin state of mind. This whole altercation brought back battles I wished I could forget. But Zaedrix's and now Xithoz's comments about my shift into soldier mode made it difficult to keep my mind off the reality.

I swallowed, sucking in a long, quiet breath through my nose. "There are some things we sometimes can't ever leave in the past."

The demon nodded, his expression solemn. I never learned how the bone demon had been summoned. Nor did I know the life he lived since that moment. But by the way he looked at me, I knew he understood because he, too, fought the shades of his past.

A dozen more Crimson Sanctuary members swarmed in, forcing us to focus. Taking a deep breath, I exhaled a hot flame. One of our enemies lifted her hand and water pulled from the air, creating a shield. The two elements collided, an explosion of steam hissing out. The hot moisture cloud spread and obscured the battlefield, cutting off visibility to the battle around me.

My lip quirked up. Or it would, had I not inherited a useful trait from my father.

Taking a deep breath, heat built in my body, rising to my head. My sight distorted and the world around me was defined by layers of color. The Crimson Sanctuary members around Xithoz and me glowed with the usual heat signatures I'd expect. But Xithoz glowed with intense colors I'd never seen before on another creature. Not even a red dragon or fire elementalist, whose bodies glowed with intensity around their flame sacs and fire origin points.

Now wasn't the time to reflect on that, though. After flicking my wrists back and forth to release some tension, I attacked the nearest enemy. Xithoz reacted to my movement by attacking as well. *He must be able to see past this fog, too.*

The Crimson Sanctuary members were easy to dispatch, unable to defend themselves while blind. As Xithoz tore into the last enemy, a hard wind whipped through, blowing away the fog. I sucked in a tight breath when more heat signatures swarmed in. Canceling my ability, I got a better feel for their distance—right on top of us. *Shit...*

I exhaled a flame, nothing strong, as I didn't have the time to take in the breath needed, but it was enough. Taking a hold of the fire with my hands before it extinguished, I intensified the blazing element and tossed it around—some aimed at people on their feet, as well as at others at the ground to stick and burn. There wasn't any strategy behind my throws, except to keep my enemies far enough away for me to think. That didn't work out for me at all.

Crimson Sanctuary members continued to multiply and soon were able to easily break through my fire on the ground. I backed into Xithoz and chewed the inside of my cheek. *Well, this is a shitty position to get myself into. Nice going, Eira.*

I cranked my neck to peer back at Xithoz when he chuckled. Had the bone demon lost it?

"Don't scream," he murmured.

Before I could ask what he was talking about, blurred shapes barreled into our enemies. Spines, claw, wings, and tails—Xithoz's clan had come out of nowhere and now viciously tore down our enemies. *Man, these demons are giving us an edge I didn't expect.*

"Eira, now!" Xithoz barked.

My brows pulled together, and then I noticed the opening that had been created in the bloody chaos. The bone demon gave me one nod before throwing himself back into the fray. I was sprinting into motion before my brain could come up with an excuse to stay and help them. They were doing this for me, to keep up the distraction as long as I could. I wouldn't let them down.

Enemies and allies flashed past me, my speed rarely faulting, not even when blades scraped my skin and elements assaulted me. I managed to dodge gunfire, though I couldn't be sure it was for me or someone else, especially since Zalia appeared in my vision briefly, popping off her yet-again newly acquired gun, and then teleported again. It made me wonder how my other soul-lives were handling everything.

There was so much chaos I hadn't thought about them, worrying more about my own hide. And I still wasn't used to their lack of presence in my mind. I couldn't believe I was admitting it, but a part of me did miss that familiarity, as annoying as it was, knowing my thoughts were never private.

Darkness flashed past me. I cranked my head back in time to see Kharis expand his large shadowy Guardian body around a cluster of enemies. A rock Guardian barreled through another grouping, and a Guardian made of wind whirled through, flinging Crimson Sanctuary combatants in all directions. Kharis turned and nodded his nearly shapeless head, promising to protect me.

I tripped when the earth underneath me shifted. Hitting the ground hard, I did my best to roll. Hands grabbed my midsection and I thrashed, trying to defend myself.

"Easy, Sweet Thing," Telar murmured, hauling me up. "I'm here to help."

I stopped struggling, allowing him to pull me close. Energy pulsed out from him and advancing enemies flew back. In my moment of reprieve, I leaned against his warm, muscular form, my breath coming in short, quick spurts. My lungs burned and fatigue weakened my body. I wasn't sure how much longer I could keep this up.

"Are you okay?" he messaged telepathically.

"Exhausted…"

He nodded and flung out his arm, throwing more tenacious enemies back. *"When I tell you to, bank a right toward the gods. You'll see an odd-shaped boulder beyond them. We sent Nisha and Isis there to rest. Bends a few rules, but no one said we couldn't take advantage of their protection of the time arches. You need to go there, too."*

I bit my lip. *"Everyone else is putting in their all. I already took a break earlier. I can't take another one when so few take one of their own."*

Telar lifted a man into the air, strangling him with an invisible force. *"You're more vulnerable than us. We haven't had our souls split over a dozen times. Plus, the Crimson Sanctuary has it extra out for you, given the stunt you pulled. You take a moment to slip somewhere they can't get you. Trust me, it'll help us all out."*

I took a slow breath of air. *"All right, fine."*

"Get ready, then." He didn't release his hold, most likely to not draw attention to me. Energy built around us and my eyes widened. I'd never

experienced such powerful psychic energy before. The back of my neck prickled as his power rolled over me and I had to fight the urge to run. *Telar is way more powerful than I've given him credit for.*

That wasn't to say I had labeled him as weak. On the contrary, after Seda and Nioush, I ranked him and Avila as the most powerful psychics I knew. And this just proved it.

"Now!" His elbow lifted just enough for me to slip out of his embrace and bolt. My arms pumped hard and my feet dug into the hard ground with each step. My lungs burned with each breath I took.

Almost there. I only had a few more yards to go when the ground rumbled underneath me. *Shit, no!* I was so close and I honestly didn't have it in me to take on an earth elementalist. They were difficult for me when I was at full strength, no way could I take one on my own at this rate.

A wall of earth shot up behind me and curled along my path, but didn't come at me. I caught a glimpse of Ir'esh before his earth cut me off from sight. My heart leapt and I sent a prayer to Valena for bestowing her power on the elven man.

Reaching the time arches, my legs nearly gave out under me, but I pushed on, my eyes focused on the weird-looking boulder Telar mentioned. When I came in range, I dove for cover behind it, not caring how desperate I might have appeared to anyone watching me.

Well, gawking was more accurate, based on Isis' and Nisha's startled expressions.

"You okay?" Isis asked slowly.

I leaned against the boulder next to Nisha, breathing hard. Unable to speak, I just nodded.

It took several long moments for my breathing and heart rate to return to a more acceptable level. "How are you two?"

Isis frowned. "I'm okay. Been stuck here a while after I ran out of arrows, and couldn't pick up any good ones from the ground. I tried to be helpful with my fire breathing, but I couldn't even manage that. Sorry…"

I shook my head. "You did what you could, and that's what matters. Kir isn't just your problem, he's all of ours. And even with Celesta pulling strings, we'll crush him and his Crimson Sanctuary."

My first soul-life didn't look convinced, but also didn't voice an argument. I turned my attention to Nisha. "What about you?"

She let out a sorrowful grunt and glanced down at her hand. "I've had better days."

My eyes followed her attention shift, and I gasped. Her hand and fingers were twisted in ways they shouldn't have been, blue runes glowing on her skin. "What happened?"

Her lips twisted. "Magical backfire. I was using too many complex spells back to back. I knew better, but I didn't think the smaller spells would be helpful, wasting my mana."

"Mana?" I blinked. The only time I'd heard that word was for a particular female dragon's name.

"It's an energy pool mages use to tap into the arcane energies around us."

I pursed my lips. "How does someone obtain this energy pool?"

"You just have to learn how to harness the energy of your soul. That's how names like our friend Mana came about. It means *Life Energy*."

My eyes widened. She said it so matter-of-factly, like it wasn't a serious thing to use your soul energy as a weapon. "So… anyone can become a mage?"

She shook her head. "Not exactly. While most could figure out a simple spell or two, mages are individuals who are able to properly harness the soul energy. This is why you can channel memory magic with my assistance, but nothing more."

I slowly nodded in understanding. My eyes slipped to her hand. "Seems like it's a lot more dangerous than people give it credit for."

Her lips twitched back and forth as she thought how to answer. "There is a danger in learning the basics of mana harnessing. But the real problem is with the spell casting. Arcane is a volatile element, and if you don't use it properly, it can seriously harm you."

"You need to see a healer," I said. "I can get Chameleon to take you up above the Temple. There's an elven woman who can help."

Nisha shook her head and pointed to the runes on her hand. "See these? They're pulling out the arcane trapped in my hand. Once the backup is fixed, Raina said she'd pop over to give me a quick heal. Then I'll get to crafting some magic arrows for Isis and jump back into the fight myself."

I pursed my lips. "Raina can heal?"

Nisha nodded. "It's a secondary skill for her, so more akin to Shva'sika's healing ability, but that's more than enough for this."

Isis peeked around a dip in the boulder. "How is it out there? We heard your little stunt, and Celesta's tirade."

I sucked in a breath through my nose. "Honestly… I don't know."

Isis ducked when a flaming boulder flew overhead and crashed into the mountain, out of sight. Her lip curled. "They've started up that tactic again. Like our exhausted psychics don't have enough to deal with as it is."

I closed my eyes, the aches in my body overwhelming me, along with bubbling despair I struggled to keep at bay. What I did against Kir and Celesta had been a decent enough distraction, but it didn't help our position the way I'd wanted it to. We were still outnumbered, and unless we got reinforcements sometime soon, I struggled to believe we'd make it out of this alive…

"Eira…" a rough growl of a voice whispered in my ear.

One of my eyes cracked open. It was faint, as if I'd been hearing things, but there was strange familiarity about the sound.

"Eira…" it called again.

This disembodied voice wasn't from the battlefield. They couldn't be living, but… why would a spirit be whispering to me? With the spiritual plane open, they could just pop in and talk to me.

My heart slowed. *Unless…* Taking a steady breath, I centered myself, aligning my spirit with the spiritual plane. I was too weak to cross over, and I didn't want to risk anything given my soul was fractured at the moment, but I was connected enough to communicate. "Anir?"

I wasn't sure if I was speaking out loud or in my head. With all the training I'd done, it was becoming more and more difficult to discern where I was on the lines of the planes if I had not fully crossed through.

"Eira." He sounded relieved. "I was afraid Acadia would cut me off again before I could get through."

My brow creased, eyes still clamped tight. "Anir, what is it? You wouldn't take this risk unless it was important."

A long time ago, Anir had lived during a time I had and apparently loved one of my soul-lives. But she wasn't destined for him, and out of anger he'd made a pact with Nazir, which subsequently branded his soul to be sentenced to hell. I was fuzzy on the details beyond that; I didn't even know which of my soul-lives it had been.

The black dragon didn't come off as a soul that should have been sentenced that way. Rashta even told me that a lot of Nazir's deals don't result in those kinds of judgments. And given how Anir treated me when I met him in hell, besides being angry, and how he'd made several attempts to help me by finding holes in hell to lend what assistance he could, I couldn't see him as an evil dragon deserving an eternity of damnation.

"You need to convince Arcadia to let us out."

The back of my neck prickled. "What?"

"Listen, Eira. I can help. I'm strong. If I'm given a corporeal form, even temporarily, the deal I made with Nazir will reactivate. I'll be stronger than normal. Same with the other souls I've rounded up. We're loyal to you, no matter what the gods say. You need us."

He was right, we did need the help, but as much as I was sure I could trust Anir to help, these other souls he mentioned… *And then there's the matter of convincing Arcadia.*

Something squeezed my arm. My eyes flew open and I looked at Nisha. Tears bubbled in her silver eyes.

"Is… are you really speaking to Anir?" Apparently I was speaking out loud and not in my head.

I tried to swallow, a knot forming in my throat. It'd been her. Nisha was my soul-life Anir had loved. And from the emotions registering on her face, his loss hadn't been easy on her. "Yes."

She took a shaky breath and then grasped my hand with her good one. Her eyes clamped shut. "Anir?"

I froze. Was she trying to communicate through me?

"Nisha…" his reply came out barely a whisper.

My eyes widened. She'd somehow managed to tap into my connection.

Tears broke free and rolled down her cheek. "It is you…"

Anir took a moment. "Nisha, listen to me…"

He rattled off the same request to her. Nisha swallowed and then nodded, as if he were in front of her. "I'll do my best."

My brows pulled together. "I'm not saying no to the idea, but this is Arcadia we're talking about. Even if every soul volunteering to help wouldn't cause issues, she wouldn't allow a single soul to leave hell."

Nisha's lips pressed into a determined line. "Doesn't mean I'm not crazy enough to try."

That makes two of us… She hauled herself to her knees and I followed, though my body protested, begging I let it rest. Poking out over the boulder, Nisha called out, "Arcadia, I have a request that is within your power to grant."

The goddess turned, as did several other gods. Her pale eyes pinched at the corners. "Do you want to be spotted? We can't stop you from hiding behind us, but we can't stop anyone from skirting around to you three."

"I don't care about that right now," Nisha replied. "You need to open a gate for hell."

Arcadia let out an amused snort. "I think you should make sure the arcane spell hasn't spread past your hand."

To Nisha's credit, she didn't flinch at the goddess' insult. "I'm serious. Anir is offering his power. He's collected other—"

Arcadia's eyes narrowed, a scowl twisting her usually sullen expression. "No. Nisha, he's playing with your emotions. He was sentenced there for a reason. He—"

"No, he wasn't." Venom laced the mage's words. "What he did didn't warrant a sentencing of eternal damnation."

My pulse slowed. So I wasn't the only one who questioned that. And given she was separated from me, no one could claim she had influenced my thoughts in any way.

Unfazed by Nisha's reaction, Arcadia shook her head. "My stance stays. Those sentenced to hell remain there for all eternity."

Nisha worked her jaw, and I stepped in. "Arcadia, look around you. We're outnumbered, even with spirits helping us. Reinforcements aren't coming."

"Help will arrive," Sela said, her attention not on me, but Zion and Celesta. "You just have to hold out."

My hand slammed on the rock, my attempt at handling this calmly reaching a breaking point. "At what cost? More will die! We need whoever is willing, even if they come from a place you'd rather not."

Arcadia's lip curled. "You do not know what you ask of me to do. You don't understand the consequences."

I took steadying breaths. "If something goes wrong, you can lay the consequences on me. But right now, I need my army."

Arcadia's jaw set, but before she could deny us again, Genesis spoke up from her kneeling position by Rashta, who still had yet to complete her purification. "Open the gate, Arcadia."

The spirit goddess' eyes widened. "But Genesis—"

"It's time to see if the judgments were just or not." The way she worded that made my skin prickle and did nothing to squash my wavering confidence in their ability to judge a soul without Rashta.

Arcadia clenched a fist and looked about to argue, but then resigned to the older goddess' command. She lifted her arm, flat palm raised, and her eyes glowed. Beyond the safe zone they created, and far enough away from the time arches for Arcadia to be comfortable, an enormous black portal formed. It swirled with white energy and an eerie black fog spilled out of the vortex.

My heart thundered in my ears. This was it. Either I'd be wrong and this was a mistake, or it was an advantage we needed. "Anir, now!"

A massive black shape shot out of the hell portal. Heavily plated scales coved the dragon's body and large, bat-like wings propelled him through the air, though the tears in the membranes made me pause and wonder how it was possible.

After Anir, a wave of spirits rushed out, weapons or elements forming in their hands, and they joined the battle, engaging with Crimson Sanctuary members, as promised. Oddly though, two spirits didn't enter the fray. They wore heavy armor of ancient warriors and held halberds in their hands, the weapons crossing each other, as if barring entrance. *Or… are they forbidding exit?*

I peered harder at the portal, and caught a glimpse of two more spirits on the other side, mirroring the position of the spirits outside of hell. They were guarding the portal. Whatever compelled them to act in this manner, they were upholding the deal to not allow any spirits from leaving if they didn't intend to help. *At least we won't have to deal with Zarda again…* I shuddered at the thought of having to face my creator so soon after destroying him. I wanted him to become a terrible memory and nothing more.

Anir swooped down in the middle of Kir's army, unleashing a terrifying onslaught of lightning. The chaos of battle drowned out the screams of his victims, but I could see it—the pure destruction he caused. My nails scraped against the boulder's hard surface, my lungs struggling to take in air. I couldn't lie, the ferocity of the attack was frightening. If this was the kind of power Nazir had bestowed him…

"He's not even tapped into the power he bargained for," Nisha said as if she were reading my mind, her voice hardly above a whisper. "He was always a powerful dragon. That's why it surprised me he bargained a deal to begin with. Then I saw the destruction he could cause after it'd been struck."

She closed her eyes. "But, even after witnessing that, I never feared him. As terrifying as his new power was, I knew he'd never harm me. I was only disappointed he'd made the decision to go that far."

"Do you… regret the choice you made?" Isis asked tentatively. "None of us have ever had the guts to ask, since it's such a touchy subject."

Nisha swallowed, her silver eyes fixed on her other favorite dragon. "There was hardly ever a day I didn't ask myself if there hadn't been another way that would have saved us both so much pain."

Isis and I gazed at her sympathetically. I could almost put myself in her shoes, given my past relationship with Tannek. Had he not died and Raikidan came to look for me, I wasn't sure how things would have gone between the three of us.

Nisha sucked in a tight breath when Anir veered away from the ground battle and shot into the sky. He angled for a blue dragon grappling with a red.

Anir slammed into the red dragon, yanking him away from the blue, and tore his massive teeth into the enemy dragon. The blue shook himself and then exhaled a thick vapor that looked as though it were hot. *Steam?*

The red dragon writhed and jerked when Anir bit into his neck, as if he were being electrocuted, and then went limp. The enemy dragon dropped from the sky and crashed into the ground, leaving Anir and what I now realized was Aser, Nisha's mate, facing each other.

Nisha tucked her arms in close, her fists pressed against her lips. Fear tightened her eyes. "Don't fight. Don't fight. Please don't fight."

The two male dragons hovered in the air for a moment before both nodding and diving toward the ground. Nisha let out a shaky breath, and I also exhaled, not realizing I'd stopped breathing.

The battle raged with no signs of stopping. Steel clashed, elements flew wildly, and guns blasted. Some enemies got alarmingly close to the temple.

I ducked instinctively when another flaming boulder shot over us. "We really need to do something about those trebuchets."

"That's been the goal of my father and his mages," Nisha said. "Unfortunately, there's a magical barrier protecting them. If they could get closer to the artillery, they'd have an easier time removing the magic, but as it stands, it's taking a while, and I'm fairly certain they have their own mages actively fortifying the trebuchets, which doesn't help matters."

Great... My nails dug into the boulder. I wanted to be out there fighting alongside everyone, but my body still needed to rest. And if I was honest, as much help as these hell spirits were, it still wasn't enough. Sela said reinforcements were on the way, but how long would we have to wait? And would they be enough?

Two white dragons dove from the sky, spewing ice over Kir's army. Enormous spikes of ice stuck out of the now-coated ground. It took me a moment to register the attack, and even longer to notice something was different about the dragons.

Isis spoke up. "Um, neither of those dragons were spirits.

"And they weren't Xanthus or Razeth," Nisha added.

I turned to them, my brow furrowed. That couldn't be right. White dragons were extinct. They had to be spirits if they weren't Raikidan's past soul-lives.

Then, a commanding dragon roar pierced the air over the clash of battle, and the ground rumbled deep below.

14
CHAPTER
(RAIKIDAN)

My teeth ripped into the soft exposed flesh of the black dragon's neck I grappled with; the metallic tinge of his blood flooded my mouth. A strangled roar tore through him, and he raked his claws over my armored hide, but my scales were tougher. I thrashed my head, tearing his skin.

Slicing my talons into him, I inhaled through my nostrils, the burning sensation of my internal flame intensifying. I exhaled without releasing my hold with my teeth, fire spewing across this dragon's exposed flesh. He roared and writhed in agony, lightning shooting out of his mouth in a desperate attempt to free himself as his life slipped away.

My muscles ached from exhaustion, yet I refused to let go. He wanted to harm Eira—my Lazmira—my everything. I wouldn't allow any of them to take her from me. It didn't matter how many of these worthless filth I had to rip from the skies. I would protect her.

With one strong yank, I tore my teeth through my adversary's neck—crimson blood and gore sprayed, coating us both. The dragon gargled, thrashing wildly, though not with any conscious attempts to retaliate. His blue eyes lulled toward the back of his skull, his life slipping away. I released my grip on him and beat my wings hard, using them to propel me just right to angle my tail to strike him one last time as he crashed to the earth below.

Heaving breaths flared my nostrils. My throat burned with the weight of my exhaustion. Aches of the battle plagued me, wounds inflicted from older dragons throbbed and bled freely. Yet, I had come out victorious each time.

I'd take on Zion himself if it meant keeping Eira safe. No one had the right to claim she was worthless and unworthy of life. They hadn't seen what she'd gone through. They hadn't watched her grow and overcome so much to become the woman she was now. I had. I'd experienced her nightmares—watched her relive those memories. I'd stood beside her as she overcame that darkness. I'd been there to help her see the light she deserved to feel. Even to this day, she struggled at times to overcome the darkness that still clung to her. But still she fought, never willing to give up. And no one would take that from her.

A pulsating sensation flowed over my body—not the pull of the mate-bond I had with Eira. No, this one was different, newer—a sensation that had sprung up when Zion split my soul to bring out my past soul-lives. *My soul-lives.*

I had struggled with this knowledge over the last year. To know your mate was host to a god, and many lives over for that matter, was difficult enough to wrap your head around. But to know you were wrapped up in that eternal cycle, too, destined to find, love, and protect her each time, that was another thing entirely. Even when Rashta had pulled that mind-stunt last year, to prove Eira wasn't jerking my leg, it wasn't easy to come to terms with.

This soul-splitting only made my head spin more.

"*Raikidan, behind!*" someone called out.

I whirled around in time to grapple with an attacking red dragon. My enemy snapped his yellow teeth at my throat, the stench of his fire-tinged breath off in a way that made my skin crawl. His red scales were dull, and his eyes had an unsettling red glow about them. *Revenant.*

The undead dragon snapped at me again, unable to break free of the grapple and compromise my defense. He wasn't the first one I'd fought in these skies, but it was no less difficult to deal with. When I had battled my first, it surprised me. I thought only humans and elves could be revenants. But as the skirmish raged on, I'd come to understand that any creature could hold that much twisted darkness in their soul. The only saving grace we had was that these dragons didn't seem capable of inflicting that R-poison Eira had warned me about. That, or they didn't use it, as if it made them more dishonorable than they already were.

Whatever the case, they weren't easy to deal with—impossible for any living dragon to kill, at least. The only thing we could do was damage them enough for Eira's psychic twin lives—Lutha and Lina—to take over and annihilate the souls with their disturbingly lethal mental powers. I'd only ever witnessed such an attack with Telar, when the Crimson Sanctuary boldly attacked the Underground when we still fought against Zarda. I understood then why psychics could be so feared, and that respect was no less for Eira's twins.

They'd explained to me during this battle they couldn't technically destroy a revenant the way Eira could with her spiritual power when she was whole. But the weakened state we dragons could put them in allowed the twins to destroy their ability to take a physical form for a while. And then shamans hidden within the temple would strike. Those spirit walkers waited for the revenants to appear on the spiritual plane where they were dealt with properly, in the way only shamans could. I had no idea the shamans were so important until Eira explained their original purpose to me. And as I snapped my teeth and struggled with this revenant, I respected them even more for the dangerous task they'd volunteered themselves for. It was not a path for the weak-minded.

A massive red body collided with the revenant dragon, strong gleaming teeth stained with blood easily piercing the undead dragon's scales. The revenant roared and struggled, trying to shake off his secondary attacker. Taiegh, my previous life, clamped down harder, his attack centered at the base of the dragon's wings. He intended to cripple this dragon, using my grapple to his advantage. I let him, breathing hot white and red flames on the undead dragon as a diversion. While not immune to fire, red dragons were not so easily affected by flames, due to their innate connection with the element. But my flames weren't normal dragon fire.

Like Eira and her enhanced powers, my draconic connection to the elements intensified with each rebirth. It was why my flame was so intense, more than it should be for my age. Not even Zaith, who was older than me, and proved to be more battle capable in a fight we had over a year ago, could hold a candle to my fire.

The revenant recoiled, crying out in agony. A tearing sensation hit my ears—Taiegh ripping the tendons of the dragon's wings. The undead dragon thrashed, slamming his skull into mine. The jarring hit broke him free of my grapple and dislodged him from Taiegh's hold. But the damage had already been done. Unable to use one of his wings, he spiraled out of control.

One of my other past soul-lives, Reve, shot toward the revenant out of nowhere, exhaling acid over his body. The twisted dragon roared as the acid ate at his flesh. Reve's twin, Zetan, hovered nearby, watching rather than engaging. I could audibly hear Zetan's terrible breathing. Earlier in the fight, I'd noticed he struggled to exhale poison and acid like the other greens. Something about his health issues involved his lungs, an important organ for dragons, but especially greens.

I could see he was pushing himself too much, just as his mate had worried he would. Even still, I understood why. He'd protect her, no matter the cost, and no health issues would stand in his way.

Taiegh's wings beat hard next to me, his powerful breaths showing his fatigue as well. My eyes assessed the larger dragon. Even though his life had been cut short, he was older than me. In fact, I was the youngest of all my soul-lives, and it showed.

While they'd altered their age appearances when in their non-dragon forms to match up with Eira's past soul-lives, there was no way they'd do so with their natural shapes. Unlike humans and their ridiculous views, dragons had no concept of age-gap concerns with mates. It only mattered that both were of mating age. And with age came status. As long as you weren't ancient and suffering from end-of-life deterioration, you were stronger and more capable of protecting your mate. And as such, female dragons weren't picky about age, either. As long as the gods made a good match for us, they cared only to devote themselves as we did to them.

I banked left when a dragon body fell from the sky, the red scales coated in dark blood. The familiar scent of Hyberian clan crossed my nose. My chest constricted when the dragon slammed into the ground and remained unmoving. Another dragon fell from the sky, Taiegh pivoted and shot after him, only to veer off, shaking his head, and let the lifeless body fall.

The angle I flew at gave me a broader view of the dragons that had fallen, along with those fighting on the ground. It wasn't just Crimson Sanctuary, either. So much loss. I knew Eira would take much of the blame onto herself, too. Even though she wasn't responsible for Kir and his ilk's actions, or the actions of those who chose to fight, it wouldn't stop her. I wished there was a way to stop the inevitable, but I knew the only thing I could do was to fight harder and prevent as many deaths as possible.

Cranking my head up, I spotted four dragons barreling toward us. I bared my teeth and streaked toward them, grappling with and snapping at my opponent. Taiegh, Zetan, and Reve, took on the others. Three more enemies swooped down, these ones larger and older than our current adversaries, unbalancing the odds, and putting us at a significant disadvantage. Their overall numbers dwarfed ours. Fighting more than one dragon at a time had become a common occurrence, even for me. But this was more than any dragon could successfully handle.

No dragons came to our aid, all too caught up fighting their own opponents. *We can't keep this up.*

I shouldn't think so negatively, especially as I'd fight to my dying breath, even with a fractured soul, but I knew these stacked odds weren't doing us any favors.

Teeth snapping, talons raking, and elements flying everywhere, my soul-lives and I battled these dragons the best we could. I flexed the muscles of my spade-shaped club at the end of my tail, separating the malleable spikes from the base, and jammed the sharp points into the soft underbelly of an opposing dragon. He roared and jerked away, raking his talons across my face. I snarled and exhaled fire onto him.

My energy drained the longer I fought. Taiegh and I managed to take down the dragon together, only for two more to take his place. Frustration mixed with my adrenaline and need to fight. Where were those reinforcements we desperately needed?

I knew they'd be mostly grounded warriors, but if they brought a few guns, especially ones designed to kill dragons, it could help us tremendously.

Black and red scales barreled into the dragon taking a swipe at me. Green and black scales sped past Taiegh and me on the other side, latching onto a smaller dragon who was taking advantage of the confusion. Ebon snapped at his opponent, and Corliss breathed poisonous gas over the small dragon. The smaller opponent coughed and sputtered until he went limp and fell to the ground.

The added numbers of my family gave me a small reprieve. Breath coming heavy, my eyes darted around to take in our enemies. They'd swarmed in and surrounded us. I sensed out my mate-bond, finding Eira very much alive, but distressed. The need to fly to her aid tugged harder than it ever had before in my life. But I couldn't get to her—not without exposing myself and the others to these dragons, and potentially her if they followed me in the event I managed to slip through. *What do I do?*

A dragon behind me swooped in for an attack. I whirled to meet his strength when a blur of white barreled into the dragon. I would have assumed it to be Xanthus, my surprising extinct white-scaled past soul-life, had it not been for another streak of white slamming into another enemy. My eyes widened at the sight of two white dragons, rather young ones at that based on their size, tearing into our adversaries.

White dragon spirits weren't a new sight to me in this battle. They'd come from some open gate Arcadia made, or something like that. But these dragons were very much alive. *Where did they come from?* Why in Zion's name were there suddenly two more dragons of an extinct color here?

A commanding dragon roar pierced the sky. Most dragons in the vicinity stopped and turned toward the call, even our enemies. My eyes widened. A legion of dragons—blue, white, and violet in color—sped our way. *It can't be… it's impossible.*

A rumble sounded below us. I swiveled my head just as brown dragons erupted from the earth, grabbing unsuspecting victims and dragging them into the depths. *They're not extinct…*

Numbness crawled over me. All the stories… wrong.

My senses returned when shaman portals opened on the battle field, hordes of people rushing out and engaging in battle. To the south, fast-moving shapes vaulted over the mountains and descended on the unsuspecting Crimson Sanctuary from behind—Xithoz's demon clan. The reinforcements we so desperately needed had finally arrived.

Something heavy collided into me. Sharp talons raked across my hide, my attacker older, his claws stronger than my plated scales. I roared, the pain excruciating, snapping and thrashing against my assailant.

Ebon came to my aid, clamping his toothy maw down on the attacking dragon's flank, and attempting to claw at his underside with his back feet. *Mother did say he embodied his striped-scale pattern in more than one way.*

But still, the two of us combined were not enough for the larger, and less exhausted dragon—until a black and red dragon landed on him. While small, it tore at the enemy dragon with alarming ferocity.

My nose twitched, the scent of this new dragon hauntingly familiar and—*that's a female!*

The black and red female dragon unleashed a heavy breath of electricity. I reeled back the best I could from the biting sparks, though her intended victim wasn't so lucky. His agonized roar hurt my ears. The dragon released me, turning to swipe at her, but I wouldn't allow it. I lunged, clamping my teeth over the softer scales on his neck and tearing his flesh out. Not to be outdone, Ebon exhaled lightning on our enemy. The female did the same again.

The dragon gasped and writhed, then went limp, his lifeless body falling to the ground. But my attention didn't fixate on our fallen enemy. The female dragon flying with Ebon and me was small, though clearly not young by the way she held herself. Scars gouged her scales, black that turned to red in a gradient pattern on each individual scale. I stared at her, recognition dawning on me. A ghost from the past… a female I'd since thought dead after we hadn't heard from her in a century. "*Vorsy?*"

She fixed mismatched green and blue eyes on me, a golden and silver ring wrapping around the pupils of each eye respectively, though the blue one was dull and almost lifeless, as if she couldn't use it. Based on the large scar on that side of her face, I guessed she was blind in that eye. A grin pulled back her lips, showing off her sharp teeth. "*Hello, little brothers.*"

Numbness fell over me but I didn't know why. I should have been happy, feeling elated our sister was alive. But the scars marring her small body filled my eyes. They gouged deeply; some no doubt had been potentially life-threatening. What had she gone through since she left our family territory? What kind of monster had willingly harmed a female so badly?

It wasn't easy being half-color. Explaining such things to Eira in the beginning had been difficult, both because she didn't understand why dragons acted as though mixing colors was so terrible, and because it brought up so much pain from the past.

Females also suffered, when they shouldn't. I knew, because our parents had enough clutches of mixed-sex offspring and the three of us were the only ones left. But never had I seen firsthand the kind of treatment that befell them, too.

A chromatic dragon, one who had betrayed his flight and turned on his duty to protect, spiraled down on us, aiming for our sister. Before he reached her, though, a blue mass struck him, sending him off course. The massive blue dragon swung his barbed tail onto the chromatic dragon before breathing out a scalding stream of steam. The chromatic cried in agony as his hide burnt and boiled.

Rylar appeared out of nowhere, grabbing onto the enemy dragon, and exhaled his unusual time breath, causing his opponent to wither before our eyes until he was a smoking corpse—like we'd seen of Riket after he'd been attacked during his timeline check.

The dragon dropped lifeless to the ground.

The blue dragon turned to Vorsy. In that instant I realized it was neither of my past soul-lives Aser or Roan, but a new dragon. The wing membranes that attached to his body, acting as webbing when in the water, showed old damage—signs of past battles, where my soul-lives didn't exhibit such injuries. Next to Vorsy, he dwarfed her. She had always been small. No one knew why, but she never let it stop her from getting what she wanted. She'd annoyingly nip at your heels if it was necessary. *"Vorsy, are you—"*

"Fine," came her terse reply. *"I could have handled it."*

He shook his head, as if this kind of conversation with her were normal. *"I will still protect you where I can, you know this."*

His unfamiliar scent wafted into my nose, the smell briny but not entirely unpleasant. I realized it came off my sister as well. My gaze drifted to the base of her neck, spotting the faint lines of a mate mark where most females received theirs. This dragon was her mate. My sister was mated to a color we once believed to have died out during the Great War. *How long has she known about their existence? Was this why she had disappeared?*

Vorsy gave an indignant snort and then breathed lightning onto a nearby enemy fighting Corliss. *"You should help the water-blessed below.*

They are pulling up from the springs to aid in the fight. It would benefit the rest of the colony."

A rumbling chuckle came from him. *"Ever the keen eye. Do not get too reckless. You know this is hard on me as it is."*

He sounded like me when speaking to Eira. Understanding fell over me. My sister's experiences had made it impossible for her to stay where it was safe, as our culture expected—just like my Eira. I hated knowing she put herself in harm's way, most of the time willingly, as if a part of her relished fighting even if her mouth said otherwise. But I'd come to accept that side of her, as did this dragon with my sister.

He nudged her shoulder with his nose and then dove down without another word. Vorsy turned her attention back to us. *"I know you have questions. But this is not the time to answer them. We have to eliminate the Crimson Sanctuary and protect the Dragon-Phoenix."*

So she did know what was going on. How, I couldn't begin to fathom. But like she said, that was for another time, after Kir was obliterated.

She darted away, her small form easy to maneuver in the sky and charged toward an enemy engaged with Peacekeeper Reiki, the other female dragon who ignored our wishes to stay safe. Though, I'd seen her fight today. She channeled the spirit of a broodmother in her ferocity. No one was idiotic enough to tell her to stay back.

I should help them, but I struggled with my body. It cried out with so much exhaustion. I wanted to land and take a moment to rest. Maybe even assist Eira. I had intended to fight alongside her like I always did. But when the dragons had descended, I thought it better to protect her from above. And the one moment I was able to help her, after she pulled some reckless stunt against the deranged goddess below, didn't feel like I'd done enough.

How I longed to be near her—protecting her physically from any harm.

An echoing crack caught my attention, an unsettling sensation crawling up my spine. That sounded like rocks breaking, and it came from behind me, where the temple was. Whirling around, I set my gaze on the protected area. My blood ran cold.

The cliff that protected the temple had cracked. Element-touched enemies assaulted the formation, as if knowing there was something precious hiding within. *Stella. Ryder. Est'la.* Even little Panga, the orphan girl I'd seen playing with Stella today. The same one who wanted me to tie up her hair all the time no matter how terrible I was at it.

I should be concerned about the Birth Heart, the direct connection to our prime goddess whose comforting words still caressed my skin. But my mind focused on the brood Eira and I had together. It wasn't like what I'd expected when I finally gave in to my desire to pursue her. Taking in offspring of others to care as my own hadn't ever crossed my mind until that moment, because loving Eira meant accepting Ryder. I thought that would be the only time. And yet, that had been the only way our family grew right now, and I was all right with that. Eira was happy with the choice, and so was I, even if she doubted that sometimes. They were mine. And they were in trouble.

Folding my wings tight against my back, I dove for those threatening what was mine. The wind whipped past me, the cold air biting at my eyes and exposed wounds, yet it didn't deter me. It'd take more to stop a dragon.

More Crimson Sanctuary filth attacked the temple walls, the gods watching on in horror. I snarled at their inaction. How dare they call themselves all-powerful beings for those here and just stand watching this all go down? I didn't care about this Celestial Law they claimed held them back. What was the point of us worshiping them if they wouldn't help?

This whole time, I'd only seen Nazir, arguably the most hated god here, lift a finger, and that was to protect Genesis as she controlled the bodies of the dead because, as he proclaimed to everyone who could hear, she was his daughter.

Some might say Arcadia had finally done something, allowing spirits to come from hell to aid in the battle, but Zetan had heard her arguing with Nisha and Eira over the choice before giving in. While it was a valid concern, trusting those of corrupted souls, Eira wouldn't make such a choice carelessly. And they'd proven themselves loyal to her and her soul-lives, especially the black dragon Anir, who fought alongside Aser.

Fire streaked out at the defilers, Eira and her former life Velsara coming into my sight. Soot, sweat, and blood coated their skin and clothes, and even from this distance I could see their heavy panting. This battle had taken a toll on them as much as it had me. Yet they refused to fall, their resolve to fight until the bitter end as strong as mine.

The two shaman women joined forces to push our enemies back. It wasn't wholly effective. Our enemy's swarmed numbers still outdid ours, even with the extra help. More of her lives jumped in to assist, but it wasn't enough. The Crimson Sanctuary easily pushed the women back and continued with their disgusting assault. I couldn't understand why they were so keen on getting into the temple, but I wouldn't let them.

Tucking my legs in tighter, I picked up speed. I vaguely sensed something trailing me, but I wasn't about to stop and find out what.

The ground grew closer and closer, until the defilers were in reach for me to unleash a torrent of hot flames. I swooped low, torching the ground and creating a fire wall to stop our enemies. Another blast of fire scorched the ground behind me. It was then did I glance back, finding my first life, Anshur, hot on my tail, assisting me in protecting the Birth Heart. He'd joined the Hyberian clan for Isis, and thus, it was his sworn duty to protect Lumaraeon's conduit.

Eira and Velsara took hold of our flames and used their frighteningly strong elemental control to force the Crimson members back. As much as I admired her abilities, I couldn't deny Eira's power unsettled me at times. And as I took a sharp turn to bank back and saw the fury burning in her eye, my heart skipped a beat.

Her determination was something I truly loved. Her passion, a quality I never tired of. Her playful and alluring looks she tossed my way, irresistible. But her anger… her rage was something so terrifying it even made me second guess many things in my life. And seeing the broodmother rage within her, even after she was so insistent she was not a good parent and could never be affected by such a need to protect her offspring, she was not an enemy I'd ever want to face.

I snarled when more Crimson Sanctuary members rushed in, unafraid to die in their attempt to destroy something so precious and sacred. The need to protect what was mine propelled me forward. I exhaled a hot inferno on our enemies, narrowly missing their retaliatory attacks.

Then, something hard slammed into me, jolting me enough to send me off course. And then gunshots rang in my ears. A roar tore through me as pain coursed through my body. Usually, bullets were little match for a dragon's hide, but with my open wounds, they made me an easier target, even if they were mostly grazing me.

Pain tore through my wing and it gave out, sending me careering into the ground. I vaguely heard Eira scream my name before I crashed.

Agony raked over me and my body became unresponsive. Even though my mind screamed to get up and continue fighting, I couldn't move. My eyes cracked open after another moment of lying there, my vision blurry.

Fire raged. A dark figure stood some ways in front of me, moving as if fighting. But they didn't approach me, so they couldn't be an enemy. Unless our enemies thought I was dead.

I blinked several times before my eyes finally cleared. The figure was Eira. She fought her hardest to save our children and the Birth Heart while also trying to protect me.

Fury burned within me. *No.* My muscles cried out as I forced them to move. She shouldn't be the one always protecting. She'd done enough before I came along, and even through the rebellion. She put everyone else before her, never valuing herself just enough to think selfishly. But now, it was me who needed to shoulder that burden, to give her the rest and peace she deserved. To show her she was everything I found worth fighting for.

With a mighty roar, I unleashed another flame. Eira was directly in front of it, but as if knowing what I'd do, she grabbed a hold of the flame's essence and bent it to her will. The sensation of losing power of my own fire as I breathed it was still unsettling. If I hadn't felt her do it before, I might have even panicked a little.

My fire split around her, spanning our enemies while she remained unharmed. The light of the flames licked at her features, casting harsh lines. Her fingers twisted in my flames, as if she were coaxing and playing with them. Eyes burning with ferocity, her lips curled with eager satisfaction.

She took joy in eliminating our enemies. I should have found that concerning, a potential slip back into a past I still didn't have a full picture of. But in this moment, I found it ultimately alluring. I blamed the stress of battle and freshness to our mated status. Especially that last reason.

Rarely did she do anything now that didn't drive me wild. Every look, small smile, or touch, no matter how innocent or intentionally maddening—I wasn't sure if that was the effect of our mating and whether it'd die down in time, or it was just how things were now that she didn't hide anything away anymore.

Eira turned her head, a vivid green eye turning to me. Poorly timed desire sparked up. Who was I trying to fool? It was just her who did this to me. And my instinct to protect her—protect my claim—only heightened my response to her.

My flames died from my lips when my lungs emptied. But before I could breathe out more, something bright and moving quickly in the sky caught my attention. Turning my gaze up, my eyes widened in horror at the sight of flaming boulders sailing toward us. And it wasn't just three, like the twins had dealt with at the start of this conflict.

Six flaming rocks sailed through the air. Two veered off, much like how Lutha and Lina had dealt with them before. But the other four continued. One more went careening off course, but I could tell, the psychics were exhausted. Otherwise, all six projectiles would have been dealt with.

Something had to be done to stop them. Bunching my muscles and collecting what energy I could, I leapt into the air. One of my wings hung limply, unresponsive to my attempts to use them as I tried to propel myself straight for the flaming boulders. Even with use of just one wing, my trajectory veered off course only a little. Tensing and preparing myself, I turned my body toward the falling projectile and braced for impact.

The boulder slammed into me, pain raking all of my body. Eira cried out my name as I crashed to the ground with a sickening *thud*. I didn't feel the impact, my body already overloaded with pain. The boulder I'd stopped landed mere feet away from me, the heat of the flames licking at my scales.

I tried to move, screaming internally that there were more to take care of. But my body lay unresponsive, agony pulsing through every fiber of my being.

My blood ran cold at the sound of something large slamming into rock and a woman screaming. It wasn't Eira, but it was familiar. *Isis.* Somehow I could still recognize the woman's voice. I wasn't sure how, when today was the first time I'd ever heard it. Maybe it had to do with my past soul-life, maybe it was something else. Whatever it was, that allowed me to catch her terror.

Then more collision sounds, and more screams.

I weakly raised my head. My eyes widened at the horrifying sight of the flaming boulders sunken into the wall of the temple. Chunks of the sheer cliff face had broken off from the impact and fallen to the ground. One of the projectiles sunk too far into the cliff for comfort.

One of Eira's lives, Nalia, used her earth-touched abilities to throw the boulders away. More of the protective wall broke apart from the action, leaving it even weaker. And then, the worst happened.

Four more flaming boulders slammed into the cliff. At the same time, enemies touched by the elements assaulted the weak points the previous attack had caused. Cracking and snapping echoed over the chaos of the battle, and then everything fell from beneath me as the temple collapsed.

15
CHAPTER

I stared, unmoving—unfeeling—shock numbing me. The temple had fallen. Those who had sought refuge, now buried. My children… *No… No… No, no, no!*

This couldn't be happening. This was a trick, a well-crafted nightmare that I'd wake up from. But deep down I knew… this was reality.

Rage boiled up through the numbness and I roared, hot flames tearing through my throat and onto the battlefield. *How dare they? How dare they be so vile!*

My back spasmed and my arms twitched. The cusp of draconic transformation rolled over me and I didn't fight it, my anger so strong I could only think of one thing—they would pay… with their lives.

Skin in various places of my body morphed into blue, red, and purple scales. My backside lurched and convulsed as wings and a whip-like tail sprang forth. Black horns forced their way out of my skull, curving backward. My hands jerked as they became bonier and my nails turned into something akin to talons.

My face twisted as my teeth shifted, my canines elongating, and my sight distorted a minute amount, indicating my transformation had changed them as well, to their wider and more reptilian appearance.

I barely processed the Dire Wolf howl of Rylan, triggered into transforming as well due to our bond, before another feral roar tore through me, this one more bestial than previous. I lunged for the closest enemy, talons outstretched.

Startled by my sudden attack, my prey could only scream as I tore into him, my talons plunging deep into his chest. Hot blood splashed over my skin. The smell teased my predatory senses, luring me back to the chaotic, uncontrolled mess I used to become when exposed to the vital fluid. But my rage was stronger.

More beings attacked nearby enemies, my focused vision detecting their shapes as being similar to my now-transformed one. My siblings? They'd taken this same form alongside me before. Or… maybe my past soul-lives? Connected souls forced to transform alongside me.

I tore into another enemy, my fury making it too difficult to focus on such questions. My anger and building grief took over everything, and I didn't fight the emotional spiral. My awareness came in spurts. Enemies would fall by my claws one moment, and then another I was aware of the dying exhale of flames from my lips. Still, I didn't try to wrestle control from my spiral.

Not until I heard the unmistakable crumbling movement of earth did I pause. Whirling, I watched the collapsed temple heave up, small rocks clattering to the ground. Then it exploded, rocks flying every-where, along with water, fire, and all manner of elements.

I flattened myself to the ground when a boulder shot my way, nar-rowly missing me as it crashed into the army behind me. Xephrya's large head reared out of the gaping hole. Fire blasted out of her maw, scorching those foolish enough to stay in her line of fire.

The female dragon's eyes burned with a fury I had just experienced myself—the broodmother rage. Even from my vantage point, mostly obscured by jagged rocks, I could see the people she protected curled up to her.

Aria and Pheydra, transformed into their dragon-altered meta-morphoses like me, jumped up onto a vantage point together. Water swirled around Aria and balls of liquid surrounded Pheydra. In grace-ful movements, blades of water shot out from Aria's arsenal, slicing through bodies as if they were paper. Pheydra, not to be outdone, flung her water balls at enemy faces, wrapping the liquid around and cutting off their ability to breath, slowly drowning them.

My breathing came slow and my rage subsided as I processed. *They…*

they made it… Est'la sprang out of the temple, fists blazing with fire. I blinked slowly. *They're alive.*

With my fury lessening, my ability to think improved. *Of course!* I wanted to smack myself. If something had happened to those inside, I would have known because some of my soul-lives had been hiding in there.

Est'la attacked Crimson Sanctuary warriors who got too close and pride welled in my chest, threatening to burst through. As much as I didn't want him to ever need to use his abilities in this way, he was doing exactly as he promised without hesitation.

Taking a deep breath, I forced my transformation back. It wasn't that I was ashamed of it—not anymore—but I wasn't as accustomed to the features. They got in the way a lot of the time, especially the wings.

A chilling scream sent alarming prickles down my spine. *Stella!* I whirled to find several Crimson Sanctuary members climbing into the temple from a collapsed side. Xephrya snapped her razor-sharp teeth at them, but they retaliated with elemental fire, and one readied a gun. *Oh, no you don't!*

Taking hold of Xephrya's fire burning the nearby ground and bodies, I hurled it at the warrior. One caught fire while the others jumped away. Xephrya snatched the one with the gun into her maw. Bones cracked and blood sprayed everywhere.

Ryder and Zalia appeared, Ryder grabbing one of the warriors with his now-bare hands, both freezing and heating the unlucky sod's skin. Zalia threw a punch and upon impact, lightning sparked from her fist and through her target. But even still, our enemies persisted, aiming to eliminate the vulnerable like the vile, spineless cowards they were.

Stella continued to scream, the sound grating my nerves and kicking up my need to protect her. I needed to save her.

I took one step forward, only to freeze at the sound of a bizarre racket echoing from the mountains. My gaze flicked up and I stumbled back at the sight of a black mass shooting down the mountain. The closer it got, the better I made out the individual bodies that made it up. *Crows?*

The corvids swooped down and attacked. Allies dove for cover. Enemies screamed and the black birds pecked and clawed at them, swarming in impossible numbers until they were overwhelmed. I swallowed hard as I watched these people collapse.

Then, Stella stopped screaming. A moment later, the birds flew off. In the absence of the racket the corvids caused, the silence was deafening, even with a battle still raging behind me. My ears picked up Ryder calming his sister down. *Had she—*

I paused and licked my dry lips. There was no need to question. Stella wasn't the basic nu-human we thought her to be. Sure, she loved nature and all kinds of animals, and she'd befriended some local crows by feeding them, but none of that would have made me think she had some latent power.

My awareness to my surroundings returned and I whirled in time to roll out of the way of a sword swing. *Focus.* I could concern myself with my daughter's power development another time. For now, I needed to eliminate those who sought to stop her from ever realizing her full potential.

Clashing with my opponent, I took him down. Another two swarmed in to replace him, when a black and red dragon head snapped out and crushed them in his jaws.

I smiled at Raikidan. It seemed he'd finally recovered from his heroic boulder slam, though he was in rough shape. Spitting out our dead enemies, he dipped his head and nudged me with his nose. I rested a shaky hand on him, my breath coming in bursts. I'd really overdone it in my rage. My whole body trembled.

Fiery energy burst through the battlefield—the warmth powerful, and intensely familiar, jerking my attention away from Raikidan. *Rashta.* My head snapped up just as she shot into the sky, her black wings spreading wide, golden eyes gleaming and intent on the battle before her. Radiant fire illuminated her in a powerful aura.

A relieved smile spread over my lips. *She's been purified.*

My elation fell. But could she do anything to help? The other gods weren't permitted to interfere, not even Genesis and Zoltan. And if she didn't suffer from any corruption, she'd be bound to Celestial Law in the same way as them.

My eyes fell to Celesta when I heard her giggling. The corrupted goddess' eyes sparkled with a child-like excitement that I couldn't quite understand. Why did Rashta's purification cause this reaction?

When she'd lashed out at Zion, she more or less gloated that Rashta's state was the fault of her own inexperience. I'd gotten the impression she thought Rashta deserved this punishment.

Maybe the timeline goddess' unhinged nature was causing her to react weirdly to the other gods' ability to fix Rashta. It was honestly hard to say, because there was nothing predictable about this unstable woman.

"Kir." Rashta's voice boomed over the battle field, commanding all to turn her way. The cove stilled, all sounds of battle dying off. My heart thumped in my chest. I'd never seen an altercation of this magnitude cease so quickly. "You have brought a great travesty upon Lumaraeon. Kir Alissard, corruptor of spirits and architect of the Crimson Sanctuary. I command you to step forward and face your judgment."

A low chuckle came from the army of our enemies. Then Kir slipped out, his eyes gleaming. "You command me, Rashta? A goddess who bound herself to a mortal soul out of sheer ignorance? The judge who failed to protect the people from the other gods' foolish behavior? I don't think so."

Rashta inclined her head, undeterred by the revenant's insults. "You will be judged for your crimes."

He chuckled, far too confident for something to be right. It was clear Rashta was going to enact something potentially similar to what she'd done with Zarda. So why was he confident he was safe?

My gaze slipped to Celesta again and my pulse stalled. Her personality had shifted to that more mature side. The only thing that wasn't typical with that side, her usual malice wasn't there. She genuinely appeared happy, and that was the most unsettling thing about this change in her.

Energy coalesced around the goddess' fingers. *What is she doing?* She couldn't possibly be planning to use her magic on Rashta, could she?

I narrowed my eyes. *No.* She was gathering her energy, but her body wasn't poised to attack. My feet moved before my mind could catch up with what needed to be done. I dug my toes into the blood-stained ground and sprinted toward the goddess.

The energy in Celesta's hand flashed just as I grabbed a hold of her torso for a ballsy tackle, and then swirling color filled my vision.

CHAPTER 16

My senses were thrown into disarray. I didn't know if we were moving, falling, or floating. The bright lights around us hurt my eyes. I tightened my grip around the timeline goddess, afraid to be lost in her magic if I let go.

Then, when I was afraid I'd lose myself, the swirling disappeared. I was unceremoniously deposited onto grassy ground when my arms let go of the corrupted goddess.

I swiveled my head around, taking in our surroundings. We'd come to a small glade in a mountainous forest. A vague sense of familiarity washed over me, though I had no idea where we were.

"Foolish child," Celesta hissed. She was several paces away. Her eerie eyes bored into me. That mature side of her was present, and for once since meeting the goddess, it seemed the strongest side of her, as if she had more control over herself. "What did you think you'd accomplish by doing that? You couldn't stop me from casting my magic."

"I know." I hauled my weary body to my feet. "If you knew me as well as you claim, you'd know I wouldn't let you teleport somewhere unsupervised."

I glanced around some more. "Where did you bring us?"

She sniffed and turned her gaze to our surroundings. "You don't need to worry your pretty head. You can't stop me, and once I accomplish my mission, you won't matter."

A muscle in my neck tightened, but I tried to appear indifferent to her dismissal. "Well, since I'm not going to matter, why not enlighten me? Can't hurt, can it?"

The goddess continued to focus around us, muttering to herself instead of acknowledging me. "Where is she? I couldn't have gotten my timing incorrect."

I drew my favored dagger and readied myself. "What are you planning, Celesta? Tell me, now!"

Her dark eyes flicked to me. "You're such a nuisance. Go back to your time to say goodbye to those who won't exist in a moment."

Won't exist? My grip on my dagger tightened. What did she mean by that? It seemed I wouldn't find out, as the corrupted goddess flung her hand toward me and her eyes glowed with the same light as before when she cast her time spell.

I braced myself for the inevitable push, cursing myself for being too hasty in confronting her, but then nothing happened. Celesta's brow creased and her face twisted as she concentrated harder.

"Why can't I send you back?" she roared.

My eyebrow quirked up. What could stop a goddess of her caliber from using her magic on me?

Her face twisted with fury. "You have a time relic on you, don't you?"

I blinked. *Time relic?* Those were rare. I'd only seen a handful in my life time. But I didn't have a—*Wait.* An image of Naloth messing with my hair surfaced in my memory. He'd specifically touched my hairclip. *Did he turn it into a time relic?*

I lifted my shoulders in a halfhearted shrug, not wanting to draw attention to my hair piece in case she knew how to break it. That was the last thing I wanted. "Maybe you're just losing your touch."

She bared her teeth. "No, you have a time relic on you. I can sense it."

Shit. I should have guessed her domain allowed her to locate such items. "Why would I carry one on me? I don't know what time relics do."

Celesta snorted. "You've had enough contact with that whelp Naloth to learn I can't touch them or anything they're connected to."

I blinked. How was that even possible? I really didn't understand the unusual limitations gods faced. "Well, I suppose I should thank you for telling me that information, given Naloth and I never had long enough contact until today to really get to know one another. He'd only broken the rules a trivial amount up until now."

Her face scrunched, her confusion evident. Seemed she'd done more speculating about me than actually watching.

The expression didn't last long. Her face went slack a moment later and she shifted her gaze behind me. "It doesn't matter. She's almost here, and you won't stop me from completing my goal."

I readied myself again for a fight. "And what makes you say that?"

She chuckled, her eyes twinkling with glee and confidence. "Because even you can't disagree with what I'm about to do."

Before I could demand she explain herself, fast-moving footsteps crunching in leaf litter caught my ears. A moment later, the sound of a woman breathing heavily followed.

I turned just as a woman of light complexion and red hair burst through the trees. Shock coursed down my rigid spine as the woman slid to a halt and stared at us. "Isis?"

17
CHAPTER
(RAIKIDAN)

My chest lurched. One moment I'd seen Eira rushing toward Celesta for some reason, and the next, they were gone.

Silence permeated the air as everyone processed what just happened. Even Rashta, as commanding as she had been a moment ago, hovered in the air, wide eyes set on the spot the two women had once stood.

When my senses returned, fear tore through me. I roared and limped to where Eira had last been. I pressed my nose to the ground and inhaled deep. Bizarre smells assaulted my senses. I shook my head out of reflex, my mind trying to make sense of the odors. Eira's familiar scent was there, as was Celesta's less familiar one. I also recognized the time smell from being around Zion and those time portals earlier.

I froze. *Time.* Where had Celesta taken Eira?

Kir's insufferable laughter broke the silence. I snapped my focus to him. He had placed his hand on his face as he lost it.

"That stupid woman! Did she really think she could stop Celesta?"

My lips pulled back as he continued to laugh. He knew what happened to my Eira. I lunged for him.

Kir's laugher ceased, but neither alarm nor fear crossed his face as I came for him. He merely smirked, as if I couldn't harm him. How wrong he was.

When I came into range, I shifted, no painless feat with my injuries. I swung my fist toward his gut, and just as it made contact, my armor pulsed with energy, a light glow emanating along with it. My hand collided with his body and he doubled over, choking. I swung my other fist into his jaw. Kir stumbled and I followed him, slamming him two more times before he fell over. I grabbed him by his armor and hauled his top half up, my eyes burning into him. "Where is she?"

Kir chuckled, a lazy grin slipping up half his face. He grabbed my arms, and the sensation of him trying to poison me hit my skin. In an instant, my armor glowed again and the R-poison didn't take.

The revenant's eyebrow lifted and he tried again. My armor flared again. My armor wasn't ordinary, not any more. After my last experience with his poison and not being able to tap into spiritual energy, the shamans went to work on an enchantment that would not only protect me, but allow me to assist Eira with revenants.

"Clever," Kir nearly purred out. "But it doesn't matter. You've all lost."

My grip tightened and I bared my teeth. My voice lowered to a snarl as fury pulsed through me. "Where is she, you motherless cur?"

"It doesn't matter. She's not coming back, and none of you will be around to mourn her." A cackling laugh threw his head back. "None of us will be here when Celesta completes our goal. You were so focused on something so trivial as this moment to *save* your life, you never thought to think ahead. Now, it's too late for you."

He's insane. Nothing he said made any sense. Except this time stuff. I turned my attention to the nearest chromatic dragon, not letting Kir go. The dragon happened to be Naloth, the one dragon I knew would try to save Eira has hard as I would.

Naloth's eyes were glazed over, a sign he was already at work. "Can you see her?"

His search didn't cease, neither did he answer. Rylar stepped up in his human shape, his attention here in the present instead of hunting. "None of us can find her or Celesta."

My fists tightened on Kir's armor. Fire burned and licked at my throat, demanding I unleash my frustration on the revenant. But I knew better. He still had information I needed. "Why can't you find her?"

"We're dealing with the goddess of timelines. She can stop anyone from finding her, that's how she's evaded recapture. Not even Zion can overpower her domain control."

The muscles in my neck tightened. So we had to just stand here and wait things out? Eira was on her own with an unstable goddess that would wipe her out from existence?

Isis gasped, ripping my attention away. She'd dropped to her knees, her head tipped skyward. Her eyes were wide and her mouth hung agape. Ansur rushed to her side, and when he called her name, she didn't respond.

I dropped Kir and limped her way. Ansur tried to engage with Isis again, yet she still didn't respond. Her eyes flicked back and forth, as if she were dreaming.

Rashta flew over to her and placed a hand on the woman's shoulder. "Isis, speak to us."

"I see her," Isis said, her voice slow and trance-like. "She was there… in the part of my memory… I couldn't recall. When I'd left the temple to sacrifice… myself."

Ansur's grip on her shoulders tightened and he turned his attention to Rashta. "What's going on?"

"I'm… not sure," the goddess said, her brow creased.

Realization dawned on me. I turned back to Naloth, who was still in the timeline search. "I think he does."

Eyes turned to the chromatic, who didn't respond for a few moments. When he did, he chuckled as he shifted to his nu-human form. "Celesta isn't the only resourceful one."

An unusual glow enveloped his eyes as he walked toward Isis. "It just so happened, I foresaw a potential in the timeline before Kir arrived. Not enough to know this would happen, but I'd taken a small precautionary measure that would outwit her."

A precaution? An image of him fixing Eira's hair earlier flashed through my mind's eye. Had he done something to Eira in that moment?

"But what is this about Isis seeing Eira?" Ansur asked. "She's not psychic or a chromatic."

"It's because Celesta jumped to a moment in the main timeline while her soul is now active both in the past and present. Isis' mind went back to the memory on its own because of the subconscious link to the moment they'd both appeared in. And I latched on."

Was he saying Eira influenced the past of her own former life? I scrubbed my face. This time magic didn't make any sense to me. How could your future self influence your past?

The chromatic dragon knelt in front of Isis, cupping her face with his hands. "Isis, keep that memory stable. We're going to use it as an anchor to get the two of them back."

"I will… try," she said in that same unsettling tone.

"I need a few psychics to help bolster my connection with her mind," Naloth said.

Lutha and Lina stepped forward. Seda and Nioush did as well. Given they were descendants of Sela, their power would be the best help. Unsurprisingly, Telar and his sister Avila also joined the circle. As much as I still didn't trust Telar's intentions, I knew his power was something to fear. And I could count on him to save Eira, no matter his personal reasons to do so. And Avila… I didn't know anything about her, but I could admire her insistence to help, even in her weakened condition. It not only showed her commitment and loyalty, but if no one would protest her involvement, it meant she, too, was powerful.

The psychics spaced themselves evenly and then all held their hands up to the people on each side of them. Even without touching each other, from where I stood, I felt the power building between them.

"You're wasting your time!" Kir shouted. "It's too late."

"Shut your mouth," Aria snarled before sending a blade of water at him.

All of Eira's shaman soul-lives jumped in. That would keep him occupied and prevent him from escaping once we foiled their plan.

Rylar slipped into the circle the psychics made and knelt behind Isis, his eyes glowing the same way Naloth's were. "I'll keep the bridge open as long as I can."

Bridge? What in Zion's name are these dragons doing?

Naloth nodded and after a moment of waiting, pressed his forehead against Isis'. "Keep that memory, Isis. I'll be back."

Then in a blink, he was gone. Rylar gripped the woman's shoulders and she mumbled out, "Hurry…"

I took a step forward, confused about the chromatic's sudden disappearance. Two sets of hands grabbed my shoulders, my past soul-lives Madorai and Vesser pulling me back. Understanding registered on their faces, but they would make sure I didn't get too close and screw up our chance to retrieve Eira.

I turned back to the cluster around Isis. *Come back to me, Lazmira.*

18
CHAPTER
(EIRA)

A soft breeze swept through the glade, teasing the grass and rustling the tree leaves. Isis stared at Celesta and me, her breath coming in hard bursts from her run, her golden-ringed green eyes open wide. What was she doing here? How was she here? Did one of the chromatics bring her? But if that were the case, why was she alone? *And why does she look so surprised?*

My eyes took her in. Something about her was different, but I couldn't quite place it. "Isis, what are you doing here?"

The woman's brow creased. "Who are you?"

I paused. What did she mean by that? How could she not know who I was? I blinked slowly, realization coming to me. *Unless…*

"Isis, you must go back," Celesta said, her voice far too kind. I glanced her way, finding her face soft and attempting to be warm and under-standing—as much as it could be with those corrupted eyes of hers.

Isis took a step back, swallowing hard. "W—who are you?"

My gaze flicked to the base of her neck, where her soul glowed. Where I would have seen a dimmed, fractured soul-light, I saw a whole one. That proved it. This wasn't the Isis I knew. Not yet, at least.

"Someone who just wants to help you."

My lip curled at her lie and I stepped in front of Celesta, my dagger poised. "Don't you lie to her."

Celesta's eyes darkened. "Do not get in my way."

She moved around me with unnatural speed and grace. Isis took another step back. Even if she didn't know Celesta's face, and the goddess didn't emit the same aura her non-corrupted counterparts did, like anyone, Isis knew a god when she saw one. "I… I have to go. I have somewhere to be."

"Child, please," Celesta said, her voice still hushed in that soothing tone that didn't fit her. "I'm only trying to help you. You're making a mistake."

My past soul-life hesitated, her eyes darting to the adjacent tree line. "I have to do this. It's the only way…"

The goddess shook her head. "What you're about to do won't achieve the result you're hoping for. It will cause so many more problems. Just go back to the temple and wait things out. I promise, that will achieve the true result you seek."

That's when I heard it. Distant, but familiar. The sounds of battle, but not the one I'd just left. My heart thumped hard in my chest. I now knew where Celesta had brought us. She was trying to stop everything from ever happening. *But why here? Why not stop Isis' parents from finding each other?*

I adjusted the grip on my dagger and lunged for Celesta. It didn't matter why. It was up to me to stop the goddess. Everything I knew and loved hung in the balance. That was why she told me knowing wouldn't matter. Even if I didn't know how altering time affected things, I knew that if this moment didn't happen, my entire existence would cease to be.

My dagger plunged deep into Celesta's side, the goddess not expecting such an attack from me. She screamed and stumbled, her arm flailing until she backhanded me in the face. With a grunt I jumped back, but angled out a swift kick to her gut, sending the goddess crashing to the ground.

"Isis, go!" I shouted, turning my gaze to her. "Do what needs to be done."

The woman hesitated again, but for a different reason this time. "You're… a fellow Birth Heart Guardian. But you're not of the clan. I don't know you."

A knowing smile crossed my lips. "No, not yet you don't."

Celesta groaned and propped herself up on her hands. I kicked her in the face, buying myself more time as she was sent sprawling.

"Isis, you must go," I said again, my eyes firm on her.

"But… am I making the right choice?" she asked, clearly conflicted now because of Celesta. "If this isn't going to do what I think it will—"

"Isis." My words came out calm but commanding. Her back straightened, a flicker in her eyes registering something about me, though it was clear she had yet to interpret what it was. "It is your life. You are the only one who can make choices for it. Do you understand?"

I took a moment to let her process my words before continuing. "No one can tell you the right choice here. Only you can decide that. And when you make that choice, do so with conviction and no regret. Do not waver."

"You don't even know what I'm going to do…" she said, barely above a whisper. Though she said the words, her eyes said otherwise. She was sharp enough to know that these mysterious people she'd never met before now knew more about her plan than anyone else in existence.

I smiled to reassure her. "I don't have to. If you think this is the only way to fix things, then I trust you."

My past soul-life swallowed and then sucked in a steeling breath. Her eyes hardened with determination and she nodded.

I turned away from her to face Celesta, who was now getting to her feet. "Now get going. I'll hold this one off as long as I can."

Isis' only answer was the sound of her feet as she ran off.

"No…" Celesta wailed. "No!"

Her eyes burned into me as she struggled to her feet. "You're ruining everything! Don't you understand I can't do this a second time? This is the only chance I have to fix this wrong."

I readied myself into a fighting stance, knowing full well I couldn't defeat a god. But that wasn't going to stop me from delaying her until it was too late, or help arrived. *If it ever does.* "There was no wrong committed today, Celesta. I don't know what you think you'd accomplish by preventing my soul from fusing with Rashta, but you're wrong if you think changing the past would solve anything."

"You are an ignorant child. You don't know what I've seen. You have no idea how much better this would have been if the others had just listened to me." The goddess sucked in a long, tight breath, more clarity coming to her features. I watched as for the first time, the seeds of corruption slowly disappeared. Neither her face nor her personality shifted, but her eyes focused, though they retained their creepy quality. It was as if her resolve bolstered her true emotions—her true motive—enough to show her real intent.

"All of this could have been prevented," she continued, her voice unusually calm. "You wouldn't have had to suffer. Your friends and loved ones wouldn't have had to suffer." Her face twisted with several types of emotional pain. "All Lumaraeon had to do was give Zion and me a child first."

My face twisted in disbelief. "This is what everything is about? You're throwing a time-altering temper tantrum because Lumaraeon wouldn't give you a baby?"

"Silence!" Celesta barked, her lip curling into a snarl. "Do not act as though my actions are selfish and petty. True, I begged for a child because I felt we so desperately deserved one. We were the first true mixed-race pair. But we were gods, so we didn't count in the eyes of mortals."

Her eyes softened, a wistful smile spreading over her face. "I was so happy, I didn't care about their opinions." Sadness overtook her features. "I was only pained when Lumaraeon told me my womb would remain barren—a side effect of my domain. Did you know chromatic dragons are so rare because of this very issue? Their time magic makes it difficult for them to conceive. Even Zion, as a chromatic elder dragon—he, too, would have had trouble giving me the child we sought, even if my womb could have allowed it."

A chromatic elder dragon? Is that why he's different from the other chromatics? While my knowledge of elder dragons was lacking, I knew it was claimed they were a precursor race of dragon. But now that I knew dragons came from humans, I suspected elder dragons were an offshoot of the dragons still around today that couldn't be sustained, thus they went extinct.

Celesta's lips quivered, and I wasn't sure what to do. I wasn't about to attack her—not while she was sharing something so personal; it helped to keep her distracted from her goal at the same time. But emotional situations… not my strong suit. I didn't know how to comfort her, if I was supposed to at all.

"But then Lumaraeon showed me the mortal pair who was destined to have the child that bridged the two races again. She told me the union would bring the races together again, and more would follow. Half-breeds of all kinds were destined to come into existence."

Her pain morphed into fury. "I was so angry she would allow a mortal to have this child instead of me. She was Lumaraeon, the prime goddess. She could do anything, including give me what I wanted—what I deserved for my faithful service."

Celesta closed her eyes, as if trying to maintain focus. I stood there, unmoving… unwilling to stop the woman from babbling, revealing her pain and what led her to this drastic plan. "Then I saw the timeline. I saw what would happen if a mortal had this beautiful child. You, Eira, can't possibly comprehend the anguish I experienced in that moment."

Her fists clenched. "And Lumaraeon had the audacity to accuse me of lying when I warned her. She brushed away my words as you had, as jealousy."

"And your child would have been treated better?" I tried to keep my tone neutral, more curious in her story than skeptical, but my true feelings still slipped through a bit.

Celesta's eyes flew open and bore into me. "My child would have been loved! I saw it. I searched and searched until I found the timeline that proved how much the mortals would have loved her. Had Lumaraeon listened to me, none of this would have happened." She gestured to the unseen battle behind us somewhere. "That would have never transpired. Isis would have never had to make the choice to sacrifice herself so others would no longer kill each other over her existence. I would have never been branded a traitor—corrupted—and taken from my love."

My face distorted with disbelief. "And yet you aided the very man who is out there right now trying to kill Isis!"

"Because Rashta forced me to!" The time goddess' eyes grew wide in her desperation to get me to understand whatever screwed-up thought process she had going on here. "Rashta's choice to save you fused your souls. Don't you see? I couldn't fix anything until that was undone. Kir was the only way I could achieve that. He drove your lives to the paths I needed them to take."

My jaw clenched. "And what path was that?"

Her face slackened. "You really don't know, do you? How can you see all the signs and still not understand?" She let out a disbelieving huff. "How could you be so ignorant of the very moment you broke the cycle?"

The ground fell from underneath me. *Broke the cycle?* "What… what do you mean I broke the cycle?"

Celesta gazed at me, as if seeing for the first time just how little I really understood of my situation. "Your soul sacrificed herself to stop the pain of others. Life after life, you continued this cycle. You put your life before everyone. You sacrificed it all before your Champion could ever stop you. That left him to mend and care for you if you survived. Until now.

"Your Champion's choice to put his life before yours in the very moment you would have sacrificed yourself for those around you, Eira, is what was needed to free Rashta."

Rashta is free? We broke the rebirth cycle? My head swam. Was that true? Was that why I was having the soul vision? What did that mean when my soul-lives and I were put back together? Would Rashta still be stuck with me until I died, or could she be removed?

Celesta gestured to me, as if that would explain where her words were failing to reach me. "Don't you see? You freed her, which allowed me to come back here to stop the cycle from ever happening. You must stand down, Eira, and let me fix the past. Stop all the pain that followed the moment Rashta fused with your soul. You can stop countless lives from so much suffering if you just step aside."

I closed my eyes and exhaled a long breath. My eyes flew open and I stared her down. "No."

Celesta paused, unsure she'd heard me right. "N–no? Did you just tell me you want history to remain as it is, full of death and pain?"

"Did you not hear the idiocy that just came from your mouth?" I mocked. "Instead of showing the mortals they were wrong and that halflings had a place in life, you helped the one man who started this whole mess! You helped him grow stronger as a revenant. You allowed him to teach others his dark, twisted ways. You allowed him to harm thousands upon thousands of innocent people who had every right to live peaceful, fulfilling lives."

"No!" she shrieked. "I needed a way to fix the cycle you and Rashta caused. Kir was the perfect pawn. I made him believe if he followed my path, I'd eliminate you. He thinks I planned to stop Isis from ever being born. But I don't want that. Even if I had the power to stop her birth, I never wanted to erase that moment. I only wanted to fix the wrong Lumaraeon and Rashta created. After I fixed it, all of those who suffered would have been erased. Their suffering wouldn't exist, and Isis could be the first and only half-breed until the mortals were truly ready."

Her mind was definitely not all there. For a moment, I wondered if the corruption had been a façade. But now I saw it had truly taken hold, born of her emotions. It created a chaotic mind that couldn't truly justify her actions, which didn't quite add up.

I slowly shook my head. "You have no right."

Celesta blinked. "Excuse me?"

"You heard me." I bared my teeth. "You have no right to dictate such things. You may hold dominion over the timelines, but you don't have the right to decide how the timeline goes just because you don't agree with our choices. Those I love have every right to exist right now. Even if they were born because of events you created in your misguided attempts to *fix* past events, they deserve to continue to live the lives they currently have now."

Celesta roared, stomping her feet. The child-like, corrupted side of her was trying to take over. "You're not listening to me!"

"I listened, Celesta. I just don't agree with you."

Fury twisted her face and she lunged. I readied my weapon and met her halfway, slicing my dagger toward her abdomen. The goddess deftly maneuvered out of the way with her uncanny speed, but she wasn't quick enough to stop me from jumping back in front of her. While I wasn't sure if Isis had made it to the battle yet, I promised I'd keep Celesta away. And there was no way I'd allow her to rewrite history, no matter what reason she'd professed to me. She didn't have the right to change what mortals did, just to create what she deemed an ideal world.

The timeline goddess eyed my blade. "That weapon… it shouldn't be able to touch me. No mortal weapon can harm a god." Her eyes narrowed. "That's your time relic, isn't it?"

"Not even close." I flicked the weapon out, willing it to turn into the shape of a falchion. While a longer weapon wasn't ideal for my fighting styles, I was going to need a little more reach if I stood any chance of touching her.

Celesta's eyes focused even more on my weapon. "What do you have there, fractured soul? What is this weapon you carry that I've never seen in the timelines before?"

I chuckled. "Wouldn't you like to know?"

Pivoting quickly, I swung at her. She sucked in a tight breath as she jumped away, but she wasn't a fighter. Celesta moved the wrong way and lined herself up for a well-timed follow up kick to her gut. Air *whooshed* out of her lungs as she stumbled.

Pain crawled through my body and I did my best to hide my wince. While a good hit on my part, I forgot about my injuries and had extended in a way that aggravated them.

Celesta snarled and strafed to the side, her movements almost too quick for me to keep up with. *How is she so fast?* I swung my falchion and missed when she ducked around the swing.

The goddess slipped under my defenses and landed a hard blow to my stomach, following up with a backhanded slap that not only had its place as an insult, but sent me spinning. *Damn, for a non-fighter she knows how to hit hard.*

I righted myself and caught her running for the trees. She seemed to be moving impossibly fast to catch, though. No matter how hard I tried to increase my speed, it was as if I couldn't go any faster.

That was when I noticed how slowly my surroundings were moving. The trees swayed in the wind, but in unnaturally slow motions, the movements elongated. The breeze hit my skin, but in a way I hadn't even noticed it was blowing, even though the trees indicated otherwise. The sound of the grass under my feet even didn't hit my ears right.

Realization dawned on me. She wasn't fast, she was just manipulating time around her. And I had no doubt that if it weren't for my hairclip, I'd be stopped in place completely, unaware she'd moved.

Frustration boiled in my chest. How was I supposed to stop her from getting away? My hand gripped my sword tighter, and even though I didn't think of it, the weapon morphed, changing into a war hammer that looked more like a gavel.

Its weight pulled on my arm, yanking me forward. I lurched and then found myself moving faster. Not enough to break free of her time manipulation, but that apparently didn't apply to the weapon. Despite the spell, the hammer was left unaffected by the time warping, giving me an idea.

Taking a deep breath, I wound up as much strength I could muster and flung the hammer at the goddess. Celesta turned just as the weapon arched down and slammed into her leg. She crashed to the ground, sprawling in an undignified manner.

The world around me returned to its normal pace and I raced to my weapon. I grabbed it just as Celesta was shakily pulling herself to her feet, groaning in a bit of pain.

The goddess' eyes popped when she set her focus on it. "T–that… that…"

I grinned. "You like? It belongs to Rashta."

"How did you get it? I hid it in time to punish her for her foolish mistake."

I gave a halfhearted shrug. Rashta had told me at some point in this last year that it'd gone missing shortly after she fused with my soul. And it wasn't until my current life that it'd been found and somehow ended up on Ryder's workbench to tinker with. Celesta's revelation only pieced together the missing information. "I guess you didn't hide it well enough. It was presented to me as a gift. Not in this form, of course."

"How did you get such a weapon? God weapons are Maker creations. Only they have the ability to alter their creations."

A wicked grin spread across my lips. "Didn't you know, Celesta? I have a Maker for a son."

The words slipped from my lips so easily. In the past, I'd denied all claims and speculations Ryder was a Maker. Sure, he made some crazy things and couldn't ever explain how he created them, but it was so hard to believe he was one after they'd been missing for long.

And yet, the more time went on, the harder it was to deny it. Especially after the scholars caught wind and started taking him on their expeditions as part of his training to get his unique elemental abilities under control—the very abilities he'd had all his life and never told me about until he couldn't hide them anymore.

"There are no Makers," Celesta spat. "Not anymore. I saw to that."

My gut churned, dread creeping through me as those words sunk in. "What do you mean, you saw to it? What did you do, Celesta?"

"They would have gotten in the way. I couldn't allow them to ruin my plans. So I removed them from time."

I stared at her with uncontained horror. How could she do such a horrible thing? "You really are corrupted…"

Celesta let out a wordless shriek of fury, but before she could lunge for me, a body crashed into her. I stared at the familiar nu-human form of a particular chromatic dragon now pinning the goddess to the ground. "Nal?"

He'd come? Someone had finally come to help?

Naloth thrust his hand to me, too far to grab. "Eira, hurry!"

My feet moved before I could think. I reached for him, and Celesta shrieked and thrashed. A moment before I grabbed his outstretched hand, a bright beam of fiery light shot up to the sky in the distance. I paused, my eyes glued to the sight.

"No!" Celesta cried. She shoved Naloth off her and clambered to her feet, trying to run at the same time.

Naloth was quick to recover and grabbed her. "Eira!"

I was in motion again, though my eyes wouldn't tear away from the light. Pride swelled in my chest as I crashed into the time dragon. I'd done it. I'd kept history intact. Isis took my words to heart and stuck to her conviction. All was as it should be.

The light of Rashta merging with my soul was the last thing I saw before swirling color filled my vision for the second time today.

CHAPTER 19

Disorientation hammered my mind, as did the sensation I was falling. This was nothing like when I'd hitched a ride with Celesta. I was more aware of Naloth and Celesta's presence, but it was certainly more difficult to keep myself focused on not letting go of my chromatic dragon and getting lost in the time stream. *How do these time wardens manage to do this all the time and know where they're going?*

The magic assaulting my eyes suddenly disappeared, as did Naloth's presence when I lurched away from him, my grip failing. I tumbled ass over teakettle across blood-stained ground. Raikidan shouted my name, but it wasn't like that was going to help me as the world spun.

The sound of something cracking hit my ears, then I came to a sliding halt, splayed out on my stomach. My breath came in gasps, and my body shook. Violet locks cascaded over my face, catching my attention. *What… how…* Running a shaking hand through my hair, I found something precious missing. My eyes widened and panic shot through me.

I jerked my head up and saw two things: Naloth wrestling with an enraged timeline goddess, and my hairclip resting several feet away from me in two pieces.

Celesta broke free of Naloth's grip and sent him spinning with a strike to the face with the back of her hand. I launched to my feet, blocking out the pain of my exhausted muscles and took off in a full sprint, ignoring my abandoned hairclip.

Weapon miraculously still in hand, I whipped the hammer at her. She didn't expect it, the heavy weapon slamming into her abdomen. Celesta choked and stumbled back, her dark eyes turning to me.

"You…" Her lip pulled back. "You ruined everything!"

I continued my sprint, closing the distance far faster than my normal pace. A part of me guessed I was still under the effects of Naloth's time magic. *Works for me.*

I swung my leg out and nailed Celesta in the side. Using my momentum, I arched low and retrieved my weapon, now transformed into its inert dagger form, just as I needed it to be. Without missing a beat, I made a wide movement with my hands and split the dagger into two pieces.

Celesta gasped when I came at her with more fury than I had before. She struggled to dodge my strikes, my movements still faster than normal. The goddess hissed in frustration, managing to knock my arm away and throw me off balance. But instead of taking the moment to retaliate, she thrust her hand toward someone else. "Enough of that!"

From the corner of my eye, I noticed Rylar flinch back. Realization sunk in. He was using his time magic on me. Not only did that increase my speed and ability to keep up with Celesta, but without my hairclip, I was more vulnerable to the goddess' abilities. And without someone protecting me, I was a goner for sure.

I wouldn't take Raikidan's past soul-life's help for granted. Arching my next attack wider than normal, Celesta was taken by surprise from my quick recovery. She screamed in agony as my blade sunk deep into her side. Following up with a shorter strike, my second dagger sliced across the skin of her belly.

Rage filled the timeline goddess' eyes, and for only a moment I had the ability to realize how careless I'd gotten. Energy flashed off her in a single burst. The world around me slowed, and Celesta yanked herself free, blood spurting out of her wound. She maneuvered around my molasses-slow form, throwing a punch to my exposed back. It took moments longer than it should have for the pain to register, but before I could cough up a painful cry, she struck me again, lower this time.

Again and again she moved and struck, her movements too fast now that she'd overpowered Rylar's ability and slowed me down with her own magic. Each blow registered later than it should, the pain doubling as my senses were overloaded.

Then all at once, the world returned to normal. I choked on the pain slamming into my nerves. My legs gave out and I crashed to the ground.

"You're going to pay for your insolence!" Celesta seethed.

She aimed to slam her heel down on my back as I struggled to my knees, when a bulky form crashed into her, sending her stumbling back. I glanced up weakly to see Raikidan, battered all to hell and looking as bad as I felt, taking a protective stance in front of me. A weak smile tugged at the corner of my lips. *He would.*

Even though it was forbidden for a male dragon to harm a female, Raikidan wasn't going to let someone beat the shit out of me if he had a say in it, even if it was a female god dealing out the punishment.

"You," she growled. "Stay out of this. This is her penance to bear."

"You will not lay another hand on my Lazmira."

My heart skittered and my breath hitched. I wanted to groan and verbally reprimand myself. Why did my brain have to react every time he acted like this? And using my name like that just wasn't fair.

Surprisingly, though, his words gave Celesta pause. Whether it was his actions or her thoughts going to Zion, I couldn't say, but it caused her to pause long enough for the dragon god in question to come up behind her.

Zion wrapped his arms around Celesta, pinning her to him. She gasped and thrashed, to no avail. The dragon god frowned and he spoke in a hushed tone, as if trying to speak only to her. "I hope one day you can forgive me for this, but you've left me no choice, my star lily."

Celesta stilled, her eyes wide. Her lip quivered. "No, please don't."

My gut clenched. I didn't know what he was about to do to her, but the fear causing her voice to shake set my nerves on edge. I knew I wasn't going to like what happened next.

Zion opened his mouth, exposing sharp canine teeth, and then bit down hard on her shoulder by the base of her neck—the spot where mate marks went. Celesta's corrupted eyes popped wide open, her mouth falling open.

My stomach lurched. The forceful nature of this action didn't sit well with me at all. And from the corner of my eye, I could see Rylar and Naloth turning their heads away, faces pained. *What the hell was this god doing that felt so… wrong?*

Celesta's face suddenly went slack, her eyes hooding instead of rolling back, as if she were in a trance of some sort. Her body went limp in Zion's arms and he finally unhinged his mouth. Holding her close, he mumbled something into her ear, too quiet for any of us to hear. Celesta, the most compliant I'd ever seen anyone in a long time, nodded, no emotion to be found in her eyes, as if she were compelled to agree.

Then the two disappeared.

Silence strained the air, until Ayuma broke it. "What the hell was that?"

No one spoke. The only sound to answer her question was Raikidan wordlessly helping me to my feet.

"No, seriously, what did Zion just do?" Ayuma said, not willing to let it go.

Leaning against Raikidan for support, I looked to Naloth and Rylar. "You two know what's up, spill it."

Naloth worked his jaw. "There's a reason dragons are the only species who have the mate voice and mate mark, and it's a history that is darker than any would want to believe now."

He paused a moment, then continued. "The mate mark manifested on its own—an ability to bind your soul to another, for better or worse, for the entirety of your life. We don't know why or how, it just did." He grimaced. "The bond also didn't need the consent of both parties to work. And with a skewed female-to-male ratio, males outnumbering females four to one, not only was it common for males to fight for females, but for males to force the mate bond onto them."

Raina gasped. "That's barbaric!"

He nodded. "That's why the mate voice was created. It might have taken away the ability to choose a mate superficially, but it actually enabled a female's only guarantee of having a choice in the end."

"But… what exactly did Zion do?" I didn't want to ask, but I had to. "They were already mates, according to Arcadia."

Naloth closed his eyes, though he seemed to struggle to continue. Rylar picked up for him. "Zion forced a new mate mark on her. Elder dragons received the mate voice, but their mate marks still acted like the marks of old, before the mate voice altered it. This means he can, for a small amount of time, force his will over Celesta."

My mouth dried out and my grip on Raikidan tightened. While I was glad dragons couldn't do that now, I didn't like the idea that they could have controlled their mate through that mark in the past.

Taking a slow breath, I straightened and turned away. *Doesn't matter. What's done is done.* We'd gotten the answer we'd asked for, and there were still some loose ends that needed to be handled. With Celesta now removed and her plan foiled, that left one last individual to deal with.

Kir stood several yards away, his face slack. Around him, his army faltered. From the looks of it, the battle had come to some sort of cease-fire for some reason while I'd taken my joy ride with Celesta, though our forces remained mingled, as if no one were ready to give an inch in case the signal to resume called.

My daggers firmly gripped in my hands, I stalked toward Kir, attempting to hide a limp brought on by so much abuse to my body. Pain pulsed in my chest, but I ignored it. "It's over, Kir. Accept defeat with what little dignity you still possess."

The revenant's face twisted with rage. "You... insolent wench! Do you understand all the hard work you've just destroyed? Do you know how long I've waited for this moment? You couldn't leave well enough alone and accept the fate you were intended to have! You were never meant to exist. None of you were. You've destroyed the one chance we had to fix this timeline, you foolish child."

I spat on the ground, a bit of blood mixed with saliva. "You're the fool. Celesta had never intended to stop halflings from coming into existence. She played you."

He squinted and growled out, "What are you talking about? She guaranteed she'd fix this timeline."

I nodded. "Yes, she did try to do that, in the way she thought would fix it. And her vision was not the same as yours. She didn't go to kill Isis or stop her parents from meeting. She went back in time to stop Rashta from fusing with our soul. Her intention was only to stop the rebirth process." I grunted. "I doubt you were even aware that she wanted to change time only so she could have birthed the first halfling child."

"That betraying bitch. I knew I should have gone after you sooner, rather than let her control your life." Kir bared his teeth. A blue vein under his ashen skin bulged and the light red glow in his gray eyes intensified until they glowed crimson. "I should have just done this from the start. You could have saved yourself a lot of pain and suffering if you'd just let her rewrite history, half-breed. So many of you and your ignorant supporters could have been spared so much pain."

He chuckled—a deep, sadistic sound, coming from him. "I do thank you for sealing revenants away instead of destroying them. No one thought to make sure Celesta couldn't get to them. Now you're going to find out just what you created by allowing us to build our power for so long."

I paused. The hair on the back of my neck rose, and a prickling sensation crawled up my spine as I picked up energy rolling off him in waves; each one growing more powerful than the first.

Someone behind me gasped. I whirled to find other revenants who had tried to assault the temple earlier, doing the same as Kir. There was something about this energy and the way these unbound spirits were now acting that was eerily familiar.

A lump formed in my throat when the demons started casting glances to each other and the revenants. This new development was making them react in a way I wasn't sure I understood—or more accurately, didn't want to know.

Arcadia's belief that Kir was aiming for ascension to further his twisted goals, regardless of the fact he was dead, may not have been anywhere near close to reality. I felt in my gut that the truth may be even worse somehow.

Shaking off my apprehension, I steeled myself and lunged for Kir. *Whatever they're doing, it needs to be stopped.*

With inhuman speed, Kir dodged my swinging weapon and thrust his sword at me. I sucked in a tight breath when the blade sliced my cheek, my reflexes not quite fast enough. I swiped at him in my side-moving momentum, trying to keep close enough to minimize his ability to use his weapon to the fullest, but he had reacted far too quickly. Not even a longer weapon would have helped me with how fast he moved. *It's like I'm trying to fight Rosa all over again.* Slowing her and Zaedrix down the first time Raikidan and I encountered them had not been a fun experience.

Kir came in for another attack when a sizable chunk of earth flew at him. He repositioned and threw up a wall of earth, jumping away as my soul-lives swarmed in to assist me. Raina summoned roots and other plant matter from the ground, while Nalia shot off more rock chunks. The earth attack was about as successful as the previous one she threw at him, and a sense of déjà vu hit me when Kir maneuvered around Raina's plants with ease.

Goose bumps rose over my arms when the air around me dropped in temperature. Snowflakes swirled around me, forming into hard shards of ice, and then shot at Kir like tiny daggers. A spray of ice stuck in the ground as the revenant ran.

Aria jumped in, flinging blades of water his way, slicing up walls of rock Kir brought out. They didn't completely destroy his barriers, her breath coming heavy. She was doing the best she could with her limited experience fighting, not that I was complaining. *I wouldn't want to be hit by her attacks.*

Sylvia suddenly appeared behind Kir, Atria leaping from her arms, long daggers poised for his kidneys. Kir chuckled and winked out, only to reappear a few feet away. I ground my teeth. *He's toying with us.*

A thin bolt of fire streaked through the air, slamming into our enemy. He hissed and tugged on the object protruding from his chest. It looked like an arrow, but was made entirely of fire—*No, it's got something else in there, too.*

Turning my head, I spotted Isis standing with Nisha and Xenia. Isis nocked another arrow, Nisha holding a batch in her glowing hands. Xenia's eyes flashes a few times, as if tapping deep into her spiritual power. Nisha had mentioned that she was going to create magical arrows. She must have figured out a way to create them, combining three different types of magic. It explained why Kir couldn't remove the projectile.

Isis fired again, her arrow narrowly missing when her uncle managed to duck out of the way. However, it gave Velsara an opening and she rushed in, lobbing fireballs at him. Kir snarled, his body smoking from the direct hits. But still, they didn't stop him.

Of course, we didn't know when to quit.

Isis volleyed more arrows. Velsara and I singed Kir with fire and Raina whipped him with roots. Xenia sliced him with sand when she wasn't channeling for Nisha.

The attacks were more annoyances for him with his speed, but even I could see it taking its toll on the revenant.

Kir put some distance between us and him, his eyes darting around to assess his odds. Whatever he had planned to do with his big reveal, hadn't gone according to his plan, with our souls still being tenacious as ever.

"Get them," Kir snapped, aiming his words to his army.

I ground my teeth. He would be so cowardly as to throw them at us like this.

But the attack never game.

Kir whirled around and glowered at his petrified army. "Is there blood in your ears? I gave you all an order."

Still, none moved, their fear rooting them in place. Without Celesta bolstering them, and me and my soul-lives showing no fear of any of these super-powered revenants, their confidence in winning this fight—for this cause—had plummeted. They still had the numbers over us, but that wasn't the only way to win a war.

"Useless," he muttered. "I should have handled this all myself from the start."

The energy he'd built earlier returned, sending a prickle down my spine. Dark tendrils of… something… leaked from his skin, and the red in his eyes intensified. Then he launched at us, his speed exponentially heightened.

We went on the defensive, making sure he didn't touch us with his hands. Sure, fighting off R-poison would be a cinch given how many of my soul-lives were shamans, but I had an uncomfortable feeling in my gut that this super-powered side of him was more than just a speed upgrade.

My breath came in hard bursts as this dragged out, and the pain in my chest from earlier pulsed again, harder this time. Lina and Lutha also pitched in where they could, but most of their energy was spent. I didn't know what put them in such a state after I'd taken my trip through time, but they looked haggard.

It wasn't until Sylvia pulled a surprising maneuver that we gained the upper hand.

Metal shot from her body and slammed into the super-powered revenant, cutting through his legs and anchoring him to the ground.

No blood gushed out of his wounds, given he wasn't alive, but he cried out in agony nonetheless.

I blinked, unable to process that the woman had pulled such a move. She'd said she had some elemental metal control, but from that display, she had more than she truly understood. My knowledge of metal mastery was limited to what I'd learned through Arnia, but it was enough to know it was no easy element to bend to your will, due to its refined nature.

My stun faded quickly and I launched in, igniting my blades with fire and pumping spiritual energy through my body. Nalia slammed stone into Kir, further pinning him down on the other leg, and Raina followed up by wrapping thick roots around the hardened earth, holding it into place against Kir's elemental-touched abilities.

He thrashed and struggled against his restraints. His body flickered as if he were trying to phase away, but the arrow in his chest pulsed, canceling his escape attempt. My daggers plunged deep into his body, one into his back, the other slicing down behind his clavicle. Kir choked and then screamed when I pumped spiritual energy into him.

He writhed and thrashed, trying to break free. I sucked in a tight breath when his hand swiped at me, those inky tendrils lashing out from his skin. Instinctively I jumped back, and I mentally swore when I yanked my weapons out of my prey.

No longer assaulted by my spiritual energy, he fixed his crimson gaze on me and swiped his hand again, this time earth shooting up from the ground and slamming into me. I choked and hit the ground hard, bouncing and rolling. Pain raked my body, blocking out Raikidan's furious roar.

I pushed myself onto my knees, finding it difficult to breathe. I pressed my hand to my chest, the pulsating sensation intensifying. *The hell?* What was with this feeling?

My head snapped up when my other lives moaned. They, too, clutched their chests. *Oh, shit.* There was no way that was good.

A wicked grin spread across Kir's face, as if he knew exactly what was going on. More power built in him, and soon, his elemental shackles shattered, rock, plant, and metal flying in all directions. He ripped out the arrow in his chest, as well as the two others Isis had sunk into his arm and leg, as if they weren't fused with spiritual energy anymore.

I tried to climb to my feet when pain shot through me. I gasped and fell back down. My whole body spasmed.

Raina, Velsara, and Nalia all dropped to a knee, their faces twisted in pain. My other lives didn't fare any better, collapsing from the pain they experienced, their falls less dignified.

Kir chuckled, his eyes still fixed on me as he slowly approached. "Foolish girls. You overdid it. You stressed your soul too much and now you're paying the consequence. Now I'll get my chance to eradicate you once and for all. And what better way to do it than to re-corrupt your youngest life? Poetic, no?"

I took staggered breaths, the pain too much for me to spit out a retort. He was so twisted.

Through the pain, I heard other footsteps running toward me, but as Kir closed the distance, I knew they wouldn't reach me in time. *Stupid! Stupid! Stupid!* How could I have allowed myself to land in this position? The gods had warned me to be careful, yet I'd gotten careless… overconfident in my abilities.

Kir's boots stopped inches from my face. I tried to summon my spiritual energy, but it fizzled when the energy only intensified my agony. I lifted my gaze, hatred burning through me. I just needed to move—to fight a little more and we could win against him. *We were so close!*

With a cocky grin, Kir reached for me. I sucked a tight breath through my nose, internally screaming at myself to fight the stress of my soul and move my sorry ass.

However, he never reached me. A fist flew out of nowhere and slammed Kir square in the jaw; the revenant yelped and staggered back. My eyes widened, my jaw hinging. The face of the familiar man standing over me sent my mind into a buzz. Tall and muscular, with short dark-brown hair, nicely trimmed facial hair, olive-tan skin, two sets of ears, and chocolate brown eyes—usually warm and caring, now blazing and hard with protective rage that made my heart stutter. "Tannek?"

"Don't you dare touch her, Kir," he snarled.

Kir righted himself. "Foolish boy. You really think you can protect her? You don't have the—"

A glowing fist collided with his face, his form distorting. "We can, and we will."

I blinked at Raikidan, watching him follow up with a second strike, his muscles rippling under his skin. His armor glowed with the enchantment we'd placed on it, allowing him perfect contact with the revenant.

Before Kir could recover, Raikidan struck again, slow but powerful. The intensity of his eyes made my heart skip. Both my past mate and current were here defending me. That just wasn't fair to my already-strained soul.

No, I don't need them to protect me. I struggled to lift even my top half off the ground. I was strong enough to fight for myself. I could defeat Kir. I could—

Tannek knelt in front of me and rested his hand on my shoulder, the touch simple but achingly familiar. "Don't. Between the fighting and time travel, you've stressed your soul to the max."

"No, I can still… fight," I managed through gritted teeth. Pain pulsed in my chest the more I fought.

"Eira, you're going to kill yourself. Please stop and for once in your life just let us protect you."

I clenched my teeth, my chest aching in more ways than one as his plea wrapped through my being. All my life I'd learned to rely on myself. It was the only thing I believed I could count on to ensure I lived. And after Tannek gave his life to protect mine, I promised myself no one else would die for me.

And then Raikidan had to swoop in and pad after me like a lost puppy, teaching me to let others in—let them take some of the burden. But never all of it—I couldn't allow them to take that extra step. Not Ryoko. Not Rylan. Not Raikidan. I couldn't willingly let go and allow someone to step in front of me.

Until now.

Lip trembling, I grasped his hand and nodded. I couldn't do this alone. *My soul-lives* and I couldn't do this alone. Not anymore.

Hot flames burst out over my head. I snapped my gaze up in time to spot Del'karo leaping over my collapsed form, fire snaking up his arms and determination creasing his face. Then my father sprinted past, barreling right into Kir. Something on his arms glowed, and I realized he had somehow obtained enchanted armor.

But he wasn't the only one. Pyralis, also equipped with this armor I thought was unique to Raikidan's situation but apparently wasn't, rammed into Kir, sending the revenant skittering.

"Father…" Velsara mumbled.

Kir scrambled to his feet, his breath coming in bursts as he darted his gaze between the men who'd come to our defense, as well as Raikidan's past soul-lives taking up positions over their mates. While he made his calculations to get through to me and my soul-lives, the shadow at his feet warped. A tall man in black leather with salt-and-pepper hair and an eye patch rose out of it. *Shyden!* His visible golden left eye gleamed in the light of an unusual arrow clutched in his hand.

"Did you really think we'd let you touch our girls?" he hissed in his deep and raspy tones before lodging the arrow into the revenant's back.

Kir howled and thrashed away from my assassin mentor. Shyden disappeared into his shadow before the revenant could retaliate. The spiritual arrow pulsed, jolting his body. Kir cried out again, frantically trying to grab the embedded projectile. But Shyden had even greater skills than me. He knew how to ensure Kir wouldn't be able to pull it out on his own.

One of the Crimson Sanctuary members tried to rush over to assist his leader when a twister of water swept him up and tossed the cultist into a group of his unsuspecting allies.

Gravel crunched at my side. I turned my head to find my mother standing with me. She slammed her weapon into the ground, water swirling around her. More allies advanced, those not caught up with defending against the other revenants, and were determined to protect me and my soul-lives and make sure Kir was dealt with.

I didn't even recognize some of these people. Maybe my past soul-lives did, particularly ones who positioned themselves to defend those lives.

Kir's lip curled, seething hatred flashing in his glowing eyes. He had been so assured in his victory, he hadn't anticipated my allies and friends would have the resolve to face him and his super-powered revenants.

A wogron snarled, and then one with brown fur lunged for him, large claws extended and sharp canines bared. I recognized the clothing. Ryoko had transformed, either by chance or she'd figured out how to take the form at will. Either way, Kir wasn't able to rely on his speed with the arrow lodged in his back, and she sliced into his torso.

Kir cried out and staggered back. This arrow did something to him. I wasn't entirely sure it weakened him, but it did reduce a great deal of the advantage he had over us—and he knew it.

Eyes darting back and forth, Kir weighed his options. He couldn't take us all on, and it was clear his army was too demoralized to finish what they started.

He scowled and reached into a back pocket. "This isn't over."

My heart skipped when he lifted a cylindrical object into the air, and it took my brain a moment too long to realize what it was. Kir pulled a pin and tossed the grenade. Out of reflex, Tannek threw himself on me, and Ryoko swiped at the explosive device to send it back at the revenant, but she wasn't quick enough.

Before it hit the ground, the grenade detonated. A blinding flash of light and an ear-splitting *bang* enveloped the senses of those around me. Tannek's body did little to lessen the blow on me. It took several seconds for my vision to return, but when it did, my eyes couldn't focus. An afterimage of my surroundings sent a splitting headache through my brain, accompanied by the ringing in my ears. What I could see was Kir's cowardly ass running away, his Crimson Sanctuary following suit.

"No," I moaned, trying to move even though Tannek's heavier weight still crushed me.

Tannek clamped a hand on my shoulder, refusing to budge. "Don't move, Eira. You can't fight him."

"He's getting away!" I struggled against my former mate's hold. "Get off me. I need to… stop him."

Tannek refused. Even at the cost of Kir getting away, he wouldn't compromise my safety in this moment. Rage and despair stormed inside me.

Ryoko shook her head and snarled as she tried to lift herself to her feet. She wobbled, and when she went to take a step, her disorientation sent her stumbling. In her place, the Asholta pack charged after the retreating army, as did the demons and other allies not affected by Kir's stun grenade.

Crimson Sanctuary warriors pulled the pins on more grenades— some concussion, others smoke, creating a slowing blanket against the pursuing ground force. Dragons swooped down and took on some of the warriors, their wings allowing them to outfly the blinding smoke. An enormous green dragon, one I was sure was the size of Zion, laid waste to a section of the retreating army with an acid breath. While difficult to see, I was sure I spotted branching horns on him. *Is that another elder dragon?*

I shook my head, trying to clear it. The billowing smoke covered the battlefield, obscuring my sight from my position on the ground. Kir had disappeared behind the shield, and deep down, I knew our forces had failed to prevent his escape.

20
CHAPTER

Breathing in slowly, I sat on my butt, legs crossed and one palm pressed into the dirt. Raikidan crouched next to me holding my other hand, while Tannek knelt behind me, his fingers kneading the tension out of my shoulders. Gina stood in front of me, her glowing hands hovering inches from my body. Normally I'd enjoy the moment of pampering, especially since Raikidan showed no signs of possession with Tannek so close, but I barely noticed any of them, my mind drained and buzzing.

Kir had gotten away. There had been pursuit, including Rashta flying off in search, but I already knew they'd come up empty-handed. Not even captured Crimson Sanctuary members were willing to turn traitor on the revenant they so foolishly followed. Hell, I'd learned more about Zephyr's history as a doctor and his former halfling opposition stance than we'd gotten out of the prisoners.

We came so close to finishing this once and for all, and we failed. *I… failed…* It was my job to finish Kir. It was my responsibility to fix what I'd created many lifetimes ago. And I failed to do so.

Despair and failure plagued me. I could only stare at the sky, running the last moments over and over, trying to find where I could have done it all differently to avoid this terrible mistake.

The glowing around Gina's hands ebbed and then faded. She took a quiet breath before stepping away. "That's all I can do. Rest is what yer soul needs now." Her eyes swept over my other lives and assessed them. Their mates were also glued to their sides. "My healin' took care of yer split souls, too. But if ye are feelin' any extreme discomfort, tell me now."

My soul-lives murmured their lack of need for further treatment. The goddess nodded and turned to the other gods. "Reformin' the soul will have to wait until it recovers."

"How long do you think it will take?" My gaze turned for the first time at the sound of Zion's voice. He had returned and had taken his dragon form again.

Gina clasped her hands in front of her. "Some time. Ma healin' is good, but there's only so much I can do."

Zion exhaled through his nose. Before he could say anything, Zoltan stepped toward him. "Is Celesta better bound this time? Is the Dragon-Phoenix safe for the needed recovery time?"

Zion nodded. "She won't be attempting any escape anytime soon. If we need to, I can refresh the power of the arches once more."

Gina shook her head. "The soul should recover before then."

"You're sure she will recover?" Satria asked.

The healing goddess blinked. "Of course. It's not like ye to question my assessment."

Satria lifted a placating hand. "I didn't mean it to come off that way. I wanted to be sure Kir didn't infect her. We still don't know what he and those revenants were attempting to do."

"That's… not exactly true," a quiet voice said.

The gods turned to the source of the voice. I did as well, concern overpowering my loathing. What had Kir done? Had we not pushed him and his revenants back quickly enough?

A mousy-looking human woman in North Tribe clothes stood nearby. Her shoulders were hunched, as if overwhelmed by all the attention. The woman shuffled her feet, taking a few attempts to speak. "There's… there's an issue… with those who were injected with… R-poison. They…" Her head turned over her shoulder. "We can't… remove the poison."

A chilling sensation crept into my chest. "Then ask Arcadia to do it."

The woman's eyes fell to the ground and she wrung her hands together. "She's trying… but… it's not working…"

My pulse came to a screeching halt. I turned my concerned gaze to Gina. She'd pursed her lips. "Bring me to them."

The North Tribe shaman nodded and gestured for the goddess to follow her. I tried to rise to my feet and follow, but Tannek squeezed my shoulders. "You need to rest."

My eyes cut to him and my lip curled. "I'm capable of walking."

To his credit, he didn't flinch at my harsh tone, no doubt desensitized because of my past shameful behavior. "I'm not saying you can't. But this new situation might be too stressful."

Raikidan squeezed my hand as if to indicate he agreed. While a part of me appreciated their concern, my defiant side was rearing its ugly head. I shrugged them both off and climbed to my feet, noting my chest still pulsed with pain, though it'd ebbed to a dull, persistent ache.

I trailed after the pair, Raikidan and Tannek close behind. Tannek's continued presence should have seemed strange to me, as well as my calm reaction to him being around. I hadn't had any contact with him since I'd been in the tower cell prior to my impeding execution. And that'd been the first time I hadn't gone into an emotional panic experiencing his presence in any way from grief. I was sure that under different circumstances, I'd be struggling with him being here. But right now, he and Raikidan both were exactly what I needed to get through whatever shit-show today still had planned to throw at me. I didn't have the capacity to handle any more without them to lean on—the two men I'd ever learned to depend on for anything.

The shaman woman pushed through a gathering of other shamans and came to a stop by a man lying on the ground. Arcadia crouched next to him, her hand grasping his arm. A blackish-purple mark crawled over his skin, the telltale sign of R-poison, but there was something… not normal about it. It was in the way the infected areas pulsed, as if there was more life than decay in the toxin.

Gina rushed to his side and began her attempt to heal him where Arcadia couldn't. I watched on, unease crawling through me. There was just something not right about this affliction. And something… familiar.

My unease only grew when Gina ceased her healing attempt and shook her head. "I can't heal him. I don't know what this is."

"I don't, either," Arcadia said.

I swallowed hard when the mousy woman spoke up again. "Um… there's something more you should… know."

She turned and the crowd parted to reveal a spirit sitting on the ground, propped up by a shaman. Her arm and neck were also exhibiting the signs of this poison. "The living aren't the only ones affected."

My stomach dropped, as did the feeling of the world falling from under me. R-poison was lethal for the living, but it had no effect on spirits.

At the sight of Gina and Arcadia exchanging concerned glances, my blood ran cold. I didn't need the ability to read minds. It was clear, this wasn't the standard R-poison we were used to.

The flapping of wings caught my ears. I spun around. Rashta descended, the demons and dragons who had pursued the Crimson Sanctuary with the goddess not far behind her.

"I'm afraid Kir has managed to escape," she said, her words not in the least surprising. "I know it's not news you wanted to hear, but it seems the damaged he sustained wasn't enough to"—her words stopped when she noticed the mood—"Something happened while we were gone."

I merely gestured with my eyes, unable to find the ability to articulate the situation none of us really understood. The winged goddess ran to the man the other two surrounded. And to my surprise, Zaedrix approached the infected spirit. The other demons gathered closer, all of them exchanging glances, something unspoken passing between them. Xithoz and Nemora watched on, their expressions grim. *What do they know?*

My feet moved toward Zaedrix before I could process what I was doing. I stopped behind the incubus, gazing down at him. He didn't touch the spirit, but his eyes critically examined the unfortunate soul.

"Gina says she doesn't know what this affliction is," I told him. "Neither does Arcadia."

"She said that, did she?" he mumbled. He didn't take his eyes off the spirit, but there was a slight disbelieving tone to his words.

"But you demons seem to."

"We do." The demon's eyes narrowed. "And that means your goddess lied."

I tilted my head. What did he mean by that? I shifted my attention to Arcadia, who was now standing. While she rested her arm over the hilts of her swords with a relaxed posture, I noticed the tightness in her eyes.

"Tell them, spirit speaker." Zaedrix turned to the goddess, his teeth clenched. "Tell them how my kind came into existence because of your incompetence. Tell them how you condemned us because you refused to fix your mistake."

His golden eyes gleamed with malice as he stood to his full height. "Tell them how your newest mistake is repeating the last."

Energy buzzed through the onlookers. I stared at Arcadia, hardly able to comprehend Zaedrix's accusation. "What is he talking about?"

The goddess' hands clenched and it almost appeared as if she was about to refuse to answer, but then she did. "The spiritual plane as mortals and spirits know it today was not my first creation attempt. I made one before it, and made a grave miscalculation."

Nemora snarled. "Miscalculation? Don't you dare dismiss what you did as something so trivial!"

Arcadia's jaw flexed, though her eyes refused to meet any of the demons'. All this time I'd thought her attitude toward them was because they were beings of dark creation from some unknown place. But now I saw it was more than that. "Explain, Arcadia."

A mortal ordering a god around was ballzy, but that was just the kind of mortal I was. She couldn't evade this. Either we heard it from her mouth, or the demons would reveal her great sin.

Arcadia took a deep breath. "In my attempt to mirror the living plane, I miscalculated the distortion needed and created it incorrectly. This plane was full of chaos and unfit for a spirit to survive on. Unfortunately, I also accidentally sealed many souls and living who were assisting me on this new plane."

"We worshiped you," Zaedrix said, his voice low and growling. "We devoted ourselves to you in both life and death, and you betrayed that loyalty by abandoning us!"

My eyes widened. She didn't… she didn't just leave them there… But the twist in her expression confirmed the incubus' words. "You… you didn't pull them out of there?"

The goddess clenched her fists. "I tried. But I wasn't able to undo the binding because of the amount of distortion. Not then, at least.

It took time to learn where I'd gone wrong. I thought they all would have been destroyed by the chaos, yet I still checked on them in case I was wrong. They were easy to locate, much to my surprise, but it was too late. The plane's distortion had warped all the trapped souls, changing them into what they are now."

"And you still left them there…"

Her eyes blazed. "I couldn't allow what they became to enter Lumaraeon!"

My fingers curled. "No, you just couldn't face what you'd done, so you tried to hide the truth."

Now I knew what Shiva meant by "learning the truth." She, like the rest of us, had been told lie after lie about demons, until she somehow became enlightened and gave up her hunting ways, because she knew killing them in cold blood was wrong.

From the horrified looks on the other gods' faces, Arcadia had done a damned fine job of hiding that truth, even now. "And you succeeded until someone made contact and found a way to summon them back."

Arcadia took a step toward me. "It was my job to protect Lumaraeon and all those who inhabit her. I did not make my choice lightly, so do not throw such ignorant accusations at me."

Zaedrix positioned himself in front of me, as if to use his body as a shield against the goddess. He didn't speak, but his silence was a message in itself.

"What does this all have to do with the afflicted?" Tla'lli asked.

My jaw flexed. The words nearly lodged in my throat. "Because it's not R-poison injected into them. It's demonic energy, right, Zaedrix?"

He nodded. "This is the process of demonic transformation."

I'd come to the realization rather quickly. It was why the demons were able to identify the affliction so easily.

Raina stepped forward, horrified eyes set on Arcadia. "Tell me they're misinformed. Tell me the revenants you promised to purify have not become demons."

"They're not demons!" Arcadia snapped. "And I did as I vowed. Many of the revenants we sealed away had successfully gone through the purification process and moved on."

"And yet, there were even more who remained locked away," I said. "You abandoned them to this separate plane just as you did the first time."

"There is no distortion in that plane! They are not demons."

"No, but they're becoming them." There was no doubt in my words.

"No they're not." The spiritual goddess was not going to relent. She would continue to refuse to see the truth in front of her. Her pride knew no bounds.

I had once believed she was a goddess who wasn't as easily swayed by such things. But that was just blind ignorance on my part. The signs were there. Whenever I asked questions she didn't like, her demeanor would change. And today, she'd gotten far too testy with my own revelations.

Instead of arguing, I turned to the demons. "Is there a way to stop this?"

Rosa shook her head. "No. Once you accept the transformation, it cannot be stopped. This was iterated to me several times when I made my choice to become a demon."

"But they didn't accept it, it was forced onto them," Isis said.

The succubus nodded. "That is the perplexing part. We can't force the transformation on anyone."

"So, you're saying we're dealing with an entirely different breed of potential demons," Nalia said.

"An even worse breed," Nemora said. "We demons rely on souls because of the way we were created. Being away from our sealed realm requires our own souls to be powered. Even if one of our kind goes on a killing spree and enjoys the thrill of it, they will consume all the souls. There is no going back to the realm we were sealed in, so if we do not feed, we die."

Her eyes turned to Rosa and then to the incubus who had conversed with us earlier when we'd checked in on Talon. "And those who were created by us here in Lumaraeon, they are under the same constraints as those who originated from our plane."

"But Kir and the revenants aren't like that," I said, understanding what she was getting at. "They don't need to feed because they weren't sealed in the same way. Celesta was easily able to break them out. And with them able to force demonic conversion on the unwilling, there is nothing stopping them from wreaking havoc across the land."

Silence blanketed the cove. No one knew how to react to the revelation. How did one fight a being that had the powers of a demon and revenant? How did we protect ourselves from such a fate?

"So, there's nothing we can do for the afflicted?" Raina hedged. "We just have to watch as the living become demons, and the dead… what, become something akin to the monstrosity Kir has become?"

"They will undergo the same transformation." Zaedrix gestured to the infected spirit. "With your current soul sight, you can see it. The soul is being called to their spirit."

My eyes flicked to the woman. As he said, a slight glow at the base of her neck had formed. It was weak, even more so than my split soul, but if he was right, that wouldn't be the case for much longer.

"When the soul and spirit merge, the demonic conversion will commence. The same will happen to the living. When the power kills them, their soul and spirit will transform."

I bit the inside of my cheek. It was all making sense now. Revenants didn't separate from their souls. It was part of their refusal to move on. That's why I wasn't surprised to see a soul within them, twisted as it may have been. And since demons also retained their souls after their transformation, it wasn't hard to see how a revenant could warp into one if they fought the pull to rest long enough.

Of course, all this knowledge of what was going on didn't help us figure out how to stop it.

My attention snapped to Raikidan when he muttered something and then rushed to the exposed Birth Heart. One of her branches had been snapped when the temple collapsed, but otherwise she appeared okay. *So why—* My pulse sped up, remembering the revenants had attacked those not combat trained after their ordeal with the temple collapse. Were they okay? Had the revenants gotten any of them? I hadn't thought to check how many had been afflicted.

And that was when I noticed how open the temple had become in the collapse and fighting. Even where I stood, I could see easily inside. Particularly I couldn't look away from the red dragon spirit lying on her side, breathing heavily, with her black dragon mate crouched beside her—Raikidan's reason for running off.

Numbness pricked my fingers and spread through my limbs. No. No, Xephrya wasn't going to become a demon. They hadn't infected her. She was just worn out from protecting the Birth Heart after the collapse…

My eyes darted around, taking in the faces of those unmistakably afflicted with the demonic power. And when I saw two people in particular, the ground dropped from under me.

Me'kunar knelt next to his father, who had been propped up on a jutting rock. Blackish-purple poison crawled over his arm. Lo'shen's chest rose and fell as his soul refilled his body, the glow easily visible to me. Me'kunar turned to me, as if knowing I was watching. Pain and despair constricted his eyes. A knot formed in my throat. This couldn't be happening. He couldn't be infected, too.

My gaze darted to my brothers and sister, all clustered around our sibling, Elgren. Yára looked at me with the same expression Me'kunar had.

Emotions roiled within me, none of which I could pin down to feel singularly. My chest tightened with the tide of feelings crashing against my very being. Breathing became more difficult and my eyes struggled to focus on anything in particular. This couldn't be happening. I couldn't be losing such important people in my life, not after everything we'd gone through.

"Eira." Tannek's voice barely registered in my ears as I fought against my swirling mind. "Eira, you need to remain calm."

I couldn't do that. Picking that state of the tide of emotions was impossible. It was impossible, because this whole situation was my fault.

My fingers threaded into my hair, nails grazing my scalp. If I'd dealt with Kir sooner, none of this would have happened. Had I taken his threat seriously, I would have gone searching for him myself in this last year. Mating rites could have waited. I'd basically thrown that tradition out the window six months in, and yet I'd become complacent.

Muscles in my back and arm twitched. A power deep beneath my feet pulsed and called in a way that caressed me down to my bones. Tannek spoke to me again, but his words were muffled in my emotional spiral. The power beckoned more strongly, and this time tugged at my chest. Unable, or maybe even unwilling to ignore its call, I allowed power to build up in my body. My soul pulsed in warning, trying to remind me of my current state, but I didn't stop.

Heat rose through me, taking away the numbness that had spread. Awareness returned to my mind. Realization came along with it when Rashta, Tannek, Raikidan, and Phyre all shouted my name at once. But it was too late. I'd already summoned the power deep beneath the earth.

Taking a deep breath, I released my grip on my head and shot a hand out away from those gathered. The power I'd called reacted instantly to the shift. A moment later, the ground erupted several hundred yards away, hot magma bursting from the earth.

I took a staggering breath as the power within me died down, though my nerves remained on edge. Not only had I lost myself to my emotional spiral, I'd almost killed everyone without even realizing what I'd been about to do.

Raikidan curled his fingers around my shoulders. "Eira, take a deep breath."

I did my best to comply, my constricted chest making it difficult.

"The Ambassador needs to do more than that. She needs to get her emotions under control. That's no way for her to act." Arcadia's cutting words hit me like a splash of ice water.

"Quiet, Arcadia," Rashta snapped. "This is hard on everyone right now."

Her voice came from behind me, making me more aware of how surrounded I now was. She, Raikidan, and Tannek circled me, while Phyre stood a few feet away, intently assessing me. Even Zaedrix had stepped closer, though his eyes were a mix of concern and unease. I didn't doubt my display had unsettled quite a few. It wasn't every day an elementalist was able to control lava. Not that my ability to tap and willingly control it was something to brag about. But I'd still managed to show how destructive I could be inadvertently. And how easily I could lose control of myself.

"She is still responsible for her emotions and actions," Arcadia said, her tone as cool as before. This time I didn't experience a visceral reaction, my emotions already showing they were equalizing.

Ryoko, now reverted back from her wogron form, stepped forward, her teeth bared. "And you have no room to talk, when this bullshit is your fault to begin with. Not that you could acknowledge and admit such a thing with your inflated ego."

The spirit goddess ignored my friend and walked toward my and Raikidan's time arches.

My brow pulled together. "Where are you going?"

She didn't turn to look at me or even stop. "While we think on how to halt the infection, there is another pressing matter I need to address before it becomes another problem."

Something in my gut twisted from her wording, and my feet moved before I realized I was in motion. The goddess set a course for a cluster of warriors and a black dragon I was quite familiar with. My stomach dropped. She was going to send him and the others back to hell. I wasn't ready for that.

Too many unanswered questions about them swirled in my mind, especially with how they not only aided us in this fight, but upheld their promise and waited without causing trouble. This was their first time feeling the warmth of the light they'd been cut off from for so long, and they were behaving, even knowing they'd have to go back. How could someone in their position truly have deserved their judgment?

Footsteps crunched on loose pebbles behind me. I didn't have to turn to know my soul-lives followed. My soul pulsed with warm acknowledgement. It knew its pieces.

"Your time outside your prison has ended," Arcadia said, her tone neutral. "Enter the portal to hell."

"Wait," I called out.

The goddess turned to me finally, her brow tucked together. "And what reason do I have to stall?"

"Because something doesn't add up, and I expect answers before they take a single step." I paused when my soul pulsed, though not with pain. This time, I sensed strength returning to it, bolstering my resolve to challenge the goddess.

Arcadia, to my surprise, waited for me to continue.

"They helped us. Every single one of them pulled their weight when we needed them most. A few even made sure the least savory souls didn't escape hell in all the chaos. And now, they stand here, observing like the rest of us and not causing anyone trouble or making attempts to flee. Everything we were taught by you gods conflicts with their current behavior."

"And you believe one good deed outweighs the severity of their past deeds?"

My brows pinched together. Was that really how she interpreted my words? Or was she trying to force me to drop the topic?

"Are you stupid, or deflecting?" Ryoko advanced until she stopped by my side, her arms crossed, and aggression and readiness to fight the goddess if needs on clear display. "Laz didn't say anything about erasing their past actions."

Anir chuckled. "You two love to cause such trouble."

Like with Zion, the fact we understood him as if he were speaking clear common was odd. On the spiritual plane, language barriers didn't exist. But we were on the living plane. "We didn't do this to amend past transgressions. We did it because we are and always have been loyal to the Dragon-Phoenix, even if certain choices may be questionable to that claim."

"That's the point Eira is trying to make," Nisha said, coming up on my other side. She rested her hand on the back of my shoulder. "Your supposed transgressions don't fit your sentencing."

Ryoko pointed at one of the hell-bound spirits. "That one there is the only reason I'm not also turning demonic. Someone who is evil wouldn't do that."

Arcadia's face remained impassive as we tried to argue the sentence. My fingers curled. She didn't care what we had to say. What I didn't understand was why? If she thought we were being too emotional about this because of the on incident, why didn't she just offer a clear explanation instead of being quiet? Why did it feel like she was acting out of the ordinary? Or was I being paranoid?

"What exactly did they do that was so horrible to be sentenced to hell?" I asked. "Give me a reason to let this go and not question your behavior."

This time, her eyes narrowed, her suspicion clear. "Question my behavior? In the absence of Rashta, because of the stunt *you* pulled all those millennia ago, I stand in her place of judging souls. You, a mortal, have no place to question me."

I furrowed my brow. I wasn't imagining the attitude she was spitting out. "You sound like Celesta."

Her eyes flashed. "Don't you dare compare me to her."

Black wings flashed in my periphery, and Rashta gracefully glided over to Arcadia. She disregarded personal space and leaned right into the spirit goddess' face. "I advise you watch your attitude, Arcadia. Eira is welcome to make callouts as she sees them. All mortals are. We like to pretend we're infallible, but that isn't reality."

"And it's quite clear you're feeling threatened for some reason," Atria called out.

Arcadia took in a deep breath. *Atria is right.* I wondered if it had something to do with me constantly testing her today. Hell, I had just exposed one of her darker secrets. But that wasn't going to deter me from getting to the bottom of this feeling I had.

It turned in my chest, something different than my healing soul. I wanted to say it was intuition, but this was a distinctive sensation that set it apart—something newer, but somehow just as innate.

"Anir," I said, turning my attention to someone who would give me answers without fuss. "Tell me the exact deal you made with Nazir and what you did with the boon."

The black dragon gazed at me for a moment and then nodded. "I bartered a deal to make me stronger. I used that power to lay waste to the Crimson Sanctuary. My goal was always to protect you. And, even after our argument, I had selfishly hoped you would have reconsidered your choice of Asher over me if I could prove I could protect you from them."

Nisha's fingers dug into my shoulder as he continued. "It was that persistence where I inevitably met my end. I'd destroyed almost two dozen of the Crimson Sanctuary's largest camps before they'd managed to kill me." His gaze burned. "I regret nothing of my choices. Removing so many camps made you safer. Not even my sentencing could make me lament my actions."

"Did you ever harm an innocent life?" I asked.

Anir shook his head. "If I had, I am unaware and it would have never been intentional."

I felt it, his conviction and sincerity. There were no lies on his tongue. Turning to a warrior in armor that made me think of Raina, I stared at him expectantly.

The man removed his helmet, revealing the sharp features of an elf. "I struck a deal to improve my ability to protect Lady Raina. My family had shielded her family for generations. I was not a particularly skilled member of my family. On many occasions, I'd been told to take up a different profession so as not to embarrass either family. Protecting Lady Raina was the only goal I had in life, so I was willing to strike up a deal with Nazir to make me better. I was willing to live that lie as long as I could keep her safe."

I could understand that position. But just like Anir, nothing about his reasoning screamed that he deserved eternal damnation. "And can you say your actions after sealing the pact were of good intent?"

"The intent, yes. But I was a soldier. I can't say all my actions were pure."

That I could empathize with.

I turned to one other warrior, a half-elf from the looks of it. He looked to be from a time with higher technology. "And you?"

"I can't say it was anything altruistic like the other two," he admitted. "I've never met any of your incarnations. It just so happens our goals align, as my pact was formed to protect my family from the Crimson Sanctuary. I did whatever it took to keep them safe."

Though he didn't give details as to how far he'd be willing to go, it couldn't have been any worse than things I'd ever done before. My jaw clenched as I tried to process this. "The three of you said nothing that would warrant a sentencing as harsh as the one you received. None of you did something so corrupt that you were deserving of eternal suffering."

I shifted my attention to Rashta. "When we are separated after my life ends, you should be able to evaluate the souls that were sentenced to hell in your absence. That's what Arcadia told me once. So why is it they didn't get a second sentencing?"

The goddess struggled with words. It was something she didn't want to admit. But Arcadia did. "Because there's a time limit."

I stared at the spirit goddess, unable to believe those words actually came from her mouth. "A time limit?"

"Yes. If your soul lives longer than that time limit, there is nothing Rashta can do."

Fury swelled in my chest. She spoke in such a matter-of-fact tone, like it wasn't a big deal. "So, that's it? They just get stuck in hell because you made the wrong choice and some arbitrary time limit came about while Rashta was fused with me, the sentence can't be revoked?"

"I didn't make a mistake. They made deals that corrupted their souls."

"Did they? Did they really corrupt themselves, or is that your own bias?"

She stared at me, somewhat confused.

"You heard their explanations of their choices and pacts. They did nothing compared to someone like me, who, according to Rosa, has a soul branded as innocent." My fingers curled. "My actions are far from it, even without a pact. So, what would you do about someone like me? When I die, do I break the cycle of rebirth and go to hell for the things I've done, or because I'm fused with Rashta, I get a free pass?"

"You've done nothing wrong."

"Nothing wrong? I murdered innocent people for a tyrant. I slaughtered children gripped in the arms of their mothers begging for their lives." Pain raked my body as my past surfaced. "I felt nothing when I spilled their blood. I never hesitated to execute my orders—regretted nothing, all because I broke and shut down. I detached myself from everything."

My voice cracked, the shame of who I was and relief of letting out this last bit of bottled pain swirling and clashing within me. "For years I walked in darkness, barely surviving but never living—a shell for someone to puppeteer."

"You were a victim."

"I made a choice!"

The goddess flinched.

I knew I was a victim of Zarda's. But that didn't change how I felt about the actions I made. "I chose to shut myself down. I chose to keep living for reasons I never understood, wondering if my life was punishment for a wrong I'd committed in the past. It doesn't matter that someone else pushed me that far, I still chose to jump off that ledge." I clenched my fists. "And if someone else were in my shoes, you would judge them as you have these other souls, wouldn't you?"

Arcadia didn't respond.

"Wouldn't you?" My voice rose, my fury unable to be restrained.

The goddess took a controlled breath. "There's nothing that can be done."

My lip curled. *How dare she!* How dare she think she could just not say the words we all knew, as if ignoring them denied how she would have handled someone in my position in place of Rashta. "Fuck you and your 'there's nothing that can be done.'"

I stalked toward Anir. I had no idea what I could do, but hell if I wouldn't try to figure this out. This situation bothered me deeply for a reason. I saw souls for a reason. Today the ability equalized for a reason. I'd be foolish to ignore all the signs now.

Anir watched me with calculating eyes, but didn't try to reason with me. Either he knew it would be a futile effort to argue, or he wanted to sate his curiosity.

"Can you shift?" I asked when I reached his feet. He was a massive creature. An impressive specimen any female dragon would wish the gods to bless her with as a mate. Between that and his unyielding devotion, I could see why things had gone so wrong between him and Nisha.

Anir thought for a moment. "I will see if it's possible."

He closed his eyes and stilled. A moment passed and then his body warped until he'd taken the shape of a tall elven man of tan complexion with dark facial hair. He ran his hand through his medium-length black hair that had been pulled back on the top section. His blue eyes gleamed. "Looks like it worked."

I agreed, though the jerk was still far too tall. That was the nature of elves. "You'll need to kneel. I'm not as tall as Nisha."

A grin slipped up half his face as he chuckled and did as I asked. "As you wish."

Okay, this is stupid. Even knelt his face nearly came level with mine, if a little shorter. "Next time I'm going to tell you to take a short race form…"

He chuckled, though said nothing more, allowing me to focus. Nisha hovered over my shoulder, and I sensed my other soul-lives gathering. My attention honed in on Anir's soul—a twisted glow, but not like a revenant's or a demon's. It swirled with dark and golden light. *I was right, he's not corrupt.* Not entirely, at least, and I couldn't say how much hell had altered his soul's purity.

I reached out and pressed two fingers against the hollow of his neck. The coldness of his skin seeped through our contact, but it was Anir who shivered, his eyes widening ever so slightly, as if my warmth chased away the darkness he'd walked in for so long.

What am I supposed to do? It wasn't like I could have planned out my next steps.

My head twitched a degree when something nearby cracked; it sounded like wood splitting. I blocked out the distraction to keep focused on Anir's soul. A warm sensation built on his skin, a stark contrast to his temperature as well as my own.

Someone gasped, and just as my head snapped up to find out what was going on, a familiar, warm voice that sent weakness into my limbs spoke. "You're almost there dear, but some guidance is needed still."

My breath caught and I took a step back. A woman glided my way. She had umber skin with pale patches. Dark hair flowed behind her, the strands sparkling like stars, and revealed pointed ears. Crystalline forward-curving horns grew from her head.

A pink and blue dress hugged her curvy figure, the translucent ends flowed in an ethereal wind. Dark red paint covered her smiling lips. Her eyes, glowing and devoid of irises and pupils, still exuded a warmth that accompanied her welcoming posture. *Lumaraeon?*

With each step she took, light flared underneath her, and magical plants sprung to life and then disappeared.

Those she passed in her path toward me collapsed to their knees and either bowed as deeply as possible, or gazed at her with awed reverence, their limbs quivering in the presence of such a pure entity. I couldn't blame them, given my first experience with her had been difficult. And as she walked my way, my legs threatened to buckle underneath me.

Anir bowed his head, his whole body trembling. I couldn't imagine the thoughts swirling in his mind—a soul deemed so corrupt that he only deserved to wallow in the dark and never see her pure light again.

Lumaraeon stopped inches from me. I dipped my head, struggling to fight against the instinct to grovel at her feet. She was here to speak—it'd be rude to do that. "Lumaraeon…"

"I don't have much time with this avatar," she said, her voice just as warm and caressing as before. "But it should be enough to get you through these two tasks."

Two?

Lumaraeon gazed down affectionately at Anir. She reached out and stroked his head. "Don't worry, my dear. I will guide her through this process to ensure a perfect execution. Nothing terrible will befall you this day."

The black dragon blinked and then slowly raised his head to meet her gaze, his eyes filled with questions. I doubted he expected such kindness to come from her. "I'll be free to move on? I'm allowed that?"

The prime goddess continued to smile. "You were never meant this fate. But no one until now could change it. Of course, it won't be an instant change. There will be a binding—your soul to her will. A slow process of purification must be undergone due to your extended time in hell. When Eira deems you ready, your service will be complete and you will move on as you originally should have."

She turned her attention to me. "Ready?"

I swallowed and nodded. I had no idea why this was my task, or even how, but I couldn't find the words to ask questions.

"Good. Place your hand on him as you had before," she instructed.

I took a steadying breath and touched the base of Anir's neck with my fingers.

"Now, concentrate. Feel the power of the soul. Connect with it."

I took a slow breath and closed my eyes. The warmth I felt before from his soul had returned. It crawled up my fingers, caressing my palm as if greeting me. I mentally reached for the soul, wrapping my mind around its existence. I was rewarded with a blooming of warmth through my body, and the sensation of several arms wrapping around me.

"It's time your suffering ends. One last trial awaits you." The words rolled through my mind without thought. Concentrating harder, I forced my will over the soul. There was a moment of resistance—not of the soul, but something dark and hungry. *Hell…*

The power Arcadia had placed in its creation gave it a type of life. Nothing so sentient it could be an entity like Lumaraeon, but something akin to the Eternal Library—which I'd learned was an extension of Imera, goddess of literature and knowledge.

Holding fast to my conviction, I forced my will against hell's grasp. Anir would be free. I would see to it he no longer suffered because of us. Not after what he was willing to sacrifice.

Power built in my chest, my strength bolstering and hell's grasp slipping. Then, a sensation of something breaking, like a taut rope being cut."

"Now, Eira!" Lumaraeon's voice penetrated my mind's focus. "You must think of a binding, something tangible, and force the soul into it. Do so quickly, or you will lose your hold."

Something tangible to bind to? Like what? I wasn't ready for this kind of pressure.

I needed to think of something that wouldn't need to be carried. That'd be too cumbersome. *Something to be worn…* Taking a deep breath, I formed a binding in my mind. The soul responded by twisting, the warmth of its existence pulsing in what felt like glee.

Just as the binding finished forming in my mind, an image of an amaranthine butterfly flashed. Then, stillness came.

Slowly, I opened my eyes. Anir stared up at me, his eyes flashing with various emotions he couldn't articulate. I pulled my fingers away, revealing the collar now wrapped around his neck. At the center, the symbol of the butterfly it'd thought of last minute, the same design incorporated into the Dragon-Phoenix crest, glowed on the neck ornament with the light of his soul. It wasn't the most unique of bindings I could have thought of, but it worked.

"It's done," I said. "Anir, your will is mine to command until you've completed your trial."

Anir reached up and touched the binding collar. He closed his eyes for a moment and then the corner of his lip quirked up into a sly smile. "I will ensure you are pleased."

Raikidan let out a warning snarl his way. I rolled my eyes. "Behave, both of you."

I turned to Lumaraeon, who was smiling, and I swore she was suppressing amusement. "Very good, dear. You performed that perfectly. Now it's time for the other Dragon-Phoenixes to do the same."

My soul-lives exchanged perplexed glances before choosing a hell-soul to attempt a binding on. I watched, careful to understand this process from the outside. When each of my past soul-lives completed the binding, the spirit's soul twisted before my very eyes, taking the form of a collar. Each of the hell-souls received the same binding as Anir. And with each binding, my chest pulsed.

By the time all of my soul-lives had completed their tasks, my chest ached, as if some of the energy I'd recovered in these last few minutes had been depleted.

"Very good," Lumaraeon praised. "Unfortunately, due to the state of your soul, that will be all you can accomplish for today if we are to complete the other more urgent task." She turned her glowing gaze on Arcadia. "You will send the rest to hell, but when Eira has recovered her strength and calls on your assistance to complete this task, you will heed the call. Is that understood?"

The spirit goddess nodded, her expression more subdued than I'd ever seen it. It was as if Lumaraeon's presence had silenced whatever issue Arcadia had before. "Of course. I will guide her as needed."

Lumaraeon's glowing eyes shifted to Rashta. "Do you have any objections to these proceedings?"

Rashta shook her head. "It is your will. I look forward to it coming to pass."

My brow quirked up. *What are they talking about?*

A silent nod was the prime goddess' response before turning her attention to the nearest demon-infected person, an elven individual with androgynous features. Lumaraeon glided over to them and knelt. They reached for her. The prime goddess clasped their hand between hers.

I took careful steps toward them. "Lumaraeon… is there anything we can… do for them?"

She was quiet for a moment. "Yes, there is one thing that can be done."

I crouched beside her, fighting the urge to want to curl up like a child. "What can you do?"

Lumaraeon shook her head. "*I* can't do anything. But…" She lifted her gaze to me. "You have the ability to help them."

My brow pinched together. What could I do? That trick with the hell-souls was new, and I still wasn't clear what I'd done exactly, or even how. The only other things I could do were elemental or spirit-walking based, and neither of those would help.

"I don't want to disappear," the elf said in a shaky voice.

My heart lurched in my chest. That was right, I could do… that…

Lumaraeon hushed them softly and stroked their cheek. "You won't disappear. I'm not asking Eira to rend your soul."

I swallowed. "Then… what are you asking?"

She smiled. "To perform the same task you had on Anir."

I blinked, my brain taking a little too long to try and process what she said. "I'm sorry… what?"

"It seems you haven't quite realized what you did, or even what's going on." The prime goddess chuckled. "That's all right. It's all new to you. This affliction affects spirit and soul, as you know. There is no way to cure it. However, if the soul moves into the rebirth state, the demonic energy cannot follow, effectively purifying the soul."

My lips pressed together. "But, there aren't any gods who have dominion over rebirth, and I still don't know what that has to do with me binding a soul… and I still don't understand why I was able to do that."

Maybe it was all the stress, but I really wasn't getting it. And I had to assume that behind the kind smile she outwardly showed, she was thinking about how much she wanted to smack this stupid child in front of her upside the head.

The glow of Lumaraeon's eyes shimmered, as if showing amusement. "No god can send a soul into rebirth, but you can. That is what you've done to Anir and the other incorrectly judged souls. Once you deem them worthy to move on, they will not go to the spiritual plane. Their souls will enter the rebirth process and they'll start a new life, one where they can prove their soul was worthy of continuing."

My mouth unceremoniously fell open. I could do, what?

"Wait, seriously?" Ryoko said. "Laz can do something the gods can't?"

Lumaraeon gave a knowing smile. "There's a reason Eira is capable of rending a soul when others cannot. And there is a reason she can bind a soul and send it on a path of rebirth." Her gaze shifted to various afflicted souls. "However, time is of the essence, and an extensive explanation will have to wait. What I can say is, this is due to how intimate her soul is with the rebirth process. No soul in existence has experienced rebirth as hers has."

That made some sense, though I still wasn't clear on why I had this ability. Of course, she was right about our time constraints. "So, how do I do this? You said it was the same as Anir, but I'm guessing I don't picture a binding object."

She nodded. "That's correct. The binding for the hell-souls was only a slight alteration, due to the need to disconnect them from hell and heal the damage done during their time sentenced away. These souls, you will only need to make the connection and wish them on."

I took a steady breath and then turned my attention down to the elf. "Are you ready?"

Uncertainty flickered in their eyes. "I suppose… I don't have much choice. I'm not keen… on becoming a demon."

I put on my best brave smile for him. "We'll make sure your family gets the closure they need."

They closed their eyes and took a pained breath. If we could hold this off for them to say their goodbyes, I certainly would. It wasn't like we could arrange a spiritual walk for their family in this situation. "I'm ready, then."

Taking my own slow, steadying breath, I placed my fingers on their throat, over the soul, and closed my eyes. Their soul pulsed with warmth under my touch and then it bloomed just as Anir's soul had.

Latching onto its presence, I caressed the soul, feeling its pain and longing. *"It's okay… the pain will end soon. It's time to move on and try again."*

The soul pulsed in response and then flared before its presence disappeared.

My eyes flew open and I looked down at the elf. They lay in Lumaraeon's arms, unmoving, the color in their face already leaving, as well as the visible corruption that had plagued their life.

Lumaraeon brushed a strand of wayward hair out of their face. "It is done. The soul is on its way to match with a new vessel."

"How long will it take?" I asked, touching my chest when an ache spread through it.

"There is no set time," she said. "A vessel must be prepared, and with such a sudden rebirth process, long before that soul was planned to leave the living plane, it could take… a week… a month… even a few years."

My brow lifted. "Is that considered quick?"

She nodded. "It's not uncommon for souls to take decades or even centuries to prepare for the transition. Preparing a vessel that resonates with the soul isn't easy, especially old souls that have experienced several lives."

That was more complicated than I thought the process was. It seemed so simple on paper.

My gaze shifted to those around us still afflicted. "So, how many can we save before I have to stop like with the hell-souls?"

"I stopped you and your soul-lives because of this task. You will have just enough energy without damaging your soul to help them all. But you mustn't dally. The infection will not cease its spread until their soul is sent on. And there will be a point it is too late and the transformation can't be stopped."

I rose to my feet. Even with sixteen parts of my soul working, this would take a while. There was no time to waste.

21

CHAPTER

My breath came in ragged puffs. The spirit I'd sent off had disappeared, with no body to leave behind. That'd been my seventh soul, my past soul-lives each sending off about the same number so far. We all felt the strain, but there were just a few more souls left to save.

Rising on weak legs, I staggered over to the next victim. Her large red-scaled sides rose and fell with the tides of pain coursing through her.

"Xephrya…" I murmured. Raiden and Raikidan hadn't left her side, and her other family had gathered around her, as well as a new black and red dragon and a blue I'd never seen before.

Even in her pain, her eyes sparkled. "I got them back, don't you worry."

I took in the demonic energy consuming her. It was clear she'd been infected more than the others. I didn't doubt she'd put up a good fight to earn it. I saw what she'd done when the temple fell. She wasn't a dragon I ever wanted to cross in my lifetime.

I reached out and brushed my hand along her scaled neck. "I don't know what to say."

A chuckle rumbled through her. "There's nothing to say, dear. I did everything with conviction. I have no regrets, and I am ready."

Raikidan, Ebon, and the unidentified third mixed-colored dragon sucked in a harsh breaths and Raiden shifted, his eyes flicking through so many emotions that the stoic dragon struggled to express.

I pressed into her under her cheek and spoke in a low tone. "I'll keep them all safe. You have my word."

"That I have no doubts. And know, I am so proud of you."

I bit the inside of my cheek and blinked back the tears bubbling in my eyes. I had to keep it together, for their sakes.

Placing a soft kiss on her scales as my final farewell, I closed my eyes and concentrated. I wasn't near her soul, but the way she lay made it difficult to reach, so I hoped my proximity would be enough.

The soul flickered and then bloomed. Tendrils of warmth wrapped around me, as if to give me one last embrace. I clenched my teeth, the tide of emotions crashing against my psyche. I held her soul against me a little longer than I should have before finally letting go. *It's time. New happiness awaits you.*

The soul caressed me one last time before slipping away. My eyes flew open and I sucked in a tight breath. Xephrya's form stilled and then began to fade.

The most agonizing sound tore through Raiden. I jumped back when he lunged for Xephrya's fading form. The black dragon tried to grab a hold of her, as if he could defy the rebirth process with sheer willpower. But her body faded regardless.

Raiden pressed his head into the ground, his talons gouging the earth. I took a quiet step back. He would have to go through one final grieving process, and I was in no position to ease him through that. I doubted anyone was.

I blinked when Raikidan's tail swept around me. Turning my gaze up, our eyes met—his pained and mournful. I outstretched my arms in invitation and he took it by lowering his head. But to my surprise, instead of pressing his nose into my smaller form, he shifted and pulled me tight into his hard body.

I wrapped my arms around him and nestled my face into his shoulder. Raikidan bent his head into my still-loose hair and inhaled a deep whiff of my scent. Neither of us said anything; it wasn't needed. I was already giving him the best thing for him right now.

He, too, would grieve for some time, but I'd be there to help him through, in any way he needed.

"*Raikidan*," Ebon mumbled.

My faithful dragon inhaled deeply once more and then released me. "Yes… I know. You still have a few more to go, right?"

I swallowed hard. "Yeah."

"I'll go with you for those."

My eyes flicked to his father for a moment. "Are you sure?"

Raikidan nodded. "I should have been with you for this whole ordeal."

I shook my head. "You were exactly where you needed to be. But if you want to be there for the rest of this, I won't say no." *Honestly, it may make this next part easier.* Marginally, but still more than if I were to do it alone.

Entwining our fingers, Raikidan fell into step with me toward the next suffering soul. As we did, feet crunched on the broken-up ground behind me. Turning, I caught Tannek following. My heart thumped in my chest seeing the man I'd loved so long ago.

His posture showed his hesitance, and I understood why. Before, my poor state warranted his assistance. Now, my head was clear enough to process his presence.

But the hurt from seeing him after all this time didn't rise up like either of us expected. Being around him didn't bring back all the painful memories and longing what-ifs. I extended my hand. I just wanted to be near him, as if nothing had separated us.

Tannek hesitated, his eyes flicking to Raikidan. My dragon's jaw flexed and then he nodded. Tannek didn't take this permission for granted. He closed the distance between us in several quick strides and tangled his fingers with mine.

My chest swelled and I tightened my grip on both my holds. I had them both with me. Even though I should have felt awkward, I didn't. I wanted this moment. I was selfish and wanted them both. And in this short moment I had that.

We drew closer to Me'kunar and Lo'shen. A woman had joined them—Me'kunar's sister. A few children, including Panga, Stella, and Sethal clustered in a small group with them. Other scholars and West Tribe shamans had also gathered. An internal battle took over my happy moment, and I had to fight to keep proceeding. This had to be done, and it was only right I did it.

Me'kunar lifted his gaze when he noticed our approach. Somber, pained eyes met mine and I had to swallow the wave of emotions that slammed into me. This wasn't going to be easy.

I slipped from Raikidan's and Tannek's hold, and knelt next to the infected elven man, taking his hands with mine. "What the hell, Lo'shen. Seriously."

He let out a weak chuckle, squeezing my hands. "Those foul spirits had no honor, targeting the children. I wasn't going to stand for it." He coughed. "I thought my healing abilities would do me some good, but…" He closed his eyes and shook his head. "I regret nothing."

"He hit the mean man with a big book, momma!" Stella said, her eyes wide.

"And threw ink in his face," Lo'shen added, pride and mischief glittering in his eyes. "Don't forget that."

I choked. "Well, if that's not the most scholarly attack, I don't know what is."

"I didn't have an entire bookshelf to drop on him," the elven man said.

I shook my head when his daughter gasped and scolded him for thinking about abusing so many books.

Lo'shen winced when the demonic change pulsed. "I'm out of time for more jokes, I'm afraid. My wife won't be happy when she finds out I'm going to be even later for dinner on the spiritual plane. I hope she can forgive me." He smiled weakly. "It would have been nice to see her face again, but another lifetime isn't that long. Gives me something to look forward to."

Stella knelt next to him, frowning. "Do you have to go now?"

My heart clenched even harder. This wasn't the first time she'd seen someone die. Unfortunately she'd been at her mother's side at the time of her passing. I'd hoped she'd never have to see that again. Today was supposed to be a good day. She and the kids should have experienced something special. Instead it'd been full of fear and death. And the worst part, I was needed for such time-sensitive things that I couldn't stop to help her through it all.

Yet, as she sat by Lo'shen's side, I saw the brave little girl we'd been raising. She just wasn't a spirited child who lacked fear of things she should. No, she understood it well. She just didn't let it stop her.

Lo'shen reached up and affectionately patted Stella's cheek. "Yes, dear, I do."

Her lip quivered. "I'm going to miss you."

Stella enjoyed the company of most people of the village. But the scholarly residents were some of her favorites. She loved their stories and the treasures they'd bring back. Lo'shen and Me'kunar especially would involve her at the home front. It was one of her favorite activities. And it made her grow close to them.

"Don't worry. We'll see each other again. I'm sure of it."

"Promise?"

Lo'shen smiled. "I'll bring new stories with me, too."

Stella leaned in and gave him a farewell hug and kiss on the forehead. "Bye, Grandpa."

Shit. I bit my tongue and sucked in a tight breath through my nose, the waves of emotion flooding me. I hadn't realized she felt that strongly.

The biggest smile I'd ever seen on the old elven man's face appeared. "Well, at least one of my kids gave me a grandchild." He shot an accusatory glare at his son and daughter, who both rolled their eyes. Lo'shen then pulled Stella into a tight hug. "Be good for your mother. And keep befriending the crows everywhere you go."

My daughter snuggled into him. "I will…"

He patted her on the back. "Good girl. Now hold your chin up and smile, for a new day doesn't start when the sun rises, but when we do."

Stella sat up, tears streaking her face. She held her head high and put on the bravest face she could muster. My heart lurched in my chest. I wanted nothing more than to reach over and pull her into my arms and take her pain away.

"*Until… morning…* light," she attempted in Elvish, though had to finish in common.

He smiled. "*We sleep under the stars tonight.*"

Stella wiped at her tears, but they tumbled into a full sob. Raikidan swooped around and pulled her into a comforting embrace. He also snagged Crystal, attempting to use her to help our daughter.

Lo'shen gazed at Stella one last moment before turning his eyes to me. He beckoned me closer with his fingers. I complied, slipping my arms around his shoulders and pulling him into my lap.

The elder elf patted my hand when I rested it on his chest. "This is not goodbye forever."

"I know," I said, my voice quiet and hoarse, giving away the emotions

I struggled to hold back. Tears welled in my eyes, and I desperately blinked them away.

His grip tightened. "Promise me, dear… Promise me, no matter what face I take, no matter the name I go by, you'll watch over me."

"Always." The words tumbled out of my mouth before I could think about what I was promising.

"I'll hold you to that." He pushed my hand up to the hollow of his neck. "I'm ready."

But was I? I took a deep breath. It didn't matter. Time wasn't on our side here. Like Stella before me, I placed a soft kiss on his forehead before connecting with his soul. Much like how Xephrya's soul related, his sprang to life at my touch and wrapped around me.

My chest constricted and I bit the inside of my cheek. I caressed his soul, memorizing it the best I could. Throughout this ordeal, I'd come to realize each soul had a different presence. I wanted to be sure I had a better chance at finding him and Xephrya in their new lives when that moment came.

It's time, my dear friend. A new adventure awaits you. Keep learning, and relish new discoveries.

His soul pulsed in a final goodbye before slipping away.

The tears broke free and rolled down my cheeks. Death was painful, but mostly to those who were left behind.

I held Lo'shen's lifeless body close. First Xephrya, and then Lo'shen. It hurt too much to fight back anymore. It wasn't fair. They weren't warriors. They weren't supposed to face the same threats we did. Lo'shen had so much life left in him, and Kir took it all away.

I took a steadying breath, and blinked away the tears. Kir would pay for this.

Tannek, who at some point during my emotional release come up behind me, grasped my shoulders and kneaded his fingers into my tense muscles. I was grateful for his more subtle attempts to calm me down.

No one uttered a word to me as I dried my eyes and returned Lo'shen to his children. Once that task was taken care of, I turned my attention to Stella. She stared at me from her place still in Raikidan's embrace, her cheeks stained with drying tears.

I opened my arms and she immediately broke free and ran for me, leaving Raikidan to keep an eye on the cat. I wrapped her up in my arms and held her close. "Are you okay, sweetie?"

"My heart hurts," she mumbled in my chest.

"I know. Mine too." I pressed my face into her head. "Where are your brothers?"

"Checking on Uncle El. Brother Ryder said he was now sick, too." She sniffed. "Is he going to die, too, Momma?"

I worked my jaw. I wanted to desperately tell her no, that he was okay and she didn't have to feel this pain anymore. But I couldn't. Not even a lie to protect her for a moment would work in this situation.

Someone approached, drawing my attention before I could answer. Isis stood a little ways away, her face showing a perplexing mix of emotions. "There's been a development with your brothers you're going to want to be involved with."

It took me a moment to register the plural use. "Brothers? More than one?"

She nodded. I shot to my feet, Stella still in my arms. My heart raced. "What do you mean? What kind of development?"

She opened her mouth, then closed it. Opened again, and then closed. Finally she jerked her head in the direction of my family. "It's better if you're there."

I didn't have to be told twice to follow, my steps hurried. Were we too late? Had we taken too much time on the others to get to him and those who remained? Or was the demonic energy doing something else to the afflicted?

My pulse quickened at the sight of so many gathered around my family. In particular, there was a high demon presence, including Zaedrix and Talon crouching next to Elgren, and Rosa and Nemora inspecting two of my brothers. In total, five of my brothers who had died prior to today showed signs of affliction, and Elgren was the only current living one to exhibit the same signs. Somehow I'd missed the others in my assessment earlier.

Puzzlement hampered my full instinctive response to panic outright, though, when I noticed Trigon was red in the face, glaring at Elgren, who was returning the look.

"You're being an idiot!" Trigon snarled.

"It's my choice," Elgren said in a much calmer fashion, though his voice had an edge to it. "*Our* choice."

"And it's a stupid one."

Elgren's lip curled. "It's not yours to make, so butt out."

Trigon noticed my presence and shot a pleading stare at me. "Tell them they're being dumb and not go through with it."

"It's not your decision!" Elgren snarled, unable to handle our brother's stubbornness on… whatever they were arguing about.

My concern from earlier was ebbing. No one else around us was panicking, just watching with mixed emotions about the situation I wasn't clued in on yet.

"Tell them, Sis!" Trigon demanded, desperation creeping into his words.

I set Stella on her feet and held up my hands. "Back up. I need to be told what's going on."

Elgren opened his mouth to speak, but Trigon beat him. "He *wants* to become a demon. All six of them do!"

I blinked, not quite sure I'd heard my brother right.

"I'm not being reborn," Elgren said.

I took careful steps over to him, letting the situation sink in properly. By the time I crouched next to Elgren, I had my mind in the right place for this conversation. "Are you sure this is what you want?"

He hesitated, his eyes showing it was from surprise rather than conviction. "You're not going to try to stop me?"

I shook my head, and made sure to shift my attention between him and my other brothers so they understood my stance was for them as well. "I have no right to. If you want to be reborn, I'll make that happen. But if you'd rather become a demon, then I won't try to change your mind. It's your soul. I merely want to make sure you are certain. There's no going back."

Smiling, Elgren grabbed my hand. "I want to protect you. I want to make Kir and his ilk pay for what they've done. I can't do that if I'm sent to be reborn. I don't know how long it'll take for me to obtain a new body. And then there's me growing strong enough to help. Of course, that's if I remember this past and my desire to fix things, which I'm not putting any faith in."

He took a steeling breath. "If I convert into a demon, I can remain helpful. I'll have to get used to my new situation, but I can handle that."

My other afflicted brothers murmured similar statements.

I nodded my understanding. I had no idea what this choice of theirs would do to them. I didn't know if it would damn their soul or if they'd even be the same person in the end. But I'd support their choice.

"I can't believe this…" Trigon murmured. "Why am I the only one who thinks this is a bad idea?" He turned to several of my soul-lives, hoping one disagreed with my stance. "One of you has to think differently, right?"

My past lives shared some glances. Raina spoke up. "We agree with Eira. We don't have the right to force a rebirth on an unwilling soul, and in the end, the choice is theirs."

"Others beyond your brothers are also choosing this path," Atria said. "We must respect the request."

Trigon sucked in a breath and desperately searched for someone to speak out against this choice. He even looked to our parents. Our mother shook her head. "You're passionate and mean well, Trigon, we understand that. But you must step back and respect your brothers' wishes here."

Trigon curled his fingers into a tight fist. For a moment I worried we'd have to get physical with him, but Rhaec and Bone each grabbed one of his shoulders. Our brothers gave him a look I didn't understand, but Trigon did. His shoulders relaxed and his hands fell to his sides. "Okay. I'll let it go."

I hoped he understood that just because no one was trying to force Elgren or our brothers to change their minds, it didn't mean they agreed with the choice. I couldn't even say I approved of the decision, but this wasn't a situation where we had any place telling them how to handle it.

Elgren grabbed his chest and clenched his teeth. The demonic energy coursing through him grew along his skin. Zaedrix tilted his head, assessing my brother. His attention slipped to Rosa, who nodded, my brother supported by her also experiencing pain. "It's begun. There is no changing of minds now."

I looked up when a large presence loomed over us. It was Xithoz. "It's time we take them."

I opened my mouth to question him when he continued. "The transformation isn't pretty. It can also be dangerous for those around, depending on what type of demon they become. And we don't know if they'll become something new, given the nature of their transformation and their mixed-species bloodline."

His eyes swept over his captive audience. "For the safety of everyone involved, we'll take them to our clan and help them through the transition. When they are ready to see you once again, we will call on you."

Solid reasoning. I wanted to find a flaw in it, but that was just me being selfish. I wanted to be there for my brothers. However, I'd also do anything to ensure they had the easiest transformation possible.

Zaedrix and Talon helped Elgren to his feet while other demons helped my other brothers. Talon spoke to Xithoz. "We can use the portals. It'll be safer for everyone."

The bone demon agreed and then his attention shifted beyond us. Turning, I spotted Lumaraeon lounging by her tree. The elderly healing elf woman from earlier lay in her lap. Bliss filled her face, though her weariness was evident. The short time she claimed she had left had run out.

Xithoz stared at the prime goddess, as if waiting for some sort of objection from her. However, Lumaraeon merely smiled at him. "I know what you expect me to say, but you won't hear those words from me. The choices of mortals are theirs."

Lumaraeon lifted her hand, and a small glowing orb appeared in her palm—a soul. It glowed gold, like other pure mortal souls, but this one had swirls of orange. Those around me gasped.

"In time, all uncompromised souls return to me. Even yours."

The bone demon blinked slowly and then dipped his head to her. I couldn't stop a small smile from spreading over my lips. In a time where most beings feared and hated them, even the gods they once adored, their prime goddess still loved them.

Xithoz turned to me. We held each other's gaze for a moment before he grinned as if he saw something, and extended his hand. I took his offer, being mindful of his sharp claws, and rose to my feet. "It was good to battle alongside you, Eira. We'll see each other again."

"I look forward to it. Make sure these new demons behave themselves. My brothers, especially."

Elgren muttered a complaint about me never giving him a break and Xithoz let loose a deep, rumbling laugh. "We'll be sure to make them into fine demons."

I kissed my each of my brothers' cheeks in farewell and watched as they were taken away. Talon organized a portal move, however didn't go with them. I suspected he'd stayed to help with the other part of the battle aftermath.

My eyes swept over the sacred ground. Where lush grass once spread, rocks and gnarled plants broke up the landscape. Fires continued to burn in patches around the battlefield; water from elementalists and still-melting ice pooled in the gouged earth. Bodies littered the blood-stained dirt, many having already been moved for identification and then later, for either burial or cremation.

The gaping hole in the mountain where the Crimson Sanctuary had stormed through loomed over it all, leaving the sacred grounds exposed and less protected.

My eyes hooded. No, that wasn't quite right. My father had even said the mountain had been raised up to protect the place during the War of End. An image came to my mind's eye. The night of my shaman test on the Plane of Between, after it was over, I'd gazed out at the damage that'd sundered such a pristine place. And yet, it hadn't been ruined. Rather, it'd been shaped anew, as the gods utilized the elements used during the test to create something even more spectacular.

My gaze shifted from the old, worn cobblestone of Isis' time, to the protective maze route created by dragons and shamans after her, and then to the open hole that would freely allow entry to anyone.

Lifting my hand, I attached my will to one of the nearby blazes, pulling it to my palm. I stared at the hot flame. This battle hadn't just reshaped the land, but the people here, too. And what better way than to show it than by preserving a part of the old and ushering in the new?

"We're with you," Aria said.

I looked up, realizing my soul-lives had gathered. Our mates had as well, though clearly not in the loop as to what we were sharing through our soul link.

"You're fine to proceed," Tyro called out to us. "Your souls are stable and strong, given you didn't have to expend all of your energy for the rebirth cycles."

Well, if anything was going to stop us, it would have been that. Or the gods, but they didn't seem keen on stepping in. It wasn't like we'd planned to destroy the Birth Heart. And what better way to honor her temple than by making it welcoming and open—something worth protecting to all who saw it.

My soul-lives and I collaborated through the use of Lutha's and Lina's combined psychic powers to ease the burden on them, while also making this a fun secret for all the confused onlookers.

When we'd come to an agreement, Lutha and Lina relayed to our mates their part in the plan. Using them would further reduce the stress on our souls. Raikidan shot me an arched look but didn't try to argue his part. He kissed me on the head before taking to the skies with his other winged soul-lives. Rhaegos slithered below the earth again.

A presence lingered behind me. I canted my head to look at Tannek. He chuckled. "I'm going to make sure you don't overdo it."

I rolled my eyes, making him laugh. I did, of course, appreciate his concern, but my reaction to him felt natural to me. After making peace with his death, it felt right to be so okay interacting with him now. I didn't feel the same level of guilt as I used to, and I had been able to appreciate what we had even more—I could appreciate this last moment with him and be at peace with the wholeness I felt, without the guilt of knowing my heart still belonged to him as much as it belonged to Raikidan. It was big enough for them both.

Raikidan, Anshur, Verrak, and Taiegh swooped down and unleashed hot flames, scorching all remaining plant life in their path. People around us gasped. My father shot me an alarmed look, and I held up a placating hand. He should know to trust me by now.

Once the four fire-breathing dragons had finished their task, they perched on the mountain by the opening, waiting for their next needed moment. It was my and Velsara's turn. We grasped onto the strong infernos and pulled them to us, leaving behind blackened earth.

Taking calming breaths after getting my portion of the flames under control, Velsara and I nodded to our psychic soul-lives and they gave Rhaegos the signal. The earth trembled deep below, then his large body popped out of the ground and then disappeared back in, like a whale breaching the surf. In his wake, the earth churned and softened, swallowing the burnt plant life and blackened topsoil.

Fire was destructive, but it also brought life. In the ashes of nature, they'd act as fertilizer for new growth that would cultivate stronger. And the breaking of the earth filtered out the scars of war and made it easier for the new life to take hold.

Rhaegos breached again, but he wasn't the only one. A second brown dragon popped out of the earth, performing the same movements as Raikidan's soul-life. And then another appeared. I blinked, realizing a little late in the stress of the corrupted souls, I'd completely forgotten about the dragons who had come to our aid.

I took a breath. That could wait until later. If a few helped with this task, it wouldn't be a problem. It was a lot for Rhaegos to do on his own, and Nalia was needed for something else, or she'd help right now, too.

When the dragons had completed their task, the earth stilled and the browns poked their heads above ground, not ready to extract themselves in case they were needed again.

Ryoko laughed to herself. "They look like prairie dogs."

I choked and the gathered crowd roared. To add to the scene, a few of the dragons turned their heads similar to how a prairie dog would.

So as not to be derailed and drag this out any longer, I nodded to my other soul-lives to start the next phase. Nalia rocketed across the ground on rolling earth, pushing the ground out and up in her straight line from the former temple. Hard earth formed behind her in the shape of a cobblestone, and parts of the path sides rose up in high, even increments with a matched pair on the other end of the path.

As she moved, the earth shot out from her across the cove, creating winding gouges that hardened into rocky gullies. While Nalia continued toward the mountain opening, Xenia raised her hands and closed her eyes. Sand flew through the air, forming together into streams of coarse silt and settled into the gullies.

Xanthus and Razeth dove down and exhaled ice into the channels until a thick layer filled it. Aser, Razeth, and Roan were hot on their tails, exhaling a scalding steam onto the ice, melting it in an instant. Aria and Pheydra were next, rushing up some of the outcroppings Nalia created and taking hold of small portions of water. They tossed the liquid up, where Aser, Razeth or Roan dispersed it farther, acting as an artificial rain shower.

With the earth prepared, Raina knelt and connected with the plants. High above, Reve, Zetan, and Vesser began to chant. I didn't know the ancient dragon language they uttered, but Mana had used it in my greenhouse many times to encourage my plants to grow healthier.

I tilted my head when a deeper voice joined in. The chant vibrated deep into my bone. I realized it was the large green dragon I'd spotted earlier during the battle. From his size and branching horns, he was unmistakably a green elder dragon. I blinked when I noticed Mana sitting next to him, and Corliss to her other side. They, too, appeared to be chanting, but their words were drowned out by the elder dragon's overpowering words.

Taking in the sight of both her and this mysterious dragon, I realized why Mana's form was so different from the other dragons I'd seen. She was related to this elder dragon. *Is this her grandfather?*

I tore my attention back to the reconstruction. There would be time for those answers later. My brow rose at the sight of the progress already made.

Lush grass carpeted the ground and beautiful flowers were springing up. The brown dragons had disappeared, but from the rumbling in the distance, I suspected they were aiding Nalia with the entrance. Brooks babbled and converged into a main stream that Aria was channeling down the path toward the temple square, detouring onto offshoots that led to resting areas. She moved like a dancer. It was quite mesmerizing.

Lutha and Lina rose into the air and flew over to the time arches. The gods eyed them carefully, but no one stopped them from lifting the ones created for Ryoko out of the ground. The twins flew off with them until they were near the entrance of the cove.

They positioned the time arches over four hills of earth and then lowered them. The earth shuddered and then split—Nalia's doing—accepting the stone arches. When the stone pillars were secure, my psychic soul-lives returned and hovered in front of the gods. This was the trickiest part of the transformation. Getting our time arches moved.

The gods looked to Zion for direction. His eyes were closed as he contemplated. "I like the look of your plan. Sela and Tyro will move them, and Valena will secure them into the ground. This will ensure no damage comes to them."

The twins dipped their heads in thanks and moved out of the way. The three gods got to work, setting up our time arches in the other mounds Nalia had created.

In the distance something cracked, and then small projectiles flew through the open space toward Sylvia. Lina stopped them before they could strike the woman, and we got a good look at the wooden discs. Sylvia reached out for them, not looking up from the work she had strewn about her. Unlike the rest of us, she didn't have much in the way of elemental capability that could contribute to this transformation. However, enough metal had been used during the battle that she wanted to craft something memorable. No one refused her idea.

More cracking echoed, and then the brown dragons lumbered back into the cove, massive trees in their mouths, their roots still intact and dirt wrapped around them to aid their transition. The dragons picked strategic locations Raina and Nalia had coordinated, as well as some places of their own choosing, it seemed, and tore holes into the ground to plant the trees.

"Who knew oversized prairie dogs also made good landscapers?" Ryoko said.

I bit my lip while my friends laughed. As much as I wanted to join in their merriment, I needed to keep control of this dragon fire. It wasn't easy, and there was a strange life to it that I wasn't used to. I chalked it up to being the first I'd ever harnessed four different dragon fires at the same time.

Nisha chanted her magic spell near me, arcane sigils appearing all across her arms. It would take her and Madorai a bit of time to complete it. How they were able to work on the same spell together, and at such a distance, was beyond my understanding, but I wasn't going to question it. Their contribution would be a great addition to the otherwise natural ones.

More cracks drew my attention to the entrance, where Nalia moved stones to create an intricate archway, the work detailed by Raina's plant abilities, a spectacular display of distance control since she had yet to move.

A breeze blew in from behind me, and on it were petals from the Birth Heart. I turned to see Lumaraeon holding up the broken branch from the great tree. An ethereal new one replaced where it had once grown, and now, in the hands of the prime goddess, the limb began to break apart and scatter into the wind with the tree's blossom petals.

Or, more accurately, they scattered across the cove. The particles landed in the grass, on empty outcroppings, and around the created paths. Then before our very eyes, they sprung up into trees of their own. Smaller than the Birth Heart, but similar in nature.

Lumaraeon smiled, her eyes sparkling. This was her contribution—a sign she approved of the change. And boy, did it add to the landscape.

Nalia was now returning, brown dragons in tow. They walked under the time arches that had been successfully positioned. As she rejoined us in the temple square, stone lanterns sprung up from the ground along the temple path and in the square. Atria, Zalia, Ayuma, Rinneth, and Isis rushed down the line and each inserted their element into the light compartments, making sure to alternate and leave a few blank for Nisha when she and Madorai finished. Nalia also created benches along the paths, in the branched resting areas, and in the temple square.

The mages still weren't ready, so I gave the go-ahead to Nalia to start the process of transforming the altar room for the Birth Heart. We hadn't been sure during the planning when that side of things should be done, as it depended on Nisha and Madorai.

Nalia nodded once and positioned herself in front of what once was the wall of the temple. Taking a controlled breath, she shifted the stones and earth. The broken boulders fused with others. The walls rose and fell, some twisting into tall, intricate pillars, and the rest opening the former cave to be a spacious outdoor temple. The ground flattened and shifted to designed stonework leading all the way up to the Birth Heart, accentuating her large roots and ensuring all those who came to speak with her would have easy access to do so.

Pheydra focused on a pool Nalia created, and concentrated. The ground rumbled and then water sprung forth from the ground, filling the basin. Then my past soul-life connected the natural spring to the other streams, ensuring they'd never run out or go stagnant. I didn't doubt that she, Aria, and the blue dragons had tapped into others as well. I'd overheard about their use during the battle.

Raina was next to contribute by bringing life to the temple. Vines and flowers crawled up the columns and stretched out to the next. Bushes popped out of the ground, as well as other flowering plants. When she finished, she nodded. Now we waited for the arcane spell.

"Not much longer," Lutha sent to us telepathically. *"They're on the last set of incantations. Be ready."*

Nisha warned us that once the incantation completed, events would happen in quick succession. Our timing couldn't be off or it'd fail, and given the state of our soul, it wouldn't be good to attempt again.

I took a strong breath and coaxed the fire in my hand. Its warmth pulsed and then seemingly came to life as tendrils of flame pulled out of the main mass until it curled around me, taking the rough shape of a serpent-like dragon. *Man, this is powerful stuff.* I had barely begun to imagine the form I wanted it to take, and it'd already responded.

Velsara had a similar situation going on for her fire, though hers had taken on wing properties.

"Get ready," Lutha said.

Taking another breath, I readied myself to let this flame dragon go. Xenia swirled snow around her, eyes intent and focused, and Velsara also prepared herself. Pheydra and Aria both pulled water from the stream, the former creating floating balls and the latter swirling the element around her body. Above us, Khalon, Zephyr, Xanthus, Razeth, Aser, and Roan took position in a semi-circle.

Nisha's and Madorai's words became more punctuated, and just before they uttered the last two words, Lutha gave us the signal and elements flew. Xenia's reflexes were insanely quick, her snow transforming from a casual snow swirl to a violent vortex of tiny ice shards hurtling toward the dragons above us. Pheydra and Aria unleashed their element at the same time, and Velsara's flame wasn't far behind, flying from her hands in the same upward direction. The dragons were the next to react, unleashing lightning, scalding steam, and ice breaths.

I was last. My fire pulsed in my hand and flickered wildly, as if I was losing control over its will. I still sensed my domination of the element, so as to not lose the flame when we'd come this far, I pushed it skyward. A moment before the element left my hands, it again pulsed and then changed shape, soaring up in the form of a fiery bird rather than a dragon.

The arcane incantation left the magi's lips, and massive runes flashed over Nisha and Madorai's bodies before vibrant vortexes of energy shot out of them, aimed at the converging power. Magic and elements collided and burst into a shower of power particles.

Gasps and other bewildered and excited sounds came from the crowd as the magics fell from the sky. Sparkling arcane attached to the trees and grass, dripping like water and shining like dew, but never disappearing, while fire, ice, and larger orbs of arcane landed on flowers, taking over their form. Motes of elements and arcane magic hovered in the air, runes encircling them, much like the guardian greeting I knew.

Nisha sucked in a deep breath and then shot off a few more sparks of arcane, lighting the remaining lantern. Sylvia, now completed with her little project, lifted her wood and metal wind chimes. Lina took them with her telekinesis, and hung them from the boughs of trees lining the main temples path. Thin paper charms hung from the chimes, painted in a language I couldn't read, but know were words of welcome to new travelers.

And then my soul-lives and I stilled to take in our work for a moment. It wasn't quite done, but we wanted to see our vision in the life it had taken. Even though we'd come up with the idea, not even our collective minds had prepared for the beauty that lay before us.

My father, in a stunned state, took several steps forward, gazing around. "Lazmira… what did you all… do?"

I grinned. "Father, if you could stay back, we're not finished yet."

He blinked, unable to process my words. Mother rolled her eyes and yanked him back. With him taken care of, I turned to Lutha, Lina, Nalia, and Sylvia. "Ready?"

The twins rose into the air. "We have the permission needed and will begin the move."

Sylvia held up sheets of metals, all with names scrawled across them. "I've got many plaques done, but nowhere close to all we need. There are still names to be added, but any metal elementalist can do that once everyone is accounted for."

"Once Lutha and Lina move some of the bodies, I'll know where to start with the memorial bases," Nalia said. "And where to create extras for when the time comes for the rest of the names to be added."

I nodded. They had it under control, and I had no other input. I wasn't able to do much more than watch now.

"Moving bodies? Memorials?" My father said. "Lazmira, what are you all doing?"

"Patience, Father," I said. "It will make sense shortly."

He let out a resigned sigh and waited, though not for long. My twin soul-lives lifted Riket from where Genesis had laid his body after using her necromantic abilities on it. The dragon's weight was difficult for my soul-lives to lift, but they managed, resting him in between the two closest outcroppings Nalia had created earlier next to the temple path.

Once the chromatic dragon had been set in an aesthetic pose, Lutha and Lina quickly moved to a red dragon, positioning him on the opposite side of the path to Riket. Unprompted, Seda and Nioush jumped in to help, and before I knew it, all psychics present were lending their abilities. At this point, it wasn't hard to understand the goal now.

"Don't forget us," an ethereal voice whispered in my ear. I closed my eyes to feel the presence of the departed. It took time for a spirit to separate from their soul and be able to take a form we could see on the spiritual plane. It was the only reason we had been at a disadvantage when we lost our living numbers.

I turned, seeing shamans already moving. Bodies of the non-dragon fallen were plucked out of the lineup and carried to the temple. Nalia created burial spots for them around rest areas, while other bodies were laid to rest along the temple path. When the earth was pulled over their bodies, a stone figure rose out of the ground in front of each grave, a depiction of the one buried.

With everyone working together, all the dragons were moved, and non-dragons who wished to be buried here were put to rest in record time. Lo'shen had been among them, Me'kunar making the decision on his behalf. While it broke family tradition, and it meant he wasn't buried next to his wife in the family mausoleum, Me'kunar felt it was something his father would want. And there was still the option to erect an appropriate substitute in the family tomb at a later time.

After that decision had been made, it was also decided that the others who had been reborn would receive the same treatment, unless anyone knew of any previously desired burial or cremation plans.

Nalia and Sylvia worked on the final touches with the metal memorial plaques, which, to my surprise, also included several plates naming those who had fought and lived—her way of celebrating those who ensured that today wasn't the dark day Kir had hoped for.

We all stepped back. One final task was left.

I turned my attention to Rylar. He was Raikidan's only soul-life still hovering in the air, the others having taken perch on the surrounding mountains. One nod was all he needed.

Rylar swooped down and exhaled a pale golden… time mist… whatever it was. I still wasn't up to speed on chromatic abilities. What I did understand was this breath he now exhaled would cause time to stop for everything it touched. The plants, the dragons bodies, even the stone walking paths would be preserved forever in time.

More chromatic dragons joined him, accelerating the process in no time at all. When the dragons completed their tasks, they perched on the mountain, holding their heads high, proud of their contribution.

"It's finished," I announced, gazing at the finished result. It'd turned out better than we imagined.

Xenia nodded. "The temple of Lumaraeon is made new."

"And open again to anyone who wishes to commune with her," Isis said, a big smile tugging up her face. "Hope you don't object, Rizgar."

My father chuckled. "A little late for that." His attention flick to Lumaraeon, who gazed around at our work. "And our goddess seems quite pleased, so as long as she is happy, we will adapt as we always do."

My focus fell to the old woman in her arms. Her eyes sparkled with a life I'd not seen, but felt when Seda gave her my sight temporarily at my shaman celebration. *Lumaraeon, is there nothing you can't do?*

"I am the prime goddess." Her words came clear in my mind, startling me. She chuckled and spoke again. *"Would you come to her? It would mean a lot if all of you saw her off."*

I had no objection to the request. However, before I could comply, Ryoko called out, "Hey, Laz? Is that fire supposed to be burning still?"

I looked at her and then shifted my gaze to where she pointed. Tucked behind one of the trees Lumaraeon had grown close to the square, a fire freely burned. My lips pressed into a thin line. I'd noticed a larger-than-expected flame burst out with the magic explosion, but I hadn't realized it had landed in this state. With the chromatic dragons breathing the time stopping breath on it, did that mean this fire was a permanent fixture? I hoped not.

I cocked my head when Stella scurried past me. She hopped on the larger stones of the square, heading straight for the burning flames.

"Stella," I called out. "Stella, stop. Don't go near that."

She slowed, but not because of my command. The young girl approached the fire with caution, eventually crouching and still inching forward.

"Stell—" Raina held up a hand to silence me. I sent a questioning look her way.

"Wait," she said. "I have a feeling I know what's going on. Just wait and see."

I pursed my lips, not a fan of this idea, but I also didn't want to question my older past soul-life.

"Hey, it's okay to come out," Stella said. "You don't have to be scared."

Raikidan left his perch and flew down, shifting to his nu-human form a few feet from Stella. He approached, but she waved him away. "Papa, no. You're gonna scare it."

He stopped and turned a perplexed look to me. I shrugged. Like I had any clue what was going on.

Stella crawled closer to the inferno. "It's okay. You can come out. We won't hurt you."

My back straightened when the fire flickered and then shrunk. Stella scooted closer, until she was nearly on the roots of the tree. The fire continued to die down until it disappeared. Stella gasped, and a moment later, *chirp*, *chirp*. My eyebrow arched. *Is that…*

Stella reached over the tree base and scooped something off the ground. Cupping her hands carefully, she held something tiny close to her and ran back to me. "Momma, momma, look, look!"

She stopped at my feet and opened her hands to reveal the tiny fluff of a bird cradled in her palms. I blinked. The little chick had orange down feathers, except two adult red, orange, and yellow feathers, one on its head and the other a long tail feather. It gazed up with molten eyes and then chirped.

"Is that…" I wasn't sure I could finish the sentence.

Raina squealed with uncharacteristically childish delight. "It's a phoenix!"

I stared at her, too stunned to say anything. I didn't doubt her, given she had raised one of these magnificent birds herself. It'd been claimed she'd cared for the last one in existence, but she confirmed with me that wasn't the case. They were just rare creatures of her time, so people hardly saw them if they hadn't attached themselves to an individual. Though, as far as anyone could confirm now, they hadn't made it through the War of End.

"Are you sure?" Stella asked. "Phoenixes are supposed to be big and majestic. This one is so small."

Raina got herself under control and smiled. "Yes. You have a baby phoenix in your hands. In time, it will grow to be as majestic as all the others that came before it."

Stella's eyes sparkled. "Wow, you mean it?"

My past soul-life nodded. "I raised one myself, and saw him through many rebirth cycles. Trust me, the little one in your hands will be big and strong in no time."

My daughter's mouth fell open. "*You* had a phoenix pet?"

Raina shook her head. "No, not a pet. A companion. Phoenixes are intelligent creatures and would be insulted to be considered pets."

Stella gasped and stumbled out an apology to the small bird. As I watched her, I struggled to understand how the bird came to be.

"Phoenixes are born of dragon fire," Phyre called out. "Most find their first life after a strong battle, such as this one."

That explained the unusual life I felt when containing the fire before the explosion. The mythical bird had already come into being. I had unfortunately stalled that in my ignorance. *I hope I didn't cause it any harm, given the way the fire had been used.*

The chick chirped. *It sounds lively and unharmed, so I shouldn't stress too hard.*

"Stella," Phyre said. "Can we trust you to raise this new phoenix?"

My daughter's eyes went wide as saucers. "Really? You mean it?"

The fire god nodded, his eyes twinkling. I squinted. I trusted that man about as far as I could throw him. *What is he up to, leaving the bird in a little girl's hands?* But when Stella turned to me for my blessing, I couldn't find it in me to deny her. "You've got a lot of responsibilities now. You'd better take them seriously."

A big beaming smile spread across her face. "Thank you, Momma Eira!"

She did an excited little dance, and then rushed over to Me'kunar when he called for her. Seemed he wanted to help her with securing a suitable carrying pouch until we got the creature home. Panga and Sethal joined them, eager to help out.

Something tugged me, and I knew that was Lumaraeon's way of getting me to refocus before it was too late. Despite her being a prime goddess, I was sure she couldn't stop someone from dying just because she wanted it. Otherwise, we'd all live forever.

My soul-lives and I walked toward the goddess and the elderly elf. Those who knew the woman had also gathered. I frowned at the sight of seeing such young children among them. While this woman's death was naturally caused, it hurt knowing these kids were exposed to such things so early.

Velsara rushed ahead, and the old woman's eyes turned to us upon hearing the approach. A bright smile came to her lips, and she greeted my past soul-life with the familiarity I expected. She had told me once that she'd been a child when the last Ambassador was alive.

My soul-lives and I surrounded her. The woman's smile grew, and tears pricked her eyes. "I have lived a blessed life. I've seen so many things, met so many amazing people, and have been given many grandchildren. And even a great-grandchild as of recent. I thought knowing both Ambassador Velsara and Ambassador Eira, along with their Guards"—she winked at me—"was the biggest highlight of my life. And yet, here you all are. So few will have the chance to say they had the pleasure of meeting all the Dragon-Phoenixes."

She turned her gaze out to the meadow. "If it's all right, I'd like to be laid to rest here. I may not have fought, and am coming to the end of my life naturally, rather than because of some pesky revenant, but it would be an honor nonetheless."

"Eh?" Sylvia said. "You, a blind old woman, saved Eira's ass. That takes a lot of balls."

"She's right," Velsara said. "You're deservin' of this choice."

The old elf woman smiled gratefully and pointed out the spot of choice. "There, under that tree."

I turned my head sideways to align my gaze with the tree that had grown horizontally on an outcropping over the main temple path near the entrance.

Velsara laughed. "That's perfect for her, no?"

Even though I didn't know the woman well, I agreed. There was something about her that said there was no better tree.

The elf woman smiled—a dreamy, loose one. "Good, good… I'm going to… rest now…"

Her eyes drifted closed and each breath came slower and slower until her chest stilled. We bowed our heads respectfully before Taiegh swooped down and landed in his nu-human form. He carefully cradled the elder elf in his arms, and with Velsara and Nalia in tow, headed for the tree. Her family followed in a procession behind them.

Lumaraeon rose to her feet with unnaturally liquid grace. The rest of us remained silent, watching as the woman was laid to rest. When the earth was closed over her, Lumaraeon raised her hand and the trunk of the tree above them warped, a familiar shape taking form. She looked out toward the entrance, her arms open in welcome. *Fitting.*

The prime goddess pressed her hand against her chest and closed her eyes, as if feeling the soul returning to her. That's when I noticed something strange. The skin on her hand had shifted. It no longer appeared natural, but a bright light of color, like what dripped from her tree, and her fingertips were missing.

I caught a flutter of color in my periphery, distracting me. Swiveling my head, I caught the sight of a butterfly swarm. But not just any butterfly—the ever elusive Amaranthine. Isis gasped and took several steps toward the fluttering insects, holding her hands hopefully.

Naturally, the swarm spread out, landing on various plants and inviting surfaces, but several fluttered over to Isis, landing on her outstretched hands. The brightest smile I dared say I'd ever seen in my life lit up her face. And in that moment, I realized something. "You're the reason they are associated with our crest."

She nodded. "Cultivating their color, and unintentionally, their species, was a project of mine and my mother's. Nisha and Aria both took on stage names in honor of me."

Nisha and Aria both grinned. *How ironic.* Or was it? Was it my engineering that altered my hair color, or the gods sending a sign? Was it coincidence Raikidan associated butterflies, toxic ones like the Amaranthine at that, with me?

"My time in this avatar is up," Lumaraeon announced, drawing me out of my musing. She turned her attention to Zion. "The rest I leave in your capable hands."

He bowed his head. "I will be sure it's done right."

The goddess nodded. "Also, four."

My brow ticked up. *Four? Four what?* Whatever she meant, Zion understood from the way his head bobbed and he rose to his full height.

"My children," Lumaraeon said, her voice carrying easily. "It was so good to spend time with you. Remember to be good to each other and yourselves. And know that I am proud of each and every one of you."

The prime goddess' form began to dissolve into light, and I called out, "Lumaraeon, wait!"

She turned her gaze to me, though didn't stop her leave. "Yes, dear?"

"Is it true what Celesta said to me? About the cycle being broken?"

People around me gasped and murmured. The only ones not surprised were the gods, including Rashta.

Lumaraeon nodded. "Yes. You are the final Dragon-Phoenix."

I let her words sink in. "How did it happen?"

Celesta had given me her explanation, but I needed Lumaraeon to
confirm the reality.

She smiled. "A new choice. When Isis made her sacrificial decision,
she died in the arms of her mate. Helpless and unable to do save her,
he relied on Rashta to do so. In all subsequent lives, similar choices
were made. Dragon mates attempted to intervene, but they were
always too late. Until Raikidan. By taking that bullet in your place,
in the manner you had attempted to sacrifice yourself, he effectively
broke the vicious cycle your souls were lost in."

"If it's broken, then when Laz's soul is put back together, does
Rashta not go with them?" Ryoko asked.

"No. They are still bound in their usual manner for a while yet."

I pressed my hand to my chest, feeling the beat of my heart against
my ribcage. So this was it then. Whatever happened, our souls would
finally rest and Rashta could resume her position as a free god.

Before our eyes, Lumaraeon's form dissolved into sparkling lumi-
nescent particles and scattered, taking form into different flora and
fauna just as the lights from her tree did before disappearing altogether.

That left us with the other gods, and whatever Zion had planned
for us.

22
CHAPTER

It is time," Zion announced, his voice echoing off the mountains. "The Dragon-Phoenix soul is strong enough to withstand the reforming process. Dragon Phoenixes and Champions, gather together—Rashta as well."

We clustered in the temple square and waited expectantly. Zion gazed at us, but when he didn't speak after several moments had passed, I pressed him. "Well?"

He chuckled. "Patience. I am preparing. The time arches are one-way, that is why I permitted their move. However, I must connect to the power within them to release the binding, though I must do so properly or it could cause your soul damage."

My lips twisted. This was way more complicated than I figured it would be. "Then what? How do we reform if there's no time arch we need to walk through?"

"You just have to kiss your Champion," Rashta said for Zion, allowing him to focus.

My brow spiked. "That's it?"

She nodded. "A kiss was the final act that sealed me into Isis. Therefore, a kiss is needed to reseal."

Zion grumbled, drawing our attention. "Ah yes, *that* issue…"

"Uh… what?"

He composed himself. "Before I can perform this, there is one task that must be done first. That gods-forsaken bond Zarda forced on you and the wolf-boy. It must go."

I tried not to laugh at the exasperation leaking into his words. "Oh, okay. Not complaining about that concept, but I'm curious about why it has to go first, and how you're going to do that."

The god let out a heavy sigh. "That man, in his attempt to create psychic bonds, somehow managed to replicate the mate bond instead."

My heart stopped. *That* was what Rylan and I shared? Well, it certainly… explained a lot.

"Zarda, of course, didn't find out until after, and that was why the project was scrapped. Unfortunately the damage had been done, though far more than if the wolf-boy had been paired with someone else."

I cocked my head. "Why's that?"

"As you were intended to mate with your Champion, a dormant mate bond already existed within you. This forced mate bond latched onto your mind, however could not fully connect. It was why your experience was different from his, and why his was so much stronger than it should have been. A proper bond is far more bearable to experience."

I chewed my lip. "So, when it's removed from me, my body will properly experience my bond with Raikidan?"

Zion nodded. "That is correct."

I sucked in a breath and clapped my hands together. "Great. So, how do you break it?"

"I do not." I opened my mouth to question him, when he continued. "Mate bonds cannot be broken by force. They must break down on their own, and then the two must agree to separate. You two almost achieved this on your own." He sighed. "Until a meddlesome child convinced you to rekindle it."

"Hey!" our Genesis called out. "How was I supposed to know it was a bad thing? And I'll have you know, it saved Rylan's life, thank you."

Zion let out an unhappy growl and Naloth laughed. "He really hates this created bond. He's been ranting and raving about it for eons."

The dragon god narrowed his eyes at the younger dragon. "A gross exaggeration, I can assure you of that. Nevertheless, the bond's removal will happen."

I pursed my lips. "You just said it can't be broken."

He nodded. "Yes, that is correct. However, I can move it to another."

I blinked. He could give it to someone else? *I suppose that's possible… somehow.*

"Rylan, step forward," Zion commanded.

He left the safety of our friends, Ryoko accompanying him. "Well, at least you called me by my name this time."

Ryoko jabbed him in the side. "Don't be like that. It's cute."

Rylan narrowed his eyes at her. "Don't encourage him."

"It also goes with the name I have for her: little wogron girl."

Ryoko smiled. "Aww, I love it. It's adorable."

Zion directed where they should stand. "Thank you for realizing I intended to give this bond to you. Saves me time."

She held up a hand. "Well, if you were going to give this mate bond to someone else, I was going to have to fight you, so I figured it was a good guess I would be chosen… you know, his real mate."

A chuckle rumbled through his chest. "Eira, you will also be needed."

I stepped away from my soul-lives and joined my friends.

Zion assessed us. "Now, the three of you will want to sit. This should be a seamless process, but in some potential instances someone might faint. I wish to reduce any risk of injury."

We quickly found places to sit.

The dragon god lifted a talon and hovered it before me, his eyes beginning to glow. "Good, now hold still."

With a light bump, his claw touched my forehead. An impressive feat, given his size. The bubbly sensation of the bond in the back of my head pulsed, and then slowly disappeared. I closed my eyes, feeling the bond leave, until emptiness was left in its wake. *So… strange.* Even after the bond had broken down, I could still feel a lingering presence. And for a moment, I wondered what it'd be like to start living with it gone—when I remembered I was supposed to be able to feel my bond with Raikidan.

Zion pulled away; something glowing on the tip of his claw went with him. *Is that it?* It was possible the bond had some sort of physical form when a god touched it. He then shifted his talon in front of Ryoko. She closed her eyes for her part, and when Zion touched her forehead, the glow disappeared into her head.

Ryoko sucked in a tight breath through her nose. "This… is a new sensation."

"It will become more bearable when I connect it to your mate properly." The dragon god moved on to Rylan, and touched my friend's forehead only briefly before pulling away. I didn't need to second guess if it worked.

Rylan also sucked in a breath, his eyes dilating. I watched, waiting to see how they'd handle the new experience.

Ryoko giggled and placed a hand on her chest. "This is… I don't know how to describe this."

"It's nothing like I had with Laz," Rylan managed to confirm. "It's stronger, but in a far more subtle way."

I snapped my fingers. "Oh, damn. I was hoping Ryoko would be able to give you emotional whiplash."

Ryoko threw her head back in laughter. Instead of getting irritated with me, Rylan smiled at his mate, unable to hide just how much he enjoyed feeling this. He pulled her into his lap and pressed his forehead to hers, gazing into her eyes. "This feels right. More… whole."

Ryoko's ears twitched and she kicked her legs happily. I pretended to gag. "Get a room."

Ryoko kicked her legs at me in retaliation. Chuckling, I left the two lovebirds and rejoined my soul-lives, though my mind wandered to the fact that my head still felt empty.

"Eira," Zion said. "Your bond will strengthen. It just needs time."

I nodded. I'd do my best to be patient, then. It wasn't a big deal if I didn't feel it like my other lives, but it'd be nice… to feel like I had a proper bond with Raikidan. At the very least, it'd be better on Raikidan. I knew it bothered him that I couldn't feel it like I should. I suspected he wondered if he were to blame in some way. And with my bond with Rylan gone, if mine with Raikidan didn't cultivate like Zion claimed it would, I wasn't sure if that doubt in him would ever disappear.

Zion assessed me and my soul-lives, then nodded. "Yes, everything is now in order. We can proceed with the unification."

Rashta nudged Raikidan with her elbow, and he didn't have to be told twice to approach me. He stared down at me so intently I nearly forgot how to breathe.

Raikidan wrapped his fingers around my hip and pulled me into his hard body, cupping my chin and claiming my lips with his without hesitation. I snaked my arms around his neck and embraced the warm emotions blooming in my chest, sending warmth through my body.

But it wasn't just emotions rushing through me. I could feel each of my soul-lives meeting up with each of Raikidan's and then uniting with my piece of our soul. My soul swelled and felt more whole with each life. Then Rashta's voice laughed inside my head and everything felt right.

Our lips parted, our foreheads pressing against each other, and the words tumbled out of my mouth before I could think. "I love you."

Raikidan's grip on me tightened and crashed his mouth into mine so hard I saw white. My breath left me and I found myself unable to stop myself from kissing him back. My fingers threaded into his hair, locking him close. Raikidan's fingers dug into the skin near my spine, sending a tingling sensation through me. Our tongues wrestled and a hunger I wasn't quite familiar with took over me. All I knew was that I needed him, right then.

"Get a cave, you two!" Corliss called out.

"Yeah, what he said!" Ryoko said.

Laughter erupted all around and I raised a middle finger in a direction I assumed one of them was in. Though, I couldn't be sure why. They were right. This public display wasn't like me at all.

"Savada, stop it," a smooth, deep voice said.

Well, that explains it. I managed to tear my lips away and snapped my attention to the gods nearby, my breath coming out in heavy bursts. The woman, a human, had milky skin, long brown hair that curled in large ringlets, and a figure that would make just about every head turn her way. The man with her, also human, had a lean, athletic build and medium-length black hair that had been tied back at the top. His violet eyes contrasted against his reddish-brown skin.

"What? Why are you blaming me, Rasmus?" Savada held up a hand, the other tucked under her bountiful chest as if to support it. I nearly snorted. As the goddess of sex and seduction, there was no way she wasn't involved in all that.

Rasmus, the god of love and fertility, and Savada's partner, shook his head. "You've meddled enough with them."

She snorted, her deep brown eyes rolling hard. "Can you blame me?" She gestured to Raikidan and me. "They danced around each other so long, I can't help myself." Her gaze shifted to me. "Honestly. You two were so stubborn, I thought I was losing my touch. Which is saying something considering the trouble you, Eira, gave me when it came to Tannek." She laughed. "I thought I was going to have to get craftier than I have in millennia."

A deep grin spread over her plump lips. "If involving my precious little Ryoko wasn't considered as such."

My brow lifted and I turned to Ryoko, whose eyes were wide and she had a finger pointing to herself. "Me?"

Savada chuckled. "Oh, yes. You were instrumental for my plans. And you did so marvelously."

Ryoko's ears drooped. "So, those ideas I had, they weren't mine?"

"Oh, no, dear, on the contrary." Her devious grin from earlier returned. "All those delicious ideas you had were all yours. I just influenced which ones you chose to ensure greater success."

Ryoko held up her hands. "Woo! Everyone heard it here. I was justified in my meddling. A goddess just confirmed it!"

I couldn't help but laugh. Not just because of her reaction, but Rylan's as well. He sighed and shook his head. He'd never been a fan of her meddling, and now she had reason to rub it in his face. *As if Raikidan and I becoming mates in the end wasn't enough of a reason.*

Savada let out a long breath. "Of course, I can't say you two were the most difficult case I've ever had to work." Her eyes cut to Nazir. "There are two on my list that are trying my patience."

He crossed his arms. "Don't look at me like that. I'm not the one causing issues."

Savada turned her eyes back to me and I grunted. "Look, I've made my attempts, too, with her. She's proving to be even more stubborn than me, insisting there's nothing going on when it's obvious there is."

Given the way they were talking so freely, I saw no reason to hold my tongue on the matter. If it was that obvious and open with the gods, then Rashta was the only one causing the holdup.

Ryoko gasped. "Hold the communicator! Are you saying the Goddess of Judgment and God of Death have a semi-secret thing going on?" Ryoko's golden eyes gleamed. "Scandalous."

Savada winked. "Those are always my favorite ones."

"All of you need to stop this!" Rashta roared. *"You're all delusional."*

Savada wagged her finger in my direction, her tongue clicking. "Tsk, tsk, Rashta, love. You just need to stop being in denial."

Energy welled up in my chest and Rashta sprang out. Her face was a mere inch away from Savada's, her wings allowing her to hover above the ground, as if it would help her seem to be more imposing.

Rasmus sighed and pulled Savada back by the shoulders. "Alright, you've had your fun. Stop antagonizing her."

The sex goddess pouted. "Don't be like that, my love. You feel it, too."

"I know when to not push, and allow things to be handled naturally, whichever way it goes." He lifted her chin with his finger. "It's something we still need to work on with you."

A hunger gleamed in her eyes. She wrapped her arms around his neck and kissed him. The wind picked up, sparkling flower petals from the Birth Heart swirling around them. And then, they were gone.

"Well, no surprise guesses what those two have gone to do," Blaze said.

I sputtered out a laugh, as did many others, though my attention lingered on Rashta. She stared at the place the two gods had previously been, her eyes almost unreadable, except... *There...* I caught on to traces of pain.

Her eyes darted to Nazir for a brief moment before she shot back into me. As the warmth settled, I placed a hand on my chest. *"Rashta? Do you... want to talk about it?"*

"No." I caught traces of the lingering pain I'd noticed in her eyes. *"I just want everyone to stop bringing it up. And to accept... it cannot be."*

I frowned, realizing now a little too late, there was more to this than simple denial.

"Laz?" Ryoko said in a quiet voice. "Is... everything okay?"

My lips remained downturned and I shook my head. "We need to move onto a different topic."

"Then we will discuss the matter Lumaraeon entrusted to me," Zion said. "Souls come into existence by Lumaraeon's will, and souls are reborn around this. However, the need to force souls to be reborn wedges them before souls already on their way into the life cycle. Life cannot be burdened with too many souls, and thus the forced rebirth has caused not only a disruption, but an imbalance."

The enormous dragon swiveled his head. "Amara and Jasmine, please step forward."

Murmuring spread through the crowd. I flexed my hands. What did he want with them? What did they have to do with this fixing of the disruption? A muscle in the back of my neck tightened. I tried not be concerned, but I couldn't keep the reaction at bay. Not when those two were involved.

Of course, I could attempt to ask Rashta, since I had no doubts she had at least an idea of what was going on, but I also knew she'd just tell me to be patient. That was reassuring in itself. She knew how protective I'd be of my mother and aunt. If something bad were going to happen, she'd warn me."

"I may be a goddess who wants you to figure things out on your own, but I'm not cruel."

In a strange way, it was comforting to hear her voice in my head. I'd become so used to it, having her missing these last few hours had been too... unnatural.

My mother and aunt approached Zion. My mother appeared confident and almost aware of what was happening, while Jasmine took more careful steps, her shoulders having her characteristic hunch when she was nervous. Of course my mother heckled her a bit. It was a normal sight, one that brought a smile to my face.

When the two assembled in front of Zion, he gazed down at them with sharp, calculating eyes. "When it was foreseen the Dragon-Phoenix's rebirth path had been altered in a way we did not expect, we took it upon ourselves to ensure the rebirth happened. Amara, you were chosen to be Rizgar's mate. A perfect balance to his sometimes impulsive and rash behavior." The god chuckled. "A trait his eldest daughter inherited."

I crossed my arms and glowered. Yeah, sure, it was true, but he didn't need to call me out like that.

"However, due the altered path, it would not have been as natural a meeting as we would have wished, and there were dire consequences to ensuring the Dragon-Phoenix came into being, for both her and for you." He paused for a moment before continuing. "Satria agreed to bring you a request: agree to be Rizgar's mate when he chose you during the peace treaty deal. This choice would ensure the Dragon-Phoenix would be born as she needed to be, but it would also condemn you to an early death."

My heart lurched. She knew she was going to die if she picked my father? The words she spoke to Rizgar earlier today resurfaced. She had sent that message with Largren to lessen the inevitable pain.

"Amara, you did not hesitate to agree to our request, even before we could offer you a reward for doing so. And when we did, you claimed having the Dragon-Phoenix as your daughter was a reward enough."

I pressed my hand against my tightening chest. *Mom…*

"Still, we have sought a way to repay you for your sacrifice, for your life ended far too soon, and you were never truly able to indulge in your mate bond, which you so eagerly embraced beyond our request."

He turned his attention to Jasmine suddenly. "Your life was not the only one we needed to approach. Xephrya was chosen to be the mother of the Dragon-Phoenix's champion. But in order for the proper match for her to be made, Xephrya's couldn't be as ideal as we would have wished."

I wanted to cringe. Raikidan had mentioned a few times his parents' relationship wasn't great. I had tried to reassure him on a few occasions that his mother had to love his father if she stayed instead of leaving him. But now I was concerned it was the promise of having my Champion as her son that kept her…

"She, like you, Amara, agreed quickly, accepting no reward. And even though the match was not what we called ideal, she was happy."

I relaxed. That made me feel better, and a little less awkward knowing Raiden was hearing he wasn't exactly *Mister Right* for the mate he'd devoted himself to.

"All of that was not the most difficult part of the request. Xephrya would unfortunately also meet her end for the sake of her son, but also the Dragon-Phoenix, for we needed her to be the catalyst for the pact Zarda sought. We required her to ensure she was at the location needed on the specified day to die."

My stomach churned and I found it hard to swallow. I knew those words were coming, but to hear them, it just… The way Xephrya spoke to me in the past, it was clear to me now she had made this difficult decision of her own free will. She knew the long game, and while she no doubt would have preferred to live, she instead accepted her fate, so I could be born and her son could have me.

"Xephrya was intended to receive her reward, but as she is now in the process of rebirth, we are giving it to another who is just as deserving." His eyes remained fixed on Jasmine. "We have chosen, you, Jasmine, to be that recipient."

"Me?" She was about as confused as I was. "Why me? I'm nowhere near as worthy as someone who made that kind of choice."

"This was the wish Xephrya whispered to Lumaraeon just before entering the rebirth cycle. And Lumaraeon agreed with the choice." He chuckled. "Because you are wrong on your worthiness. You, Jasmine, with no prompting of us, made selfless actions to protect the Dragon-Phoenix at all costs."

"Yeah, so?" my aunt said. "She's my niece. Of course I wanted to protect her."

The dragon god shook his head. "You meddled in Zarda's intended design, refusing to allow him to defile who she was intended to be, even without knowing how important she was beyond being your niece. You continued to meddle, at the risk of his continued abuse. And you ultimately sacrificed your life so she could escape his clutches, knowing full well going into your plan the chance of you making it out alive in any calculation you made was only five percent. Jasmine, you are worthy, because your reasons were pure of heart and done so with no regret."

Jasmine opened her mouth to protest, but my mother elbowed her in the ribs. "Just be quiet and accept the offering. You're not going to change their minds. And you're being stupid for arguing."

My aunt sighed unhappily. "Alright, fine. What is this reward you're giving us?"

"It has been decided, in order to obtain life balance and reward such worthy souls, time will be turned back and a second chance to live will be granted to the both of you."

Silence. Not even a single gasp at the proclamation. I could hardly begin to register the numbness spreading from my fingers to the rest of my body, let alone what the god had said. *Turn back… time?* Was that possible?

"Quite possible," Rashta said.

Jasmine echoed my question, in a way. "How… how are you able to defy something as set in stone as death? That's not… logical."

I choked on a laugh. While the rest of us were surprised the gods would even attempt something like this, my aunt, of course, was concerned only about the logical aspect of the action. She had always been that way. It was why she made a good scientist.

"As the Keeper of Time, I hold dominion over many aspects of time in Celesta's absence. This does include the meticulous task of rewinding time on an object or individual. Of course, an equal exchange must be met to do so. Lumaraeon has deemed the exchange will come in four reversals."

So that's what their last exchange meant. I did a rough count of the number of souls my soul-lives and I had sent into a rebirth process. It was over one hundred and twenty. Four soul reversals were equal to that many rebirths. I wasn't even sure how to understand the logistics around that balance.

"It's an intensive process to reverse time on a soul," Rashta said. *"The energy expended is what causes the cost to be so great."*

I supposed that made sense. It couldn't be a one-for-one exchange if the power expended was so great. But if it screwed the exchange, why not choose something more one-to-one?

"Are you really complaining about your family coming back to life?" Atria asked. *"Of course not!"*

"Then stop questioning this and go with the flow," Pheydra said.

"If you had this power to begin with, why didn't you turn back time on those afflicted before the rebirth could have been forced onto their souls?" Jasmine asked, her lips pursed. "An equal exchange wouldn't have been needed, or at least needed to a lesser extent by my calculation, and it would have had a more favorable result."

Zion's lip twitched, as if her insistence to question their decision amused him. "This magic cannot touch immortals, which demons are, due to their nature. Once a soul begins the demon transformation, it takes them out of my domain of influence."

Jasmine worked her jaw, trying to come up with more ways to argue. Zion loomed over her and my mother, his eyes calculating. When Jasmine couldn't conjure another way to stall the gods' decision, the dragon god inhaled deeply through his nose and then exhaled a pale golden mist.

The haze engulfed them and a moment later, the two women gasped, air filling lungs. Their skin practically glowed with their renewed life. A light breeze teased their hair, drifting their unmuted scent toward me.

My mother pressed a hand to her chest, feeling its rise and fall with each breath. Jasmine stared at her hands, lavender eyes wide.

I took a step forward. "Mom? Jasmine?"

My mother looked at me with sparkling green eyes. "Who would have thought the sensation of breathing would feel so unnatural?"

My chest swelled and tears pricked my eyes, a flood of overwhelming emotions cascading over me. *She's... alive again...*

"Go to her," Rashta whispered.

I didn't need to be told twice. I sprinted to my mother's open arms and nearly tackled her to the ground. "Mom..."

She held me tight against her. "I'm here, my Little Phoenix."

Tears trickled down my cheeks as I buried my face into her neck and embraced her warmth. She was here... She was really here.

"Are you crying?" Raikidan asked someone.

"No, course not," Ryoko replied just before she sniffled.

My mother chuckled and it wasn't long before I was dissolving into laughter alongside her. When we finally got our fit under control, my mother wiped away a lingering tear with her thumb. She then rested her forehead on mine and I closed my eyes, relishing the feeling of contentedness pulsing within in me.

I looked over at Jasmine when I'd had enough time to bond with my mother and snickered. She was looking her body over slowly. *Overanalyzing this, like usual.* "Aunt Jasmine."

"It's not logical," she murmured. "None of that was logical."

I shook my head and then hugged her. "Shut up for once about this logic crap."

She grunted. "Of all people to tell me to not think logically, you are not at the top of my list."

"Today is just one upside-down day so you're going to just have to deal with it."

Jasmine wrapped her arms around me. "All right. I'll think logically later."

"And by later, she means in about ten minutes!" Ryoko yelled.

The lot of us burst into a fit of laughter. No one doubted the claim would be true. Jasmine was too logic-focused for her own good sometimes. Even she admitted that.

I wheezed when someone ran up to us all of a sudden and pulled my mother, Jasmine and me into a tight bear hug. "Uncle, let go!"

Zane laughed. "Why would I when three of my favorite ladies are alive and finally in one spot?"

I squirmed until he huffed and put us down. My mother nudged him with her elbow, a sly grin on her lips. "Where's your favorite lady, huh?"

Without hesitation, he turned and gestured to Shva'sika. In the giddiest action I'd ever seen from her, my mother clapped excitedly and held her arms out for the elven woman. Shva'sika rushed over and the two embraced before my mother gushed about the ring. I knew how excited my mother was about my uncle finally finding someone. She'd always heckled him about his pickiness in the past.

I backed away when the floodgates of everyone else wanting to see my mother and aunt burst. Most were my siblings, but I caught Ryoko, Rylan, and a few other friends among them. The only person I didn't see was my father. Instead, I found him hanging back, watching—waiting.

I was surprised by his restraint. I expected him to try and take off with her to make up for all the lost time—not that I really wanted to think of my parents in that way.

When things calmed down around the women, Rizgar finally had his turn. He approached with surprising calm, and all the confidence of a clan leader. But my mother threw out whatever smooth plan he had when she practically jumped his bones. I took a step back, taken by surprise over her lack of restraint. My eyes flicked to the gods, checking to see if Savada had returned, but she and Rasmus were nowhere in sight.

"No, I'm pretty sure your mom is just thirsty," Sylvia said. *"Can't say I'd be better behaved if I had a moment like this with Rylar."*

"Perhaps you wouldn't," Raina said. *"But some of us understand there is a time and place for such lack of restraint."*

"Hey, get a cave!" I called out.

The two completely ignored me. I rolled my eyes and turned to Zion. "While those two are causing a scene, you mentioned four souls. Who are the other two you plan to perform this on? Are they here, or somewhere else?"

Zion grinned. "Oh, they are here. Lazei, please step forward."

The ancient elf knight appeared from a cluster of spiritual warriors and approached us, though rather warily. "You've chosen… me?"

The dragon god nodded. "You gave your all to protect Raina and did not complain when she appointed you guardian of Imera's Eternal Library. Your dedication did not end upon your own death, as you sought Raina out to bind you to the very spot with a crystal. Even after she had passed from this world and experienced many lifetimes of rebirth, you persisted with your protection. Not even Arcadia could convince you to rest. Your dedication to your duty moved us. We have deemed you worthy of a new life. While a rebirth into a world so different from your own would be our preference, you have demonstrated great resilience and adaptation. We are confident you will be able to thrive in this second life."

Lazei blinked slowly, and then bowed deeply. "I humbly accept your gift with the utmost gratitude."

Zion nodded and breathed life back into him. I made a slow approach to the elf warrior as he adjusted to the feeling of life again. Raina's presence bounced so hard against my mind I thought she might manifest beside me.

"Lazei?" I said.

He turned his attention to me. "Lady Eira."

I bit back the knee-jerk reaction to correct him about using formal titles with me. This was a lot for someone to handle, especially someone who wasn't even from this time, and if he was most comfortable using the title, then I'd let him. "How are you feeling?"

He worked his jaw. "I'm still figuring that out. I had expected to go back to my duty as a spiritual guardian. Now I'm a living one. If… I'm allowed to be a guardian anymore."

His eyes flicked to Zion briefly when he mentioned his past duty, but the god gave no indication as to whether any expectations would be placed on him. And for that, I was grateful. He had the chance to start a new life if that was his wish.

I closed my eyes when Raina's presence became too much to ignore, and she shared with me her memories spent with Lazei. They gave me a good feel for his character, and I quickly picked up on a concern I knew she was trying to convey to me.

"Lazei of house Ravadi, son of Naertho," I said, hoping I'd recited that correctly.

The elven warrior's spine straightened and he held himself at attention.

"The gods have left no expectation or condition for you. This new lease on life is yours to decide what you will of it. However, as the Dragon-Phoenix, I have a condition for you." I paused to make sure I would word myself correctly. "I will not deny your services if you request it, nor will I persuade you to abandon your duty as guardian of the Eternal Library. But, I will ask of you to not squander this life, and for you to choose to live for yourself this time."

My eyes softened, Raina's compassion channeling through me. "You sacrificed so much for the sake of my name and duty. I do not wish to see you repeat those choices again."

Lazei bowed his head, taking in my words. "I would be honored if you'd have me at your command should you have need of it, my lady. I do not wish to live a second life where I am not permitted that ability." He lifted his head. "And I will do my best to adhere to your conditions. I merely ask for your patience, as you know that condition was not my strongest trait."

I reached out and framed his face with my hands. "You have an open invitation to stay with the shamans until you know what you wish to do. There is no pressure to make decisions right away."

He grasped them with his, smiling gratefully. "I will take you up on that offer."

After sharing a few more words with him, I turned my attention back to Zion, expecting him to announce the last soul to receive this amazing gift. The dragon god looked at me but when he didn't speak, I tilted my head. "Well?"

He chuckled. "I am assessing you, to make sure you are ready for this last soul's revival."

My brow furrowed as I pursed my lips. Why would I have such a strong reaction that he had to be concerned?

The god didn't break eye contact with me when he spoke, "Tannek, step forward."

My heart stopped and the ground fell from under me. *Tannek?* I turned my wide-eyed gaze to Tannek, who stood stock-still. The entire gathering had quieted, and even my parents had ceased their antics.

"Boy," Zion rumbled. "Step closer."

Tannek's eyes darted to me, and then to the god, yet his feet remained rooted in place.

Zion let out an exasperated sigh. "Mortals… trusting us to know what we are doing every now and then would not kill you."

I choked, breaking me free of my shocked state. Tannek chuckled, also freeing him from his state. Zion smiled as if that were his intent, and repeated his request for Tannek to step forward. He did this time, though his gaze did shift to me again.

"I suppose I should ask the obligatory question of why you chose me as the last recipient of this gift," Tannek said, obviously trying to use the moment to calm his nerves. It was a better attempt than I would have been able to manage.

"We have you to thank for ensuring the Dragon-Phoenix is here today," Zion said, his tone even and leaving no room for doubt. "Not only did you teach her how to defy the unfortunate training Zarda attempted to instill in her, and show her how capable she was of love and compassion, you gave your life to save hers."

The god closed his eyes for a moment, as if he were seeing the moment we all knew he spoke of. "While it has been long believed she would have been protected by the armor she wore, that was not the reality. Had you not stolen the shot from her, Eira would have been left permanently paralyzed. And I do not think I have to explain what Zarda would have done to her had that happened."

I pressed my hand against my chest. This whole time, I'd lamented Tannek's death because I foolishly believed he died for nothing. But had I been left unusable in Zarda's eyes, I wouldn't be here today.

"If Eira had died before the purification process, catastrophic repercussions would have occurred. Your selfless sacrifice out of love, Tannek, saved more than you could have ever anticipated. That is why we have chosen you." A grin pulled back Zion's lips, showing off his sharp teeth. "And she will have need of you in her coming trials."

Coming trials? He probably meant Kir. Though I wasn't sure how Tannek could contribute to that situation better alive than as a spirit. He was only a medic.

"For now," Rashta said in a rather ominous tone.

Before Tannek could finish processing or even verbally accept the boon, Zion exhaled the pale time mist onto him. Tannek pressed his hand hard against his chest as he inhaled his first breath of life, his eyes wide.

I took a tentative step forward. "Tannek?"

He lifted his gaze to me, still taking long, slow breaths. I took several more steps, reaching out and brushing my fingers against his cheeks. Breath left my lungs in a single *whoosh* at the touch of warmth on his skin hit me. "You're… warm."

Tannek cupped my face, the callouses on his fingers biting into my skin. "You're warmer, Chickadee."

The sound of a long ago conversation we once had seeped deep into the fog of my mind. Overwhelming joy burst in my chest. I threw my arms around his neck, burying my face to hide the tears streaming down my cheeks. *He's back… my Tannek is back.*

His strong arms crushed me into him, one of his hands threading into my hair. The embrace was so familiar it hurt. And yet I could remain like this forever and be content to never let go.

However, that's not what I got. Tannek shoved me away suddenly. Bewilderment fogged my mind. *Why did he do that? What did I do wrong?*

A body crashed into Tannek, and a moment later my brain caught up and processed Azriel holding his older brother in a death grip. Andariel, whom I had no idea was even here, appeared shortly after. The three brothers embraced, and Azriel even kissed Tannek on the forehead a few times.

I smiled. Even though Andariel was the most arrogant and asshole-ish one, he loved his older brother just as much as Azriel did. The three of them had a strong dynamic back then. It really wasn't until Tannek died did things fall apart and Andariel became so insufferable.

My smile faded when familiar footsteps crunched behind me. My gaze flicked from Tannek, who was now calming down and refocusing, to Raikidan. Nisha's presence surged, hovering on the line of my awareness, and now racing emotions.

I'd longed to have Tannek back. Even when I had shut myself off from everything, there were still times I wished I could go back and have just one more moment with him. Having him back now was that dream come to life.

I had learned to accept the loss and make room for a future without him—with Raikidan. But that didn't mean I'd stopped loving Tannek.

Nisha pressed against my mind, as if trying to reach out and hug me. Pain pulsed in my chest, my attention continuing to flick between the two men I loved. I was going to have to choose, just like Nisha had. And even though logic said the choice was obvious, my heart couldn't bear making one.

Raikidan rested his hand on my lower back. "We'll work this out."

My mouth fell open. Even Nisha's presence paused. *Did I hear him right?* Was I seeing this right? There was no tension in his touch, body, or words. There were no possessive hints at all that I would have expected from him. "You mean it?"

He easily turned his attention to me and nodded. The softness and sincerity in his eyes made my heart swell. I wrapped my arms around his torso and murmured, "Thank you."

He ran his fingers through my hair in response. I pulled away when Azriel began heckling Tannek. "You've got permission, go tell her what you'd intended to before you died."

Andariel grinned and nudged him with his elbow. "Yeah, take advantage of it before someone changes their mind."

Tannek narrowed his eyes at his brothers. "Knock it off. Now isn't the time for that."

My brow arched. "What are you three talking about?"

Tannek shook his head. "Ignore them."

I crossed my arms. "That's easy when it comes to Andariel, but you really think Azriel would allow that?"

The three brothers burst with laughter. That was a *no, of course not.*

After rolling my eyes, I quelled my curiosity. If I really wanted to know later, I could. In this last year I'd learned to be more open with what I wanted, and how to entice Raikidan if he wanted to be stubborn. Tannek wouldn't be able to resist me, either.

I turned to Zion. "Any more surprises for us?"

A throaty laugh rumbled through the dragon god. "Not quite for you, but for our guests. Of course, due to their long absence, I'm sure the rest of you would like some answers."

He swiveled his head toward the four dragon colors watching on. None seemed impatient to leave. On the contrary, one of each color had already assembled closer. What caught my eye among them were the white dragon and blue dragon. The blue was significantly smaller than the other three, and appeared quite small compared to some of the other blue dragons gathered. The white was a little smaller than the brown and violet, but what caught me about this one was the body shape. *Are they... female?*

I was still terrible at discerning the two sexes from a visual standpoint. I'd been assured it wasn't easy even for dragons, and most relied on scent, but it still irritated me. The only thing that gave me the impression these were female was their size and sometimes their body shape. While not always the case, female dragons were usually smaller and leaner than their male counterparts. This blue showed both of those traits, while the white exhibited the slightly smaller stature and frame, but their musculature made it difficult to come to a sure conclusion.

"You're right about your assessment," Lina said. *"White and blue dragons are a bit... unique."*

"What's that supposed to mean?" I asked.

"Just wait. You'll either see or catch on soon enough."

The four dragons approached and shifted to humanoid forms. The brown dragon changed into a stocky nu-human man with terracotta skin, braided brown hair, and amber eyes. The violet dragon shifted into a tall, light-skinned, violet-haired elven man with silver eyes, and the blue dragon shifted to a buxom woman with bronze skin, wild blue hair, and copper eyes. The final dragon, the white, shifted into a tall and impressively muscular woman with porcelain skin, white hair, and violet eyes.

Recognition dawned on me as I stared at the familiar-looking blue and white dragons. "You've got to be shitting me."

The white dragon crossed her massive arms and grinned, speaking in a low alto tone. "It's good to see you again, Eira."

I sensed eyes falling on me. Even Raikidan turned a flabbergasted look to me. Ryoko spoke up. "You met extinct colors and didn't say anything?"

"I had no idea I'd met a blue and a white dragon before."

Ryoko crossed her arms and narrowed her eyes at me. "Yeah, sure."

"What the hell do you want me to say? 'I'm sorry, my dragon senses weren't tingling and had to go into the shop for repair?'"

She and many other laughed.

"An' that's how we wanted it," the blue dragon drawled. "Honestly, we were surprised ya'll kept yer mouths shut."

My brow spiked and then I turned to Shva'sika. She'd been the one with me when we ran into these two. My friend shrugged. "I figured it out rather quickly, as I knew a few key signs. They were convinced I'd out their existence, even when I swore I'd never tell a soul, not even you. They of course didn't believe me. Clearly they don't know me."

"So, *you* knew this whole time?" Ryoko said. This big secret really seemed to bother her for some reason.

I held up a hand to stop her from saying any more. "Let's calm down and allow them to explain. I'm sure it'll answer the most burning questions and clear things up."

Books cracking open and pages flipping echoed through the gathering. I pinched my nose while the white dragon laughed. "Scholars never miss a beat."

When she calmed down, the violet dragon spoke up. "As you can all witness with your own eyes, our flight colors are not extinct. Rather, we had gone into hiding for our own preservation. We violet dragons were the first, as our numbers were hit the hardest during the War of End. We spread rumors of our supposed demise and have since kept low profiles and worked to bolster our numbers to a more sustainable level before revealing our existence again."

He nodded to the other three colors. "The other flight colors had suffered greatly during that war as well, but fortunately still managed numbers that were stable enough to remain in the open. Until the Great War."

The white dragon spoke up. "While we knew it was foolish for us to involve ourselves, as we had still not recovered, I could not allow my flight to sit idly by."

"Wait, back up," I said. "Your flight? As in…"

The blue dragon giggled. "Unlike the rest of the color, the females call the shots for blue and whites. We share some ideals and philosophies with the other flights, but not all."

I blinked. *Well, that's different.* A good different in my eyes, of course, but I'd been so accustomed to hearing the singular beliefs Raikidan and the others held, I never thought any others would pop up.

The brown dragon cleared his throat, and spoke in a deep, bone-penetrating voice. "All three flights understood the risk of fighting in the war. However, none of us could stomach the Crimson Sanctuary's behavior, and we wouldn't allow Velsara and Taiegh's sacrifice to be in vain. Even if it cost us everything. In the end, we found ourselves in the same predicament as the violet dragons, and spread misinformation about our fate to protect those of us left."

"So, since you're here, your numbers are good again?" I asked, a bit skeptical with how little time had passed. It was a significant amount for a human, but not dragons, especially given their low conception rates.

The violet dragon shook his head. "Not quite. We caught wind of the plan of attack and found ourselves unable to ignore our desire to help, knowing full well it could destroy us once and for all."

I didn't know what to say. They'd showed loyalty to a degree I'd never seen before.

My soul-lives all pulsed in my mind. I pressed two fingers to my forehead, feeling them out. *Is it just me, or is this easier to do now?* "We're all grateful for the risk you took. Without your help, none of us would be here now." My hand dropped. "I wish I had a way to repay you all for your loyalty."

"That is where I come in," Zion said, lowering himself to the ground. He curtained his wings in front of his face. Nothing seemed to happen, but when he pulled his wings away, a medium-sized nest with eggs laid on the ground before him. My feet were in motion before I realized it, closing the distance until I could kneel and touch them. The eggs were about two feet tall and clustered by type. There were four types total, with about ten eggs per type.

One type was brown and grey, and hard and jagged like stone. Another was white with blue ice encasing them, making them cold to the touch. The third type of eggs were a deep violet color, and their surface swirled when touched. The last set of eggs was the strangest type of them all. It had a tough, clear outer shell, and inside bubbled some type of water or embryonic fluid. Stranger more was the ability to see the tiny creatures growing inside these eggs—a dragon.

I looked up at Zion. "Dragon eggs?"

CHAPTER 23

Before the god could respond, I jumped when Mana popped in next to me. We watched her paw over the eggs, inspecting each one and even pressing an ear to them, as if she were listening to something.

Her eyes sparkled. "They're all so healthy! I've never felt such healthy eggs before. Not a single one could possibly not hatch."

I noticed the four dragons exchanging excited glances. "Um, can I be brought up to speed? Mana, you can sense the health of eggs?"

"It is an ancient technique," Zion answered for her. "It was common when green elder dragons were more prevalent. But between our kind's slow extinction and the War of End thinning the numbers of greens with the skill, Mana's training from Xeren makes her one of the few left."

Xeren? Was that the name of her grandfather?

The ground rumbled and we all turned to see the green elder dragon I'd spotted earlier approaching. He shifted, taking the form of a tall, tan-skinned human man. His wild, wavy green hair cut at the tops of the shoulders, framing his strong-featured face, and branching horns grew from his head. Striking golden eyes fixed on me as he smiled.

"The skill was highly sought after, as it could tell a pair which eggs to focus their efforts on, or if one needed a longer incubation time than usual, reducing the chance of early abandonment," he spoke in smooth, soothing tones. "Of course, we never gave our assessment without coin or some other treasure payment."

His eyes cut to Mana when he said this, as if reprimanding her. Mana pressed her ear against one of the brown dragon eggs. "This is my contribution. I don't make a habit of giving this information away for free."

Her grandfather shook his head and knelt beside her, making his own assessment.

"So, what do these eggs have to do with repaying the dragons?" I asked Zion.

"Their willingness to risk everything for your soul has earned them a reward. Ten new dragons plucked from time. They will provide the needed bloodline boost for each color to flourish."

"When will they hatch?" the blue dragon asked, her voice indicating their eagerness.

"In the next few days," Zion said. "By my calculations, you should all have at least one pair of mated dragons who would take them as their own."

All four dragons turned to their flights and conversed quickly to make sure that would be the case. It didn't take long for several mated pairs of each flight to ask to be chosen, most wanting all the young for one large brood to call theirs. Their leaders wouldn't decide right here how they would work it out, but at least Zion was right. And I was happy he'd given them this. None of the flights should live in fear of dying off, so if these eggs gave them the boost they needed, then I hoped they'd all grow up to be strong dragons.

"Child," Zion murmured.

I refocused my attention on Mana, who was still touching the eggs. Longing glazed her gaze. My heart clenched in sympathy. She yearned for her own brood, and for her to witness other dragons being handed one, especially a large one, I couldn't imagine how much she wished she were in their place.

"Your time will come," Zion said to her.

She nodded. "I will be patient."

"Zion," Jasmine spoke up. "Not to question your ability to secure the bloodline diversity, but as a geneticist, I have some concerns."

I pressed my lips together and bit back a snarky remark. Of course she would find possible issues. I swear her brain never stopped.

"I wouldn't be surprised if she dreamed about that stuff," Ayuma said. *"Zephyr did all the time."*

The dragon god swiveled his head to face her. "You are a talented woman, Jasmine. I value your input over my pride."

That was quite the compliment.

My aunt adjusted her glasses. "My calculation is based on an estimated number that could be assumed is a barely sustainable number around such a long-lived species that are generally monogamous by nature. I haven't mathematically factored in some adult dragons taking different-colored mates, or if some of the acquired eggs come from the same mated pairs, but it is a theoretical concern that did get factored into my prediction."

She paused and then shook her head. "I'm sorry. I almost started rambling the technical side of the calculations that either bore or go over the heads of most. So as not to do that, trust me when I say, unless great care and meticulous planning for future pairs, ten won't be enough to prevent genetic dilution, inbreeding, or extinction."

The four lead dragons exchanged concerned glances, and rightfully so. Not even I could disagree with Jasmine's assessment.

"Can we obtain more eggs, Zion?" the white dragon asked. "I don't want to sound ungrateful for what you've already done, but I can't deny more dragons added to our flight would help us greatly."

Zion shook his head. "It was hard enough to convince pairs to give these ones up. And Lumaraeon has forbidden me from approaching adult dragons to time travel. I need to think about this." He closed his eyes for a moment. "Thank you for bringing this oversight to my attention, Jasmine. These unborn dragons will be cared for as planned while I reevaluate this error."

"Well, I'm not actually done," Jasmine said. "I have a solution that, while slow, will work fairly well."

Zion stared at her intently. "Go on."

"It's no secret Dalatrend was well known for its the extreme experimentation that went on under Zarda's reign."

Murmurs of agreement in the crowd confirmed her words.

"Naturally, that stopped upon his demise, and the laboratories have been converted to ethical research, as well as continued healing wards for experiments, and the occasional civilian who opted into experimental research."

It sounded like Jasmine had been checking in on things over the last year.

"That all being said," she continued. "The technology and resources to grow a living creature remains accessible. There has been discussion to opening this technology up to aid the infertile, as it's more robust than what is available in the medical market now. I propose we put that idea into motion by growing dragons. Not to full adulthood, mind you, but to an age and size typical for hatchlings."

I stared at Jasmine, as did most others. It was a brilliant idea.

"You can do this?" the violet dragon asked. "You can grow dragons?"

Jasmine nodded. "Viable, living animals were created many times before humans were ever grown." She gestured to me and then my siblings. "We've also grown half-dragons successfully. I'm confident we'll be able to grow dragons. It will take some time, of course. We'll need to gather information from heat cycles to internal egg formations, and then external growth. The more we understand dragon biology, the more successful our results will be."

Mana cocked her head toward me. "Does she talk like this all the time?"

I shrugged. "Pretty much."

"What can we do to assist in this project?" the brown dragon asked.

"A plan will need to be drawn up. It'll have to cover all the stages of study we'll need. One thing we'll need immediately is the ability to study these dragon eggs, given they're bound to hatch at any time." She turned to look at the blue dragon. "Your eggs would be the easiest, given we can do most of our monitoring externally, minimizing the need for technological interference."

The dragon gazed at her warily. "Do you need all of them?"

Jasmine shook her head. "Two would be fine. And I'm sure there's an imprinting process upon hatching, so we can work together to ensure that is not interfered with."

The blue dragon's unease was settled and she agreed to the terms.

"What else is needed?" the brown dragon asked.

Jasmine crossed her arms. "DNA."

"DNA…"

She nodded. "It's what will keep the bloodlines new. Blood, reproductive cells, even bone and scales can work. While reproductive cells would be optimal, and honestly preferred, I understand that can be hard to obtain for some species, so the next best source would be bone or scales, as the DNA for those last the longest. We can take the DNA from the donor and splice it with another and create a new viable life to grow that will introduce new genes into the pool. I won't bore you with the specifics, but that's all we will need to grow these dragons. And more space and tanks, but we can handle the renovation process."

Zion gestured his head to someone, and Naloth spoke up. "We can handle that."

"You'll work through this process from start to finish?" the white dragon asked Jasmine.

She nodded. "I'll return to Dalatrend to head the project. This is what I know best, so if I'm working on a second life, might as well make the most of it, even if it's based around what I'm familiar with."

Maybe on another day I might be concerned about her decision, but really, I struggled to see Jasmine doing anything else. She loved her work. It was just Zarda who'd made her miserable. My concerns, though, centered around her mental health if she were to go back to that place. I hoped she knew what she was doing.

"We have a plan," Zion said. "I have nothing left that needs discussion, and this search takes precedence." His wings unfurled. "It was a pleasure meeting all of you. We may meet again in time."

"Zion, one last thing from me," I said before he could leap into the air.

His muscles bunched for the jump, but then relaxed. "What do you have for me?"

"A request, based on a conversation Celesta and I had about Makers."

The dragon god lowered his head so one of his eyes was level with me. "Why were you speaking about Makers with her?"

I drew my altering dagger and morphed it back into its original shape, from before it had been reworked for me—Rashta's hammer. Zion's eyes widened. "Rashta's gavel…"

Warmth bloomed in my chest, and the goddess in question popped out. She nodded to confirm.

"How… where did you find it?" the dragon god asked. "What did you… how did you alter it? Only—"

"Only a Maker could." I turned and looked Ryder's way. "And it happened to find its way to a Maker's workbench."

Ryder ran his fingers through his hair. "So we're on the same page with that now? 'Cause that was the thing I was going to tell you about later. We discovered concrete evidence in the latest expedition."

"It was hard to keep ignoring the signs, and then when Celesta told me god weapons are Maker creations, I knew I couldn't deny it anymore." I squinted. "My question is, how did you get Rashta's weapon, and why did you alter it?"

Ryder nodded his chin toward Phyre. "He came to me."

I raised my eyebrow. "You entrusted a child to play with a god weapon?"

He held up a dismissive hand. "I wanted to know if my hunch was right. If he wasn't a Maker, the weapon would be untouched. If he was, he'd be able to do as I asked."

"How did you find it?" Zion asked. "And why didn't you say anything?"

"Given its mysterious disappearance shortly after Rashta's fusion with the Dragon-Phoenix soul, I had a few guesses as to what happened to it. Had I known Celesta had hidden it right under our noses, I would have retrieved it sooner. However, I suspected it was due to Celesta's meddling, and with her escape, I didn't want to bring attention to the find by handing it over to Eira, as she didn't need a bigger target on her back in her vulnerable state. The same goes with formally identifying the boy. Speculation on the mortal's part in this wouldn't trigger anyone to investigate him, so I deemed it better to keep it that way until I was sure it'd be safe to reveal."

"What is a Maker, exactly?" Raikidan asked.

Zion closed his eyes for a moment. "They were rare, unique beings with a near limitless ability to craft. It was because of them, civilizations thrived. They were nothing like anything we'd ever seen before." The enormous dragon let out a heavy sigh. "However, there was a drawback to their abilities. Makers were unable to teach others their ways. It was so intrinsic to their being, they could barely explain how they created their creations. And then…"

"And then, what?" Tannek asked.

"And then Celesta made them disappear," I revealed.

Zion snapped his gaze to me. "What?"

I nodded. "That's what she told me. I don't know how removing someone from the timelines works, but that's what she did."

Zion snarled, startling me. "Why would she do that?"

"She claimed they'd get in the way of her plans. I'm guessing their unique abilities would easily disrupt them, and I've no doubt they would have sided against her quite easily."

The dragon god bared his teeth and gouged the ground with terrifying talons. I frowned. "Watch it. We just got this place looking nice."

He looked down at the damage and swept his claws over the ground, the earth fixing itself. "I apologize. I am just struggling with the notion that she was so far gone she'd take such drastic actions. I do not know if I'll be able to find the Makers she sent away, but I will make it my focus. The chromatic flight will handle the DNA collection."

The dragon looked to Ryder. "I am glad you evaded her sight. Maybe she was too vain to believe a severely diluted bloodline could produce another."

"Is that how it's possible for him to be a Maker?" I asked.

He nodded. "You exhibit many Maker qualities, though you are not one. The same goes with Rylan, to a lesser extent. It is of no surprise the two of you created a Maker offspring."

"Laz, if you want to donate another Maker baby contribution, I'll raise it for you!" Ryoko called out. "While we're at it, I think we need to paint a giant S on your chest, since you now check the following boxes: Maker blood, host of a god, and extremely talented in a lot of things."

I rolled my eyes while others laughed.

Zion rose to his full height. "I shall take my leave to deal with this matter."

Not allowing anyone to stall him, the large dragon leapt into the air and flew into the starry vortex above. Chromatics took to the skies and followed the god until only one remained. The swirling maelstrom slowly disappeared until the atmosphere returned to normal, leaving Naloth behind.

I spiked an eyebrow as he slowly approached me. "Not going with them?"

He gave a one-shouldered shrug. "I can get home whenever. That whole thing was just for dramatics."

"I figured as much. That's not really what I was asking, though."

Instead of answering, he held up my hairclip, the hair ornament still in two pieces. My stomach knotted and I reached out to take the parts from him.

"I'm sorry," he said. "Because I made it into a time relic, I can't turn back time and fix it."

I twisted the pieces in my hands. It had always been my most precious possession. There was hardly a moment I could remember when I didn't have it on my person. *Sometimes we have to let go of the past to move on in our future.*

Working my jaw a moment, I offered him one of the pieces. "I want you to have this."

His brow knitted. "Are you sure?"

I nodded. "A keepsake to remind you how many times you saved my ass."

Naloth smiled and accepted the gift. "I'll treasure it. I should get going. I have some body parts to collect."

I snorted. "Don't be a stranger, okay?"

A cocky grin spread up half his face. "Oh, you can't get rid of me that easily."

Then, in a blink, he was gone. I took a step back and blinked. Rashta and Phyre laughed. Seemed that was a normal thing for a chromatic to do. Or at least Naloth.

"Oh, it's definitely a color trait," Sylvia said. *"Rylar loved doing that to me. Especially when I was in the middle of lecturing him."*

I laughed, gaining a few strange looks I was now used to when interacting with my soul-lives. I then threaded my fingers through my hair. "Guess I need to look into a replacement."

"No, you don't," Raikidan said.

I turned to him and noticed an older elven man standing with him. He had short salt-and-pepper hair and wore clothes similar to the North Tribe, though with some differences to its clear elven origin, telling me he was from the area around them. There was dried blood smeared on his face and clothes; a sword hung from his belt on one side, and a gun was holstered on the other. In his hand he carried an elegantly crafted wooden box.

Curious about what the hell Raikidan was up to, I ventured over.

The elf dipped his head in greeting. "It's a pleasure to meet you, Eira. My name is Aelrindel of the Ravcan family."

Aelrindel? I knew that name. "You crafted my hairclip."

He nodded, smiling. "And its sister."

That was right. My mother had one, though I wasn't quite sure what happened to it after her death.

"It's a pleasure to meet you finally," I said. My eyes flicked to the blood on him. "I apologize for the unfortunate circumstances that came before this."

He let out a hearty laugh and then patted his weapons. "No need. I needed a good workout."

The corner of my lips quirked up. I already liked him.

I slipped my gaze to Raikidan. "So, what's going on? I'm not dumb enough to think he showed up by chance."

Raikidan grinned. "Well, if you were allowed to slip away whenever you wanted this past year, so was I."

I lifted an eyebrow. "*You* slipped away? Mister Clingy?"

He gave me a long, unamused look. "I had something made for you."

"I heard of the meeting when doing work with some North Tribe shamans," Aelrindel jumped in, clearly assuming a lovers' quarrel was about to transpire. "Raikidan was to meet with me in a few days for pickup, but I thought today would be a better choice." He smirked and offered the box in his hand. "I was right."

I accepted the object, taking in the details carved into the woodgrain before glancing between the two men. The elf smiled, and Raikidan gave me his subtle "hurry up" eager-and-impatient look.

Lifting the lid, the box hinged open, revealing violet satin and something gold, green, and sparkly lying on top. My mouth fell open. It was a hairpin made of emerald, much like my hairclip, but it had golden detailing accents. The stick was made of gold with an emerald ball at the end. I removed the ornate hairpin to give it my full appreciation.

Elegant detail had been carved into the curved base, depicting vines and other flora. The holes for the hair stick were lined with gold, and a large flower ornament of a lighter shade of green, maybe a different gemstone altogether, had been designed on the top as a center and striking visual.

"It's… beautiful." I paused and then looked to the craftsman. "He paid you, right?"

Raikidan released an exasperated breath and Aelrindel let out a hearty laugh. "Don't worry, I know how to deal with dragons. They're frequent customers of mine."

Well that was good. Dragons didn't steal all the time. Bartering was a fairly common practice, but that didn't mean they didn't try underhanded tactics every now and then.

"Now if only I was in a more presentable state, I'd be able to wear it properly."

The violet dragon flight leader muttered something and then snapped his fingers. I gasped when the dried blood, dirt, and other traces of battle disappeared. "Now, that's a handy spell."

Taking advantage of my cleaned-up state, Raikidan snatched the hairpin from my fingers and slipped behind me. I didn't stop him for pinning up my hair. "Perfect."

I smiled up at him. "Thank you. I love it."

He grinned back, and brushed my cheek with his knuckles. He suddenly frowned and touched my ear. Sharp pain caused me to hiss and pull back from the touch. "Your earring was ripped out."

I tentatively touched my ear, noting it was my bell earring that was gone. "Shit."

"I've got it!" Valene called out, running toward us. "Seda noticed it was missing, so we went looking for it."

I sighed with relief, taking the piece of jewelry from her. The sapphire stud and golden bell were miraculously unharmed, though the rest of it was another story. There would be no saving the mangled pieces, but that was okay. I could either have the chain recreated or change the style up. One that kept the bell closer to my ear might be a good idea.

"You need to get your ear checked out," Raikidan said. "How it escaped all the healing you've gone through is beyond me, but it's not something to ignore."

I shook my head. "It's fine. Nothing a healer can't handle later."

Tannek took a few tentative steps toward me. "No, he's right. You don't want that getting infected."

I rolled my eyes. "You two worry too much."

Zoltan laughed from where he still stood with the other gods. "Well, while you three bicker about that healing treatment, we gods will leave you to the rest of your day. May we meet again under more pleasant circumstances."

They began to disappear in their myriad methods. My mother left my father's side and rushed over to Satria, who had joined Phyre's side. "Satria, wait."

The goddess turned to her and smiled. "Yes?"

My mother pulled her sword from her back. "I have this to return to you."

"Wait, hold on," Ryoko called out. "You can't be saying that's *the* Tamashi, and not a replica, right?"

Satria smiled. "No, that's exactly what she's saying. As a gift for agreeing to our request, I gave her my sword to use in battle. Its magic accepted her as a wielder, allowing her to use it in ways others wouldn't have been able to."

Both my and Ryoko's mouths fell open. That was one hell of a bombshell drop. It explained so much, but still… it was hard to believe.

Satria turned her attention back to my mother. "Keep it a while longer, Amara. You've certainly earned it. And it may still be useful in the days ahead."

My mother placed the flat side of her fist against her chest in salute, a habit that would take her quite some time to break. "I'll continue to take care of it."

No hesitation. No second-guessing the goddess' choice. It was the exact behavior I expected from my mother. She was as fluid and adaptable as the water she controlled.

The war goddess gave a respectful nod.

Phyre held up his fist to me. I smirked and bumped mine with his.

"This isn't the last we've seen of each other," he said.

I snickered. "Planning on messing with more carnival attendees?"

The fire god shrugged. "It's not off the table. It'd be nice to walk among mortals a little more often."

There weren't any laws that kept their contact with us at a minimum. I figured that given how long they lived, it was just easier for them to be distant to handle the pain that came with mortality.

Phyre wrapped his arm around Satria and then they disappeared in a puff of smoke. The last of the gods were quick to follow—all except Nazir. He stood off a little ways, conversing with his daughter.

I glanced to Rashta. "So, what's the story? I have a feeling it's not as black and white as, 'He gave humans his DNA so a clueless demigod could run around.'"

Rashta frowned. "You're right, it's not. It's quite sad, really. But it's not my place to tell."

Nazir turned to us. "I had every intention of raising Genesis myself. When I was a mortal mercenary, I was happily married to an amazing woman who could give me a run for my coin purse."

The corner of his lip twitched up, as if remembering something about her for a brief moment. But it didn't last long as his expression grew colder. "When she was with child with our first, I was drawn away from our estate to handle a situation. It was a ruse. I was betrayed by my closest allies, and she and our child suffered the price."

My stomach clenched. That had to be the event he'd vaguely mentioned to me last year that had changed how he'd come to obtain the fearsome reputation that led to his ascension. I could sympathize.

Nazir continued. "When the humans started their experiments, I saw it as an opportunity. As much as I could visit my wife on the spiritual plane, I couldn't bring her back to life. But now I could have a piece of her with me for the time a mortal body would allow. It was then I intervened with the humans and made them a deal. I'd give them the ability to craft the perfect human and I would take the first child, one who was made of me and my wife."

He closed his eyes. "I angered Lumaraeon in doing this. She couldn't stop my deal, as it'd already been struck, but she did prevent me from retrieving Genesis. I was forbidden from having any contact with her. She wasn't to know of her connection to me, and I couldn't plant any clues to tip her off."

I worked my jaw. "That explains why Genesis' lab information went missing."

He nodded. "To ensure the secret remained, I was instructed to take anything that would lead her to me and make sure the humans forgot the deal was ever struck, and believed they had created the new humans without outside assistance."

"Did you anticipate that reaction from Lumaraeon?" Genesis asked.

"Some of it. But I never anticipated she'd command me to leave you." He frowned. "Had I known, I would have handled it all differently."

She nodded and rubbed her arm. "Well, for what it's worth, I don't hate you."

Nazir chuckled. "That's reassuring. I appreciate that."

"I don't know if I'll continue our agreement about the training. As I've learned more about my abilities and used them, I've become less fond of them. But you're still welcome to come by, if you like."

The shocked expression on his face was priceless. When he finally recovered, he smiled and rested his hand affectionately against the side of her head. For a moment I thought he might try to hug her, but it seemed he thought better of it until they had a more solid relationship.

His fingers slid through her long hair as he pulled away, and an ornate feather hair wrap manifested. "Perfect. I will see you later, Genesis."

The god turned, passing Rashta one last glance before walking off and disappearing. Ryder bent close to Genesis' ear and spoke quietly to her, my ears catching his compliments of her new hair accessory.

With the gods now gone, along with the threat of impending doom, weariness was settling in. I felt like I could sleep for days. Rashta reentered my body as to not tax me any further.

Shva'sika and some other shamans approached the white, brown, blue, and violet dragons, offering to assist in the moving of the eggs through portals to ensure their safety. None of the dragons refused, grateful for the offer. The violets especially were interested to see the ancient tech. No surprise, given their origins predated the War of End, and only select families still held the knowledge on how to construct them.

I smiled. This kind of outreach would help cement relations we were aiming for across Lumaraeon. It also reminded me I had one other task to handle, and he was approaching.

Anir nodded in acknowledgement. "Arcadia sent the non-bound back to hell."

"I suspected as much. The moment I'm back to full strength, I'll be sure to go and bind them. I don't want them trapped there any longer than necessary."

He smiled. "They know. They'll be patient either way. You've given us something we never thought would come to us. We'd all wait centuries as long as it meant it would eventually be possible." Anir shook his head. "But enough about that. What would you have us do for you now? We're happy to go hunt down some Crimson Sanctuary."

I chuckled. "I'm sure you would be, and that will be one of the tasks, but I have one that I believe will be more pressing. Dalatrend sits in a peculiar location where the living and spiritual planes naturally thin and nearly merge. Kir utilized this space to more easily shift in and out of the living plane, when spirits would otherwise require more time and energy to do so."

Anir's eyes narrowed. "This sounds like a dangerous place."

I rocked my head back and forth. "In itself, it's not. I used to use the location as my personal getaway when I needed to de-stress. However, I'm concerned about continued use, and not just at this one. I have no doubts there are more out there, but I don't know where to begin searching for such mergers."

One of my other bound spirits approached. "You'd like us to find them, then, yes?"

I nodded. "Who better to task this with than spirits? You're able to travel farther distances faster, and would sense the thinning areas sooner than the living. Not even I realized what the place was for a long time."

"We'll do it," Anir said. "But what about the established one? Who is keeping an eye on that one?"

"Shamans," I said. "There's a dual purpose to me tracking down these locations. The thinness provides an opportunity for those without the ability to communicate with the dead. There are only so many shamans around to help the grieving and to ferry messages between the living and dead. I proposed erecting a communal spot to ease those burdens. I still have to speak with the Dalatrend Council to finalize the request, of course, but so far everything looks to be in order to start building."

"What about the other ones we find?" a spirit asked. "No doubt they'll be located in other lands."

I shrugged. "Then we'll need to have talks with them as well. Given it's a matter of safety, as it reduces the chance of revenants and other ill-intended spirits from coming and going as they please, and it benefits their people, it shouldn't be too difficult."

"Says the non-people person," Atria teased.

"We'll head out at once," Anir said.

I allowed them to leave. They knew how to find me, and I didn't doubt I had ways of checking in on them. I'd figure that out later.

Tannek approached, his steps still unsure. I smiled and held out my hand. It took him a moment to slip his in with mine. I then did the same with Raikidan, tightening my grip when I had them both.

This was going to take some time, for all of us. Hell, I didn't even know how this all worked. But my soul had past experience, so I was determined to figure it out. I was a selfish half-dragon and I would fight to have them both for as long as I could.

"Momma Eira," Stella called.

I turned to see her, Sethal, and Panga approaching. Es'tla trailed behind them. Seemed he chose to keep an eye on the trio, and somehow ended up with Crystal in the process. Around Stella's chest, she had some sort of cloth sling that budged in one spot.

"Momma, my baby phoenix is all tucked in now," she said, pulling open the distended area of the cloth. Inside was a nest made up of all manner of material, and the phoenix chick. Its eyes were closed, showing it'd settled down for a nap.

"The blue lady helped warm up some rocks to keep the chick warm," Panga said.

My brow rose. "Blue lady?"

She nodded. "Her breath was really warm, like steam from a shower."

"Oh, a blue dragon."

The young girl nodded. *That was nice of the female to do.*

Stella's focus shifted to Tannek. "Who are you? Why are you holding Momma Eira's hand?"

"Stella, this is Tannek," I said. "He was my mate before Papa was."

She cocked her head. "Why did he stop?"

"I died protecting her," Tannek said.

Stella pursed her lips, her nose scrunching. "But you're alive."

"Zion gave me a second life today."

"I don't get it..." She scratched her head. "Momma, is he going to be living with us?"

I glanced to Tannek, then Raikidan, wondering if one of them was going to object to the idea. I wanted Tannek close so we could try and pick up somewhere close to where we'd left off, but if he wasn't comfortable, and Raikidan wanted to take things slower, then we'd work something out.

"Yes, he is," Raikidan said.

"He's taking this a lot better than I anticipated," Rashta said.

She wasn't the only one.

"Do you cook better than Momma?" Stella asked Tannek.

He chuckled. "Yes."

"Not that it's difficult to cook better than me," I mumbled. Honestly, I had no idea what was wrong with my ability to cook for non-dragons. I still wasn't clear on why my food was appealing to dragons at all.

"Okay, then you can stay," Stella proclaimed.

I laughed. "Thanks for your permission, hon."

"Can Panga stay with us, too?" my daughter asked. "She doesn't have a momma or papa, and I really like her. She says I'm older than her, so she could be my little sister, and I won't ask for one from you anymore."

"The two have been glued together for half the day, I swear," Es'tla said, almost exasperated. But I noticed the humor in his eyes.

Panga's eyes went wide and then hopeful. I blinked and then looked to Raikidan. That put us in a tough spot. We hadn't even gotten Es'tla home and settled in. Were we in a position to take in another child? Was *I* ready for that? *Hell, can I say no and disappoint the poor girl?*

"She does need someone to do her hair for her all the time," Raikidan said, the corner of his lip curving up.

I pressed my lips together. Of course he'd say it that way. "Well, we can't have her running around with inferior hairdos, so I guess we need to find Raid and Mocha so we can get the paperwork done so she can come live with us."

It took Panga and Stella a moment to register the agreement, then they exploded with glee. Panga wrapped her arms around our legs the best she could, before running off to find Raid or Mocha for us. Stella scurried on after her, and Sethal took off after them after taking a moment to realize they were gone, calling after the girls to wait up for him.

"So, who wants to hold the cat next?" Es'tla asked.

I laughed. *What have I gotten myself into with these kids?*

The next few hours flashed by. Gina hadn't actually left with the other gods. She'd set out to heal the dragons, given that shaman healing didn't work on them. I made sure Raikidan got in on the treatment. He tried to hide the pain he was in, but I'd seen the damage he'd taken in his dragon form. And his nu-human form was battered to hell as well.

The Crimson Sanctuary members had been hauled off during this time. I wasn't sure if we'd get anything out of them, or what we'd do with them, but I was going to leave that to those who made those calls.

My father and Del'karo officially met Shyden. The three hit it off nicely, which I was grateful for. I also managed to catch up with them and my other assassin-turned-mercenary students.

I finally got to finish catching up with people, living and dead alike, including Lord Taric. He apparently helped in the fight as well, to which I was immensely grateful for. I also got to amusedly witness him give Argus a lecture about taking good care of Seda while oddly praising him for it at the same time. According to her, Taric had done this a few times while he oversaw the establishing of the new governing system for Dalatrend.

Daren introduced me to his family, who were wonderful to be around. They showered me in endless compliments that didn't once feel like brown-nosing. And they really wanted to see Rashta's weapon. I was more than happy to show it off to them. If anyone would appreciate a Maker's work, it'd be the dwarves.

Atria complained in my head about how unfair it was that I got the weapon when she could have used it. That triggered quite the bickering between her and Rashta, who didn't approve of Atria's prior profession, and seemed to get on her case about it about as much as Atria's own mother had.

Raikidan also introduced me to the scarred dragon I'd seen earlier with them—Vorsy, his long-lost sister. She was a scrappy one. I liked her a lot. And she had a blue dragon for a mate, which explained why she'd disappeared.

I also got to meet many of my past soul-lives' family as well. Not all of them, though, as it appeared many were living new mortal lives somewhere. But it was nice seeing where I'd come from.

Mana insisted I officially meet her grandfather, as she deemed our prior conversation not good enough. Given he'd met some of my past soul-lives before I could understand her insistence. Though, I felt bad he didn't get the chance to speak with them again when my soul was fractured. Xeren insisted seeing them from afar was enough, however I chose to act as a messenger on my soul-lives' behalf to ease the guilt.

As the afternoon faded to evening, the gathering wound down. Many left inebriated from all the ale the dwarves shoved into people's hands. I saw Ryoko, Rylan, and the Asholta pack off, Ashnard mentioning he looked forward to seeing me in the next peace talks with the Dalatrend Council. Seemed Ryoko and Rylan had told enough stories about me that they were anticipating more lively meetings in my presence, and I knew the alpha wogron meant it in a more troublemaking sense.

I said goodbye to my other friends, promising it wouldn't be the last they saw of me. And we came to an agreement with Raid and Mocha to finalize the needed paperwork for Panga to move in with us tomorrow. They trusted us enough that we weren't required to follow the usual protocols, and liked the idea of settling Panga in immediately.

The only two I didn't get the chance to say goodbye to were my parents. Rizgar had whisked my mother away at some point. It didn't bother me. They deserved this time to catch up. And it surprised me more that he'd waited as long as he had.

The West Tribe shamans gathered together; Kharis also joined us. It seemed he wanted to continue to protect me as he'd sworn to do. Many other guardians chose to do the same, while others asked my permission to roam and protect those who needed it. The idea of them off on their own made me uneasy, mostly because I didn't know if they'd be met with hostility by those they wanted to protect, but I wasn't going to deny them their requests.

With my now-bigger family gathered around me, we headed home through a portal. Well, to the village. Getting to the house took a bit more time, as I wanted to allow Es'tla, Panga, Lazei, and Tannek to take in some of their new home.

Stella elected herself as the official "tour guide" and showed them many places, though I was sure to keep her from going overboard. They'd need to absorb it in small bursts, and it was getting late. There was plenty of time for them to explore tomorrow.

Daren, Valene, and Vanessa, who had been using the spiritual gateway to not only assist in the battle earlier, but now spend time with the two, showed Lazei to the inn where he was allowed to stay until he knew what he wanted to do. Genesis, who'd been renting a room when she wasn't out with the scholars, followed them. Ryder planned to join her, but after the move-in. I knew it was in case I needed help. It was a big transition.

I managed to herd my family toward the forest path leading to our house. Shva'sika and Zane split off from us when they reached their home path. Shva'sika promised everyone would at least have beds within the next few hours. I wasn't overly concerned. We had couches, blankets, mountains of pillows, and sleeping bags. I could work something up in a pinch.

"Wow," Es'tla said when we reached the house. "This is bigger than I thought it'd be."

"You'll learn quickly Shva'sika's family doesn't do things by halves or know the meaning of simple," I said.

He laughed. "That sounds about right, from what I've heard of the Lightshines."

Raikidan opened the front door, leading us into the spacious foyer. He set Crystal down, allowing her to explore, and then put her supplies in the kitchen until we figured out where they'd go.

Tannek remained by my side as we walked into the living room, gaping at the opulence. "This… feels too luxurious for you."

I glanced at him. Didn't he know this layout?

"I don't believe he's been around for the whole year," Rashta said. *"I never sensed him once."*

That was strange to think about. I knew he'd given me space when Raikidan and I first mated, but I figured he'd struggle to not keep secret tabs on me afterward. "I didn't decorate. This was all done by a certain elf."

He chuckled. "That I can see."

"Is it going to be a problem?" I asked.

He blinked and then shook his head. "No, of course not. It'll just be something else to get used to."

I frowned. I didn't like how he worded that.

Tannek poked the corner of my mouth. "Don't do that."

I wasn't sure what to say to him. We needed to get the kids settled in before he, Raikidan, and I talked about how things were going to work, but at the same time, I wasn't sure if talking about it tonight was the best idea. We were all exhausted and still trying to process.

Stella tugged on my skirt. "I'm going to show them where they can pick their room."

"We get to pick?" Es'tla said, clearly skeptical. "You haven't already picked it for us?"

I smiled and rested my hand on his cheek. I wasn't sure the kind of choices he had while staying in the North Tribe. They were better than when he'd been with his father, that much I could confirm. But here, he'd have vastly different rules placed on him. I wanted to do my best to allow him freedoms but still give him proper boundaries. "Of course we haven't. There are plenty of empty rooms to choose from, so go take a look."

His face lit up, and he rushed up the stairs, his long legs skipping every other one. Stella complained about him getting ahead of her, especially since she had to be careful with her chick, but the half-elf teen didn't listen to her.

Panga kept pace with Stella, and I followed behind. By the time we'd reached Stella's room, Es'tla had already figured out the one he wanted. A room with a large window that overlooked the west side of the house. It was quite a bit away from the other occupied rooms, but if that was the room he wanted, then he'd get it.

Tannek wandered a little ways to pick out a room for himself.

Panga glanced around, clearly overwhelmed. Luckily Stella noticed and was all too eager to help. "Want to stay in my room?"

Panga smiled wide. "Can I?"

Stella nodded. "I got lots of space. We can share the bed, too, until you get yours."

The two ran off and I took a breath. This was turning out easier than I expected.

I turned when Raikidan came upstairs. He slipped up next to me and wrapped an arm around my hips.

"Sounds like it's all going well," he said.

I nodded. "Smoothest it could have gone. If we had the right number of beds, it'd been perfect."

He tightened his grip, pulling me closer, and he bent down to speak against my ear. "If you'd allowed Shva'sika to fully furnish the house like she'd wanted, this wouldn't be an issue."

I suppressed a shiver that ran down my spine, triggered by the rumble of his voice, by rolling my eyes. "I wasn't going waste my time keeping unused furniture clean. Besides, this isn't so bad. One night with improvised accommodations won't kill them."

He grunted as if I wasn't quite getting something he was trying to imply. I shrugged it off. I was too tired for subtle hints.

Pulling away from him, I went to check on the girls, only to find them trying to search for a good place to put Stella's phoenix. They were being smart in trying to pick the perfect spot for both them to care for it, and keep it out of Crystal's reach. So far, she hadn't tried to eat it yet, even when Stella insisted on introducing the feline to the chick, but no one was willing to take any chances.

I gave the two a hand, finding the perfect temporary box until we could get something better. We'd just have to keep Crystal out of the room until then.

Our final task was moving Stella's bed and other miscellaneous items she had left out so Panga's bed could fit. Not too difficult, but a fun little puzzle for the girls. Panga didn't have much in the way of her own things yet. Mocha promised to pack up what little she had and have it ready tomorrow for me to pick up.

When I turned around, I found Raikidan leaning in the doorway, his arm propped over his head. His intense sapphire eyes watched me. I didn't stop myself from drinking in the sight he presented. My bottom lip caught in my teeth, desire pooling in my core. I had it bad for him when he stood like this.

My gaze slipped to Tannek when he appeared in the hallway. He leaned against the wall. It was now that I got a good moment to take him in, and I realized what Zion really meant about turning back time. He looked exactly the same as the day he'd died, just as he always did when I saw him as a spirit. Age, military uniform and all. *He still looks good in uniform, that's for sure.*

Raikidan's hand clenched, his eyes shifting briefly to Tannek before going back to just me. *Oh...* I understood now why he was just standing there. He'd reached his limit today. No doubt that was why he didn't insist on moving the bed instead of me. I'd expect him to behave in front of the kids, and if he didn't trust that he could, he'd make deliberate space between for as long as he could manage. But now I needed to take of him—once I figured out how to not broadcast it in front of the family.

Ryder came around the corner with blankets spilling over his arms. He paused when he spotted us in this weird stand-off arrangement. Before I could discreetly ask for his assistance, Tannek spoke up.

"Ryder, mind showing me how to get to the greenhouse? I noticed it from the room I chose."

My son nodded. "Sure. Stella, why don't you help? You can give everyone a tour around the outside of the house and show them the stable that's in progress."

Stella gasped. "Yes! Panga, we're getting horses."

The young girl's eyes went wide. "I get one, too?"

Stella nodded. *Gee, thanks for deciding that, Stel.* But I couldn't rightfully give Stella a horse and not Panga.

The two girls rushed out of the room and down the hall. I walked over to Raikidan and slipped my arm around his waist, but didn't go any further as Ryder called for Es'tla to follow. The teen, while confused, didn't object.

Stella made it to the stairs when she realized Raikidan and I hadn't followed. "Momma?"

"Go on. Papa and I have to talk about something. We'll be down after."

The young girl shrugged and took off again.

"That extra horse is going to cost a pretty coin," I said to Raikidan casually.

He bent close to my ear, the heat of his breath sending a shiver through me. "If you asked for a whole herd, that's what you'd get."

I tipped my head up, smirking. "I don't need that many. I've got my hands full with the other herd we're growing."

He pulled me closer, his fingers pressing into my back that was different from how he'd touched me before. I bit my lip. The touch was in no way unpleasant. Strangely, Velsara stirred, as if the contact called her.

"That's Taiegh's touch," she said, her voice breathy.

"Our brood is growing," Raikidan murmured, his mouth curling up half his face. He reached up and caressed the corner of my mouth with his thumb. "And your broodmother rage is as enticing and frightening as I expected it to be."

"Hmm, is it?" My hand glided over his abs, his hard muscles flexing under my touch. "Tell me more about how you're feeling."

A groan rumbled in Raikidan's chest, and the sapphire hue of his eyes deepened to a molten glint. I gasped when my back hit the wall. "I'd rather just show you."

I swallowed, fighting the rising desire building in me. "Do you have enough restraint for us to at least make it down the hall?"

His hand curled around the back of my neck, pulling me hard against his mouth. A quiet whimper escaped me and I pressed into him. I didn't expect words to be his choice. He was a dragon of action, and that worked for me.

Our lips synchronized, and our hands roamed each other's bodies. My insides melted with each touch, desire crashing over me in waves. His musky, ashen scent surrounded me.

Raikidan gripped my hips and lifted me up. I wrapped my arms and legs around him, squeezing tight. His heavy steps barely registered through my haze of needy desire as he walked us down the hall, our kiss never breaking.

The door of our bedroom slammed against the wall. My back hit the plush comforter, Raikidan's calloused fingers underneath me, dragging down my spine. I moaned, and Isis stirred in the same way Velsara had earlier.

I expected him to get rough and start ripping at my clothes. They were always his most-hated barrier and first goal. But his kisses trailed down my jaw and neck, and over my collar bone, the pace needy, but slow and surprisingly controlled. Sylvia surfaced in my mind, summoned by the touch.

"I thought I was going to lose you," Raikidan murmured against my skin. "I thought the moment you disappeared through time, I'd failed to protect you. And then Kir almost corrupting you…"

His teeth grazed my shoulder, hands roaming my sides in a way I'd never experienced, but Nalia seemed to know this touch by the way she now stirred. "I need this last moment to have you to myself."

My desire fizzled. *It did bother him Tannek was back.* I took a quiet breath and lifted his gaze to meet mine. "Raikidan… if Tannek being part of my life like he had before is going to be a problem, then—"

"I'm not going to make you choose." The intensity in his eyes made my pulse skip. "I made that mistake once before. You weren't the same after I forced that decision on you. It was like a part of you died with him."

I swallowed, his eyes showing something I'd never seen before in him. Nisha whimpered, longing lacing the sound. "You're speaking as if you remember that time yourself. The way you're looking at me…"

"They're not going away this time, Eira." Raikidan said. My heart nearly stopped. He could communicate with his past soul-lives again? "It's different this time. I hear their voices again—share their memories as they offer them to me. I sense their presence as an extension of myself. Even now, they press against my mind, willing to be channeled. And this time, it's permanent."

I propped myself up, my breath coming quick. "Why didn't you say something earlier?"

He leaned in and kissed me—hard, but slow and deliberate. My hands fisted the blankets, desire quickly returning. "Because it's not something you can help me with. I need to learn to live with this now."

Raikidan kissed the corner of my mouth, then under my jaw, sending a wave of weakness through me. "And we thought this might add a little more fun."

A quiet moan left my lips, all my lives stirring this time. His voice… altered in a way; layered, as if he was channeling his soul-lives all at once.

"We'll ensure you're always pleased," he murmured against my throat.

I sucked in a tight breath when he nipped my skin. My pulse quickened as he trailed kiss after kiss down my chest and between my breasts. His hands traced my sides, the touch familiar and foreign at the same time.

He continued lower, a kiss just below my ribcage and then on my stomach, eliciting a slow inhale from me through my teeth. He trailed back up after nipping my skin below my navel. I tried to speed up his agonizing pacing, but he pinned down my arms beside my head. My back arched when his lips found the sides of my breast again. Need thrummed through me.

Raikidan's grip on my arms lessened as he slid his hands down. His fingers traced my collar bone and then migrated down. The clasp of my top popped open and my supple breasts spilled out into his hands. I gasped and then moaned quietly with hooded eyes when his fingers rolled over my aching nipples—pinching and tweaking them.

Need pooled between my thighs. This agonizingly slow pace was new for him. Our time together was always fevered, frenzied lust. But I liked the change. I liked the feeling of slow and strong building desire for him.

Raikidan's tongue flicked out, caressing my aching buds before slipping one into his mouth and sucking hard. My fingers threaded into his hair, locking him in close. Raikidan kneaded and sucked in a rhythm that pulsed my need in a maddening mix of the right amount and not enough.

Desire fogged my mind, mixing my past soul-lives' presence with my own conscious thoughts.

My breath came in heaving gasps between moans the more my need built. I didn't dare release him until the building ache in my core became too much to bear. I couldn't do this slow pace anymore. Fussing with the belt of his armor, I undid the buckle and yanked the armor off, tossing it carelessly.

Raikidan's eyebrow quirked up, a pleased grin slipped up his face. "Have I frustrated you, Butterfly?"

"More than you realize," I said, my voice heavy with the desire built up in me.

My hand hands slid over his hard abs, memorizing every peak and valley of his muscles. Raikidan let out a low grown when I reached the waist of his pants. "Ladies first."

He slipped his fingers into the band of my skirt and shorts, and in one impressive motion, I found myself lying bare and on display beneath him. Raikidan gazed down at me with hungry appreciation. He slipped off the bed when I reached for him again, and his pants hit the floor, his erect member springing forth.

I caught my tongue between my teeth and allowed myself to drink in the view. I'd never tire of this—of him. Lifting my finger, I beckoned him back, spreading my legs in invitation. He didn't need to be asked twice.

Raikidan crawled over me and claimed my lips, his hands finding my hips. I dragged my fingers down his chest and rocked my hips, feeling his hard length between my thighs. He responded by reaching between us. I gasped and moaned, his fingers stroking my burning heat, sending my nerves ablaze with pleasure.

My whole body quivered, and just as I thought I would go over the edge, he slid inside me. I groaned, throwing my head back.

The frenzy of lust took over, and Raikidan thrust into me stronger and harder. My breathing quickened, my pulse pounding in my ears. My soul-lives reacted with each motion, pressing against my mind until I struggled to process where my thought started and theirs ended, as if we were all in sync and experiencing our mates together as one for the first time.

I panted and moaned, begging for more until the overwhelming sensations flooding me pushed me over the edge. I arched my back, my mouth falling open as a scream erupted with the burst of ecstasy coursing through me. Raikidan's grip on my hips tightened, losing himself into the tide of his own pleasure. He pressed his face against the side of my neck and groaned as he spent himself.

He slowly stilled and panted hard into my skin, his muscles trembling. When he couldn't hold himself up anymore, he slowly extracted himself from me and flopped down on the bed. Raikidan pulled me close, tucking me in under his arms.

I curled into him, resting my head on his chest and listening to his strong heartbeat. Pleasure coursed through my exhausted body. My past soul-lives' presence had receded in a slow and satisfied languid movement that matched my current state. Raikidan ran his fingers over a sensitive patch of scales on my hip. He always managed to bring out my dragon.

After a moment of nothing but the sound of our breathing filling the room, I spoke, "Are you sure you're okay with Tannek being back in my life?"

I knew I shouldn't bring it up. I should relish in the moment we'd just shared and be happy Raikidan wasn't going to make me choose, but I couldn't let it go just yet. I needed to make sure his needs were met just as much as mine were.

Raikidan brushed a damp lock of hair away from my eyes. "Yes. I deeply regret making you choose that first time. Since that moment, I have shared you in two lives. It does not matter that it was just our souls involved."

He traced his finger up my arm. "I can be happy with this arrangement, because it is him. Anyone else I would not accept. You never stopped loving him, even though you allowed yourself to love me. I've always known this. I know it doesn't mean you love me any less."

My chest swelled. "I do love you."

His eyes glinted. "Say it again."

I grinned and rolled on top of him, speaking in draconic this time. *"You are mine."*

Raikidan tangled his fingers in my hair. A growl rumbled through his chest. "Again."

I placed my hands on either side of his head, hovering over his lips, and ground my hips into him. *"You are mine."*

He groaned. "You're going to give me the impression I haven't satisfied you."

"With more feet running around the house, I'm taking this free moment for all I can." I chuckled. "And it can't hurt to practice more for when we want to add to our brood."

He dug his fingers into my hips. "Don't tease me like that, Eira."

I pecked him on the lips. "I'm not, I'm serious."

Raikidan stared up at me, searching my eyes, and then pulled my head down for a rough kiss. "Then you're not leaving tonight."

I nipped his lower lip. "We'll see if you can manage."

He chuckled. "I'm confident in my ability."

EPILOGUE

J asmine typed on the computer while I sat on the bench behind her, kicking my feet. Raikidan stood beside me, our hands intertwined. The tests, the waiting, we had done this before, but this time something was different. I knew the answer, just like last time, but Jasmine "had to be sure" and Raikidan was still skeptical.

Jasmine hummed to herself as she downloaded the test information to a handheld device Argus designed a few years ago, with the help of Rinneth. Over these last years, the connection with my past soul-lives had strengthened, allowing for all kinds of new abilities to manifest on top of the ones I would have normally had access to had it not been for Zarda and Kir's meddling. *Argus is lucky we let him take all the credit.* I didn't want all that attention. I got enough as it was. Besides, he and Seda were now far better off with the money he was able to bring in, not that she wasn't doing well for herself. *Correction, Eira, that's Doctor Seda now.*

Jasmine rose to her feet, no easy task with the sizable belly she sported, and waddled over to us. She shook her head and handed the device over to me. A smirk lifted the corner of my lips. I was right.

Raikidan's eyes flicked between me and my aunt. "What? What is with the looks?"

"She was right, again," Jasmine said.

He snatched the device from her and stared at the screen. It took him a few moments to respond. "This is one hundred percent accurate?"

"I ran the test three times to be sure," she said. "It's as accurate as it can be."

I leaned back, resting my hand on my rounded belly. "I told you, what I can see is undeniable."

"Yes, at least my consolation prize is I can still surprise you with the more detailed information the test provides."

She had a point. My abilities had limitations, and it'd be nice to see everything the test could say. I lifted my hand so Raikidan could hand the device over for me to look at myself. He didn't see me. His eyes remained glued to the screen. "Rai?"

The handheld device clattered to the floor and before I knew it Raikidan lifted me into his arms and spun, his face alight with a joy I'd never seen before. Bubbling happiness rose up in my chest and soon I was laughing—until the motion made me sick.

Raikidan immediately put me down, and nearly panicked as I leaned on my bench, breathing slow in hopes I wouldn't lose what little food I was able to eat today. Jasmine snatched a bucket and made sure she was ready. Luckily, the sensation died down.

I took a deep breath and sat down. "I'll be happy when *that* stops happening."

"I'm sorry," Raikidan said. "I wasn't thinking. And—"

I pressed a finger to his lips and hushed him. I wasn't going to blame him for getting excited. "Can you let me see the test so I can also know the full result?"

He paused and then looked for it. Jasmine was already trying to pick it up, her even rounder belly than mine making that task a little too difficult. Raikidan got her to sit back down and grabbed the handheld device himself.

I got most of the way through the test results when a tiny knock sounded at the door of the lab. Jasmine walked over to let them in. The person knocked again, this time a bit more frantically, and she chuckled as she opened the door. On the other side was Ryder, along with a light olive-skinned young girl around the age of five, with long raven hair. Streaks of violet accented her side-swept bangs. Two teen girls, one with russet skin and brown eyes, and the other pale with blue eyes, stood next to Ryder. A teen elven boy with a black and red mohawk and dark olive-toned skin, and a young half-elven man with light skin, blue eyes, and copper hair hung back behind them.

The youngest gazed up at Jasmine with sparkling green eyes. "Is Momma's test done, Auntie Jasmine?"

Jasmine smiled at her. "As a matter of fact, Tyra, it is. Why don't you come in so you can find out the result, too?"

Tyra bolted into the room, leaving Ryder and Jasmine in the dust with amused expressions, and ran over to Raikidan. Her hair bounced as she moved, revealing the two sets of ears she had. "Papa Raikidan!"

Raikidan picked her up immediately. "You're excited, little flower."

She nodded with enthusiasm. "Was I right? Tell me I'm right. I'm getting a little brother, aren't I?"

Raikidan chuckled. "Yes, you were right."

Tyra's arms shot up in the air. "Yay!"

I smiled and kissed her on the cheek. "And a little sister."

Our daughter gasped. "Two babies? You're carrying two babies, Momma?"

I nodded. "That's right."

"Coolie! Just like Auntie Jasmine."

Jasmine rested her hand on her swollen belly. "Yes. We'll both have our hands full soon enough."

Ryder came over and embraced me in a hug. "I'm happy for you, Mom."

"Thank you. I'm surprised, but happy. Course, in several months I'll just be miserable."

Jasmine waddled back over to her seat to rest. "Like me."

Ryder laughed and focused on me. "I'll help where I can to alleviate some of that."

"I could use that treatment, too," Jasmine said.

I snorted. "You've got the treatment. Your mate carries you everywhere you go, as if you're going break if you walk more than a foot."

Jasmine smiled. "True."

The other two girls came in, while the young men hung back to not crowd the room too much. The darker-skinned girl gave me a hug. "I'm so happy for you, Momma Eira."

I kissed her on the forehead. "Thank you, Stella. I hope you can be as patient with me as the last time while I go through my crazy mood swings."

She giggled. "Not like you don't put up with that with me."

I grunted. Teen girls were rough.

"Our family just keeps getting bigger and bigger, doesn't it?" the other teen girl said.

I went to say something when I noticed her dark hair was all a mess. "Panga, what happened?"

She pulled some of her wild hair out of the way. "Uncle Ebon and Uncle Trigon." She shot an ugly glare at the young man hanging back. "And Es'tla. They took out my braid and then took a balloon to my head."

Es'tla snickered, unrepentant of his actions toward his younger sister. "I don't know what was funnier. Her freakout, or her lame attempt to beat us up."

Panga's fists curled at her side and she stomped her foot. "Just you wait. I'm going to kick your butt one of these days."

Her older brother made a dismissive motion with his hand, irritating her further. I shook my head. *Never a dull moment in our family.*

I looked to Jasmine. "What's Ebon doing here, if I may ask?"

"Oh, just the standard daily testing we're doing with the dragons."

"Right, right." I should have thought of that. He and Nyoki had been among the many volunteers to be study subjects so Jasmine and the other geneticists could understand dragon biology better before tackling the tedious task of growing them in tanks.

It was a long study, as the first year proved there were only certain times of the year their bodies were in tune biologically. Human-and-dragon pairings were also researched at the same time, to understand how the human's higher conception rate affected their partner. All in all, it was a fascinating study.

I turned my focus to the teen elf hanging back. "Sethal, what are you doing here?"

He shrugged. "Father had business at the embassy today. Let me come along."

Ryder scrutinized the young elf. "I caught him and Stella getting up to no good."

Stella placed a hand on her chest, and made a clearly fake gasp of offence. "Big brother, that's completely untrue."

I crossed my arms, my brow spiking. It didn't surprise me in the least the two were up to something. Not only were they virtually inseparable, they had the habit of getting into trouble if left unsupervised.

Stella let out an exasperated breath. "Fine. We were just playing a prank on a few Council members."

"With the help of Viva," Ryder said, rubbing his temples. "I still don't get how a phoenix can have such a troublemaking personality."

"I blame her parent," Es'tla said, clasping his hands behind his head.

I bit back a laugh, clamping my teeth down on my lip. Jasmine and Raikidan, however, did not hide their amusement. None of this surprised me. It wouldn't be the first time the Council was the target of their antics. *Nor will it be the last.* "At this rate I'm going to get dragged into their chambers and reprimanded."

Raikidan snickered. "Just like old times?"

I shook my head. "There are some things I'd like to leave in the past."

Panga minced up to Raikidan. "Um, Dad, can you do my hair?"

He smiled, never able to refuse that request, no matter how silly she sometimes felt for asking him, still, at her age. "Sure."

He set Tyra down and went to work. Tyra latched onto my leg. "Momma! Wait until Daddy hears I'm getting a brother *and* a sister!"

Someone knocked on the door frame. I looked up to see Tannek standing in the hall. He smiled. "Did I hear the test results are in?"

"Daddy!" Tyra ran over to Tannek. "I'm getting another brother and a sister! Isn't this exciting?"

Tannek picked her up. "It sure is."

I smiled as he held our daughter and made my way over to him. He pulled me against his side, and I gave him a quick kiss. "How was class?"

He'd been working hard on obtaining his doctorate in modern medicine. This was on top of cultivating natural healing we discovered he had a knack for.

Tannek blew out a breath. "Boring. I think I'll test out of this one."

I smiled. "Whatever you want to do, I'll support you."

He rested his forehead against mine. "I know."

My chest swelled. Even after six years had passed, I never tired of his and Raikidan's presence.

The first year of Tannek being back hadn't been easy. There was so much everyone needed to learn and adapt to, it got overwhelming.

To the point I thought things weren't going to work out. But here we were, still together and with a daughter, who in all honesty hadn't been planned, and the event that really sealed our relationship. To this day, I was certain the gods had a hand in that, as if trying to tell us we needed to get our shit together.

And Raikidan had done remarkably well upholding his promise to me. We all still had days when we struggled and needed to work extra hard to keep things from falling apart, but we were making it. And he adapted to this co-parenting aspect far faster than I'd expected, becoming an amazing second father to Tyra.

I gasped and jumped back when a hand went through Tannek's face as if he were an illusion.

Tyra screamed and then complained, "Big brother! Don't do that to Daddy."

Es'tla threw his head back in a raucous laugh. I took a slow breath, pressing my hand against my chest and feeling my racing heart. I hated it when he did that.

Tannek turned to the half-elf. "You know, that does feel weird."

Es'tla smirked. "That adds to the fun."

My heart returned to a normal pace. This ability Tannek exhibited was unique to him. We weren't sure of the reason it developed, but it was clear it was brought on by his unusual return back to life, as Jasmine, Lazei, and my mother had either developed or were showing signs of developing their own new abilities.

And, as a result of Tannek's new abilities, Tyra was also showing signs of unique ones herself.

I cocked my head when Raiden's familiar face appeared in the hall. "Well, hey stranger. You here for the news, or to bother Jasmine?"

He grunted. "I'm making sure she's not overdoing it."

Jasmine rolled her eyes. "I'm fine."

The dragon didn't believe her from the face he made, but with all of us in the way, he couldn't do anything about it.

Ryder peered down the hall. "You ready to break the news to Ryoko? I think I hear her coming."

"I passed them on the way up," Tannek said. "Their eldest was having a bit of a meltdown. I guess she finally calmed down."

Ryoko and Rylan's eldest daughter was only a year older than Tyra, and was just as much of a handful as her mother. It sometimes brought out the worst in Tyra, but other than that, the two were the best of friends, which was all I could ask for with them.

"Let's go tell Auntie Ryoko and Uncle Rylan!" Tyra said, pulled Tannek with her as she left the room.

We all exited the lab and entered the heavily windowed hall facing the fortress courtyard. Viva perched on the ledge of an open window, watching the hustle and bustle below. Even at six years of age and with all her flight feathers, she was still quite small, especially when compared to Raina's companion. My past soul-life let us know she'd get to that size in time, most likely after she went through a few death cycles, which happened about once every century.

The mythical bird turned its head and chirped, flying to Stella's shoulder, where she lovingly nuzzled her companion. The two had such a strong bond. I was proud of Stella. Phoenixes proved to be difficult creatures to raise, and yet Stella had met that challenge, igniting a passion for rehabilitating injured animals.

Ryoko's voice echoed through the halls, as well as a tiny girl's voice that went a mile a minute with endless questions. *Only ten in the morning and she's already at it.* I couldn't help but snicker. Ryoko was getting a taste of her own medicine with this one.

Ryoko and Rylan rounded the corner. Rylan carried an infant with an abundance of white hair on his back, and a smaller girl bounced at Ryoko's side. Before anything could be said, the little girl let go of Ryoko's hand and charged down the hall, her wavy brown hair flowing behind her. I laughed when she came to a skidding halt and pressed her ear against my medium sized belly bump. The dog-like ears she inherited from her mother twitched as she listened. Her gaze slowly went up at me, her one gold and one blue eye wide with awe.

Her brow knitted and she pursed her lips. "Are you having a monster baby, Auntie Eira?"

The hall erupted with laughter. I smiled when I got myself under control. "No, Ayra, I'm not having a monster baby."

Ryoko coughed into her hand as she approached. "Dragon baby. Beg to differ."

I squinted at her and then looked at Ayra. "I'm having twins."

Little Ayra's eyes grew wider, but it was Ryoko who squealed with delight. "Two purple-haired dragon babies!"

I couldn't stop the laughter. She never stopped calling them that.

My attention was pulled to the courtyard when the sound of large wings flapping hit my ears. I knew them to be dragon wings, but it was a few minutes before a large red dragon landed. I grinned at the sight of my father. "Hey, Rai, want give my father a heart attack?"

Raikidan's eyes lit up. "When do I not?"

I shook my head. *Like father, like son.* The others laughed as he lifted Tyra onto his shoulder and took off for the lower levels to get out to the courtyard, our daughter egging him on. She loved her grandfather dearly, and he her, but she also enjoyed the odd relationship Raikidan and my father had and perpetuated it when she saw fit. *She's definitely my daughter, that's for sure.*

"That she is," Rashta's amused voice said.

I looked to my side to find her projecting herself next to me. The others moved on to follow Raikidan, knowing my talks with Rashta were important. Raiden hauled Jasmine into his arms, not allowing her to walk herself. Her complaints carried down the hall, reminding him she was capable of walking, and that it was good for her. It all fell on deaf ears, like always.

I smiled at Rashta and then gazed out to the courtyard again. This time, I noticed all the people of different walks of life gathered. I had seen crowds like this enough to know they had heard I was in the city and wanted to either catch a glimpse of me, or even speak with me if they could.

I sighed. "So much for the quiet life I had wanted."

Rashta chuckled. "Life is good at throwing curves at us."

"This story isn't over yet, is it, Rashta?"

"Life is made up of many stories. This heavy one may be ending, but for you, a new one is already starting. It'll be some time before your stories are done."

"Well, if this past one was any hint to the next, it'll be quite the tale. Not to mention we do have Kir to deal with still."

Rashta's eyes darkened. "Yes."

After the battle at the shrine years ago, Kir had up and disappeared again. We'd had run-ins with the remnants of the Crimson Sanctuary now and then, but so far their numbers still hadn't recovered on the surface to pose a problem for us to deal with. And with Anir and my bound spirits finding plane-thinning areas all the time, Kir's super-powered revenants had fewer avenues to easily spread their corruption.

Rosa and Xaedrix, as well as Xithoz and his clan, were also proving to be valuable allies. People were still terrified of them, but Nemora and Xithoz attended a few peace talks in hopes of working something out with the rest of the Lumaraeon races.

And I supported them. Not only because they deserved as much of a foothold here as the rest of us, but for the effort they'd gone through to helping my brothers and other newly converted demons adjust.

I took a breath and refocused my thoughts onto Kir. His absence during all this hadn't come as a surprise to me. The blow we hit him, he knew it was best to stay hidden for now.

Celeste hadn't escaped this time, her purification going much better than the last. And without her helping him, he was going to need time to combat me and the plans I was enacting. My attempts to bring peace to Lumaraeon, including the end of halfling persecution, were progressing in ways he would struggle to combat.

Another presence appeared next to me. Isis stared out beyond the fortress, her focus intense. "The smartest thing he could do is to wait out our lifespan. Thanks to Celesta, he knows the rebirth process is broken. But even though you're too strong for him as you are, he won't wait that long. You'll accumulate too strong a following, and he wants the satisfaction of destroying us himself."

I glanced down at my swollen belly. Two glowing orbs flickered in and then out of sight as if they hadn't truly been there. My ability to see souls never went away, as we predicted. It'd become stronger, and I was beginning to learn how to identify souls based on a unique energy they gave off—like the two growing inside me.

Two precious souls I'd last seen six years ago and promised I'd see again. I rested my hand on my belly and closed my eyes. *Xephrya... Lo'shen... I promise you both, you'll have the best life I can give you.*

I shook my head. "Let's not act dumb here. We all know what's potentially going on. We all see how people react when they see me. We all hear many continue to utter the title *goddess*." *And they've recently started directing such titles to Raikidan and Tannek.* "My ability to see and bind souls isn't a fluke, and not something any mortal can have. My youngest daughter has abilities normal mortals don't get."

I closed my eyes and took a deep breath. "Kir is no fool, either. He knows he can't wait this out, even if his pride allows it. Not this time."

My eyes flicked to Isis. "We've been casual about my learning of our history to allow me to live my life in the way I was denied before. I've focused on the now, trying to fix what was broken. But if we're to deal with Kir, and finally put this eon's long feud behind us, we're all going to have to sit down so you can all teach me about our past."

Isis nodded. "I agree. The more you know about how he works, and how we've dealt with him and his like, the more successful we'll be in finally ending him."

Rashta placed a hand on both our shoulders. "This will end, don't you two worry. But let's move on from this topic. It's spoiling the joyous mood." A wicked grin spread across her face. "It's time to break the news to Mom and Dad. Their reaction will be quite entertaining."

Isis and I exchanged amused glances before she vanished back into my mind. "Your parents or mine?"

"Both. Definitely both."

I laughed and we headed down the hall. No matter what happened in the coming future, one thing I was certain of, my life was going to be far from dull and quiet.

*Eira and her past soul-lives' stories continue in
the Dragon-Phoenix Chronicles*

GLOSSARY
CHARACTER

DRAGON-PHOENIX

Aria (*ARE-ee-uh*) – Human blue dragon hybrid, Dragon-Phoenix: eighth life, water elementalist. Mate to Reve and Zetan

Atria (*ah-TREE-ah*) – Human black dragon hybrid, Dragon-Phoenix: sixth life, fire elementalist. Mate to Verrak

Ayuma (*EYE-yoo-mah*) – Human black-green dragon hybrid, Dragon-Phoenix: tenth life, lightning elementalist, dream walker. Mate to Zephyr

Eira (*AIR-uh*) – Nu-human-dragon hybrid experiment, Dragon-Phoenix: fifteenth life, former rebel battle leader, former commander and assassin, sister to Bone, Rhaec, Trigon, Yára, Elgren, mother to Ryder, Stella, Panga, and Est'la. Shaman of the Rising Sun, current Ambassador. Alt names: Alt names: Laz, Laz'shika (*laz-shee-kah*). Mate to Raikidan and Tannek

Isis – Human red dragon hybrid, Dragon-Phoenix: first life, fire elementalist. Mate to Anshur

Lutha – Human white dragon hybrid, Dragon-Phoenix: third life, psychic: Battle Psychic, twin to Lina. Mate to Rhaegos

Lina – Human white dragon hybrid, Dragon-Phoenix: third life, psychic: Seer, twin to Lutha. Mate to Rhaegos

Nalia (*nal-EE-ah*) – Human brown dragon hybrid, Dragon-Phoenix:

fifth life, Shaman of the Fractured Earth, second Ambassador. Mate to Razeth

Nisha (*NEE-shah*) – Elf violet dragon hybrid, Dragon-Phoenix: second life, arcane mage. Mate to Aser

Pheydra (*FAY-drah*) – Human black-blue dragon hybrid, Dragon-Phoenix: twelfth life, water elementalist. Mate to Roan

Raina – Elf green dragon hybrid, Dragon-Phoenix: fourth life, plant-based Shaman of the Fractured Earth, first Ambassador. Mate to Xanthus

Rinneth – Human black dragon hybrid, Dragon-Phoenix: eleventh life, lightning elementalist. Mate to Vesser

Sylvia (*SILL-vee-ah*) – Human brown dragon hybrid, Dragon-Phoenix: ninth life, metal-based earth elementalist. Mate to Rylar

Xenia (*ZEN-ee-ah*) – Human brown-red dragon hybrid, Dragon-Phoenix: thirteenth life, sand-based Shaman of the Fractured Earth and Shaman of the Frozen Waste, third Ambassador. Mate to Madorai

Velsara (*VELL-sar-ah*) – Nu-human dragon hybrid, Dragon-Phoenix: fourteenth life, Shaman of the Rising Sun, fourth Ambassador. Mate to Taiegh

Zalia (*ZAL-ee-ah*) – Human black-chromatic dragon hybrid, Dragon-Phoenix: seventh life, lightning elementalist. Mate to Khalon

DRAGON-PHOENIX CHAMPION

Anshur – Red dragon, Dragon-Phoenix Champion: first life. Mate to Isis

Aser – Blue dragon, Dragon-Phoenix Champion: second life. Mate to Nisha

Khalon (*KAL-on*) – Black dragon, Dragon-Phoenix Champion: seventh life. Mate to Zalia

Madorai (*MAH-door-eye*) – Violet dragon, Dragon-Phoenix Champion: thirteenth life. Mate to Xenia

Raikidan (*RYE-ki-DAN*) – Black and red dragon, Dragon-Phoenix Champion: fifteenth life, brother to Ebon and Vorsy, cousin to Corliss, son to Xephrya and Raiden. Ambassador Guard. Mate to Eira

Razeth (*RAH-zeth*) – White-blue dragon, Dragon-Phoenix Champion: fifth life. Mate to Nalia

Reve – Green dragon, Dragon-Phoenix Champion: eighth life, twin to Zetan. Mate to Aria

Rhaegos (*RAY-gose*) – Brown dragon, Dragon-Phoenix Champion: third life. Mate to Lutha and Lina

Roan – Blue dragon, Dragon-Phoenix Champion: twelfth life. Mate to Pheydra

Rylar (*rye-LAR*) – Chromatic dragon, Dragon-Phoenix Champion: ninth life. Mate to Sylvia

Taiegh (*TAY-zh*) – Red Dragon, Dragon-Phoenix Champion: fourteenth life. Mate to Velsara

Verrak – Red dragon, Dragon-Phoenix Champion: sixth life. Mate to Atria

Vesser – Green-black dragon, Dragon-Phoenix Champion: eleventh life. Mate to Rinneth

Xanthus – White dragon, Dragon-Phoenix Champion: fourth life. Mate to Raina

Zephyr (*ZEH-fer*) – Black dragon, Dragon-Phoenix Champion: tenth life. Mate to Ayuma

Zetan – Green dragon, Dragon-Phoenix Champion: eighth life, twin to Reve. Mate to Aria

CRIMSON SANCTUARY

Kir – Leader, revenant

SHAMANS

NORTH TRIBE

Arnia (*ARE-nee-ah*) – Nu-human experiment, former rebel mole, twin to Jaybird, metal elementalist. Partner to Ven'lar

Fe'teline (*fey-TELL-een*) – Nu-human, Shaman of the Rising Sun

Jakcel (*JACK-sell*) – Nu-human, former Dalatrend Orphan

Jaybird – Nu-human experiment, former rebel mole, twin to Arnia, air elementalist

Sha'hiri (*sha-HEER-ee*) – Leader, nu-human, Shaman of the Frozen Waste

Ven'lar (*ven-LAR*) – Nu-human, Shaman of the Cleansing Spirit. Partner to Arnia

SOUTH TRIBE

Ir'esh (*EAR-esh*) – Chief, elf, father to Tla'lli, Shaman of the Fractured Crystal

Kelen – Shaman, nu-human, psychic, twin to Nisa

Ne'kall (*nay-CALL*) – Elf, son to Del'karo, father of four, Shaman of the Rising Sun

Nisa – Shaman, nu-human, psychic, twin to Kelen

Talon – Nu-human demon hybrid experiment, bone spike ability. Partner to Tla'lli

Tla'lli (*teh-LAH-lee*) – Elf, daughter to Ir'esh, Shaman of the Whispering Winds. Partner to Talon

EAST TRIBE

Nela – Nu-human, Shaman of the Dancing Lights

Se'lata (*say-LAH-tah*) – Elf, spice merchant, Shaman of the Fractured Crystal

Xa'vian (*ZAH-vee-an*) – Leader, elf, Shaman of the Dancing Lights

WEST TRIBE

Alena – Elf, wife to Del'karo, mother figure to Eira, mother of Vanya, Ne'kall, and eleven other sons, Shaman of the Cleansing Spirit

Daren – Human, Valene's adopted father, inn keeper, former partner to Valessa

Del'karo (*del-CAR-oh*) – Elf, mentor and father figure to Eira, husband to Alena, father of Vanya, Ne'kall, and eleven other sons, Shaman of the Rising Sun

Es'tla (*ess-teh-LAH*) – Half-elf, adopted son of Eira and Raikidan, Shaman of the Rising Sun

Genesis – First nu-human, formerly oversaw Rebellion Team 3, necromantic abilities, daughter to Nazir

Kharis (*CAR-is*) – Shadow guardian, elf (formerly)

Ken'ichi (*ken-EE-chee*) – Nu-human, friend to Eira, Guard and Shaman of the Cleansing Spirit

Lazei (*LAH-zay*) – Half-elf, ancient swordsman, protector of the Eternal Library, revived

Lo'shen – Elf, scholar, father of Me'kunar, reincarnated

Maka'shi (*mah-KAH-shee*) – Leader, half-elf, Shaman of the Frozen Waste, widow: former wife to Va'len

Me'kunar (*may-COON-are*) – Elf, scholar, son of Lo'shen

Mel'ka (*mel-KAH*) – Elf, elder, storyteller, Shaman of the Fractured Crystal

Panga – Nu-human, adopted daughter of Eira and Raikidan

Ryder – Nu-human wolf dragon experiment, son to Eira and Rylan, ice and fire elementalist, Maker. Partner to Genesis

Shva'sika (*shh-VAH-see-KAH*) – Elf, sister to Xye, mentor and adopted family to Eira, Shaman of the Dancing Lights. Engaged to Zane. Alt names: Elarinya (*ell-are-IN-yah*), Danika

Stella – Nu-human, adopted daughter of Eira and Raikidan

Tannek – Nu-human experiment, double ear prototype, brother to Andariel and Azriel, medic, mate to Eira, revived

Vanya – Elf, Daughter to Del'karo and Alene, sister to Ne'kall and twelve other brothers, godchild to Eira

Valene (*vah-LEEN*) – Human, daughter to Valessa, Eira's and Daren's adopted daughter, Shaman of the Fractured Crystal

Valessa – Human, mother to Valene, Shaman of the Fractured Crystal. Former partner to Daren. Deceased

Xye (*zeye*) – Elf, brother to Shva'sika, attempted to court Eira, Shaman of the Cleansing Spirit, deceased.

Ral'ko (*ral-KOH*) – Human, Guard

Ren – Elf, Shaman of the Cleansing Spirit

Va'len (*VAH-len*) – Former leader, elf, Shaman of the Fractured Crystal, former husband to Maka'shi, deceased

DRAGONS

Ambrose – Black dragon, father to Rennek and Raiden, grandfather to Corliss, Raikidan, Ebon, and Vorsy. Mate to Salir

Anir (*ah-NEER*) – Black dragon, coveted Eira's soul, purification bound

Corliss – Green-black dragon, cousin to Raikidan. Mate to Mana

Ebon – Black-red dragon, brother to Raikidan and Vorsy, son to Xephrya and Raiden. Mate to Nyoki

Enrek – Green-black dragon, brother to Corliss, infatuated with Mana

Mana – Green dragon. Mate to Corliss

Naloth – Chromatic dragon, assigned to watch Eira

Nyoki (*NEE-oh-key*) – Black dragon. Mate to Ebon

Raiden – Black dragon, father to Raikidan, Ebon, Vorsy. Former mate to Xephrya

Rennek – Black dragon, adopted son to Salir and Ambrose

Salir (*sah-LEER*) – Black dragon, mother to Rennek and Raiden, grandmother to Corliss, Raikidan, Ebon, and Vorsy. Mate to Ambrose

Xeren (*zer-EN*) – Green elder dragon, grandfather to Mana, deceased

Xephrya (*zef-RYE-ah*) – Red dragon, mother to Raikidan and Ebon, reincarnated. Former mate to Raiden

VELSARA WILDS CLAN

Anahak (*an-ah-HAWK*) – Black dragon, father to Rimu, cousin of Raikidan. Mate to Xaneth

Rimu – Black-red dragon, son to Anahak and Xaneth

Xaneth (*zan-ETH*) – Red dragon, mother to Rimu. Mate to Anahak

Zaith – Clan leader, red dragon, adopted son of Velsara and Taiegh

NORTH HYBERIA MOUNTAIN CLAN

Amara (*ah-MAR-ah*) – Nu-human experiment, General, mother to Eira, Bone, Rhaec, Trigon, Yára, Elgren, sister to Jasmine and Zane, water elementalist, revived. Mate to Rizgar

Bone – Nu-human-dragon hybrid experiment, former rebel mole, former assassin, clone of Eira, daughter of Amara and Rizgar

Elgren – Nu-human-dragon hybrid experiment, former rebel mole, former assassin, clone of Eira, daughter of Amara and Rizgar

Largren – Clan lieutenant, red dragon with black dragon ancestry

Rizgar – Clan leader, red dragon, father to Eira, Bone, Rhaec, Trigon, Yára, Elgren. Mate to Amara

Rhaec (*RAY-ek*) – Nu-human-dragon hybrid experiment, former rebel mole, brute class, clone of Eira, daughter of Amara and Rizgar. Partner to Nyra

Shora – Human, mother to Isis, sister to Kir, earth elementalist, deceased

Trigon – Nu-human-dragon hybrid experiment, former rebel mole, brute class, clone of Eira, daughter of Amara and Rizgar

Yára (*YEH-rah*) – Nu-human-dragon hybrid experiment, former rebel mole, water elementalist, clone of Eira, daughter of Amara and Rizgar

SOULCRESTAL CLAN

Vorsy – Black-red dragon, sister to Raikidan and Ebon, daughter to Xephrya and Raiden

DEMONS

Rosa (*ROH-sah*) – Succubus. Mated to Zaedrix
Zaedrix (*ZAY-dricks*) – Incubus. Mated to Rosa

XOLRAL CLAN
Nemora (*nay-MORE-ah*) – Succubus. Mate to Xithoz
Xithoz (*ZEE-thaus*) – Bone demon, Clan leader. Mate to Nemora

WOGRONS

ASHOLTA PACK
Ashnard – Alpha, wogron
Rylan (*RYE-lan*) – Nu-human experiment, former rebel, brother to Raid, former Captain, ice elementalist, experimental shapeshifter: wolf. Artificial mate bond with Ryoko (formerly Eira), Mate to Ryoko
Ryoko (*Ree-OH-koh*) – Half-wogron experiment, former rebel, brute class, former Lieutenant, clone of Peacekeeper Ryoko, best friend to Eira (reincarnation soul bond). Mate to Rylan

DALATREND

COUNCIL
Adina (*ah-DEE-nah*) – First Dalatrend shapeshifter experiment, nu-human experiment, formerly oversaw Rebellion Team 7
Akama (*ah-KAH-mah*) – First Dalatrend Seer experiment (not planned), nu-human experiment, formerly oversaw Rebellion Team 5, twin to Enrée
Eldenar – First Dalatrend war experiment, nu-human experiment, formerly oversaw Rebellion Team 4

Elkron – First Dalatrend elementalist experiment, nu-human experiment, formerly oversaw Rebellion Team 6

Enrée (*EN-ree-ay*) – First Dalatrend Battle Psychic experiment (not planned), nu-human experiment, formerly oversaw Rebellion Team 2, twin to Akama

Hanama (*HAH-nah-mah*) – First Dalatrend anthropomorphic experiment, nu-human experiment, formerly oversaw Rebellion Team 1

FORMER LEADERS

Taric – Nu-human, father to Zarda, deceased

Zarda – Nu-human, son to Taric, deceased

MILITARY

Zo – Nu-human experiment, former rebel mole, General, previously interested in Eira

Arlon – Nu-human experiment, former rebel mole, recent tank release, fan of Eira's reputation

CITIZENS

Alex – Nu-human experiment, former rebel, Run competition participant, previously interested in Eira

Aliyah (*ALL-ee-yah*) – Nu-human, former soldier, has amnesia

Alyra (*all-EYE-rah*) – Nu-human experiment, former soldier, partner to Lakon, father to Eyri, musician

Andariel – Nu-human experiment, double ear prototype, brother to Azriel and Tannek, former rebel, former medic, strip club owner: Midnight

Argus – Nu-human experiment, former rebel, inventor. Partner to Seda

Aurora – Nu-human experiment, former rebel and Underground computer tech, head of Dalatrend Cyber Security, experimental shapeshifter: vampire bat. Partner to Nioush

Ayluin (*eye-LOO-en*) – Elf, grandfather to Sumala, tries to find Eira suitors

Azriel – Nu-human experiment, double ear prototype, brother to Andariel and Tannek, former rebel, former medic, night club owner: Twilight

Blaze – Nu-human experiment, former rebel

Chameleon – Nu-human experiment, former rebel, former assassin, molecular fusion ability. Interested in Aliyah

Dan – Nu-human experiment, former rebel, former Lieutenant to Eira

Devon – Nu-human experiment, former assassin, musician

Doppelganger – Nu-human experiment, former rebel, temporary cloning ability

Elara – Nu-human, former Dalatrend orphan

Evynne (*EV-een*) – Nu-human experiment, former rebel assassin

Eyri (*EYE-ree*) – Nu-human, Lakon and Alyra's daughter, musician

Ezhno (*EZ-no*) – Nu-human experiment, former rebel and Underground computer tech

Innon (*EYE-nin*) – Nu-human experiment, former rebel battle leader, former Commander

Jasmine – Nu-human experiment, aunt to Eira, Bone, Rhaec, Trigon, Yára, Elgren, sister to Amara and Zane, geneticist, revived

Lakon (*LAY-con*) – Nu-human experiment, former assassin, partner to Alyra, father to Eyri, musician

Lara – Nu-human, former rebel, mother to Lexi, Run competition help for Alex

Lena – Nu-human, former rebel. Partner to Zenmar

Nari – Nu-human, former Dalatrend orphan

Nioush (*NEE-oosh*) – Nu-human demi-god, former rebel, psychic: Battle Psychic, twin to Seda, brother to Saléna and Nyra, grandson to Sela. Partner to Aurora

Nyra – Nu-human experiment demi-god, former rebel mole, psychic, twin to Saléna, sister to Seda and Nioush, granddaughter to Sela, partner to Rhaec

Orchon (*OR-con*) – Nu-human, former rebel, bouncer at Twilight

Saléna (*sah-LEY-nah*) – Nu-human experiment demi-god, former rebel, psychic: Seer, twin to Nyra, sister to Seda and Nioush, granddaughter to Sela

Seda (*SAY-duh*) – Nu-human demi-god, former rebel, psychic: Seer, twin to Nioush, sister to Saléna and Nyra, granddaughter to Sela. Partner to Argus

Sumala (*sue-MALL-ah*) – Elf, granddaughter to Ayluin

Vek – Nu-human experiment, former rebel, psychic: Battle Psychic, registered

Xantar (*ZAN-tar*) – Nu-human experiment, former rebel

Zane – Nu-human experiment, former rebel, uncle to Eira, Bone, Rhaec, Trigon, Yára, Elgren, brother to Jasmine and Amara, former soldier, mechanic. Engaged to Shva'sika

Zenmar – Nu-human experiment, former rebel, crippled in a skirmish. Partner to Lena

ORPHANAGE

Lyra (*LIE-ruh*) – Former matron, nu-human

Mocha – Matron, nu-human experiment, anthropomorphic: cat. Partner to Raid

Myra (*MEER-uh*) – Nu-human, adopted by Raid and Mocha

Raid – Curator, nu-human experiment, former rebel, brother to Rylan, experimental shapeshifter: dog. Partner to Mocha

Orphans (Elsa, Levi, Kelcen (kell-SEN), Alson, Ellie)

GODS

Anila (*ah-NEE-lah*) – Goddess of air

Arcadia (*are-KAY-dee-ah*) – Goddess of spirits, daughter to Solund and Lunaria, sister to Phyre

Celesta – Goddess of timelines, corrupted. Mate to Zion

Genesis – Goddess of time. Partner to Zoltan

Gina – Goddess of health and healing

Halcyon (*hall-SEE-on*) – Goddess of the sea

Imera (*eye-MEER-ah*) – Goddess of literature and knowledge

Jin – Goddess of refined earth

Kendaria – Goddess of water

Koseba (*koh-SAY-bah*) – God of shapeshifting

Le'carro (*ley-CAR-oh*) – God of lightning

Lunaria – Goddess of the moon, mother to Phyre and Arcadia. Partner to Solund

Nazir (*nah-ZEER*) – God of death, corruption, deals, trickery and deceit, father to Genesis (nu-human experiment). Interested in Rashta

Phyre (*fire*) – God of fire, son to Solund and Lunaria, brother to Arcadia, father to Rashta. Partner to Satria

Raisu (*RAY-sue*) – God of dreams

Rashta (*RAH-sh-tah*) – Goddess of judgment and rebirth, bound to the first halfling soul, daughter to Phyre and Satria. Interested in… complicated

Rasmus – God of love and fertility. Partner to Savada

Satria (*sah-TREE-ah*) – Goddess of war, mother to Rashta. Partner to Phyre

Savada (*sah-VAH-dah*) – Goddess of sex and seduction. Partner to Rasmus

Sela – Goddess of psychics, sister of Tyro, grandmother to Seda, Nioush, Saléna, and Nyra

Solstice – Goddess of ice and winter

Solund – God of the Sun, father to Phyre and Arcadia. Partner to Lunaria

Tarin – God of nature. Partner to Valena

Tyro (*TIE-roh*) – God of psychics, brother of Sela, great uncle to Seda, Nioush, Saléna, and Nyra

Valena – Goddess of earth. Partner to Tarin

Zion – God of dragons and Keeper of Time. Mate of Celesta

Zoltan – God of matter. Partner to Genesis

PEACEKEEPERS

Assar – dwarf, deceased

Pyralis (*PIE-ral-iss*) – Red dragon, former Velsara Wild Clan leader, father of Velsara, deceased

Raynn (*rain*) – Human, deceased

Reiki (*Ray-KEY*) – Green dragon, deceased

Ryoko (*Ree-OH-koh*) – Half-wogron, Shaman of the Fractured Crystal, mate to Varro, deceased

Varro – Elf, healer, mate to Ryoko, deceased

RAVENWARD

Aelrinde (*Ale-RIN-day*) – Elf, craftsman
Avila (*ah-VEE-luh*) – Nu-human experiment, former rebel,
  psychic: Seer, twin to Telar
Taryn – Half-elf, scholar. Interested in Telar
Telar (*tell-ARE*) – Nu-human experiment, former rebel, psychic:
  Battle Psychic, twin to Avila. Interested in Taryn

AZROK

Nordec – Dwarf, tavern owner
Vorn – Dwarf, old friend to Eira

ALTARIS

Reynor (*RAY-nor*) – Nu-human, Run competition commentator

SILVERCREST

Carlos – Nu-human, Run competition competitor help
Den – Nu-human, Run competition commentator
Lucas – Nu-human, Run competition competitor

UNAFFILIATED

MERCENARIES

Greeve – Nu-human experiment, assassin, shadow blind ability, codename: Shadow

Helkin – Nu-human experiment, assassin, molecular breakdown ability, codename: Mist

Salis – Nu-human experiment, assassin

Sendara – Nu-human experiment, assassin, codename: Death Angel

Shyden (*SHAY-den*) – Nu-human experiment, assassin, Eira's mentor and father figure, shadow manipulation ability

Zelmen – Nu-human experiment, assassin, codename: Reaper

SPIRITS

Jade – Nu-human experiment, soldier under Amara, deceased

Rana (RAH-nah) – Nu-human experiment, assassin, trained under Eira, vendetta against Eira, reformed ways, deceased

Raynn (rain) – Nu-human experiment, former rebel battle leader, former general, clone if Peacekeeper Raynn, deceased

Rick – Nu-human experiment, General, deceased

Verra – Nu-human experiment, General, vendetta against Eira and Amara, deceased

Zeek – Nu-human, brute class, soldier under Amara. Former mate to Ryoko, deceased

Shiva (SHEE-vah) – Elf, former demon hunter, deceased

GLOSSARY LANGUAGE

ELVISH

Elvish is an eloquent language, light on the tongue with an airy sound. Even the usual consonants of common don't hold the same harshness in Elvish. Many elves and other humanoids raised with Elvish as their mother tongue carry this light speech over in their common.

While not the easiest language to learn, Elvish is a favorite among the linguistically gifted. Those who seek to learn this language seek out elves before any other race and are taught by full immersion. Some elves will provide a few words for the humanoid to start with but it's not common to do so. The elves believe this technique is the best way to learn and creates a better understanding of the language for everyday use.

Written Elvish is just as elegant as spoken, usually written in script by native speakers. Non-natives tend to forgo the script, which is accepted by native speakers, though the handwriting is still expected to be neat, and flourished on important documents. Sloppy writing is considered an insult.

Phrases used in the series:

Éan ag eitilt – Flying bird

Go dtí go gcomhlíonfaimid arís – Until we meet again
Nuair a ardaíonn an ghrian arís – When the sun rises once more
Go dtí solas na maidine – Until morning light
Codlaíonn muid faoi na réaltaí anocht – We sleep under the stars tonight

DRACONIC

Draconic is a guttural language made up most of grunts and growls with the occasional tongue flick, exhales, or teeth clatter. It's difficult for a non-dragon to learn, as the formation of these words are foreign to most humanoids. Some sounds are impossible for non-dragons to create so other sounds are substituted as an alternative. Even dragons taking a humanoid form must make these changes. Rarely is a humanoid able to perfect the speech, even when raised among dragons.

Those attempting to learn are always taught single words before attempting sentence structures. Draconic sentence structure is similar to Common, but with a possessive edge due to the mindset of dragons. There are no contracted words in Draconic, as such, dragons who don't speak common often, tend to use the same sentence structures of their mother tongue when they do speak common.

It's not common for dragons to write in the current age but there is a basic written form of the language that was used more extensively in the past. This written form is comprised of glyphs easily created with dragon claws and easy to decipher for most dragons no matter the cleanliness of the script. Non-dragons find this writing easier to learn than the spoken language and most of the time will stop learning after they've master it.

Some words Raikidan has taught Eira in the series:

Aio – You	*Cull* – Kiss
Aion – Your	*Cyyg* – Keep
Aionl – Yours	*Diik* – Food
Ayl – Yes	*Dnyy* – Free

Duny – Fire
Din – For
Dinytyn – Forever
Dnis – From
Dnuyvk – Friend
Eny – Are
Eun – Air
Ev – An
Evk – And
Ezfeal – Always
Femyn – Water
Finna – Worry
Frem – What
Fryzg – Whelp
Fulkis – Wisdom
Fuzz – Will
Gyexy – Peace
Gyelevm – Peasant
Gzyely – Please
Id – Of
Iddlgnuvw – Offspring
Ion – Our
Iv – On
Ki – Do
Keowrmyn – Daughter
Knewiv – Dragon
Lgunum – Spirit
Lisymruvw – Something
Liv – Son
Livw – Song
Lmneuwrm – Straight
Lmnyvwmr – Strength
Lreny – Share
Lry – She
Luny – Sire
Lulmyn – Sister
Lupzuvw – Sibling

Lxezy – Scale
Lynyvuma – Serenity
Lyy – See
Mi – To
Mii – Too
Mioxr – Touch
Mrevc – Thank
Mruvc – Think
Mryny – There
Mnyelony – Treasure
Ol – Us
Pnimryn – Brother
Pnyemry – Breathe
Pumy – Bite
Py – Be
Regguvyll – Happiness
Rel – Has
Rety – Have
Rl – He
Rosev – Human
Rovwyn – Hunger
Rul – His
Rus – Him
Ryn – Her
Ryzzi – Hello
Sa – My
Simryn – Mother
Siny – More
Suvy – Mine
Sy – Me
Semy – Mate
U – I
Ud – If
Ul – Is
Um – It
Vi – No
Vim – Not

Vyyk – Need
Wiikpay – Goodbye
Wik – God
Wikkyll – Goddess
Wym – Get
Xifenkza – Cowardly
Xivvexmyk – Connected
Yem – Eat

Yenmr – Earth
Ytyv – Even
Ziaeza – Loyalty
Zity – Love
Zoxca – Lucky
Zudy – Life
Zulmyv – Listen
Zutyl – Lives

Some phrases spoken in the series:

Ion cuvk – Our kind

Lazmira, sa xruzk – Lazmira, my child

Zity, gyexy, lgunum, ziaeza, lynyvuma, lmnyvwmr, fulkis – Love, peace, spirit, loyalty, serenity, strength, wisdom

Sa mnyelony – My treasure

Aio xevvim rety – You cannot have

U gnimyxm ryn – I protect her

Lry ul suvy – She is mine

Sevugozemuty pumxr – Manipulative bitch

Aio rety vi nyez gongily – You have no real purpose

Aio eny synyza ev enmuduxuez xnyemuiv – You are merely an artificial creation

Aio gilmony mi ruky aoin finmrzyllvyll – You posture to hide your worthlessness

Mrul finmrzyll xnyemuiv rel mry detin id Zion – This worthless creation has favor of Zion

Frem pzylluvw kiyl aoin dunyzyll lxezyl rety – What blessing does your fireless scales have

U mii pyzuyty lry fuzz lety ol – I too believe she will save us

Evk Raikidan ul zoxca mi py wutyv ryn – And Raikidan is lucky to be given her

Ud ivza ry fuzz zulmyv evk wym rul gnuinumuyl lmneuwrm – If only he will listen and get his priorities straight

U ki vim mruvc fy fuzz rety mi finna epiom mrem – I do not think we will have to worry about that

U fuzz py pexc – I will be back

Py wiik din Eira – Be good for Eira
Lry ul suvy, fryzg – She is mine, whelp
Lry vim pyzivw mi aio – She not belong to you
Lry sa mnyelony – She my treasure
U myzz ryn ud xiozk – I tell her if could
Aio vim – You not
Aoi vim xeny yviowr – You not care enough
Aoi elresyk – You ashamed
U vim – I not
Muvk nyekuvw dnyec – Mind reading freak
Aio pimr cyyg ryn ledy – You both keep her safe
Lry ul usginmevm – She is important
Mryny ul lisymruvw lgyxuez epiom ryn – There is something special
    about her
Ytyv ry lyyl um – Even he sees it
Aio xvyw epiom mrul dylmutex? – You knew about this festival?
Mrymy ivxy fel e zummzy knewiv wunz – There once was a little
    dragon girl
Lry fel lmnivw evk pyeomudoz – She was strong and beautiful
Evk rek ev yay din lruva mruvwl – And had an eye for shiny things
Regga mi lyy Eira – Happy to see Eira

DEMONIC

Little is known about the language demons speak. On the surface, the structure appears complex. Some are rough and guttural, while others smooth and almost alluring, drawing in the listener. It is believed through limited observation, the species of a demon, and possibly even clan make up, plays a major role. Whether the variances witnessed are a result of dialect, more than one language used that can interact with other demonic ones, or something else entirely, that truth remains out of reach.

While ancient texts from past summoners have been found, all lack translations or comments in any known decipherable language or dialect on Lumaraeon. And due to the reputation of demons, even the most courageous scholars find themselves hesitant to get close enough to unlock the secrets first hand. Those who do, never speak of what they learned.

LOST LANGUAGES

T hought the history of Lumaraeon, language has developed and died, but some have left a more notable impact on the races. These forgotten languages hold important information lost during the millennia of turmoil making them important topics for scholars.

OLD TONGUE

O ld Tongue, also known as God speech, is the most ancient form of speech that was replaced by the various languages of Lumaraeon, ultimately dying out among the mortal races. Much of the language was lost during the War of End and with no one but the gods around to remember, the language was thought dead. Until a large find of books in the Eternal Library turned up after a new entryway was found, eight hundred years ago.

Scholars have done their best to decipher the old language and have since found new discovery sites all over Lumaraeon to help with their research. But while the tongue is researched, it is not know if the translations are quite right, and no one has thought to ask the gods, not even Imera, the goddess of literature and knowledge.

Words used in the series:

Mukarna – Makers
Spekta – Spectral

ANCIENT DRACONIC

Ancient Draconic is the most ancient form of dragon speech. Most of its knowledge has been lost to the ages, not even ancient tomes contain information about it. It's said this tongue powered magic lost to the mortals during the War of End, and what little remains, allows the dragons to speak with the elements of their scales. What speech remains is passed between dragons of the same color, never to outsiders, and none is written for others to see.

ABOUT THE AUTHOR

USA Today bestselling author Shannon Pemrick is a full-time slow-burn romantic fantasy author, fuller-time geek, and unrelenting dragon enthusiast. She owns too many novelty mugs, not enough chocolate, and maintains a forbidden love-affair with all things shiny. When she's not burning her fingers across a keyboard handing out adventures and HEAs, she's rolling dice and getting lost in RPGs or searching for brides for her dragon overlords.

You can learn more about Shannon by visiting her website at: Shannonpemrick.com